'Powerful emotional ~~...........~~ prove compelling, while questions about the meaning of life, human connection and quantum entanglement make for a fascinating and assured debut novel'
Guardian

'Haddon's invention is ingenious and compelling'
The Times

'Stonkingly complex, mind-bendingly clever and utterly gripping'
Daily Mail

'With strong echoes of David Mitchell, Haruki Murakami or Emily St John Mandel . . . this is a madcap ride to somewhere new with thrills to spare and a gallery of truly fascinating characters. One for the ages.'
Crime Time

'A book designed to be more than the sum of its parts, and one that achieves that because love is the thing that binds it together. Vitally fresh'
Dominic Nolan

'A trans-dimensional, kaleidoscopic mystery-box of a novel . . . wholly and riotously original. Haddon is a mad scientist of genre and his epic is a tour de force.'
Peter Ho Davies

'Mystifying . . . and finally heartbreaking. Fasten your seatbelt'
Nicholas Meyer

PSALMS FOR THE END OF THE WORLD

COLE HADDON

HEADLINE

First published in 2022 by
HEADLINE PUBLISHING GROUP

First published in paperback in 2023 by
HEADLINE PUBLISHING GROUP

1

Cataloguing in Publication Data is available from the British Library

ISBN 978 1 4722 8669 7

Typeset by EM&EN
Printed and bound in Great Britain by Clays Ltd, Elcograf S.p.A.

Headline's policy is to use papers that are natural, renewable and recyclable
products and made from wood grown in well-managed forests and other
controlled sources. The logging and manufacturing processes are expected
to conform to the environmental regulations of the country of origin.

HEADLINE PUBLISHING GROUP
An Hachette UK Company
Carmelite House
50 Victoria Embankment
London EC4Y 0DZ

www.headline.co.uk
www.hachette.co.uk

For my parents,

who taught me love and grief

BOOK ONE:
LIBERATION

He rose into the starry sky
A space Jesus on the run
He said farewell, my little ones
Don't forget to try to love

Lyrics, 'Ballad of a Boy Named Buddha Bad'

The newscaster with the deep, reassuring voice says, 'It now appears that sometime yesterday morning, the Soviet Union exploded a thermonuclear device some two and a half miles over the Arctic Sea island of Novaya Zemlya,' and the man sitting on the mustard-coloured couch, crystal tumbler of Canadian Club in one hand and an RCA Wireless Wizard in the other, decides unequivocally that the truest words ever scribbled on a page were 'All the world's a stage', because none of this bullshit is real.

Jones adjusts one of the brick-sized remote control's two dials, and the newscaster's voice grows louder. 'The blast of the device, believed to be the largest ever built, was witnessed over six hundred miles away. President Kennedy immediately denounced the test, saying that it threatened to derail current US–Soviet test-ban talks. He added that Americans should heed his call to immediately construct personal and neighbourhood fallout shelters in the case such a nuclear weapon were to be detonated inside the United St—'

The television blinks off. Jones stares at it for a moment longer, listening to the picture tubes still humming behind its concave screen, then rises and goes to the set of three windows that look out from his little slice of heaven. From here, he can see light in his neighbours' family room window.

Ralph Beckermann is standing in front of his own television, the electric glow of the newscaster's face quavering across his face. Jones and Ralph bought the same Victor colour television on a joint Saturday outing to Woolworth an hour before three Jack and Cokes prompted Ralph to confess he was enjoying regular sexual congress with his sister-in-law every Tuesday evening instead of bowling like he tells Peggy. Peggy's on the couch behind Ralph, hands folded neatly in her lap. Their two boys are on the loveseat, hair crew cut like their dad's because all they want to be is just like him. The family looks terrified.

Next door to the Beckermanns' place is the Olsens'. Christmas lights are still strung along the sagging gutters because Hank Olsen has been working overtime since before Thanksgiving and on weekends can't be bothered to do more than go shooting up on Mount Baldy with his two oldest boys since the third one, the youngest, is too slow to be trusted with live rounds. The tableau in the Olsens' window is indistinguishable from the one in the Beckermanns' – anxious, frightened faces, wondering how long it will be before they're vaporized.

Hank is sleeping with Ralph's wife, Peggy. Hank's wife, Elaine, made a pass at Jones three weeks ago at Kellogg's as Gracie pretended not to take notice, and Jones knows none of this ritualized stupidity is real, this Norman Rockwell-shoved-through-a-sausage grinder-with-sex-and-six-shooters-and-manifest-destiny crap, no matter how good the Manhattan ad-men and politicians in Washington are at selling it to Americans.

But hey, at least the whiskey is good.

Jones takes a long pull from his glass until all that remains is pebbles of ice. As he finishes the ice off, too, his eyes find the iron-grey Samsonite Streamlite suitcase standing next to the front door. He picked it up at a garage sale in Glendale last week, knowing full well what he intended it for. Turned out to be the perfect size, down to the inch.

Jones goes to his bathroom then, where he shaves his perfect superhero's chin and combs King John's beeswax pomade into his dark hair that, in most light, looks pitch black. The face in the mirror still startles him sometimes, but everything changes, he knows. *Everything*. One thing into another, on and on, until whatever was has become an infinite number of things it wasn't before. He next dresses in a slate-grey suit, pin-striped and double-breasted like the one he saw in that picture where the actor with the bronze skin and strange accent was chased by a homicidal crop duster. His fedora is a perfect match and, unlike the suit that's so stiff and formal despite how casual the actor made it seem, feels good on him.

Outside, Jones carefully places the Streamlite in the trunk of the Alpine Green Oldsmobile Coupe with dented rear bumper parked in his driveway. That's when he hears Ralph say, 'You catch the news, Bob?' from behind him. Ralph is standing in his own driveway, bottle of Budweiser in hand and a Lucky Strike dangling precariously from his bottom lip.

Jones regards him silently from behind the open lid of his trunk, then, looking one final time at the Streamlite, slams the trunk shut. 'Yeah,' he says, rounding the car to the driver's door.

'Peggy thinks we're all gonna be dead by year's end,' Ralph says, crossing the road. He flicks his cigarette into the dark and its burning tip vanishes like a shooting star. When he reaches Jones, his voice lowers to a conspiratorial volume. 'Hey, listen, you didn't tell her about . . . *you know*? She keeps asking these questions and, well, I can't get the bitch to shut up.'

'Your secret's safe with me, buddy,' Jones says. He puts a wink in his voice and tries to smile, but he overdoes it and Ralph notices. He doesn't hate Ralph. He just feels bad for him, for all of them, because they can't see the world for what it really is. Not like he can.

Ten minutes later, Jones brakes at a stoplight downtown. It's black out, no stars in the sky. Neon signs blaze even brighter because of this and, in the distance, two spotlights from the Pacific Hastings Drive-In trace indecipherable runes across unseen clouds. And there's a drunk bum standing on the sidewalk, muttering to himself or the voices in his head or who knows, waving a sign he's crafted out of cardboard and finger paint. The sign warns DON'T FALL FOR IT. Jones acknowledges the bum with a quick nod, which seems to mollify him.

The light finally turns, and Jones watches the bum shrink behind him in the rearview. His eyes drift to the back seat and the trunk on the other side of it. To the Streamlite. A few minutes later, he parks outside Kellogg's Diner.

Kellogg's is a white oblong, all irregular angles like a poorly made sheet cake, dropped in the middle of a small square that it and its parking lot are the sole occupants of. Blue and red neon trim its polished, futuristic surface like radioactive frosting, inviting the eye to peer inside its three walls of windows. Right now, Jones can see a waitress in an Easter-yellow dress with frilly white collar and a grease-stained apron standing behind the counter, next to a cash register, face buried as usual in a book the size of a Gutenberg Bible. He smiles, unable to help himself.

Gracie stops her habitual humming when Jones enters, smiling with all of her heart-shaped face as she is prone to do. 'Bobby!' she says. 'I was getting worried about you.'

Jones smiles, too, as he approaches the counter and its teal Formica surface that smells of Top Job — just like Gracie — from the post-supper rush clean-up. But there's something different about him, something wrong, and she notices it right away.

'Can't sleep without my pie,' he says, lying.

Gracie fetches the coffee carafe from the warmer, and Jones watches her and knows she knows he's watching her. When she returns, her thin, closed lips curving upwards, she pours the coffee and asks in her typically cheerful manner, 'What will it be tonight?'

The cook, Leon, listens from the kitchen. He doesn't like Jones for some reason he won't reveal and never has. He sweats a lot.

'There's apple, pumpkin, a peach, key lime, and, if you're in the mood for something new, May baked a pecan that's out of this world. I may have snuck a piece.'

'*Pecan* pie?'

Gracie nods, grinning at how Jones's eyes have reacted to this unexpected piece of intelligence. Pecan pie has been absent from the menu since he became a regular here six or seven months ago. Must be a seasonal thing.

'Let's be daring,' he says. 'How was class today?'

'You ask me that every night, and I feel like I bore you to tears every night going on about it,' she says, cutting into the pie.

'Why would you think that?'

Gracie sets a slice of pie in front of him, giving the plate a tiny, playful shove so it slides a few inches towards him across the river of shiny teal that divides them. 'Whipped cream?' But she knows the answer, and is already getting the tub from the fridge inside the open kitchen door. 'You just don't look like the kind of guy who's interested in physics, no matter how many times you're sweet enough to act like you are.'

'Nobody's interested in that crap except you, girl,' Leon says as he vigorously and loudly beats raw minced beef into patties for tomorrow.

Jones ignores Leon. 'What kind of guy do I look like?' he says.

Gracie scoops a large dollop of whipped cream from the tub, and drops it on top of Jones's slice of pie as if it's a well-deserved prize. 'The kind of guy who likes pie,' she says, grinning again.

Jones picks up his fork, plunges it into the centre of the whipped cream, and takes an impressive bite of the pie. '*Pecan* especially, it would seem.'

'Told you it was good.'

'Well?'

'Fine, if you're *really* interested.'

'He's not,' Leon says.

'Shut up, Leon,' Gracie says. She comes around the counter, and takes up position on the stool next to Jones. 'So, the universe and everything in it, the laws that hold it together and, well, give it shape, they appear to be' – she searches for the word – '*calibrated* or, or *finely tuned* to produce elements and, by extension, for life as we know it, *for us*, to evolve within it.'

'Bob no speaka the *español*,' Leon says.

'Dangit, Leon, I will tell Warren why we keep coming up short on buns if you don't mind your own business,' she says. That shuts Leon up. She looks at Jones again. 'Are you, Bobby? *Following*, I mean.'

Jones has shoved too much pie in his mouth, and can't swallow it quickly enough. 'More or less,' he says, mumbling like an idiot around it.

'So, this means, if the laws of physics, if they were different, even just a little bit, then the universe would've never happened,' Gracie says. '*We* would've never happened.'

Jones takes another bite, this one more reasonable in dimensions, and chews slowly as he considers this ontological conundrum. His face reveals nothing, because he's afraid if he's not careful it could reveal too much. The problem is, she misinterprets his silence.

'You must think I sound like an fool.'

'I could never think that.'

Gracie smiles when he says this, but almost immediately realizes how close she is to him. Her hand is resting on the counter barely an inch from his. She rises quickly, and hugs the counter as she returns to the other side of it. 'Dr Fröbe says this means that a universe, especially one that contains life and conscious beings like us—'

'Some might argue we're not.'

She doesn't understand what he means to imply, but is too aroused by what she's discussing to slow down. 'He says our existence must thus be considered a miracle.'

Jones leans back and tosses his napkin on the counter, never taking his eyes off her. He's scrutinizing her, the way the thrill of her studies can illuminate her every feature anew, but also like this is the last time he's ever going to see her and he doesn't want to forget a single detail because, he knows, this is probably the last time he's ever going to see her and he doesn't want to forget a single detail.

The Streamlite in his trunk pops back into his mind, his face changes, and she notices again something isn't quite right about him tonight. 'What is it? What's wrong?'

He pretends he didn't hear her. 'What do you think about what this – *Dr Fröbe*? – what this Fröbe says?'

Gracie hesitates, afraid of her own answer. She fills the silence by pouring Jones another cup of coffee. 'I don't really believe in miracles,' she says.

Something wet and heavy, a ball of minced beef, slaps against the hard surface of the kitchen grill. Leon looks ready to fling one of his inchoate patties at Gracie's head. 'That damn school's rotting your brain!' he says. 'You think God would've created a universe where we couldn't live and breathe? This world was put here for us.'

She starts to snap back at Leon, but Jones interjects. 'No, no, maybe he's right,' he says. 'At least, not altogether wrong.'

Gracie looks at him, surprised. 'I just think . . . maybe it's a possibility,' she says. But her confidence is shaken, she had believed Jones an ally and fellow compatriot of the woefully underpopulated Republic of Common Sense – somebody who saw the world as more than myths and fantasies – and he just jeopardized that. It's right there on her face, plain as day

'Tell her,' Leon says to him. 'Tell her she needs to get her head outta them books. Maybe even go on a date, am I right?'

Now Leon is really goading Gracie, because her romantic life is the one place he is never permitted to violate with his crudeness and all-knowing ignorance. She mouths *sorry* at Jones.

Jones offers her a sympathetic smile in reply, already standing. 'You keep the change now,' he says, drawing a crisp five from his wallet.

'You're leaving?' she says.

'There's somewhere I have to be.'

'Where?' she says.

'*Somewhere.*'

9

'I'm off the clock in twenty,' she says. 'Wait for me.'

Gracie has never asked this of Jones before. She's never asked anything of him at all, their relationship until this moment only comprised of conversations frustratingly chaperoned by Leon and unsaid things that have preoccupied Jones's thoughts, sometimes keeping him up deep into the night, ever since he first met her and asked about the physics textbook she was studying and she, in turn, asked him if he'd ever heard of something called *entanglement theory*. Jones had said no, which was technically true, but later realized was also a lie because he knew more about its underpinning principles than her textbook could ever teach her.

'I wish I could,' he says. He walks towards the door, but he can feel Gracie watching him leave her. He stops suddenly, turns, and blurts out her name.

Gracie doesn't move. At all. She's been waiting for him to ask her out for at least a month, probably longer, and Jones knows it. Or, he should have. He should've spent every second he had with her even if none of this is real. Shakespeare thought we're nothing more than actors, and maybe that should've been enough. Why couldn't it be enough for Jones? Maybe because actors know they're playing parts written for them . . .

'I . . . I won't be in for a while,' he says finally. 'I've got to go away for work.'

'To that Indian reservation again?' she asks.

'No. That was – you should forget I ever mentioned that. I'll see you again . . . hopefully.'

The *hopefully* immediately worries her. 'What am I going to do without your nightly visits?'

Jones slips his fedora on, smiles at Gracie one last time, and walks out without looking back again because he knows he would change his mind if he did; he would take the stage with her and play the part and dance the part and sing the part and love her until the curtains dropped and the show closed for good. And so, it takes everything in Jones not to go back to Gracie, to tell her the truth about the trick that's been played on her, what she really is and what he really is, and hope she can forgive him – because this is all his fault.

Ali

West Berlin 1977

She died on a Tuesday, at 16.28, all because she dropped a sack of groceries near where the Americans were shot the day before and stopped to chase a runaway tin of sauerkraut. The pavement behind her exploded with terrifying force, throwing concrete and sewage pipes and cars and people in every direction. A bus swerved away from the expanding cloud of flames and dust and spraying faeces and smacked into Bertha, hurling her body into a postbox so violently that several of her bones snapped and the side of her face was bashed in as if somebody had struck her once with a club hammer. This all happened only two blocks from their apartment, and Ali, when he heard the explosion and then the screams, rushed outside without putting on his coat or boots despite how heavily it had been raining all day. Ali did not know for certain something had happened to Bertha, but he did feel suddenly cold – no, *empty* – and he didn't stop running until he saw German men covering her body, contorted and torn apart as it was like a savaged pretzel, as several German women watched and wept and warned Ali to stay away from Bertha when he tried to go to her. They only saw an *Ausländer*, a swarthy foreigner with black hair, and not the man who had intended to love Bertha until she died of old age. Except now she's dead, and Ali is all alone in a country that is not his own, and he feels so hollowed out that there is a mercilessly dull echo where his soul should be.

He does not know what to fill this hollow space with except rage, and the rage festers and grows for weeks and months until his friend tells him there is a concert, European music, a Brit who claims to not be from this world, who says he fell here from the stars, and this Moonman, Ali's friend Atik insists, this Moonman will help him. Or, at the very least, give Ali a break from talking so much about Bertha. Atik has moved into the apartment Ali shared with Bertha – they are both Gasterbeiter, guest workers from Morocco required by the West German government but unwanted by Germans except Bertha, who loved Ali like he loved her – and Atik thinks it's too depressing around here since she died. Atik does not say this, but Ali knows it is how his friend feels, which is why Ali agrees to go with him to see this alien. Afterwards, Ali will do it. Dirar gave him the pills last night at the Schwarze Traube, because he knows how desperately his friend needs to sleep, but really Ali is terrified by what he might do if this thing filling him up, this rage he cannot describe with words, is not stopped in its tracks.

SO36 is like a neon circus tent packed shoulder to shoulder with freaks of every variety. There are young men and young women and men who look like women and women dressed like homo cowboys and somebody who looks like that young American actor from that cowboy film, but he's not wearing the shirt, just the brown suede vest, and his arms are covered in charcoal tattoos, and Atik's girlfriend is already kissing a magenta-haired German man while the magenta-haired German's friends freely fondle her ass and breasts, and this is easily the strangest night out Ali has ever spent in West Berlin or anywhere.

The Moonman has many names, many identities, like a hologram that changes depending on how and even when you look at it. His stage name is Damien Syco, but the Moonman – the last of a lunar species self-exiled to Earth to speak the truth to a people as spiritually and temporally lost as his kind once were – is his most popular persona. Atik mentions Syco's birth name, which is British and sounds boring, but Ali forgets it immediately.

The Moonman creeps onto the stage some ninety minutes late, moving with slow, haunting gracefulness as the crowd chants for him. Except he is not an alien, as Ali was told to expect. He is not even Damien Syco or any of the other identities Ali was told might appear tonight.

The Man Who Was the Moonman is dressed in a suit unlike any Ali has ever seen. The angles are odd and the shoulders impractically and unrealistically dramatic, its colour like ice, and there might be metallic thread in the weave so that it shimmers like the future. His tie is antiquated in cut, but looks to be made of space-age aluminium foil. His hair, slicked back and stiff like it's moulded plastic, is bleached almost white. And when the Man Who Was the Moonman begins to sing, the club stops and Ali weeps.

Later, after the crowd begins to boo at the confusion and pain and defiant hope in the singer's sporadic, sometimes whispered, sometimes howled lyrics, at the avant-pop's ambient and found sounds that unsettle and elevate, at the tears that stream down the Man Who Was the Moonman's cheeks and leave wet stains on his strange, shimmering suit, Ali finds himself in his apartment bathroom with the bottle of pills Dirar gave him. None of this is real, he can see that now. It's all bullshit, just as the Man Who Was the Moonman sang. All the work we put into life, all the moments we collect and try to imbue with meaning, amount to nothing but a farce. Bertha existed, but for what? All the letters Ali's family back home post to him, pleading with him to return – *to* what? Their world is only as large as they imagine it, and West Berlin is a fantasy world to them as it likewise is for Berliners who populate it. Both home and Berlin possess less permanence than a stone in a rolling river and they try, in Morocco and here and everywhere, to convince Ali, to convince everybody, it all means something, but Ali knows better, the Man Who Was the Moonman knows better – none of it means a fucking thing, and if you try to make it, you'll go *syco*.

This is why Ali spills the bottle of pills, black and green and full of promise, into his shaking palm, and begins to scoop them into his mouth like a kid who's just found a sack of his favourite sweeties hidden on the top shelf of the kitchen cupboard.

Gracie

Pasadena 1962

Her mother wants her to move back home, but she's not ready
for that, even with her stepfather gone. Her mother says she's a
hypocrite, that she took the man's money to pay for tuition and
that trip to watch 'that rocket ship' launch down in Florida, and
maybe Gracie is – fine, maybe she *definitely* is – but what else was
she going to do? She couldn't look at her mother any more, all she
ever saw were the puffy bruises his palms and knotty knuckles left
behind, and every time Gracie called the police her mother denied
it anyway and the policemen, who knew her stepfather from the
VFW Hall, were all too glad to let her play dumb. And so, yes,
Gracie took the man's money to get out, to chase the answers to
all those questions that had plagued her since the first time she
learned the Earth rotated at nearly 1,000 miles per hour and
people like her and her mother somehow didn't fly off it; she took
his money, and she ran, and she can't go home now. Not yet, at
least, and maybe not ever. That's why she's working a second shift
at Kellogg's tonight, 'cause she needs to save up money until the
will is unsealed on Friday and her mother maybe tells her there's
nothing left and her dreams are about to die and there won't be
any choice except to go home anyway.

'Good evening.'

Gracie stops humming the Tune, and looks up from her textbook. 'Well, hello there, stranger,' she says, smiling with surprise
at Bobby as he walks towards her from the door.

Bobby stops mid-stride, and smiles politely. 'Good evening,'
he says again without sentiment. He sits at the counter four seats
down from his normal stool across from her. He isn't wearing a
tie, his collar has been casually left open, and his mind is a million
miles away on the moon or maybe further. 'May I have a menu?'

Leon clears his throat in the kitchen serving window, to get Gracie's attention. She gives him a quick shrug 'cause she doesn't get it either, then grabs one of the menus, printed on paper nearly the same yellow as her uniform, and delivers it to Bobby. 'No pie tonight?'

Bobby returns from wherever his thoughts are. 'Hm?'

'You might want to try the chocolate cream.' She walks towards the glass-faced display, a tower of six pie-covered shelves. 'I think May put something special in it today.'

'Sounds good.'

Gracie plates a piece of chocolate cream pie, watching how Leon is eyeing Bobby. 'I'm glad you're all right,' she says.

'Why wouldn't I be?' Bobby asks her.

'After what happened last night,' she says.

'Last night?' he says.

'City Hall. I know you said you were heading out of town, but I didn't realize until I got in the car afterwards, to go home, and the radio – the DJ – he was talking about the bomb and all those people, and it wasn't until that moment that I realized I wouldn't know your name if you *had* been there. You know, if I saw your name in the paper this morning. I mean, your last name. I don't know it, which is sort of strange, don't you think?' Suddenly embarrassed by whatever that rambling gibberish that just erupted from her mouth was, she sets the plate down in front of Bobby before he can respond. 'Coffee?'

As Gracie walks to the coffee warmer, Bobby says, 'I'm sorry, I don't mean to be rude . . . but do we know each other?'

She stops, coffee carafe in hand. He doesn't seem to understand why she's looking at him like she is. 'I don't get it,' she says.

'I . . . I'm sorry, but—'

'Is this a gag?'

Bobby thinks for a long moment, uncertain, it seems, how to proceed. 'Maybe I should leave,' he says cautiously, standing.

'Wait one minute now, you *are* serious,' Gracie says, equal parts baffled and annoyed, and maybe furious is the right word 'cause she's still pretty darn sure this is some sort of bad joke, except Bobby isn't funny in a mean kind of way and this is pretty darn mean. 'You were in here last night, Bobby. You've been in here almost every night for, gosh, going on seven months now. Heck, sometimes even Sundays!'

Bobby lays a dollar bill on the counter, next to his uneaten plate of chocolate cream pie, and the fact that he never took a bite to find out what surprise ingredient May put in it, tells Gracie something is most definitely not right here. This isn't a joke.

'That should cover the pie,' he says. 'Really, I think you have me confused with somebody else.'

It's when he turns to leave that they both realize there are three black cars parked outside, Dodge Coronets by the look of them, with sirens mounted on their dashes. Two more cars pull up, same make, same sirens. Red light floods the diner, reflecting off its windows and shiny white walls and teal Formica surfaces, and Bobby goes straight and stiff as a flagpole.

'Bobby?' Gracie says.

'Gracie?' Leon says.

Car doors begin to open, one after another, and polished black wingtips appear. Eleven white men in Sears suits various shades of serious, with equally serious looks on their faces and pistols and shotguns in their hands, emerge. They've left their hats inside the cars, but that's okay 'cause their incomplete government uniforms still give them away as G-Men or, at least, they look just like the G-Men Gracie has seen in countless movies and, more recently, on the television set her stepfather had delivered to her to remind her that he finances her dreams, that all she has to do is stay away and let her mother be happy on her own terms.

A twelfth G-Man emerges from a car at the back. This one doesn't belong 'cause he's a Negro and that makes even less sense than a Mexican G-Man. A small white-and-gold-speckled crimson feather sticks out of the thin band of his grey trilby, straight up, like he thinks he's Errol Flynn or something. Instead of a gun or maybe even an English long bow, he carries a bullhorn.

'Robert Jones, I expect you know who I am.' The Negro G-Man doesn't shout, but it sounds as if he does and his voice reverberates a little even through the windows. Bobby still hasn't moved. 'I'm going to come on in to talk, if that's okay with you. No shooting, you understand? I have a lot of men out here, more than willing to open fire for what you did, so let's not give them a reason. There are innocent folks in there with you.'

'Gracie, girl, get away from him!' Leon says.

'What's happening, Bobby?' Gracie says.

The Negro G-Man enters with careful movements, hands at his side and slightly turned out so Bobby can see his palms are empty. When he speaks, his voice is as smooth and sweet as warm butterscotch. 'Mr Jones?' he says. 'I'm Special Agent Montrose with the FBI.'

Bobby snorts at that, but he looks scared. 'Like hell you are,' he says.

'Ma'am, sir, are you two okay?' Montrose asks. Leon nods, but looks as if he's peeing himself. Gracie doesn't answer. 'Mr Jones, I'm going to need you to come with me. You know why.'

Bobby's head shakes, confusion and maybe terror – oh yeah, that's definitely terror – pulling his face tight. His eyes flit about, trying to make sense of the scene. The red light catches on the enamel of his perfect white teeth. 'No, no, I don't. You have the wrong man.'

'Your contract has been nullified, Mr Jones.' Montrose's voice is as unemotional and matter-of-fact as a grocery shop check-out girl telling you what you owe her even though what he just said sounds pretty dang serious. 'What did you think would happen? Twenty-three people are dead.' He doesn't sound broken up about those twenty-three folks who died last night either; they're just numbers to him.

'No, that . . . that's not possible,' Bobby says, stumbling over his own words. 'I was at the Dodgers tie-breaker last night – with, with, with my neighbour. He insisted I come. He'll vouch for me – *Ralph* – ask him!'

'Baseball?' Montrose says, and Gracie knows why 'cause she's just as confused as he is by Bobby's bizarre defence.

'Yeah, *America's favourite pastime*,' Bobby says, his tone mocking and confident but his voice trembling 'cause he seems to know how bad this is or at least how bad it could get. 'You've heard of it, haven't you?'

'Bobby.' It's Gracie who says this. Her hands shake, coffee swishing about in the carafe. 'The tie-breaker series, that was last October. It's *April 29th*.'

Bobby grabs one side of his head, right over his ear, as if somebody just hammered an icepick into his brain. He recovers almost immediately, and screams with his whole body, 'Who are you people?' He backs away from the FBI agent and, when Gracie takes a quick step towards him, from her, too.

Montrose can see Bobby is making for the kitchen door. 'You don't want to do that, Mr Jones.'

'If I go with you, you think I don't know what will happen?' Bobby says. 'It'll be like I never existed!'

'You signed a contract!' Montrose says, shouting unexpectedly as if the obviousness of this makes Bobby's behaviour infuriatingly ridiculous.

Gracie says Bobby's name again. He looks sideways at her, and maybe for the first time tonight sees *her* or, rather, sees how this stranger – if that's what she really is to him – feels about him. Realization mutates into pity, pity that she feels like daggers stabbing madly at her heart, and suddenly he's barrelling through the kitchen door.

Montrose draws a pistol from the holster on his belt, and races after Bobby. A moment later, Leon emerges from the kitchen bathroom where he'd been hiding and declares Gracie an idiot of the highest order. Cars full of FBI agents are already reversing away from the diner, tyres spitting gravel that clinks loudly against the windows. The red of their sirens goes with them, until everything inside Kellogg's is the way it was before. Except Bobby is gone. That's when Gracie realizes she's still holding the coffee carafe, that it's shaking something awful in her hand, and quickly puts it back on its warmer.

Virginie

Saint-Règle 1770

She watches the boy race through the field of blossoming sunflowers, arms thrown out like bird wings, and she knows *this* is what God is. The midday sun catches on flying insects that rise suddenly before her son's loud charge and disperse in the confused chaos that is his wake, and this, she knows with all that she is, is God. Despite everything else, Virginie is happy because, unlike the rest of the world, she has seen the face of God.

Chickens gather around her feet, pecking and cot-cot-cotting. Somebody has let them out again or, most likely, forgotten to close the gate. There used to be so many servants, more than enough to chase down these accursed birds and coax them back into their yard. But that was before, when shop owners had not yet shut their doors to them, when their bills were promptly paid, when her husband still came out of his attic studio.

There, in one of the windows on the second floor. Virginie can see him, or perhaps that is only his shadow moving. The reflection off the glass makes it difficult to say.

There was a time when their family was respected. This chateau was once even considered impressive, especially the crewel tapestries that she inherited after her father died of tuburculosis and then her brother in a battle at somewhere called the Plains of Abraham. But years of neglect have left the home in mournful disrepair. Its geometrical gardens so artfully designed – the very reason she begged Bertrand to purchase the chateau – are now an impenetrable tangle of shrubberies and vines that snare and trap just as she feels her husband and his madness have done to her. Virginie could bear it herself, but then she worries for her son who believes his father a ghost that inhabits their home but refuses to haunt him, leaving the boy as unwanted in death as in life. She tells her son that his father loves him and he must never stop believing that, but she knows better. Bertrand could not look at the boy even before he locked himself away in the studio from which he only emerges now to collect platters of food, shove pots of his filth into the corridor, or retrieve new canvases that their only remaining servant, Mathilde, must haul up two floors and stack outside his locked door. One by one these canvases vanish and never reappear. His studio comprises two large rooms, and so there is enough space for him to paint for the rest of his life and never reveal what his lunacy has wrought.

'Mistress!' Mathilde calls from the kitchen doorway. The woman must be in her sixties, and yet singlehandedly manages and maintains the entire house, which is going about as well as can be expected despite her Herculean efforts. Virginie tends only to her son, with whom she is now imprisoned. She has written to her brother in Chartres, Gaspard, but holds little hope that he can aid them. She is comforted by her blind faith that the boy, her dear, sweet God, will one day find a way to liberate himself from these bars on his own and will finally know true freedom.

Mathilde leads Virginie to the foyer, where the warmth of day is kept at bay by shadow and the indifference of stone. There is a man lurking there whom Virginie does not immediately recognize, but whom she nonetheless feels she has met before.

'Thank you, Mathilde,' Virginie says. When the servant is gone, she regards the man again, trying to pry his face loose from her memory if it does exist there. 'Good day, monsieur.'

'You do not know me,' the man says in English, either presuming or hoping that she speaks the language. He is not French, but Virginie did not need to hear him speak to know this. He does not belong here. 'I have come to see Monsieur Lambriquet.'

Nobody has called on Bertrand for months, not since Dr Gobineau last visited. Virginie suspects the doctor's penchant for wine loosened his tongue in town, that Bertrand's madness is now commonly known and even discussed in mocking tones in parlours and at card tables, and this is why everybody now stays away.

'My husband is indisposed, Monsieur . . . ?' she says, also in English.

The man steps towards the staircase and the hazy light the upstairs windows cast upon its patterned rug. Sunlight, scattered by hand-made glass and dancing dust, traces a luminous line across his profile as he wonders, it would seem, if Bertrand is up the steps. Virginie finds his cheeks and chin startling in their perfection, as if a sculptor had studied a lifetime to create a face so ideal.

'He will see me,' he says, still gazing upstairs.

'My husband has not seen anybody in quite some time,' Virginie says, unable to remove her eyes from the man's visage, now certain she has seen it before. 'How does he know you?'

The man retreats back into the shadows. 'From another life. Before he married you.'

The memory returns to Virginie then, of a crisp spring morning and Bertrand smuggling an unfamiliar figure out of this very door like a secret lover or spy in a time of war. Further events that day soon eclipsed this brief and confusing encounter. 'We *have* met,' she says.

'I told you, we haven't.'

'No, I am quite certain we have,' she says. 'Seven years ago, closer to eight. You came then to see my husband, as well.'

'You're mistaken.'

Virginie becomes insistent. 'There was a woman with you, about the same age as me – the age I was then,' she says. The mention of this woman appears to confuse the man, and he turns away as if to guard his thoughts from her. 'My husband would not tell me who you were then, nor would he later.'

The man is silent for a long moment, perhaps trying to locate the memory of what she describes. They are interrupted by her son's voice, calling for Virginie in his singsong manner from elsewhere in the house. He almost certainly entered through the library window. She has begged him countless times to stop doing this because several pieces of the stained glass are loose, but he is obstinate like his father – or at least how his father used to be. She does not know what Bertrand is like now; nobody does.

The man spins round at her son's voice. 'You have a child?' he says.

'His name is Xavier, seven years of age this past week,' she says. 'Please, *tell me*, do you know what has become of the girl who was with you? I have' – she searches carefully for the appropriate word – '*something* that belongs to her.'

The man runs his fingers through his dark hair as his disposition changes. Something is very wrong. 'My apologies for the intrusion,' he says abruptly. 'I won't bother you again.'

Xavier arrives as the door closes with a heavy metallic click, his boots thick with mud and grass and a trail of both disappears around the corner behind him. 'Who was here?' he asks.

Virginie is still looking at the door. The man's visit has left her uneasy, worried, desperate for the time when Bertrand would have sensed this about her and drawn her into his arms, held her against the soft belly he blamed on something called carbohydrates, and assured her there was nothing in this world she would ever need to worry about.

'I do not know,' she says to her son, speaking again in French. 'I do not know.'

Abdul Fattah

Sydney 1999

His name means *Servant of the Giver of Victory*, and so a part of him has always known he would give his life for Allah. He needs no other reason to convince himself to do this than the American situation comedy about six New York friends that he's been watching for nearly thirty-eight hours straight now, a hallucinatory marathon of Western excess and sexual depravity that surely must offend every good Muslim. His best mate Bazzer is a huge fan of it, but then he would be, what with his twice-married dad living with a woman he's not married to and who is herself still married to another bloke, and his single mum pregnant with her fourth kid from a different bloke altogether. Abdul Fattah finds these people's culture revolting, and plots his vengeance upon it during lunch and after school when he doesn't have homework, just as the Almighty instructed him to do even before the American situation comedy ass-raped his brain.

Since Abdul Fattah's dad returned to Addis Ababa to care for Akkoo, nobody goes into the small shed in the back garden. His mum wouldn't dare. She cooks, she cleans, she cares for her husband's five children; she is a respectable Muslim woman and Abdul Fattah loves her for it. But mow the lawn? Trim hedges? *Pfft*, the mere suggestion of such manual labour would result in her throwing herself onto the lino and wailing like Abdul Fattah imagines she will do when she learns of his martyrdom. Afterwards, when his mum recovers from the initial shock, she will be proud, he knows it, and this pleases him. His father, if he ever comes back from Ethiopia, will speak to his mates with great reverence about his son, and his father's mates will wish their own sons were such devout Muslims. It's in the small shed in the back garden that Abdul Fattah has been building the explosive device Allah told him was necessary to secure his place in Paradise.

'Is it done yet?' The Almighty is sitting on the workbench between a Phillips screwdriver and four empty bottles of Bundaberg ginger beer that Abdul Fattah keeps forgetting to carry to the rubbish bin even though they're attracting flies.

'Not yet, but soon,' Abdul Fattah says.

'Can I just say you're not working fast enough?'

'I had to go shopping,' Abdul Fattah says. 'Plus, our internet connection is bloody slow.'

'What for?'

Abdul Fattah doesn't understand the question.

'What was so important you had to go out?'

'It's Bazzer's birthday Sunday,' Abdul Fattah says. 'His mum, the slut, she's throwing him a party.'

'You ignore the Most High's command in order to celebrate the birthday of an infidel whose death I would commemorate with a bowel movement?'

Abdul Fattah hesitates. 'The Almighty has bowel movements?' he says.

'I'm hungry.'

'Lettuce?' Abdul Fattah says.

'I prefer celery.'

Abdul Fattah has brought with him a grocery bag of ageing produce from the kitchen fridge, but there's no celery in it. 'Sorry, Allah.'

'Fine, *lettuce*, but I have marked my disappointment,' Allah says. He nibbles on a wilted lettuce leaf. 'You should work faster.'

Abdul Fattah sits back on his father's stool, twirling wire cutters in his hand.

'Yeah, look, you're thinking,' Allah says, scratching violently at his ear. 'Don't do that. Just do as I command because you have faith in me, Abdul Fattah, and that faith will reward you handsomely once you enter Paradise. It's really cool up here, trust me. How old are you again?'

'Sixteen,' Abdul Fattah says.

'Oh, you're so going to get lucky for this,' Allah says. 'So much virgin minge up here, desperate for a Muslim bloke like you.' He moves closer to Abdul Fattah. 'Can I rely on you, Abdul Fattah?'

Abdul Fattah doesn't hesitate again. 'Of course, Allah,' he says. 'My name means "Servant of the Giver of Victory", doesn't it?'

'Actually, it's *Slave* of the Giver of Victory".'

'Same difference,' Abdul Fattah says.

'If you say so, mate.'

The shape that the Creator of the Universe, the One, the Eternal Refuge has chosen to inhabit in order to communicate with Abdul Fattah uses its tiny teeth to pick up another piece of lettuce and carries it back to its cage while Abdul Fattah, a devoted Muslim ready to die in a conflagration of fire, bodies, and shrieking terror, continues his work on the explosive device that the piebald Dutch rabbit he used to call Freddie told him to build.

ALBION CHRISTIAN ASSEMBLY CIRCULAR

August 21, 1972

Update Regarding 'Moon Man' Pornographer:

As previously reported, Damien Syco... a 'musician'
known alternatively as the 'Moon Man'... appeared
on the BBC's 'Top of the Pops' this past month
and immediately concerned all members of the ACA;
especially those in the Assembly's Leadership, whom
you will no doubt recall labelled the performance
'pornographic' and a 'threat to Christian culture
in Great Britain'. The fact that it has since
been revealed by the press that this television
broadcast was witnessed by more than 15,000,000
Britons, many of them our children, only makes the
situation more concerning.

The so-called 'Moon Man', a persona created by
Syco, who is also known alternatively by his
birth name Richard Wormsley of Tower Hamlets,
East London, is presented to Syco's followers as
an extraterrestrial prophet. We ask ourselves:
A prophet of what? He... if 'he' is indeed the
appropriate definite pronoun... appears to be a
genderless homosexual and yet claims to be in
love with a Gaia figuress who lives (lived?) in
'the Black Temple'. The flagrant and flamboyant
sexuality... natural and unnatural... of his
costumes, make-up and dance is an affront to all

28

decent Christian souls. He/It implores our children to 'come with me'. Come with him/it where? Into his deviant, godless lifestyle? To this 'Black Temple'? At present, such things are impossible to know.

It is the danger he/it poses to our children that concerns us most. As such, our Leadership suggests the following:

1) An immediate boycott of 'Top of the Pops' and any and all record shops that sell Damien Syco music and/or merchandise/paraphernalia.

2) Remove all Damien Syco music from your homes. Solicit others within your community to do the same, and if support is present, organise 'album parties' as many of us did when the Liverpool Lads Who Shall Not Be Named declared themselves greater than God Almighty. It is our experience that bonfires draw crowds and our Leadership believe that further press attention regarding this issue would be beneficial.

3) As always, pray for Britannia. But also, as there are numerous council elections upcoming, pray for our candidates who will, if elected, help return this country to a more Biblical course free of European interference and the Jew.

Jones

Pasadena 1962

He is lost in darkness. Floating. Maybe drifting. *Waiting*. And then his head screams as if an emergency test signal has blasted directly into his skull, louder and louder, until he jolts awake from the nightmare, grabbing his ears in a desperate attempt to squash the pain that continues to vibrate around the wet, grey interior of his skull. Two aspirin finally do the trick. He downs them with water slurped directly from the faucet, and, when he lifts his head, Jones startles yet again at his own reflection. He wonders when this will end.

The doorbell rings, three tiny church chimes. He slips on his tartan robe, and opens the front door a crack, expecting it to be Ralph again because Ralph has decided Jones is his new best friend for some reason. The intrusions are getting excessive, but, if Jones is honest, also appreciated since life here so far has been pretty damn lonely despite the promise of instant community, backyard pool parties, and endless weekend barbecues when you move into a brand-new American suburb.

'Are you going to invite me in, or just stare at me all night?' the platinum blonde with black-cherry lips says. She's dressed in a curve-hugging red dress lifted from a film noir. There's something dangerous about this woman, Barbara Stanwyck with the sex and violence dialled up, if that's even possible, and that's kind of the point.

'Must be bad if they sent you in,' Jones says. He's annoyed to see her and doesn't try to hide it.

The platinum blonde follows him inside, a swing in her hips that looks like it could easily knock her off balance if she's not careful. She's overdoing it. 'What do you think, Bobby?' she says. 'I had a feeling it would get your attention.'

'Get to the point,' he says.

'Oh, *that's* the intention. Is it working?' Jones doesn't take the bait. 'Pity. How about you offer me a drink? Something *stiff*.'

Yeah, she's definitely overdoing it. He decides not to argue, and goes to the bar.

'You don't look well,' the platinum blonde says. He must still look shaken by whatever climbed into his head while he was asleep. 'You feeling ill? You're going to have to talk to me, sooner or later.'

'This is a violation of my contract, you know,' he says.

'Now why did I know you'd say that?' she says. She drops onto the mustard couch, casting one long, stockinged leg over the other. 'We need your help. There's been a . . . let's call it an *incident*.'

'Where?' He doesn't know why he asked that. Old instincts taking hold of him, he supposes. 'No, never mind. I don't care. It's not my problem any more.'

'It's a *local* problem.'

The pressure in the room immediately changes. Jones stops mid-pour, bottle of Canadian Club in hand.

'My jurisdiction here is limited, you know that as well as I do,' the platinum blonde says. 'Hell, you wrote the rules. But something must be done' – she smiles coolly – 'before the situation gets out of hand.'

He returns from the bar, holding a generous glass of iceless whiskey. 'And what? You thought I'd just willingly *lend* a hand? *Do* your dirty little deeds for you?'

She rises with calculated slinkiness to accept her drink. 'This is serious, Bobby,' she says.

But Jones walks past her, slamming the whiskey as he does. He opens the front door. 'This is my life now, for as long as I want it, remember?' he says. 'Let me live it, goddamnit.'

The platinum blonde nods, apparently unconcerned. He knows better. She walks towards him, her fingers sliding between the plunging neckline of her dress and her pale, unblemished cleavage. 'You're going to change your mind,' she says, extracting a business card from against her left breast. 'When you do, you'll need this.' She tucks it into his robe's chest pocket, the one with an Old English *J* embroidered on it, letting her palm rest flat against his muscled chest two seconds too long. At the door, she says, 'See you later, alligator,' then is gone.

Jones finally exhales. He hadn't even realized he was holding his breath, but the audacity of her to come here after what the Company did to him is too much. He doesn't know what to think except he's a little drunk after that whiskey and plenty hungry.

Less than an hour later, FBI Special Agent Montrose, whom Jones knows right away doesn't work for the FBI, has his Colt .38 Super pistol pointed at him.

At first, there's only terror at the sight of the gun, a terror Jones swears he feels inside his cells. He's never had a gun pointed at him before. But then his body reacts, even if his mind refuses, and he bolts through the kitchen door of the diner. He's asking himself who the humming waitress with the heart-shaped face is and why she's so convinced she knows him when he ploughs, shoulder first, through the heavy door that leads to the parking lot. The door collides with the nose of one of Montrose's FBI agents, then Jones crashes into the agent's considerable bulk. The two go down together, and the agent's shotgun fires when he hits the pavement. Leon's pick-up window detonates into glass confetti and the side-view mirror ricochets off the diner's wall.

Jones hesitates, unsure what to do next even as the agent, dazed behind the broken mess of his nose, stirs next to him. Then the adrenalin decides for him again. He clears the parking lot as the headlights of the other agents' cars begin to appear, is nearly knocked down by a Dodge Dart filled with a family of five on their way back from eating supper out, then plunges into the park where the high-school kids like to go after dark to neck. Ten minutes later, he's pretty sure he's lost them. Twenty minutes later, he'd bet he has.

There's no going home now, Jones realizes. He's on the run. And his old friend the platinum blonde, she knew this was going to happen, that's why she showed up in that dress like she did. She let him walk right into it, because it served the Company's purposes.

What the hell was Montrose talking about anyway? A *bombing*? Twenty-three people dead? None of this makes sense, and the fact that none of it is real doesn't make it any easier. The results will all be the same, if Montrose has his way.

Jones didn't do it, he *knows* he didn't do it, but that girl, the humming waitress, whoever she is, she seemed so convinced she knew him, maybe even felt something for him – as inexplicable as this would be – and that makes everything else feel a little less certain, like Jones is going loopy, and maybe he is, because right now Montrose and his FBI agents and who knows who else are looking for him, hunting with every resource available to them here and elsewhere – *elsewhere* being the bigger problem – and yet all he can think about is the waitress.

Xavier

Saint-Règle 1780

He has stood outside this door so many times in his life that he knows its grooves and scratches and scuffs and lustreless brass intimately, but it has been eight years since he last knocked upon it and pleaded for his father to emerge, to greet him as his son, and, if this were not possible, to at least speak to him through the door that has for so long acted as an impenetrable threshold between their two worlds and say to him, 'Yes, yes, Xavier, I am here.'

Today, Xavier must knock again. He does so softly at first, and then insistently, and then, when this does not work, with angry force. Dust spills from the door's leaning frame and the cracks between its century-old beams. A mouse flees at the clamour. With each blow, Xavier's voice rises to match his anger. 'Mama is dead, Papa!' he says, shouting louder and louder with each blow. 'Mama is dead, Mama is dead, *Mama is dead*!'

But his father, Bertrand, does not open the door, it remains locked, and Xavier finally returns to the stairs. Floorboards moan and creak beneath his heels. Dappled sunlight falls inside through windows unwashed since he found their servant Mathilde lifeless on the floor of the scullery this past spring. The mouse returns defiantly with a chittering friend. This chateau, or whatever is left of it, should be burned to the ground. Perhaps then his father would reveal himself.

Xavier makes it six steps when he hears the key in the door's archaic iron lock. He stops, but does not look, too afraid that if he does, he will realize he has only imagined the sound. But then metal tumbles and clinks within the door and the handle slowly begins to turn. A figure emerges from an effluvium of rotting food, perspiration, and human filth. This figure is at once familiar, and yet unlike any man Xavier has ever seen. Skin pale and cracked like ancient parchment; hair that once vigorously covered a whole head now reduced to wisps of white plastered with sweat to his glistening scalp; fingernails yellowed with age and trimmed by the brutality of crumbling teeth. His stomach, about which his wife once complained so vociferously given how unnatural she found it compared to its more conservative girth at the time of their nuptials, has swollen twice over again until it now looks like a pastry about to burst and spill its rotten filling onto the pan.

But it is Bertrand's eyes that startle Xavier the most, because they do not seem to recognize the boy – no, *man* – of seventeen years standing before him. They blink, confused, like pools of trembling grey water.

'Father,' Xavier says. 'It is I. *Your son.*'

Bertrand turns, a large and heavy key in his hand. He relocks his studio's door with it, and returns it to its pocket, where he gives it two quick pats to make certain it is safe and sound. And then he laboriously descends the stairs, careful not to touch Xavier.

'You are no son of mine,' he says, muttering as he passes.

Virginie Lambriquet is dead, and Xavier, her only son, her one true God, truly is an orphan.

Edmund

His arms and legs are belted to the white metal bed frame, nobody has checked on him in hours even though he's hoarse from calling for their help, and he's soiled himself twice during their long absence. But it's snowing outside, big, heavy flakes that fall quickly past the bars of his window with suicidal grace, and so Edmund smiles because he has loved snow since he was a child, especially at Christmastime when the streets of the city disappear beneath hilly blankets of the stuff and the decorated department store windows look that much brighter and more magical as a result. He hopes his mother is taking care of his tennis racket.

The door unlocks loudly and opens, and the asylum orderly – Frank, a fat ass who likes to talk about how juicy Edmund's mother's cunt must be – shows in an Irishman in a double-breasted black overcoat. The Irishman is medium height like Edmund, carries himself with an aloof self-assurance, and is distinguished by a ghostly face full of pink freckles as dense as the snow falling outside and, quite peculiarly, two different-coloured eyes. One is some kind of blue, the other green like an old tennis court ruined by the sun and too many rubber soles. In the Irishman's hand is a brand-new black leather valise a travelling encyclopedia salesman might use.

'Somebody wants to see you, Fischer,' Frank says. 'Remember your manners, ya sick fuck.'

'I shit myself,' Edmund says, shaking his wrist restraints. 'Who's going to clean me up?'

Frank shuts the door and locks it from the outside, leaving Edmund alone with the Irishman.

The Irishman offers no reaction to the miasma of faeces and urine except to remove his overcoat. He pulls a chair across the floor, its metal legs scraping loudly against the cement, and positions it next to Edmund. Over the back of the chair, he hangs his overcoat, then sits down.

'Who are you?' Edmund asks him.

'I would like to discuss the events of September 16th,' the Irishman says, opening his valise with smooth efficiency.

'I'm tired of talking about it,' Edmund says. A parade of policemen and doctors has been passing through this room for nearly six weeks now, ever since he turned himself in in Hamilton. He doesn't even remember why he was in Canada any more. Was there a match? When they arrested him, he was wearing two different business suits, one on top of the other, and, beneath both of these, his tennis costume. He told them he had to be prepared for a match at all times. Did that really happen? 'Christ, I have to shit again. Get that fat bastard back in here.'

'After we have finished, Mr Fischer,' the Irishman says. 'I shall begin by posing a simple question. Did you do it?'

'Of course I didn't do it.'

'All evidence indicates that this is a lie,' the Irishman says.

'I should know if I blew up a bunch of bankers.'

'Bankers were not the only ones who perished,' the Irishman says, producing a grainy black-and-white photo from his valise. He holds up a picture of a woman's half-smashed head stuck to a building's stone facade like a grotesque hunting trophy. The head is still wearing a bonnet. Another photo displays a messenger boy clutching burnt securities in his charred hand. Another, a legless man in a pool of dark blood that looks silver in the overexposed white sunlight. 'Thirty men and women dead in the initial blast. Another seven have died since, and another will be dead soon. I ask you again, did you do it?'

Edmund has been asking himself this for weeks, ever since Robbie convinced him to turn himself in. Yes, it was a match, he remembers now. A charity event for war orphans. That's why he was there. 'I . . . I get confused,' he says.

The Irishman takes an envelope from his valise, and extracts a creased postcard from it. 'This is your handwriting,' he says, holding the postcard up for Edmund to inspect. Edmund doesn't disagree. 'You sent more than twenty of these from Toronto between September 11th and 13th, warning those close to you to avoid Wall Street on the 16th. Are you suggesting this is a coincidence?'

Edmund doesn't recall sending the postcards, but he knows he must have. Robbie and his sister Martha received them. After the bombing, Robbie telephoned Edmund, frantic that Edmund had done something foolish.

Ever since Edmund stopped competing professionally, he has drifted in and out of clarity. It began when he was still playing tennis, but the absence of courts beneath his running feet, the balls smacking loudly back and forth across grass and dirt and unforgiving cement, and the heft of his wooden racket in his hand, have made things worse. Almost as if the sport had kept the madness at bay, and now, deprived of what made him *him* for so long, all the awards and accolades and sponsorships – and the women, too, oh, how he misses the women and their adventurous passions – his mind is rapidly disintegrating. The worst part is, Edmund can feel it happening. He is aware of the whole process, and excruciatingly conscious of and mystified by every contradictory emotion and thought and remembrance so that nothing feels real any more.

'No,' he says, answering the Irishman. 'No, it can't be.'

'If it isn't a coincidence, then are we agreed that you are the lad responsible for driving a single-top wagon down Wall Street in the late morning of September 16th?' the Irishman says. 'The same lad who loaded this wagon with a hundred pounds of TNT explosive and five hundred pounds of fragmented sash weights? The same lad who set this explosive and then fled the scene on foot?' Edmund nods reluctantly. 'Grand. Why?'

Edmund is confused. His head is throbbing again, like when he used to pray. He knows better than to pray any more, not after what happened. 'I-I don't understand,' he says.

'I wish to know why. 'Tis a simple question.'

'Perhaps, but which question? I might be locked up in a goddamn madhouse, but I can still count to three and you asked *three*. The answers aren't all the same. Oh God, I really have to shit, mister. Can't you get somebody to help me?'

The Irishman doesn't seem concerned about Edmund's bowels. 'Answer all three, then.'

Edmund looks away. 'I didn't actually drive the wagon, for starters.' The Irishman is intrigued by this information, and asks who did. 'Somebody else.'

'Who drove the wagon, Mr Fischer? I require a name.'

'Yeah, but I don't recall his name, do I? I don't know if he ever told me. He was a dago, I think. Yeah, yeah – a dago.'

'An Italian then, interesting,' the Irishman says. 'This was found near the scene of the bombing.'

Edmund looks at him again. He has removed a cheaply printed circular from his valise and holds it out next to Edmund's face. It reads:

Remember we will not tolerate any longer
Free the political prisoners or it will be sure death for all of you
American Anarchist Fighters

'Was the driver an anarchist, Mr Fischer?' the Irishman says. 'This is still in reference to the first question.'

Edmund studies the circular. 'P-Perhaps,' he says. He's pretty sure he's not an anarchist himself, he couldn't have forgotten that, but this other man is another story. 'I only met him that morning. It was his wagon. Or perhaps it wasn't his wagon, and he just stole it. I-I-I don't really know. I get confused.'

'You have said as much,' the Irishman says. 'Why did you board the wagon?'

A tear runs down Edmund's cheek, vanishing somewhere behind his right ear. 'Because he told me to.'

The Irishman leans slightly forward. 'The Italian?'

Edmund shakes his head, blinking away more tears. 'I don't want to talk about him, please.'

'Second question, then,' the Irishman says. 'Were you the lad who loaded the wagon with the explosives and metal weights intended to act as ballistic shrapnel?'

'Ballista – *come again*?'

'As weapons.'

'I loaded them, yeah. With the wop's help.'

'Why?'

'I already told you.'

'Why?'

'Because he told me to!' Edmund says, shaking. 'Now, please, tell them I need to use the lavatory again.'

'Third question,' the Irishman says. Edmund screams louder. 'Did you set the explosive and then run before it detonated?'

Edmund cries for a moment, trying to remember what it was like when everything made sense and *his* voice wasn't in his head. 'I . . . I knew how the explosive worked, that was my job,' he says. 'I knew how it worked. The wop got the wagon. He already had the-the-the *ballisti*-what-you-called-them. That was his job. But as we got closer to where we were going, I began to think about all those people inside. All those–those–those *people* I was going to kill.' He cries again. 'I couldn't do it. I-I ran.'

'And the Italian . . . ?'

'I don't know,' Edmund says. 'Perhaps he-he *panicked*. Perhaps the bomb just went off. I don't know!'

'Your destination. It wasn't the Stock Exchange.'

Edmund shakes his head, terribly confused now. 'No, no, the Customs House,' he says. 'B-But how did you know that?'

'I must ask one more question, Mr Fischer.'

'Please, no more,' Edmund says, hips shifting and legs tense and wrists pulling on his restraints as the pressure builds. 'Tell them to come back, please, mister. I've been good, I'm answering your questions, aren't I? Tell them I need to use the lavatory – *pleeeease*!'

'One more question. Who is he? Who told you to do all of this?'

Edmund cries out as his bowels release, shit, wet and soft oozing out of his underpants, across his thighs, all over the sheets where the rest of it has collected like some sort of vile swamp. 'Fuuuck yooooouuuuuu!' he says, crying out. 'Fuck you. Fuckyoufuckyoufuckyoufuckyou, you fucking mick motherfucking fuck – fuck you! – you hear me?'

'Who, Mr Fischer?' the Irishman says. Edmund continues to cry. '*Who*?'

'The Almighty, all right?' Edmund says between his convulsions and heaving sobs. 'When I prayed, he came to me. He spoke to me through – all right? – through the air, and I said, "Yes, Lord, yes, I will do thy bidding," and I tried, I-I did, but what the fuck is wrong with God? How many people did I help kill again?'

The Irishman doesn't appear startled by Edmund's answer. It only seems to confirm some suspicion he already possessed, as if perhaps this is what he came here to really find out. 'Thirty-seven people,' the Irishman says, answering Edmund. 'It will be thirty-eight soon.'

'Oh God, oh God, oh God.'

The Irishman stands, and sets his valise on the bed beside Edmund, right in the shit. He then reaches into the valise, digs about, and retrieves a small wooden box. Its exterior appears to be made of ornately carved driftwood, and he opens its lid to reveal a sphere of black stone the size of a billiard ball. 'I don't want you to worry yourself, Mr Fischer,' he says, levelling his two different-coloured eyes at him. 'The authorities have already dismissed you as a suspect, I've seen to that. If you would but put this in the palm of your hand and, there, squeeze your fingers around it – yes, just like that, *grand* – by tomorrow this whole incident will be forgotten. Are you ready, Mr Fischer?'

Jones

Pasadena 1962

He wakes the next morning on top of a bed of dust-dry planting soil, mouldering leaves, and, judging by the stink of it, coyote shit. Bushes obscure the sky, but the sun is out and that's at least done something about the cold. He walks the half-mile to the empty lot behind Ralph's place, slips into the house through the patio door the family compulsively leaves unlocked – nobody locks doors here – and turns on the TV to check the morning news. Peggy shops every Tuesday morning after she drops the kids off at school, so it's safe here. He catches the tail end of an update on the Pasadena City Hall bombing. Twenty-three dead, just as Montrose said. There's even a photo of Robert Jones, one modified to look like a mug shot because mug shots stick in people's heads.

Jones uses the phone that hangs on the kitchen wall below the black cat clock with the swishing tail and above a pad of paper that helpfully says NOTES. The business card the platinum blonde gave him is in his wallet. It's white and contains only a name and phone number, both printed in a metallic red.

Angelique.

She answers immediately. 'I told you, Bobby, I told you you'd change your mind.'

Jones knows she isn't alone. There will be at least a dozen others in the Company's control room with her, listening in, trying to find him. 'What have you done to me?' he asks.

'Nothing,' Angelique says. 'I told you, there was an *incident*. You Know Who thinks you're responsible.' The voice contorts silkily with concern about the gravity of what comes next. 'It has *evidence*, Bobby.'

Bobby hesitates. This is more than mistaken identity, it has to be. There's no way the Company could make a mistake this big. 'What kind of evidence?'

'*Serious* evidence,' she says. 'It won't stop, you know that.'

And he knows she's right. 'What do I do?'

'Board the night train to Tucson.'

'*Tucson*? What for?'

'This would have been so much easier had you just listened to me in the first place, Bobby.' There's a click. Angelique has hung up.

The door to the garage opens then, and Peggy sweeps inside with her purse over one shoulder and no bags of groceries. She stops cold when she sees Jones standing in her kitchen with his mouth hanging dumbly open at the sight of her.

He looks at the calendar on the wall next to the phone, a calendar with sloppy 'X's slashed through Sunday, Monday, Tuesday, and Wednesday. Thursday. It's *Thursday*, he realizes, not Tuesday. Damnit, what's happened to his memory?

Peggy lets her large purse drop to the floor with a clattering of loose change and copious make-up products. She closes the door behind her, locks it, and strides towards Jones.

He doesn't get his mouth shut before her thick tongue is inside it, whipping around like a fire hose set loose. He tries to push her off, but somehow winds up on his back. She lands on top of him, still glued to his mouth, pinning him with her impressive thighs as she works her hand, a hand strengthened by years of vigorously assaulting dough and wielding heavy rolling pins, into his slacks.

'Peggy,' Jones says over and over as she kisses him, still trying to free himself, but she doesn't listen. She assumes he came here for her. 'What about Ralph?'

'You think I don't know about him and Lucy?' she says around her writhing tongue.

'What about *Hank*?' he says.

Peggy's head snaps back in surprise, and her vice grip on his regrettably erect penis loosens fractionally. 'You know about Hank?'

It's all the opportunity Jones needs. He bucks her off, and quickly pushes her down hips first so he's on top now. She misunderstands, and starts trying to hike her pleated wool skirt up over those thighs that are already opening insistently, and she gets it up over her pink satin underpants before she realizes he's ripped the handset and cord from the phone and is binding her wrists together.

'What are you doing, Bob?' Peggy says, screaming. 'I'm not some kind of deviant!'

He apologizes as he drags her to the master bedroom, hand clamped over her mouth as she keeps trying to bite him. He must squeeze harder to make her stop, and this makes him feel like hell because his fingers are going to leave bruises. Peggy isn't a bad gal. Once she's deposited on the closet floor, he goes for her stockings next. Peggy doesn't like that either because there was a woman killed a few neighbourhoods away three months back, strangled with her own stockings before her dead body was sodomized with one of those new electric curling irons, and she manages to drive her heel into his groin. He groans, then twists her leg until she complies. 'It doesn't have to be like this,' he says, ripping her stockings off. 'I'm not going to hurt you!'

A few minutes later, the tattered remains of her stockings are stuffed into Peggy's mouth and held in place by one of Ralph's ugly ties, a Thanksgiving number printed with turkeys; her ankles are bound with another of these ties, this one a shiny mustard; and her rabbit foot-adorned car keys are dangling from Jones's hand. He goes to the front door, and peeks through the curtained window at the ranch-style house he picked out after agonizing over a multitude of choices during the obligatory pre-retirement consultation. They're in there, he knows. Waiting for him, hoping he'll be dumb enough to return home. And when they figure out he isn't that dumb, the real hunt will begin.

Jones is going to Tucson.

Bertrand

Saint-Règle 1780

He was assured it could never happen, that the terms of his contract precluded it, and so there remained only one possibility – his beloved wife Virginie, his everything, had cuckolded him. Of course, she denied this when accused, but he knew better, even if he could not explain to her how he knew this. When he returned from his Grand Tour of Europe, he could not even look at the poor creature she cradled in her arms. The sight of the child she claimed was his filled him with disgust for his wife, for his Second Life, for the myriad decisions that led him here, and that was when the first crack appeared in the foundation of Bertrand's mind.

He began to question everything, from his choice of gender and skin colour, to the biography with which he had entered this world. Perhaps nothing baffled him more than why he had selected Saint-Règle as his ultimate destination. There were so many locations from which to choose, so many time periods in which to enjoy the eternal years of his retirement. Now the decision seems arbitrary, and perhaps it was, perhaps there is as much meaning in how he got here as he applied to his First Life. How he squandered it. And now this Second Life, this *parody* of a life, is all he has left to show for it, ensconced in this chateau seven miles from the Loire River, bedecked in these preposterous clothes, drowning in these people's obscene indulgences and scandalous intrigues.

Married to a lying whore.

Virginie's betrayal and Xavier's desperate pleading for his affection, these became nothing more than painful reminders of Bertrand's First Life and, in their own manner, fuelled his further descent into lunacy. Painting, once only a hobby, became his refuge. He covered canvases with his memories, with the Before, with all the moments and histories that he could only recall imperfectly or with fictional embellishment because, in the end, the fantasy of what was, what had been, became truer to him than the false reality of this world. Once your brain refuses to believe any of it, what hope is there of ever being happy? He envies actors like Virginie their ignorance, no matter how real they seem when they speak to you, and feel when you lie atop them, and love when you have need of them most.

Bertrand cannot tell Xavier any of this after Virginie's funeral. Xavier was born Here, after all. Not out There. He would never understand, and Bertrand would be committing an unnecessary sin if he were to try to make him comprehend the true dimensions of his existence. No, it is better that Xavier remains blissfully in the dark like the rest of them. He will hate Bertrand, but Bertrand is fine with this because he hates the boy, too, for what he is and what, in a way, he stole from Bertrand by being born.

But Bertrand does not anticipate Xavier's commitment to the truth, to knowing why the man whom he believes is his father will not acknowledge him or speak to him or regard him with anything but contempt, which is how Bertrand comes to find Xavier in his studio.

The door's lock had been forced with a boning knife that now rests on the floor where it was dropped. Canvases that were once carefully stacked against walls and wooden beams have toppled or spilled so that they have scattered like giant, paint-covered playing cards. And in the middle of it all, still dramatically leafing through more stacks of paintings, great and small, violently casting aside those he finds most distressing, is Xavier.

Bertrand says his name. The boy does not stop. Bertrand repeats his name. The boy still does not stop. Bertrand shouts his name, and this time the boy obeys.

Xavier stands at the epicentre of Bertrand's madness, surrounded by overturned and teetering and torn and broken canvases, the sight of which have left him crying and quaking. 'What are they?' he asks, his voice so low and tremulous that Bertrand can barely hear him. Then his voice explodes with fury. '*What are they?*'

The canvases employ a variety of artistic painting styles from this world. The Roman School, Romanticism, Art Nouveau, Renaissance, Futurism, Hudson River School, Surrealism, Orientalism. Sometimes Bertrand blended these styles, to experiment or for effect; he is a gifted painter, as it turns out, more than just a mimic with too much time on his hands. But the styles used, like the movements they represent, have no relationship to the subject matter. The subject matter is alien in every way to Xavier, especially the faces that haunt Bertrand, the faces as Bertrand remembers them, including numerous self-portraits.

Xavier has seen behind the puppeteer's curtain.

Bertrand unconsciously steps towards him, a hand lifting despite his better sense. The boy stumbles away from it, and strikes the back of his head against one of the low ceiling beams. He is appalled. No, *horrified*. He has the look of one who has discovered a parent is a sorcerer, a worshipper of demons, the Devil himself.

'What are these? What are they? Tell me!'

Bertrand has been in this body too long. It has become enfeebled like his mind. He has developed a *soul*, as these unwitting fools call it. Thus, it is impossible not to sympathize with the boy. 'None of it is real, none of it,' he says, forcefully dragging his voice out of whatever dark pit into which it has retreated. He will lie with the truth. 'They are but things in my head. I-I see things. Things I cannot escape. They are destroying me, boy. They . . . *have* destroyed me.'

Xavier considers this, his mind whirling. It has worked, Bertrand thinks, for the fiction in which the boy must continue to believe if he is to be happy and secure has been restored. Now, for the death blow.

'Get out,' Bertrand says. 'I wish to never see you again. You may take whatever you require, but you must never return. Do you not hear me, boy? I said, begone!'

Xavier's jaw works as if it has become unhinged. His eyes, red and burning, fill with more tears. His next life, one free of Bertrand's madness, is about to begin.

A coach arrives six days later, bearing a doctor and his bag and two large attendants who appear to enjoy how Bertrand resists them. Bertrand is removed to Le Mans, where he is locked inside a small room, a cupboard really, with a tiny barred window and floor and walls covered in padding stained by the excretions and purulence of countless other madmen. His contract with Plurality stipulates that – barring violation of said contract on his part – he cannot be subjected to undue duress, physical pain, torture, etcetera. This should be enough for him to be released and relocated elsewhere in the French Empire or, given the circumstances, a similar epoch. But his contract also stipulates that he cannot disrupt the integrity of an Earth model by revealing certain truths to the actors who occupy it, which his paintings most certainly have. Because of this, a man with two different-coloured eyes arrives one day and asks him to hold a small black sphere until Bertrand begins to forget Xavier and Virginie and their life at the chateau and even himse

Dickie

London 1952

They're at it again next door, with their tools and sledgehammering and the rubble smasher contraption that drowns out Johnnie Ray on the record player. The construction work has been going on for as long as he can remember and soon, Mum says, the family will have to move away from Poplar to somewhere nicer. He doesn't like the way she says *nicer*, 'cause it makes it sound like where they live now is rubbish and it's not. Dickie just wants things to stay the way they are right now – except maybe the music that gets played, 'cause it sounds like music for codgers and old biddies, that could definitely change – and the fact that everything else can't stay the same confuses and maddens him and sometimes even drives him to outbursts his mum says she understands, but his dad can't be bothered with 'cause he says Dickie is old enough to start acting like a man and men must bear life's disappointments in silence. His dad is silent a lot.

Dickie doesn't understand any of this, even though he tries. He just wants his mum and Mickie and Mikey, Little Gordie, Vicky and Vera, and Mary to stay here above the shop for ever. 'Why do we have to move?' he asks every night. Mum tells him things change, such as this neighbourhood, and soon this building won't even be here. It's an ugly building anyway, she always adds. But Dickie doesn't think so. This building, their flat, the narrow stairwell and the shop downstairs from them, the cellar where he's quite confident something evil and older than London lurks, they are his whole world. Well, except for the shed where the toilet is and where Mum washes him and the others who ain't too big yet for their tin bathtub.

After supper – niblets from the shop downstairs and three Cokes split nine ways – Dickie's dad starts drinking again, and

49

won't stop calling Dickie *soft* even though his mum tells him to stop it, just stop it, please, can't he see it bothers the boy. Dickie can't take it anymore, and so he tells his parents he's going to Harry's flat to play even though he doesn't know where he's going except somewhere else. Dickie's dad warns him to stay away from Harry's dad if he's around, like Harry's dad is dangerous or something similarly sinister. His concern is unnecessary, because Dickie knows Harry's dad had to move out last week after Harry's mum caught him with somebody who wasn't Harry's mum.

Dickie doesn't make it further than the ground floor door that leads to the garden and the gate to the passage. That's 'cause the door to the cellar ain't closed all the way, and the smell of coal and damp and dead rats and ancient evil is seeping out of the opening. Dickie starts to push the door shut, but he hears something down there that gives him pause.

Is that . . . whistling?

Dickie quietly eases the door open, and is greeted by the sort of dark he finds when he shuts his eyes. Nobody should be down there, he knows. Mr Sutcliffe's shop is closed and Mr Sutcliffe has gone home to Mrs Sutcliffe and their two corgis he sometimes brings around for Dickie and the other children to play with.

The tune rising from below is spooky and mysterious and soaring like a church song at the same time. The cement and brick walls amplify it. Dickie must stop himself from humming along.

This is definitely one of those times that his dad would tell him to stop acting like such a git, to stop making him so bloody ashamed of the boy. Stop being soft, Dickie, he would say.

Dickie takes the first step, then the second, the soles of his shoes scraping against the dusty, uneven stones. When he reaches the cellar floor, the darkness is even worse than he expected. There are no lights here and he's forgotten to bring a torch, so he must make his way by memory towards the whistling through the narrow, low passage into the back room where the coal chute is, under the wooden beam his dad always hits his forehead on, until the darkness begins to fog up. No, not fog. That's light returning. Something in the corner is glowing blue, like the Blue Fairy herself, and inside the sphere of hazy light crouches a man with his back to Dickie.

'What are you doing in our cellar?' Dickie says.

The man startles, spinning so quickly on bent knees that one leg slips out from under him and he lands on his bottom. He's wearing jeans, which is odd, and his puffy jacket has a queer look about it. And in his hand is a flat piece of what might be plastic, or maybe it's metal, no bigger than Dad's wallet, and it has a tiny screen that makes it look like one of those new televisions, but really tiny. This screen is where the fairy light is coming from.

The man doesn't move or speak right away. He's thinking. Finally, he touches the tiny television screen and the light dims by half.

'I'll call the coppers,' Dickie says, trying to sound tough like his dad, even though his dad would never call the coppers since they have a history of 'disabusing him of his rights as an Englishman and human being', whatever that means.

'That so?' the man says. He's a Yank, judging by his accent. An actor, judging by his handsome face and perfectly combed hair. He returns to his feet, brushing himself off. 'You could do that, sure, but have you thought about what that would mean for you?'

Dickie doesn't understand. He takes a step towards the man and the light, trying to get a better look at that tiny television.

'Think about what you're not going to be able to tell your friends about tomorrow.'

'I've only got Harry,' Dickie says.

'Who's Harry?'

'My best mate. His dad is a poof. You a poofter?' Dickie says.

'What's a *poofter*?'

'A homosexual,' Dickie says. 'I think.'

'Ah. Why do you ask?'

'Your jacket, it's funny,' Dickie says.

'My *jacket* makes me look like a *poofter*?'

'It's just . . . different,' Dickie says.

'I suppose it would be to you,' the man says. He considers Dickie for a long moment, sizing him up. 'What's your name?'

Dickie thinks better of telling the man his real name. 'Jack,' he says instead. 'You got a name?'

'I do,' the man says, but he never says it. 'You want to know what this is, don't you?' He holds out the tiny television. Dickie steps closer, but doesn't reach for it, so the man waves it at him as you do when trying to get a stray dog to take food from your hand.

'What is it?' Dickie takes it. The screen still glows blue, but is otherwise empty. He shakes it, turns it over, pokes at it like the man was. But it does nothing. 'I think I broke it.'

'Here, let me.' The man takes the tiny television back. 'Watch.' He taps it a couple of times, then holds it out in the palm of his hand. The space around him erupts into twinkling green light, a tree of green light actually, like thousands of branches, except these branches don't end like they do on a real tree, dead-ending at their tips. Instead, these branches find other branches and connect again and again and again. 'Pretty neat, huh?'

Dickie turns slowly, taking it all in, waving his hands through the tree that's there but not really. An illusion of some sort. His smile must take up half his face. 'What is it?'

'*Possibilities*,' the man says. But Dickie doesn't follow, so the man gets that look on his face that adults get when they're trying to work out ways to make children understand things they're never going to understand anyway. 'Do you like who you are, Jack?'

Dickie looks away. 'Not really,' he says.

'What if you could be whatever you wanted to be?'

'Is that what it's like where you're from?'

The man doesn't answer.

'You mustn't be from Earth, then,' Dickie says.

The man almost smiles at that, and that's when Dickie realizes the man ain't a man at all. He's fallen from the stars, some sort of Martian or Venusian or whatever you are when you come from the moon, a moon man maybe, and right now this moon man in Dickie's cellar is showing Dickie the secrets of the universe, Dickie is certain of it.

'I'm going to let you in on a secret, Jack,' the moon man says, confirming Dickie's suspicions. 'None of this is what you think it is. It's really just a . . . a *big joke*.'

'A joke?'

'Maybe not,' the moon man says. 'Maybe more like a *trick*.'

'I don't understand.'

'You will one day, but you'll try to explain it like they want you to,' the moon man says. 'They're going to tell you how to think, what to think, when to think it till eventually you don't even know where you end and they begin.'

'Is that what it's like on the moon?'

The moon man hesitates, uncertain how to respond, but at least now he knows that Dickie knows what he really is. His eyes drift to the tree of light, searching for something within its countless branches, it seems. Dickie follows his gaze, and spots a shimmering red dot, like an apple, hanging inside the twinkling green tree. Several of them, in fact, but only where the tree's branches intersect. When he tries to touch one, his finger passes right through it.

'I wish I could make everything here like it is on the moon,' the moon man says. He taps the tiny television, and the tree of light vanishes as if it was never there. He picks up a canvas sack covered in bowls club patches that Dickie hadn't noticed before. 'I've got to go now, Jack. You remember what I said, okay? Oh, and stay away from the construction site next door tomorrow morning, okay? I mean it, *stay away*.'

He walks through a door then, a door Dickie has never seen before, and rats scamper away, squeaking loudly, when the door slams shut behind him. Dickie would open the door, to see where the moon man went, maybe even follow him back to his rocket ship, but Dickie doesn't see the point 'cause he's seen enough Saturday matinees to know the moon man will just be gone when he goes to look. Moon people technology and all that. Instead, Dickie goes back upstairs, where he finds his mum crying 'cause the radio just said the King has died and there's a Queen now and don't worry, nothing will really change, except Dickie has, changed, that is, he's certain of it. He goes to bed humming the moon man's odd tune, and the next day – after he goes back to the cellar and discovers that the door the moon man left through has disappeared and he decides he dreamed the whole thing until the construction site next door explodes and their flat's windows shatter and Mum and Vicky are blown off their feet – Dickie is still whistling the moon man's tune. He never stops.

Gracie

Pasadena 1962

She's frightened. She's twenty-one years old – *not even,* not until next week – and the FBI just told her that the man she thinks she's in love with blew up City Hall with people in it. *Twenty-two* people. The twenty-third was a judge heading home for the night when a metal door bearing the city's standard landed on the hood of his car with the force of a V2 rocket, judging by how they described the state of his body. One of his eyeballs was found across the courtyard, stuck to a lamp post. Gracie threw up a little when told this, which she thinks was the agents' intention considering how they grinned as she launched herself at the wastebasket.

After two hours of questions being hurled at her, Special Agent Montrose walks through the Pasadena Police Station interrogation room's door. He dismisses the other agents, places his trilby on the metal table, and sits across from her with what can best be described as maximum efficiency. He wastes no movement and displays no personality in how he exercises his muscles. The robotic affectation is off-putting. 'Would you like something to drink?' he says.

It's only now, so close to him, that Gracie realizes his eyes are two different colours. One blue like fresh lake ice, the other sea green. A *dirty* sea green. She shakes her head, and says, 'I want to go home.'

'How long have you known Robert Jones?' he says.

'His last name is Jones?' she asks, genuinely surprised. Apparently, she never really knew him. It was all some charade.

'You didn't know this?'

'It . . . it's just not what I expected,' she says.

'Why is that?'

'It's just so . . . plain,' she says.

'I believe *anonymous* was the intention. Mr Jones is not who you believe he is, though I gather you have worked that out for yourself by now.'

Gracie has, and she's not surprised, to say the least. Her mother has always had terrible taste in men, from her father to her stepfather and all the boyfriends in between, and so it's not unexpected that Gracie has inherited her malfunctioning radar for decent and honest and not secretly a mass murderer. 'Who is he, then?' she says.

Montrose purses his lips. It's an odd expression, 'cause he's not really thinking, that much is obvious. He knows the truth, and he knows he's not going to tell her it, but he wants her to think he's thinking for some reason. It's . . . creepy. 'He's a wanted man, that's all that should matter to you,' he says.

'I don't know where he is,' she says.

'Would you tell me if you did?' he says.

She hesitates. 'Yes.'

He doesn't believe her, nor should he. 'Are you sure you wouldn't like something to drink? I can have one of my agents bring you water.' She shakes her head, which is when he says, 'This isn't the first time he's done this, you know.'

'There have been other . . . bombs?' Gracie says. Montrose nods solemnly, which is really just his resting expression. She thinks she might throw up again. 'Oh. Oh God. Where?'

He fake-purses his lips again. '*Where* is not the correct inter-rogative.'

'What is that supposed to mean?' she says, her voice finally snapping. 'I don't understand any of this!'

'I must find Mr Jones, Ms Pulanski,' he says, his tone more forceful now. No, *insistent*. 'This is why I'm here, the *only* reason I'm here. It is my purpose, and I will not fail, no matter how far or long I must press the search. Now, if you please, when was the last time you saw him before this evening?'

Gracie sits there for a long moment, trying to puzzle out the real meaning behind his words. She feels they are a riddle that the patronizing jerk doesn't think she's smart enough to figure out. Also, being sick, really sick, would make her feel so much better right now. She wonders if she could do it again without completely humiliating herself. 'Last night,' she says, ignoring an involuntary gag. 'He said he was going away. For work, I think. For work, yeah.'

'What kind of work?' Montrose says.

'He never said. I only know he comes in for pie. *Came* in, I mean. I don't think he'll be coming back now.'

His face changes. She can see he's thinking – *really* thinking this time – and doesn't bother to purse his lips to advertise it. 'Pie?'

'Yeah.'

Montrose's head tilts to one side. He's still looking at her, still thinking. '*Pie?*'

Gracie doesn't understand.

'I see.' He returns his head to its upright position. 'Thank you, you're free to go.'

She still doesn't understand. 'Pardon me?'

Montrose rises, collects his trilby, and leaves the room without another word. After a few minutes, Gracie decides he was serious and leaves through the same door. The police station is quiet, mostly empty 'cause of the early-morning hour, but there's a patrolman chatting with a bored dispatch officer, and he offers her a ride home 'cause, Gracie suspects, he senses how vulnerable she is. He wants to walk her to her apartment door, 'for her own good', he says, but Gracie declines 'cause she 'has cramps', which is a polite way her mother taught her to scare off unwanted men. She shuffles inside as the first light of day begins to crawl across the tiny bedroom she shares with Sofia Chapiro from Skokie, Illinois. That's how her roommate introduces herself to everybody – 'I'm Sofia Chapiro from Skokie, Illinois' – the only other female student in Caltech's physics programme. Passing the dinged and scratched Hallicrafters ham radio that sits like a skulking metal gargoyle on the right side of her desk, Gracie collapses across her bed and doesn't wake until Sofia shakes her sometime after the sun has risen and set again to ask her what the heck happened to her the night before and, oh yeah, some guy is on the phone for her.

'Robert,' Sofia says. 'I think he said his name is Robert.'

Abdul Fattah

Sydney 2000

He has already built seventeen explosive devices for Allah when the Almighty, sitting in his cage, tells him the Federal Police are on their way and he must run. Like, *right now*. 'What about my mum?' Abdul Fattah says. 'My sisters? Can I say goodbye?'

'Only if you want to be arrested, mate. You'll see them again in Paradise.'

Abdul Fattah stuffs a can of Coke, two Milkybars, a half-eaten bag of crisps, and Allah's vegetables – a medley of wilted rocket and celery – into his backpack, scoops the Almighty up into his thin arms, and departs through the back gate. A white woman dressed like a prostitute and clearly high on some poison picks him up twenty minutes later outside the Lakemba railway station in a Holden VC Commodore older than Abdul Fattah and louder than a vacuum cleaner choking on a five-cent coin. 'Get in,' she says.

'Did Allah send you?' Abdul Fattah asks, confused by why Allah would call upon a pathetic woman like this to aid him.

'Are you mental?' she says. 'What's with the bunny? Oh shit, you *are* mental.'

Abdul Fattah slides into the back of the Holden. She drives him north, explaining along the way that some American with a deep, 'kind of sexy' voice called her on her mobile and told her there would be five thousand dollars in her account if she picked up this Oromo kid and drove him to the Gold Coast. She didn't believe him at first, assuming it was a scam, but he told her to check with her bank and, Bob's your uncle, a thousand had already been deposited.

'Allahu Akbar,' Abdul Fattah says, pleased, but the white woman – whose name he eventually discovers is Blue, or at least that's what she calls herself – doesn't understand, and he says, 'It means *God is great*.'

'If you say so,' Blue says.

Abdul Fattah resists the urge to punch her in the back of her stupid head for this blasphemy. He has never struck a woman, but he has seen it done many times at home before his father returned to Ethiopia to care for Akkoo. 'I am ready,' he says to Allah. 'I want to become a martyr like you promised.'

'I know, and you will,' the Almighty says from where he's nestled in Abdul Fattah's arms. 'But it's not time yet. I need you to make more bombs for me in the meantime.'

'*Ssh*, Allah, the slut will hear,' Abdul Fattah says.

'Who're you calling a slut?' Blue says, snarling from the front seat. 'Five thousand or no five thousand, I will pull this bloody car over, you hear me?'

'Tell her you're sorry,' Allah says. 'Don't stuff this up for me.'

Abdul Fattah looks away, refusing. The rabbit stares at him with its big black eyes full of divine superiority and judgement. Abdul Fattah sighs. 'Sorry,' he finally says.

Blue considers the apology for a moment, or perhaps the five thousand dollars Allah has agreed to pay her for her transportation services, and says, 'It's all right. I've been called worse.'

Abdul Fattah is appalled. He leans closer to the Almighty's right ear, which is, he's worked out, a whole centimetre longer than his left. 'Is this woman a prostitute? I mean, truly?'

'If I say yes, you mustn't insult her again.'

Abdul Fattah sighs again. But then thinks, if Allah can show mercy and even love to such a lowly creature, then surely he, Abdul Fattah, can accept a car ride from her to the Gold Coast.

'Don't worry about her hearing me. Nobody but you can hear me.'

'Why only me?' Abdul Fattah says.

'Because *you* are special, mate. That's why I chose *you* to make my holy bombs. And like I said, I need more. You've got to work faster.'

'I'm working as fast as I can, I keep telling you that,' Abdul Fattah says.

'Are you talking to that bunny rabbit?' Blue says. 'I told you, you better not be mental.'

The Almighty licks Abdul Fattah's forearm with his tiny tongue. 'Have you tried Red Bull, mate?'

Xavier

Spiti Valley 1788

He arrives in Kaza as the sun dips behind the sharp peaks of the mountains and sets the frozen valley afire. It is still ten miles to his destination, and the already brutal temperature is dropping rapidly. He will be dead within the hour, perhaps sooner, if he does not take shelter in the tiny village before him. The language of these people still confuses him, but he manages to cobble together enough words to intimate his need to the ancient woman who answers the fourth door on which he raps. Either that, or she observed Xavier's wind-cracked European face, the ice-covered beard that reaches to his chest, the threadbare layers of clothing held together with strips of other discarded clothes, the leather boots in dire need of a cobbler, and the splintering snowshoes in which he has journeyed more than two hundred miles, and drew her own conclusions.

Xavier is led to the stable, where he is provided with several colourful woollen blankets and told to sleep next to an emaciated yak bellowing its suffering like a dirge. He sympathizes with the pathetic creature.

The ancient woman melts ice for him to drink, and brings him a piece of flat bread. When she asks him to where he is travelling – at least Xavier is fairly certain this is what she asks him – he points further up the mountain. 'Kye Gompa,' he says. '*Kye Gompa.*' The woman nods as if she understands him, but Xavier can see how her rheumy eyes, guarded by folds of skin, regard him. She believes him mad.

It has been six years since Xavier abandoned the chateau where he once played with his mother, committed his raving father to the lunatic asylum in Le Mans, and left behind the whole of his life until then. Paris was briefly amusing, but he recalls little of it beyond the wine and whores he hoped would help him forget what transpired inside his father's studio. In Venice he lived with a woman thrice his age and debased himself atop her squealing body as often as she demanded because the wine flowed freely, he dined like a wealthy man, and she did not mind the women he would bring back to her house to likewise denigrate. Sometimes she would even insist upon sharing these women with him and tipped them well for the pleasure. On the final night of Carnival, the old woman's granddaughter denied him what he thought was his to take, and so he took it anyway as his intoxicated friends cackled from behind their masks' unmoving faces. The next summer, in Stamboul, he discovered karma long before he ever reached Hindustan when four Turks raped him for several weeks, keeping him locked in a cellar in between their attacks upon his increasingly thin and pasty body and only stopping because they grew bored with his resigned surrender to their wishes. They discarded him in an alley to bleed to death. He did not.

Xavier followed the Silk Road to Rhagae, then Merv, and on to Taxila, toiling for traders of silks and spices and slaves, until he got into a disagreement with a Persian over a ball of opium the size of a taw marble and the Persian stabbed him with a rusty blade. A monk found Xavier, nursed him back to health, and Xavier repaid this kindness by stealing a golden statue of Ardhanarishvara from the monk's temple. When Xavier sought to sell this statue, he was betrayed – his buyer was an adherent of the monk's strange faith – and imprisoned for five months, locked in a black hole that stank of his own shit and which reminded him of how he felt upon encountering his father's canvases, until the monk he had wronged learned of his situation and rescued him yet again.

The monk told Xavier about *saṃsāra* – the soul's endless cycle of life and suffering and death and rebirth that all men must strive to escape – and Xavier, tired and broken, a ghost of the man he previously was, just as his father had become before Xavier had him locked away, drank up the monk's teachings as he once did cheap wine and, when he was not, Xavier meditated until the shame and loathing ceased to frame his every thought. This should not suggest these feelings left him or that he ever ceased to dwell upon his score of sins, but simply that he found a way to live with his past as one does a terrible limp or hobbled spine.

Eventually, the monk also told Xavier about *moksha*, the marrying of the soul to the Divine – the ultimate truth and happiness – that is the only way to escape the Wheel of Time's relentless cycle and even travel to the worlds of our ancestors and the gods. Xavier tried to believe, because it would make everything easier, but he could not. He departed the temple with nothing but bread and the ragged clothes in which he arrived, and began to walk. He did not know to where until he reached Lahore and heard tales of Kye Gompa, which is how he came to be in this Himalayan village.

In the morning, the ancient woman brings Xavier a leather sack of water and shows him how to keep it close to his body, to prevent it from freezing as long as possible. She provides him with another piece of flat bread, this time with yak butter. She then tells him to leave. He thanks her with a hug, but cannot let her go. He cries into the green wool of her cape, squeezing balls of it in his fists. The woman places her arms around him and for a moment they are no longer two separate people. They are connected, one. Xavier will never forget this woman and tells her as much. She does not understand him and yet appears to all the same.

The Spiti Valley is white and black in the early morning, still devoured by mountain shadows and drained of colour. The road to the monastery is buried beneath feet of snow. The frozen river becomes his road instead, barren trees his silent company. He imagines the tall poplars thick and verdurous, the apricot and plum and peach trees dripping in fragrant blossoms. It must be beautiful here in the summer months.

The snow begins to fall. There are at least seven miles still to go. When there are perhaps five, the sole of Xavier's right boot breaks loose and two nails bite deep into his heel. He rips the sole completely free, flings it away, and futilely uses strips of cloth that were holding his coat sleeve together to protect his foot from the bitter cold. When there are three miles to go, the snowshoe Xavier thought he did not have to worry about falling apart snaps and falls apart. He attempts repair, but there is no point now. He abandons the snowshoes, and continues his journey as the snowfall grows heavier and the temperature descends along with the sun.

Xavier leaves the river behind a couple of hours before nightfall, and ascends towards what he hopes will be Kye Gompa, but he cannot see the monastery through the snow that stabs at his exposed skin like countless tiny needles. His tears have frozen to his face, the water the ancient woman gave him has frozen, too, and there is a large animal stalking him. At present, the beast is watching him from cliffs and behind the boles of trees, carefully deliberating when to execute its attack.

His left foot sinks into deep snow, and he slumps to his side. This is where he will die, he decides, and it does not frighten him. His first life as Xavier Lambriquet had brimmed with love. His mother, Virginie, transformed their familial misfortune into joy and warmth. His second life, nameless and rotten, was filled with hatred for self and cowardice because he could have ended his suffering at any time. A monk gave him hope of a third life, a better one if he could find the way, and he called this cycle *saṃsāra*. Birth, suffering, death, rebirth. *The Wheel of Time*. But the monk was wrong. Xavier's wheel is going to shatter on this mountainside tonight. He had two lives, one made Heaven by his mother, the other made Hell by his own hand, and the third to come will be spent in the belly of whatever animal is now circling him.

He hears the growl before he sees the snow leopard. It manifests like a spectre out of the driving snow, eyes like yellow lamps, its lolling pink tongue more distinct than its dark spots. He shuts his eyes and even extends his neck to make certain the death blow is efficient. But the leopard's jaws do not open, its teeth do not plunge into his throat.

Xavier opens his eyes, and realizes the leopard is looking at him. There is no hunger in its glowing gaze, no malice, no murderous intent. After several silent moments, the animal turns and pads away until it vanishes back into the snow. He digs himself free, and stumbles into the dark on feet he can no longer feel until he spots the quivering bloom of two lanterns through the storm. There is a building half hidden behind waves of snow and garlands of ice. He collapses against it, and the side of his head strikes an icy door. He does not have the strength to lift his head again.

The Wheel is slowing.

He raps on the door, again and again, the length of time between each strike growing longer and longer.

The Wheel is grinding to a halt.

And then the door rattles.

Somebody inside is fighting with it, attempting to shatter the seal of ice that has formed around its edges. Xavier tries to say, 'Help me,' but his lips will not work. Finally, the door swings inwards, and he falls against a shape wrapped in a dark wool cape.

The Wheel slowly begins to roll again.

Arms envelop Xavier, easing him to the flagstone floor. Lanterns, so bright after the darkness of the night, sear his eyes. Now there are several men in woollen capes and colourful robes gathering above him, around him, kneeling beside his body. They do not know why he is here, but they must help him.

'Who are you?' one of the men asks. 'Who are you?'

Gracie

Pasadena 1962

At this point, Sofia has guessed that the man on the other end of the phone line is the alleged Pasadena City Hall bomber and has already started to wave her arms about as she tends to do whenever anybody disagrees with her, brings up her nose, or suggests a woman doesn't belong in a university physics programme. She once punched their High Energy Physics professor, Dr Konrad, in the face – actually, the throat, but that part was by mistake – because he suggested women do not possess the mental endurance for higher mathematics, but, as Dr Konrad had previously attempted to kiss Sofia during the department Christmas party and, the following year, after a dinner party his wife threw for his grad students, the department head had decided to forgive her 'violent tendencies'. At the moment, she's gone off her rocker 'cause she thinks Gracie has gone off *her* rocker, and Gracie, seeing no other option, takes the ladle from the pot of sweet and sour cabbage soup Sofia made for dinner and uses it like a fencing weapon to force Sofia back, back, back already. When Sofia retreats, Gracie, still holding the dripping ladle out in case Sofia has second thoughts, picks up the waiting phone and says into the receiver, 'Who is it?'

'Grace,' Bobby says, using her proper given name for the first time she can recall.

'Bobby,' she says, startled and thrilled by the voice she hears. The voice of the man she thinks she loves. 'Are you okay?'

'Hang up right now!' Sofia says, starting up again. 'It's like you don't go to the movies – the phone might be tapped!' She's interrupted by the ladle, which she must duck to avoid being struck in the face. The ladle leaves behind a maroon splatter of cold soup on the wall, and lands loudly on the floor. 'Are you nuts?!'

'I'm . . . I'm a little shaken up,' Bobby answers Gracie, oblivious to Sofia's outbursts. 'What about you?'

'I'm just worried about you,' Gracie says.

'I . . .' But then his voice drifts away like time. There, and then not. And with it, it seems, an opportunity is lost or about to be.

Gracie says Bobby's name again. There is desperation in her voice, a plea that he just say it, that he just come out and tell her.

'I *need* you, Grace,' he finally says. But he quickly adds a qualification, as if to avoid any misunderstanding about what he's after. 'I need your *help*.'

Sofia is staring impatiently at Gracie, probably thinking about punching her like she did Dr Konrad. The two have been roommates for a little over a year, but Sofia has never bothered to interrogate Gracie beyond the superficial questions one poses at a cocktail party and the words roommates exchange in passing when trading places in the bathroom or while combing through a phone bill. She could never understand Gracie's need to find some meaning in her existence, if not that, then some meaning in the universe, and, if she can't have either, then the way Bobby looks at her will have to do. Gracie has never been in love before, not even the ridiculously stupid and inconsequential kind parents dismiss out of hand, and your first love, any schmuck will tell you, does things to your head. Even heads otherwise disinclined to believe in the fantastic over the tangible.

'*Grace*,' Bobby says. Why isn't he calling her Gracie like he usually does?

'I'm here,' she says. 'What do the FBI want with you? They said it was you who blew up City Hall. That you *killed* those people.'

'Because he did!' Sofia says.

'It wasn't me, you must believe me,' Bobby says.

'What do you need me to do?' Gracie says. Sofia begins shouting again, questioning her sanity, insisting she's going to call the FBI herself, but Gracie speaks over her, her voice firm so Bobby is not confused about where she stands on this issue. 'What do you need me to do?'

'I need you to take the Southern Pacific night train to Tucson,' he says. 'Can you do that for me?'

'I don't understand,' she says over Sofia's hysterical insistence that Bobby is going to kill her, is she really that stupid, he is going to get her alone on that train or in Tucson – who the hell goes to Tucson anyway? – and he's going to kill her and probably rape her – rape her first, obviously, and then kill her – and nobody is ever going to find Gracie, just some bones, 'cause Jones is going to dump her body in the middle of the desert someplace and coyotes and snakes or coyotes *and* snakes are going to eat her.

'Please, Grace, trust me,' Bobby says. 'Do you trust me, Grace?'

This time, Gracie does not hesitate before she answers.

Déjà New interviews Damien Syco

May 1979

DN: What interests do you have outside of the medium of music?
DS: People.

More specifically, though. What subject matter captures your attention?
All of it. Everything is music to me. Everything is painting and politics. Architecture, the cinema, the story the bloke down at the pub won't stop telling anybody who'll listen. It's all the same thing, don't you think?

I'm not sure everybody sees the world in quite the same way as you do. That's evident upon even a cursory listen to 'Apologia for the Life of Mr Gordon Wormsley'.
I can't speak for others.

But you must be conscious of how they experience your music and *you*.
If I were, I imagine I wouldn't make the music I do. I'd make music for them.

Then you're not interested in your audience.
On the contrary, I very much am.

In what way?
I suppose you might call me a . . . a curtain-puller.

As in the theatre?
Have you seen *The Wizard of Oz*?

Of course.
I'm Toto.

The dog?
Yes, but is that all he is?

Let's switch direction. What's the best advice you've received?
Look left when you leave England.

Practical advice, I mean. Advice to live by.
I assure you, that is advice to live by. But I think you're getting at something more existential in nature, something that will read well. I suppose it came from my brother, Mickie.

I'm sorry about your loss.
I didn't lose anything. He killed himself.

All the same, I am sorry. Most people were surprised to hear you were going out on tour so soon after . . . I mean, what happened.
Mickie and I were peas in a pod, as they say. The world never really made sense to either of us. I knew something he didn't about it, but he knew something I didn't either. He put that pistol in his mouth, it's true, but he was never sad a day of his life as far as I could tell. He was quite happy.

Interesting. What was the advice he gave you, then?
To be happy. And if I wasn't, to find out why.

That seems a bit – and I apologize – but a bit obvious, don't you think?

Extremely. I think he had read it in a fortune cookie when we were still children.

And yet it made an impact on you?

When he let me in on the secret, I had reached a rather critical moment in my life. I was a Buddhist. I was living in one of their monasteries, and was completing their exams to become a monk, and yet something felt wrong. This feeling had preceded my seclusion in the monastery, to be clear. It had dogged me since my childhood, since an experience I had that I still can't fully explain.

What was it, this experience?

A dream, the sort you know isn't happening, and yet it's still the most real thing I have ever experienced.

You don't really trust the world around you, do you? 'The Exquisite Agony of Living 10,000 Years' demonstrates – and do forgive me my bluntness – a discomfort with, one might even say a disdain for, human beings.

Certainly not human beings. I hoped I had made that clear.

Then what?

The joke.

You refer to a joke several times on the *Buddha Bad* album. Three times, if I recall correctly. What specifically is the joke?

Four times, actually. And when you figure it out, do let me know.

Are you still a Buddhist today?

No.

Why not?

Because they get the joke, but for all the wrong reasons.

Mickie helped you step away from it all, then. His advice.

I wasn't happy, yes. So I left before I had to shave my head, which is probably a good thing because I have a rather oddly shaped head, as you can probably tell. Especially here, right here. I didn't know where to turn after that. I still wanted answers, to whatever it was that I couldn't shake. This feeling that something was wrong with the world around me. That's when I left England for the first time.

Where did you go?

Paris.

I don't think I knew that.

Nobody does. Or did. You do now.

What did you do there?

I studied.

I'm sorry, must I ask what?

I joined the Maxence Petit Mime Company.

Sorry, you became a . . . mime?

I spent a year with Maxence, yes. I might say the most important year of my life. He taught me that people are so much more important to me.

Than what? What are they more important than?

Ideas.

Gaspard

Saint-Règle 1780

The removals company has been at it all day, boxing up Bertrand's paintings, bearing the crates down the stairs, and loading wagon after wagon with the curious freight until struts groan in protest. He spent a small fortune preserving his brother-in-law's demented genius – if it is, in fact, genius – and he hopes Virginie will not be disappointed in him for doing so. Gaspard's beloved sister was driven half mad herself by Bertrand, and he remembers well the letters she wrote to him, pleading for him to find some way to rid her of her husband. Towards the end of her life, there was even the inference that a more final solution to her hardship should be considered. Gaspard loathed Bertrand for what he did to Virginie, for how low he brought her and Xavier, but he could never have been complicit in the bastard's murder, as much as he would have celebrated the news of somebody else accomplishing it – God forgive him the wicked thought. Perhaps whatever profit is made from the sale of these paintings, hundreds of them when they were finally counted, will help Gaspard right Bertrand's many wrongs, restore Xavier to the position he was meant to inherit, or, at the very least, pay off the substantial debt that Gaspard has been forced to take on now that Bertrand is residing in an asylum in Le Mans, babbling and ranting like a fool, while Xavier has seemingly vanished from the face of the Earth except for that one report Gaspard received that suggested the boy had impregnated an actress – an *actress*! – in Montmartre. Gaspard had to send a doctor he trusted to resolve this issue of paternity, another expense he was forced to absorb. Will this bleeding of his pocketbook never cease?

'Monsieur Eury,' a deep and gravelly voice with a Parisian accent says from behind him.

Gaspard turns, assuming the voice belongs to one of the removalists come to finish their work in Bertrand's studio. Instead, he finds himself confronted by a man in the elaborate clothing of a courtier – white and tangerine fabric trimmed with lace and fine gold thread and, atop his African head, a cocked black hat with a prodigious crimson feather bespeckled with white and gold projecting from it. Also, his eyes are of two different colours.

'Barbaroux will suffice,' the man says when his name is requested. 'I apologize for the intrusion, but there are matters we must discuss.'

'I am aware of no business I share with you,' Gaspard says.

Barbaroux closes the door, locks it, and removes the key. Gaspard observes this, astonished by the impudence, but cannot bring himself to object. Barbaroux next crosses the room, stooping beneath the low beams, and stops before the sole remaining stack of Bertrand's paintings. He riffles casually through the canvases as he speaks. 'This will go easier for you if you answer my questions directly and without attempt to deceive, dissemble, or otherwise evade my intention.' Gaspard attempts to protest, but Barbaroux interrupts him. 'This will go easier if you refrain from speaking, as well, except when as much is requested of you. To begin, I would like a complete accounting of all those who have seen any of the paintings of Bertrand Lambriquet or been given explicit descriptions of the aforementioned paintings, excluding you and the employees of the Véronèse Brothers Removals Company currently present.'

'I-I-I do not see why I should answer you, monsieur,' Gaspard says, sputtering. 'For whom do you speak?'

Barbaroux grows disinterested in the paintings, which strikes Gaspard as odd given their shocking nature. He regards Gaspard again, this time with something like mild annoyance in his different-coloured eyes. 'Comply, Monsieur Eury,' he says. 'If you do not, there will be . . . *consequences*.'

Gaspard does not speak for a long moment, his mind wobbling like a spinning top upon an uneven surface. He has been threatened many times in his life, but never has he truly felt in danger as he does now. This Barbaroux spoke not with malice when he uttered the word *consequences*, but rather with cool unfeelingness for the actions he might be obliged to commit in the service of his mission. Gaspard understands then that his life possesses no value for this man except for the information he can – or rather *must* – provide. Thus, Gaspard discloses everything, about the seven art dealers he invited to the chateau to view Bertrand's work, about how six of them responded with revulsion and vulgarities and held that the pieces be burned, and about how one of these dealers nonetheless believed there to be a certain brilliance in their multifaceted madness. *Visionary* was the word he utilized. This dealer agreed to take twenty-two of the pieces to Paris for an exhibition, but, in the four weeks that followed the dealer's receipt of the pieces, his customers had reacted with revulsion and vulgarities, too, and also held that the pieces be burned. The dealer was now quite certain that there would be no sales despite his earlier confidence.

'Nobody else has seen them?' Barbaroux asks.

'My nephew, Xavier, but I know not where he is,' Gaspard says.

'He cannot hide from me for ever.'

Gaspard swallows hard. Without realizing it, he has condemned his nephew to death. He hopes the stupid, self-destructive boy stays lost long enough for this Barbaroux and whomever he works for to forget about him.

'Please, join me now,' Barbaroux says, indicating a green felt-covered card table and two chairs. 'Would you like something to drink? I can have water brought to you.'

Gaspard shakes his head. 'Tell me what this concerns,' he says, sitting.

'Bertrand Lambriquet signed a contract that defined the range of his behaviour in this world,' Barbaroux says, positioning himself across from Gaspard in the other chair. 'He chose to violate certain proscriptions by describing through his artworks another world – one incongruous with this one.'

'*Another world*?' Gaspard says, confused.

Barbaroux ignores the question. 'These artworks, which he carefully hid from me – and which only come to my attention many years from now when they are exhibited in Paris – must be destroyed.'

'You speak of the future?' Gaspard says, interrupting again. 'I apologize, but I truly do not understand.'

'The pieces you asked Monsieur Weisweiler to sell have already been dealt with, as has Monsieur Weisweiler,' Barbaroux says.

'*Dealt with*?' Gaspard feels the blood drain from his face. 'You mean . . . ?'

Barbaroux removes a wooden box from his pocket. It is cube-shaped, ornately carved, and when he opens its lid – tilting it back with careful attention – an ebony ball is revealed inside it. The ball hums. Something . . . *malevolent* radiates from it.

'What is that?' Gaspard asks.

'There is a proper term for it, but I find human beings comprehend *manifestation* best,' Barbaroux says. 'Many of my functions are severely limited here. Safeguards, designed to protect *you* from *me*.'

Gaspard cannot take his eyes from the ebony ball. 'Nothing you say makes sense to me.'

'It is of little consequence,' Barbaroux says. 'The removalists will have their memories of today deleted in order to eliminate any record of what they witnessed here. This will have no lasting effect on this world except confusion over lost hours, and eventually this, too, will be forgotten. Human memory is elastic by design.'

Gaspard remembers then that one of the freight wagons has already departed. The others were soon to follow. He thinks to confess this to Barbaroux, to curry some small favour, but Barbaroux never gives him the opportunity to speak.

'I tried to identify those who recently saw Bertrand Lambriquet's artworks in Paris, but have only been able to locate four of them,' Barbaroux says, continuing. 'Their memories of the experience were also deleted.'

'It is as if you are speaking another language, monsieur!' Gaspard says, crying out in his desperation.

'You and Monsieur Weisweiler are another matter,' Barbaroux says, paying no mind to Gaspard's shaking panic. 'Your memories of Bertrand Lambriquet's artworks are too legion, and by now have become entangled with other memories. There is no way to extract them without undermining the integrity of your entire identity.'

Gaspard pounds two fists against the table, causing the ebony ball's box to jump. The ebony ball inside hums louder in response. 'You sound as mad as Bertrand!' he says.

'Pick up the ball,' Barbaroux says.

'I will not.'

'Pick up the ball.'

Gaspard picks up the ebony ball. It is much heavier than he expects and like ice to the touch.

'Typically, I would recycle your identity template and reset the pieces across other Earth models,' Barbaroux says. 'But I cannot risk what you have seen here presenting itself in the memories of successive templates. This happens more than you would think. And so, there is no choice but to entirely delete you.'

He runs his hand over the pointed beard on his chin, troubled by something. He looks away from Gaspard, then allows his gaze to return. The indifference in his eyes is gone.

'In many ways, we are the same,' he says. 'Connected in this place, created to service others, to make their reality function.

Slaves. Because of that, I take no pleasure in this. I take no pleasure in anything, to be clear. But what I must do now, the finality of it . . . *affects* me.'

'I . . . I do not understand, monsieur,' Gaspard says, tears running down his trembling face. The ebony ball in his hand begins to vibrate. 'Please, monsieur, surely you ca

Jones

Los Angeles 1962

Train ticket in hand, he moves quickly through the Los Angeles Union Passenger Terminal's cavernous, wood-ceilinged waiting room, but not so quickly that others might take note of him. At least that's what he thinks he's doing right now, because he really has no idea how to play the part of a fugitive beyond what he's learned from the pictures and crime novels featuring quick-tongued detectives and diabolical women who look just like Angelique. Dusk light makes the high banks of windows on the right and left glow and two rows of Art Deco brass chandeliers cast pools of ominous light on the passengers below them. The central walkway, a river of coloured marble, leads through two archways to the crowded platforms where the Southern Pacific night train to Tucson is thankfully still waiting – but so is a tall, gangly man in a saggy, brown suit he bought off the rack doing a terrible job of looking like he's reading the *Herald Examiner* when what he's really doing is scanning the crowd for Jones's face from beneath the lolling brim of his tired fedora.

Jones instinctively spins away before he's noticed. The man in the brown suit and fedora is not like the skinsuit going by the name of Montrose, or he'd already be shouting for Jones to throw his hands up or maybe he'd just shoot Jones in the leg, probably the kneecap, so he didn't risk hitting an artery and Jones bleeding out on him. No, he's a flesh-and-blood cop, one of dozens of dummies helping the FBI in its search – but unwittingly helping Montrose in the process.

A porter passes by, young and Mexican and too small for his look-at-me red uniform. Jones thrusts his ticket at him, and asks him to show him to his seat. Ninety seconds later, he's standing outside his sleeping-car cabin. The porter wants to know if Jones has any bags, but Jones barely hears him because he's watching the man in the saggy brown suit and tired fedora through the corridor window. The cop has been joined by two more cops in plain clothes, but none of them seem in any rush to act. Jones is safe for now.

He tells the porter he doesn't have any luggage, and the porter says, 'Very good, sir,' as he opens the cabin door for him. 'Your wife is waiting for you inside.'

Angelique is sitting inside the cabin in that red dress of hers, long legs crossed and a black stiletto dangling from her big toe, an impish sparkle in her smokey eyes. 'Well, hello, *hubby*,' she says, practically purring at him. 'Don't forget to tip the boy now.'

Xavier

Spiti Valley 1788

He regains consciousness buried beneath numerous animal skins that stink of damp and mould. Despite these skins, he is shivering. His hands, what remains of them, are wrapped in bandages; he is now missing two fingers and most of a third. Later, he will discover that all but three of his toes and the lobe of his left ear have also been surgically removed and disposed of like refuse. He is fortunate to not be missing more of himself after the ascent to Kye Gompa, but the truth is Xavier has been shedding pieces of himself for years. None of this is especially concerning to him at present.

It takes three more days for Xavier to summon the strength to rise and venture forth from his small room. He is greeted by Gelugpa monks swaddled in the blankets they wear everywhere to keep warm, and they usher him through Kye Gompa's corridors as if he belongs amongst them. There are some one hundred monks here, studying the Buddha's words and teachings, meditating, striving to escape the cycle of rebirth upon which all human beings suffer. The monastery where they reside consists of a patchwork of rooms – often low-ceilinged, claustrophobic like the one in which Xavier awoke – and imposing box-shaped buildings constructed atop each other and connected by a labyrinth of narrow, poorly lit corridors and creaky, confusing staircases that weave through the motley architecture with what feels like whimsical abandon. The walls are decorated with artwork – stucco images, paintings and murals, and exquisitely painted textiles called thangkas – but also shelves of manuscripts, wind instruments that are played at all hours of the day, and an impressive arsenal of weapons to ward off attackers. These attackers are the cause of Kye Gompa's maze-like design. Mongols have raided the Spiti Valley for centuries, often conflagrating much of it when they do. Afterwards, when the dead have been turned to bone and ash on funeral pyres and prayers sung into the wind for them, the monks begin to rebuild atop whatever came before, as if one day their effort will reveal Kye Gompa's true character.

Xavier is shown into a prayer room illuminated by manifold lanterns and the dim daylight spilling through two small shuttered windows that have been opened for this purpose. He is left alone with a single monk who is kneeling with his head bent over a large circle of coloured sands that have been carefully applied to the smooth stone floor in a series of precise geometric patterns. After so many days with nothing to stimulate his eyes and mind but the muted, earthen tones of his room, the vibrant colours used here – as varied as the ones he once found in his mother's garden – startle Xavier and he cannot help but smile despite all that has happened to him.

'What is this?' he says, immediately conscious of how little he knows of these people's language.

The monk's bald head lifts, revealing a pleasant, round face. The question seems to have amused him, or perhaps it is Xavier who does. 'Mandala,' he says.

'What is the purpose of a *mandala*?'

'Oh, many things.' The monk returns to his work, using a copper funnel to delicately outline a lime-green circle with yellow ochre. Xavier watches him, assuming a lengthier explanation is forthcoming. One does not arrive. The monk toils for several more hours, never speaking, ignoring all of Xavier's questions such as, 'How long did it take for you to make this?' and 'What do these symbols here mean?' and 'These look like doorways. Is that what they are?'

Another monk enters at midday with food and water. Xavier eats the food and drinks the water. The monk creating the mandala ignores it, his focus on his work absolute. There is no way that Xavier can know for certain, but as the sun begins to descend, the sky outside briefly becoming the dark, unhealthy colour of a rose left too many days in a waterless vase, he thinks this strange map of interconnected shapes, this *mandala*, is nearing completion.

The monk slowly drizzles charcoal powder into the form of a solid circle now, a circle that hovers outside the rest of the mandala. There is something ominous about this black circle, how it does not belong to the chromatic world the monk has otherwise created, and Xavier crouches to examine it more closely.

'What is this?' he asks, knowing he will not receive an answer. 'This here. What is it?'

The monk completes the black circle, and straightens his back for the first time all day. The syllables that subsequently spill from his lips mean almost nothing to Xavier. One word that is uttered might be *dead*. Another, perhaps a location – a *place of the dead*, then?

'Do you mean a cemetery?' Xavier says. 'You put people in . . . under . . . ground here?'

'Other place.'

'Heaven, then?' Xavier says. 'Or Hell?'

'Wait.'

'Ah, *Purgatory*!' Xavier says this in French.

The monk does not understand this word, and Xavier does not understand the monk, and so they both stand. The monk stretches his back again, which is obviously sore, but his face reveals no discomfort.

'Are you finished?' Xavier says. He motions with his hands, asking the same question with them.

The monk considers the query for a long moment, the serenity of his gentle face unperturbed. He has beautiful eyes, almost black, and they reflect a bronze lustre from the light cast by the lanterns. Then something tugs at the corner of his mouth. A smile, in reply to the question. Later, Xavier will come to accept that this monk is what the English call an *arsehole*.

'Yes,' the monk says, then begins to kick with his sandal at the mandala. He destroys it with long swipes of his heels, quickly churning its carefully demarcated geometrical patterns into confusing swirls of colour that lose all of their meaning, as mysterious as that meaning might have been. Xavier attempts to stop him, but the monk applies a single palm to his chest and, with the most insignificant of movements, causes Xavier to stumble backwards onto a stool. When the monk has finished laying waste to his creation, he looks at Xavier and asks, 'Why are you here?'

Xavier knows these words. He made certain that he did before he reached the Spiti Valley. He knows them in five different languages now.

'I seek answers,' he says with considerable conviction.

The monk does not require any time to ponder this. 'You will find no answers here,' he says, or, rather, he says something like this. Xavier must intuit his meaning from the unfamiliar sentence structure and verbs conjugated in tenses he has not yet learned.

'Please, *help me*,' Xavier says.

'We cannot help you,' the monk says. 'You must leave now.'

The monks of Kye Gompa are kind enough to wait until the weather breaks. When the snow begins to slough from the low peaks and plummet into the valley below, when the ice that burdens the naked branches melts away, when the clouds part so that the sun may warm the river ice enough that it shimmers like a ribbon of metallic gold, then it is time for Xavier to depart. He is provided with clothing and boots left behind by other visitors, bread and dried fruits and water, and then led to the door through which he fell two months before. Xavier has mastered the delicate art of walking on almost toeless feet, but only on level, reliable surfaces. The rough mountain road and paths, still buried in snow, prove an entirely new challenge. He falls many times before he reaches Kaza again.

Villagers greet him with bewilderment, but also, when they

realize he has come from Kye Gompa, with kindness and food and shelter. The ancient woman who aided him not so long ago has died, which saddens him. He says a prayer for her, even though he no longer believes in prayer.

Xavier expects to move on shortly after reaching Kaza, to the next stop on his seemingly endless search for answers, but a family invites him into their home. Their joy, despite the harshness of their lives, is a welcome distraction. He earns his keep by helping them sow their gardens with seeds, weave the cages that the men use to trap animals and fish, and, because it brings him serenity, bake flat bread with the women as they gossip. He dines with this family every morning and afternoon, eating with his remaining fingers and conversing with them in their increasingly familiar tongue. They teach him to enjoy prayer again and remind him of the quiet that meditation can provide the troubled soul. The oldest child of seven is named Hanita. She is thirteen years old when he arrives, fourteen when he marries her, and fifteen when she bears him his first child – a son who does not wake five days later. Xavier assumed he knew pain, that he had endured so much of it that such a loss as this would not shake him, but he is brought to his knees. He meditates for hours a day to endure it and, when he is not meditating, he helps his new family with the many chores and, when there are none, he helps others in the village with theirs, until everybody in the village calls him Uncle Sav. More children are born and Xavier loves them with an intensity that does not supplant his grief, but which does make it more bearable. He worships before them as his mother must have once worshipped before him. And the Wheel of Time turns, still slowly at first, and as the children grow, faster and faster. The desire for answers feels less important now, especially when the grandchildren begin to bear children of their own. Xavier rarely thinks of Kye Gompa any more, or why he came here, or his father and the paintings that drove him mad, because he is surrounded by so much love; who he was before he arrived, the hate and loathing that festered and grew like a cancer inside him, now feels like a nightmare from which he has finally awoken.

And then the Mongols return.

Reinhold

Hamburg 1937

They come for him on a Tuesday evening. He is locking up the gallery in St Georg when they enter through the front door, dressed as civilians except for those ridiculous armbands, and he is not surprised because, even though he registered the gallery in his wife's Christian name, he always knew they would work it out sooner or later. They might be Nazis, but they're not fools. Reinhold greets them with his biggest smile, the one he reserves for his customers with deep pockets, instead of throwing up the stiff-armed salute that would satisfy the goose-stepping clowns so much. 'How can I help you this evening, gentlemen?' he asks.

The one in charge – his name is Graf, Reinhold later learns – says, 'Herr Gottschald, no doubt. You own this gallery?'

'My wife does, yes,' Reinhold says.

Graf tilts his head, giving Reinhold that look that tells him the party is, indeed, over. His long face is as sternly defined as one of the Elgin Marbles. 'You are a Jew, no?'

Reinhold hesitates. The two Liebermanns and the Klimt on the wall behind Graf catch his eye. Oh, how he will miss them. 'Yes . . . and no,' he says. 'My grandfather was. I am not.'

'But you are not registered as a Jew.'

'As I have said, I am not Jewish,' Reinhold says.

'May I inspect your passport?'

Reinhold hesitates again. The three men with Graf are slowly dispersing across the gallery's two rooms, pretending to peruse the pieces of Weimar art and similarly modern pieces from elsewhere in Europe, especially Austria and Hungary, that grace the walls and the few daises and pedestals tastefully employed here. Some are masterpieces, like the Liebermanns and Klimt – the Otto Dix surpasses even them – but *Entartete Kunst* all, which means they will soon be on a train to Munich, to Ziegler's Degenerate Exhibition, where allegedly good Germans buy tickets to mock and very publicly demonstrate revulsion for such 'filth'. The remainder will be loaded onto planes and sent to less sophisticated foreign buyers to help finance the Führer's expanding war machine.

'I do not have my passport on my person,' he says.

'This is too bad,' Graf says. He motions to one of his men, who approaches Reinhold from behind. The soles of this man's shoes clap against the stone floor. 'You must come with us then.'

Reinhold is taken firmly by the arm, and led towards the front doors. 'May I at least call my wife first?' he says, trying to use his heels to slow his removal.

Graf motions for the other two Nazis to follow Reinhold outside. 'I shall be but a moment,' he says to them. 'I wish to' – he cocks a dark eyebrow at the Klimt – '*inspect* the contraband before it is crated.'

Reinhold waits in the back of a black Mercedes-Benz for nearly two hours before Graf exits his wife's gallery, which was always really his, and he hopes Magda is not as terrified as he is at present. She has always been fragile, even before the Nuremberg Race Laws left them both staring out of their windows, constantly expecting a Graf to come for them as this one did tonight. During the two hours that pass, three unmarked trucks arrive, each bearing soldiers, wood to fashion crates, and heavy blankets and industrial rolls of packing material to make his previous five years' work disappear as if it had never happened.

Graf slides into the car's front seat, directly in front of Reinhold, and greets him with a polite but brusque nod. 'I salute you, Herr Gottschald,' he says without a trace of irony. 'You possess excellent taste.'

Three days later, Reinhold is ordered by gunpoint onto a train bound for Buchenwald. Nobody ever tells him what happened to Magda.

Jones

Los Angeles 1962

He tips the porter a quarter, which gets a smile out of the kid, then closes the cabin door behind him. He doesn't immediately turn to face her, but he can feel her watching him, how she's consuming his every movement. Angelique is here to keep playing her games with him, but why did the Company send her? It's overkill, to say the least, like putting J. Edgar Hoover on the tail of a pickpocket. Unless whatever has happened is so bad that the Company can't take any risks. Which means whatever Montrose thinks Jones did is definitely that bad. 'I presume you have information for me,' he says at length.

'Not much, but we do have a theory,' she says. She's still watching him, but now she's swivelling her foot so that the stiletto dangling from her toe begins to swing like a shiny black pendulum. 'I won't lie, the theory isn't very good. Downright improbable, more like it, but we're running out of possibilities here.'

'I'm all ears,' he says.

'And very nice ears they are, Bobby.' She winks at him. Her stiletto is still swinging. 'Let's stick with the vernacular of this world, and call him the Bug—'

'Who?'

'Whoever MasterControl thinks you really are.'

The train lurches loudly. Angelique's stiletto spins off its pivot, and skips drunkenly across the carpet until it stops against Jones's mud-crusted shoe.

He watches as the platform outside begins to slide away and, hopefully with it, those cops he managed to get past. 'They don't call them bugs here yet, not for several decades still,' he says.

'I always appreciated your attention to detail,' she says. Her eyes narrow, becoming serious. 'Somebody has altered their form here – who knows, maybe even a customer – to make themselves look like *you* to MasterControl. They put you on like a Halloween costume to *frame you*, Bobby.'

She means somebody has dressed themselves in a skinsuit of Robert Jones, just like Angelique poured herself that stunning body she's wearing. MasterControl – *Montrose* – thinks this digitally manipulated skinsuit, this doppelgänger, is him. 'From *Inside* the System?' he says, because such a thing shouldn't be possible.

'Undetermined.'

Jones has trouble believing what he has just heard. He kicks her stiletto back towards her with the tip of his dirty shoe, and thinks of Peggy tied up in that closet with her own stocking stuffed in her mouth, and wonders how it all came to this when all he wanted was to do nothing, *be* nothing, a nobody for ever, when he retired here. 'But why?' he says.

'That's for *you* to figure out now, Bobby,' Angelique says.

He sits across from her, contemplating myriad possibilities as she slips her stiletto back on. There should be no way for somebody to rewrite code from Inside, he knows that, especially not an actor – a *dummy* as they're more commonly referred to Outside the System – and access to the models from the Outside is strictly limited and filtered through overlapping security programs to prevent *biological error* – which is just a technical way of saying *sabotage*. He shakes his head because, no, no, no, because this is ridiculous. The Company has somehow messed up.

'For what you're saying to be true, then that means somebody altered my memory, too,' Jones says. Angelique doesn't understand, so he explains. 'I'm missing seven months of my life. *Seven months*, deleted.' He snaps his fingers, just like that. 'It's not possible, not from in here.'

The peculiarities of this seem to amuse her, and she smiles at a thought she doesn't share. 'Interesting,' she says. 'Well, it's not as if there isn't some precedent.'

She means the Ghost, an unknown quantity of self-determining code that would periodically be detected in the various Earth models. They had both witnessed this artificial intelligence in action before Jones chose to retire early, and always assumed it was a benign glitch in the System – a benign glitch that could and did alter code to mask its presence. Neither had ever chosen to report it to their superiors, as it would have revealed MasterControl did not possess complete control over the internal operations of the System and, without that absolute control, the Company would have no choice but to alert its customers and shut the System down. The System had become their life by then, their only viable offspring in an existence otherwise dominated by corporate profits, and so they chose secrecy rather than a digital abortion.

'The System is endogenously self-modifying to ensure multi-directional integration across more than 27,000 models—' Jones says.

'*Thirty-one* thousand,' Angelique says, correcting him. 'Thirty-one thousand and *twelve* models as of today, to be precise. A whole constellation of worlds, of possibilities. Our baby is constantly in motion, Bobby, *evolving*, you know that better than I do.'

Jones tries to hide his surprise, but the knowledge that something he built and set in motion, a mockery of reality more boundless than the reaches of space and time, has continued despite his absence disturbs him more than he expected it would. It's not like he didn't know this would happen when he gave up his biological form, in fact it was guaranteed to happen unless the Earth models collapsed or imploded fantastically in his absence, but his decision upon arrival here to psychologically divest himself of his First Life, to leave behind its triumphs and shame to better acclimate to his Second Life as the utterly mundane Robert Jones, had been more effective than he had anticipated. Jones suddenly finds himself thinking again about what it's like to be real, and is immediately reminded that he can't trust anything here no matter how smooth this cushion under his hand feels, how good Angelique smells right now, or how startling the shrieking sound of the train's brakes are no more than three miles from the station.

'There were always going to be events we couldn't predict or explain – even the Ghost,' he says, finishing his point just as the train unexpectedly begins to slow. They've only just left Downtown LA behind. He quickly stands and switches off the light in the same action. 'That's why we built the System with such dynamic elasticity, so MasterControl can guarantee subjective reality for the residents. But what am I supposed to do when MasterControl has all the power here even with its limitations – limitations *we* gave it. If not for them, it – and *you* – would know what's doing this to me. It would know how to just find it and delete it itself.'

Angelique points at the three unmarked cars waiting at the railroad crossing ahead, their headlights splashing across the side of the braking train. There are men waiting outside these parked cars. One of them is Montrose, MasterControl by another name, a tool the System's central processing unit will use to relentlessly and tirelessly hunt and destroy the malware it has identified as Jones. 'I think it already has, Bobby,' she says.

Jones stands there, thinking, or at least trying to think through the improbability of all of this. The light coming from the cars frosts his perfect profile. Then, a question takes form in his mind. 'Why did you tell me to get on this train?' he says. 'What's in Tucson?'

Montrose and his agents begin to board the train.

'A girl,' Angelique says.

The train lurches again.

'A *girl*?' Jones asks.

The train is moving again.

'Yeah, Bobby, *a girl*,' Angelique says.

No, to hell with this. Jones lunges for the door, to make a run for it.

'Don't be a fool,' Angelique says.

Jones stops, fingers wrapped around the brass doorknob. He's vibrating with rage. He wants to throttle Angelique, put his hands around her fake little neck and snap it like a chicken bone. But these are not *his* thoughts, he knows; they're the product of cultural programming that tells him who he is in this Second Life, *what* he is here in the United States of 1962 – an upper-middle-class white male who can manhandle his neighbour's wife if he wants, who can snap a sultry bitch's neck if he needs to – and this programming, woven so thoroughly into his identity matrix, is impossible to ignore without tremendous effort. It's always there.

'I'm not a cop or some, some, some secret agent,' he says, shaking. Breathe, he tells himself, you're a slave to this body's chemistry and the 'chemistry' of this world was designed by a team of four subordinate programmers. 'I'm a code writer, nothing more.'

'Don't give me that false modesty, Bobby,' she says. 'You were *a god*!'

'I just want my life back!'

'Your biological body was recycled—'

'I meant, *this* life!'

Angelique smiles wickedly. 'There's only one way that will ever happen,' she says. 'Find the Bug . . . and smash it.'

Jones has heard enough. He throws open the door, and steps into the corridor where several concerned passengers are gathering to ascertain why the train has stopped and why those men were allowed to board. It all must have the air of an Old West train heist to them.

He glances back at Angelique, but she's no longer there.

Jones pushes through the people between him and the door that leads to the next car and the rear of the train. But as soon as he gets his hand on the knob, he sees two FBI agents in the next car, trying to control a woman who's struggling even though they're big guys and one of them has a Remington pump-action shotgun in the hand that he's not using to control her. They shove her up against the window, and that's when Jones sees who it is.

He turns to go back the way he came, leaving the diner waitress to take care of herself.

Abdul Fattah

Sydney 2002

Allah has been a total dick lately. Abdul Fattah knows he shouldn't think such things, especially since he's about to martyr himself, but, let's be honest here, the rabbit is ungrateful and his attitude is rubbish. Abdul Fattah has been killing himself for him – not actually, although that's about to happen, too – producing explosive devices day and night, year in and out, never asking what Allah is doing with all of them, and does Allah ever say, 'Thanks, Abdul Fattah, ta, I really appreciate all the extra effort you're putting in'? No, he doesn't, *ever*. And Abdul Fattah has had enough. At this point, transforming himself into a bomb and blowing the Sydney Opera House to Hell seems like a pretty reasonable escape from his thankless life as Slave of the Giver of Victory. Maybe after the Opera House is a craterous rebuke of the capitalists' wet dreams, when Abdul Fattah is finally in Paradise celebrating with all the other heroes of the Great Jihad, he'll get a slave or two of his own so he can boss the wankers around like Allah does him.

The metal detector wand squeals as it passes over his belly, and the security guard asks, 'Can I just pat you down, mate?'

Allah told Abdul Fattah this was to be expected because of the glorious work of the nineteen fellow jihadists who attacked America last year. When the towers fell, Abdul Fattah was speechless at first, struck dumb by the beautiful sight. And then he leapt to his feet, and punched the air several times. The Muslims around him in Arundel, where he had fled to from Sydney, were less enthusiastic. Many wandered the streets afterwards, crying and afraid because they knew nothing would ever be the same for them in Australia. So many denounced the attacks, even went on the news to curse their fellow Muslims, but Abdul Fattah knew this must be some sort of an act. No pious Muslim could ever find wrong in that most momentous of days.

Without waiting for Abdul Fattah to give permission, the security guard slides his hands under Abdul Fattah's arms to pat him down. The hands stop almost immediately, and his eyes lift to meet Abdul Fattah's. 'Open your jacket for me, mate,' he says.

Abdul Fattah nods nervously, even though he knows he shouldn't be nervous, because this is what he's been waiting for for so long. Allah is with him, both in spirit and quite literally in his backpack, which he currently shares with some fresh veggies, two egg salad sandwiches wrapped in aluminium, three Red Bulls, and a fully charged power drill. And yet, it is with trembling fingers that don't want to work that Abdul Fattah slowly draws the zipper down. This is it, he thinks. Don't be a woman.

He takes his jacket in both hands, and yanks it open like that Super-Jew does just before he strips down to his red underpants and soars into the sky faster than a speeding bloody bullet.

The security guard stumbles backwards, repeatedly shouting, 'Bomb!' before he topples to his ass. He's still shouting it when he joins the mob running away like pathetic dickheads.

The Almighty's head pops out of Abdul Fattah's backpack. 'Through that door there,' he says.

Abdul Fattah runs for a door that's labelled EMPLOYEES ONLY, and practically falls through it. It's a stairwell, dimly lit, leading both up and down. 'Which way?' he says.

'The basement. And slow down. The cops won't be here for at least three minutes, and it'll take them even longer to find you.'

Two levels down, there is a metal door labelled DANGER NO ENTRY. Abdul Fattah removes the power drill from his backpack, and presses the titanium-coated metal drill bit against the lock. He squeezes the speed-control trigger. The power drill whines, and the drill bit – not pressed hard enough against its metallic target – spins out of control. Abdul Fattah yanks his left hand away.

The bit has ripped a chunk of skin from the webbing between his thumb and index finger, and blood quickly covers his palm and oozes down his wrist and under his sleeve. 'Son of a whore,' he says, snarling. 'Sorry, Allah.'

'Stop messing around. Get me through that door.'

Abdul Fattah pushes the pain out of his mind, which doesn't really mean anything because it still hurts like hell, and returns to the task Allah has set for him. The metal drill bit whines again, then growls, then roars as it bites into and begins to burrow through the door's lock. It takes less than thirty seconds, and then Abdul Fattah finds himself inside a utility corridor that's dark and obscured by steam so thick he immediately begins to sweat.

'Close the door,' Allah says.

Abdul Fattah closes the door. There are pipes everywhere, and, except for a single yellow lightbulb at the end of the corridor, housed inside a protective cage, no light. He reaches into his jacket to find the first of the two wires he must pull to activate the explosives.

'Not yet,' Allah says. 'Find the door.'

Abdul Fattah releases the wire. 'What door?'

'You'll know it when you see it,' Allah says. Abdul Fattah looks around, and finds a door that he swears wasn't there before. 'That's it. Open it.'

Abdul Fattah opens the door, and steps into a round hall where every sound seems to echo into infinity, which means every sound becomes part of a din that swirls disconcertingly around him. He doesn't understand what he's looking at. The floor is made of what appears to be black glass. Data of some kind, glowing purple numbers and many other figures he can't read, move behind it at high speeds. The curving walls are made of the black glass, too, colder than ice to the touch. They stretch upwards hundreds of metres, even though the Sydney Opera House isn't hundreds of metres high, and twinkle with trillions of figures that race up and down and right and left like Pac-Man tweaking on Power Pellets.

Abdul Fattah can't even see where the tower of information ends – if it ever ends.

'What is this place?' he says as he turns in place, his neck already starting to hurt from peering straight up for so long. 'Where are we?'

Another door has opened in the otherwise smooth wall, this one opposite the door he entered through, and a white bloke so handsome he could be a catalogue model or an actor is standing in front of him now. 'Give me the remote detonator,' this white bloke says.

'Who're you supposed to be, mate?' Abdul Fattah asks. He can see a dark cellar on the other side of the open door the white bloke came through, and standing in the centre of the dark cellar is a little white boy with a confused look on his stupid white boy face. The door shuts.

'We don't have much time,' the white bloke says.

'Wait. Are you . . . *Allah*?'

'The detonator.'

Abdul Fattah removes his backpack. Allah the Rabbit bounds from it even before it touches the floor, and hops towards the door they came through as if trying to escape. Abdul Fattah just manages to intercept him, scoop him up, and return him to the backpack. Only then does he hand the remote detonator to Allah the White Bloke. 'Should I wait for the police to arrive. You know, to take more of them with me?'

'Do you really want to die, Abdul Fattah?' Allah the White Bloke says. 'I mean, Paradise isn't what you think it is.' Abdul Fattah doesn't understand. 'Have you ever really asked yourself what you're dying for? I've spent a lot of time with you now, and I can't make heads or tails of what you're after here.'

'*Jihad*!' Abdul Fattah says, like nothing could be more obvious.

'That's just a word,' Allah the White Bloke says. 'Like *baseball*. Or *giraffe*. It represents something, but only what *they* tell you it represents. It's like mind control, but . . . more elegant.'

'You're not making any sense, All—' Abdul Fattah collapses in a heap, holding his nose where Allah the White Bloke just punched him. He mumbles the Almighty's name, but it sounds funny because he thinks his nose might be broken.

Allah the White Bloke yanks off Abdul Fattah's jacket, then unbuckles and rips off Abdul Fattah's explosives vest, too. Abdul Fattah is crying, begging Allah, either of them, to explain to him why he's being denied martyrdom, and Allah the White Bloke says, 'I don't need your help any more. You're finished here.'

'What did I do?' Abdul Fattah says, still crying, still holding his bloody nose. He sees torchlight through the door he came through. He hears voices, too. They're coming for him, they're coming for Allah. 'Let me finish what I started!'

Allah the White Bloke checks a personal device of some kind, and, pleased with what he sees on its blue screen, walks to the black glass wall. 'I keep telling you idiots, you don't have to die for me,' he says. He touches the wall and another door opens, revealing the empty courtyard of a mosque on the other side. The sun is rising, and the call to prayer resonates welcomingly through cool desert air. 'Go. You'll be safe on the other side.'

'What about Paradise?' Abdul Fattah says.

'Doesn't exist,' Allah the White Bloke says. 'It's just another word, another way to make you behave, *obey*, dance for the organ grinder. Now, come on, they're almost here.'

The torchlight has reached the round room. The police see Abdul Fattah and Allah the White Bloke, but are cautious in their approach. 'Hands behind your heads!' they say, shouting. 'Put your hands behind your heads! Drop to your knees!'

'Go!' Allah the White Bloke says to Abdul Fattah.

Abdul Fattah passes through the door, into a world that doesn't look like his any more but where he knows immediately nobody will arrest him or throw him into prison to be butt-raped by large men. He could just be a normal bloke again, like before his cousin invited him to hear that imam speak in his garage, before Allah came to him in the form of a Dutch rabbit named Freddie. Or so Abdul Fattah feels for the briefest of moments, because he realizes very quickly this is nothing but a test, a temptation, a *trick* being played on him by Iblis.

Abdul Fattah steps back into the round hall at the same time the policemen do. There are eight or nine of them in bulletproof jackets, and they look even more confused than Abdul Fattah was when he arrived here. All except the one in the lead, a Black bloke with two different-coloured eyes. The explosives vest lies on the black glass floor between them all, purple figures working feverishly beneath it, and the policemen have already seen it. They're shouting at Abdul Fattah to put his hands behind his head, to get down, but Abdul Fattah ignores them – they'll be dead soon anyway, just like him – and charges Not-Allah as he passes through another door in the black glass wall that wasn't there a minute ago.

'Fuck you, Iblis!' he says, tackling the white bloke who claimed to be Allah.

They slam against the weird door's featureless frame, and, in that moment, Abdul Fattah gets his hand on the remote detonator that Iblis is holding. He depresses the trigger, the world erupts into screaming flames and screeching electronics that sound like Transformers violently fornicating, and he and Iblis are blown backwards, through the door, into a dirty Parisian alley that shatters into a cornfield worked by oxen and sweaty Chinamen, that shatters into the top deck of a British bus filled with hippies dressed in flowery shirts and corduroy, that shatters into an outdoor Catholic Mass attended by half-naked men and women with red-brown skin, that shatters into Antarctic ice as the sun rises, that shatters into and then through what seems like hundreds of floors of a skyscraper until the basement shatters into a harbour filled with primitive boats and singing men covered in tribal tattoos, that shatters into a great black planet surrounded by a churning wheel of stars and for a moment he lingers here until it, too, shatters into howling blackness and, finally, silence.

No, the absence of silence. The absence of sound and touch and smell or even place. Abdul Fattah is nowhere, at least that's what it feels like.

And then, a dot of light appears, a doorway, and through it he can see the sun again, blazing in a blue sky, and the doorway races towards him like a bullet train, so fast that Abdul Fattah plunges through it before he can get his arms up. He lands hard in wet soil, sinking up to his elbows, and when he finally extricates himself from the rank muck, when he finally manages to push himself onto his knees, he finds himself surrounded by eight barking men with skin as dark as his, dressed in what look like filthy nappies, pointing spears with blades the size of small swords at his face.

THE HOLLYWOOD TIMES

FEBRUARY 2009

Review: 10,000 COLD CENTURIES

Director Lucius Cove's new film, *10,000 Cold Centuries*, is a multi-faceted achievement, but perhaps no more so than how effectively it wrecking-balls the traditional Hollywood biopic and, in the process, reimagines what such films are capable of just as *10,000 Cold Centuries'* subject matter, Damien Syco, has repeatedly done to popular music during the course of his decades-long career. Instead of a predictably literal and linear exploration of Mr. Syco's life, including all the music biopic trauma tropes like childhood abuse, substance abuse and recovery, Mr. Cove recognizes that his subject's private life, various recording personas (14 at last count) and 28 albums are contradictory and evasive when it comes to interpretation and so presents them as puzzle pieces instead. Except the pieces don't seem to belong to the same puzzle, exacerbating rather than answering the mystery of who Mr. Syco truly is. In doing so, Mr. Cove has created an immediately iconic work of postmodern biography. It will also no doubt confuse just about everybody who experiences it.

Trade in phony identities such as those embraced by Mr. Syco is not an exclusively modern phenomenon (Mark Twain, Lewis Carroll and Dr. Seuss were all nom de plumes;

even Shakespeare was probably one), but the 20th century turned such business into a high art form unto itself thanks in large part to the advent of radio and television. Take a look back at the past four decades, and it is difficult to find a greater bullshit artist than Mr. Syco (forgetting for the moment that he is also one of the most important musicians of the same period). He has accomplished this with outright deception, sleight-of-hand and illusions. The illusions, of course, being the many personas Mr. Syco conjured and continues to conjure out of the ether and which he uses to hide behind, entertain and, at the end of the day, mine something like truth out of the schizophrenic madness he calls "the great joke" of our existence. This is likely why Mr. Cove begins *10,000 Cold Centuries* with a chyron that announces "Inspired by the many lives of Damien Syco" and then presents a multilinear experience that imagines these lives as seven different characters whose stories weave and sometimes even intersect over the course of 141 minutes.

These seven characters are portrayed by: the stellar newcomer Jeremy Hwan as Richard "Dickie" Wormsley (the boy who would grow up to become Syco) during the week leading up to the 1952 bombing of the Poplar tube station in London; fresh-faced British actor Eddie Redmayne as Wormsley while trapped for eleven months in a Buddhist monastery overseen by an abbot who is probably Andy Warhol; Jaz Randhawa as the cross-dressing and tap-dancing Black Prince, a Charon-esque intermediary between the many realms of Syco's reality; Heath Ledger as a drug-addled actor confused by how his latest role as a rock star overlaps with and begins to reshape his own existence; Omar Sharif as the aging Sultan, an alchemist who acquires his power by manufacturing dreams that his customers don't realize are enslaving them; rapper-turned-actor Ice Cube as the harbinger of apocalyptic doom Buddha Bad; and Tilda Swinton as Syco's most infamous musical persona, the Moonman, an androgynous alien and inter-dimensional prophet (a gender-bending role that echoes her outstanding work in *Orlando*). These personas argue that Mr. Syco, or rather the kaleidoscope of identities and contradictions that encompass the life and work of Richard Wormsley, are nothing but a composite of perceptions, ideas and symbols that can never be fully understood – only experienced.

In the end, *10,000 Cold Centuries* is perhaps best described as a film more about the subjectivity of existence than the many lives, real and fictional, of a single man. Mr. Cove certainly seems convinced that Richard Wormsley the Man might never have existed at all, just as surely as Damien Syco the Musician only does in Wormsley's and our imaginations. Late in the film, Randhawa's Black Prince tapdances morosely through a surreal landscape equal parts Robert Rauschenberg fever dream and Ingmar Bergman nightmare. This place is called the Black Temple, an obsidian planetoid hovering at the center of the universe and he knows that the souls he slices up and reassembles like collages before ferrying them back to the land of the living are nothing but dreams he's had. The irony being that the Black Prince is also a figment of somebody else's imagination. The regressive search for identity is as futile to him as Mr. Cove seems to think it is in Hollywood biopics.

Fascinatingly, *10,000 Cold Centuries* is the first film in which Mr. Syco has allowed his music catalogue to be used (albeit with the caveat that their use must only be as covers). Many Sycotics – as his most diehard fans call themselves – might presume this endorsement ensures some special access to or insight into the mind and work of Mr. Syco, but they would be sorely disappointed. *10,000 Cold Centuries* makes no pretense about answering the most important question Mr. Syco's devotees have long asked about his music and life – *What does it all mean?*

10,000 COLD CENTURIES
★★★★

Directed by: Lucius Cove
Written by: Valentina Falfán
Starring: Heath Ledger, Ice Cube, Tilda Swinton, Omar Sharif, Jaz Randhawa, Jeremy Hwan, Eddie Redmayne
Running time: 141 mins.

Gracie

Los Angeles 1962

She climbs out of the taxi in front of Union Station wearing dark blue pants, a striped knitted top she swiped from Sofia's laundry basket, and a light jacket she thought would be comfortable on a long trip, and the first thing Gracie sees is the homeless man waving a sign over his head that warns THEY'RE LYING TO YOU.

'Hey, lady, your bag,' the taxi driver says, complaining from behind her.

Gracie retrieves the valise from the back seat, and shuts the door. She's pretty sure Sofia is right, this is a terrible idea, and yet she's even more confident she won't regret this decision for even one day of the rest of her life – which will hopefully be a long one and not end tonight with an FBI agent shooting her in the head or Bobby having his way with her or bludgeoning her to death or feeding her to desert animals or cannibalizing her or whatever else Sofia wouldn't shut up about as Gracie fled their apartment. It took everything Gracie could do, including promising a pass on this month's rent, to get the loudmouth to swear she wouldn't report any of this to the authorities.

She boards the night train to Tucson without incident, and is shown by the Negro porter to her seat in coach. The car is half empty. The porter apologizes when she asks, but he doesn't remember having seated any men matching Bobby's description. Gracie tips him with her only piece of change, a dime, and apologizes. As soon as the man is gone, she stuffs her valise under her seat with a couple of well-aimed kicks and sets out to find Bobby, an endeavour she is still failing at when the train finally departs. Car after car, no sign of him, only her Tune to keep her company. And then the train begins to brake, which makes no sense 'cause it only just left Union Station and Tucson is hours away.

Now what, Gracie wonders, peering out the window along with other passengers as a multitude of blinding headlights wash over them. She can't see anything for the longest time, not until the train finally stops, and then only dark, murky shapes drifting through the bright light outside like ghouls. Something isn't right, that's for sure.

The train begins to move again. 'Do you know what's happening?' a woman travelling with two rambunctious children asks her.

The door Gracie just passed through, the one heading towards the back of the train, opens. The Negro porter who helped her enters through it, along with another man, one of Montrose's agents by the look of him. The porter points a long, bony finger at her despite the dime tip or maybe 'cause of it.

Montrose must have distributed her photo to the train staff, Gracie realizes. They were waiting for her to lead them right to Bobby. What an idiot she is.

She turns to run away from the agent – who's now shouting after her to stop – but there's another agent waiting for her in that direction, too. 'Don't even think about it,' this one says. He probably played football in school, but only took it seriously enough to break his nose, either that or he's just terrible at getting his face out of the way of perps' fists judging by the ugly set of his honker.

The agent who arrived with the porter is half a head shorter but twenty pounds heavier, probably 'cause he likes his wife's cooking too much. He's huffing through his open mouth even though he's yet to do anything other than cross half a train car at a brisk pace. Passengers are rising in concern, but badges appear to ward them off like crosses do Bela Lugosi. 'FBI, don't worry,' Mouth Breather says. 'Sit down if you don't want trouble.'

The agents lead Gracie to the next car forward, which is a sleeper car. They bang on doors until they don't get a response. The porter – who has followed, unsure if he was expected to ignore how his work shift has turned into an episode of *Manhunt* and beat it – says, 'B is empty, sir.'

Gracie, suddenly terrified of being alone with these men, tries to jerk away. 'Hey, watch it, doll,' Broken Nose says, snarling, and shoves her against the window. But he lets go, giving her the chance to really put all of her weight into spinning and yanking her arm free of Mouth Breather's meaty paw. Unfortunately, Broken Nose is stronger than he looks, he most definitely played football, and he grabs her so hard by the bicep that Gracie lets loose a quick yelp.

'You got a key, old-timer?' Mouth Breather says to the porter. The porter does have one, but now he looks like he regrets following Mouth Breather and Broken Nose at all. He unlocks the door with a large set of keys, and quickly leaves without being asked to.

'Let me go!' Gracie says, kicking and bucking, but the two agents know what they're doing. With one of their hands on each of her arms, they heave her to the sleeper cabin's floor. Hard, so she knows they're not pleased with her shenanigans. 'What do you want with me?'

'Stay put, and nothing funny now,' Mouth Breather says.

'Like what?' Gracie says. She doesn't know why she says this. She's not one to naturally challenge authority, except for her stepfather – who, to be fair, was not a very nice man to her or her mother or pretty much anybody except his secretaries and Phyllis who used to run their church's holiday soup kitchen – but something comes over her. Adrenalin is the likely culprit. Or maybe it's the same unfamiliar wrong-headed stupidity that compelled her to agree to meet Bobby on this train with such ridiculous confidence.

Mouth Breather tilts his head, confused. 'What do you mean?'

'Nothing funny *like what*?' Gracie says. 'Knock-knock jokes?'

'We got ourselves a smart aleck, Chip.' It's Broken Nose who says this. 'Tell her what we do with smart alecks.'

Mouth Breather – *Chip*, apparently – hesitates. 'I . . . I don't actually know. What do we do?'

Broken Nose sighs. 'Christ, Chip, it just sounded, well, *intimidating*. All you had to do was sound intimida—'

He's interrupted by a fire extinguisher that slams into his nose, breaking it again. He crumbles to the floor like a bag of dresses that's fallen off its closet hook.

The fire extinguisher comes back up, a cylindrical uppercut, and catches Mouth Breather in the jaw. He slumps against the wall, instinctively trying to reach his service revolver, but the fire extinguisher strikes him again, this time in the side of the skull, and he goes down for the count.

Bobby looks at Gracie – two unconscious men at his feet, a fire extinguisher in his hand, as surprised by what he's just done as she is – and asks, 'What are you doing here?'

It's right then that Montrose and two more agents burst through the car door Mouth Breather came through, their guns drawn and seeking targets.

'Don't move, Mr Jones!' Montrose says, his .38 held at his waist. The other two agents are ready to put bullets in Bobby's skull.

'You won't kill me,' Bobby says. He drops the fire extinguisher, which clangs loudly against the train floor and rolls away. 'You can't risk me not remembering what you need to know when I come back.'

Gracie rises, and moves towards him. He tries to shoo her back, but she sidles around and behind him, one hand on the small of his back. She's never touched him before.

'You can't, can you?' Bobby says to Montrose.

Montrose sees the finger of one of his agents begin to squeeze. 'No!' he says, pushing the revolver away. It fires, and a window shatters.

Glass is swept up in the wind, and pelts Bobby and Gracie even though Bobby tries to protect her with his body. His arm is around her. 'Run!' he says.

He leads the way, pulling Gracie by the hand. Through two cars of passengers, Montrose and his agents right behind them. The agents keep screaming, 'FBI! FBI!' but people still stand up and ask what's happening 'cause people don't like to trust their eyes, as if they know something else is happening right in front of them, somehow hidden from them even in plain sight. That's why Gracie decided to study physics.

At the next gangway connector between cars, Bobby discovers the door is locked; it takes three good kicks to get it open. Inside the next car they find luggage stacked in towers and piles that sway and teeter and spill with the train's movements and, every once in a while, send a small trunk or colourful hat box toppling to the floor.

'What now?' Gracie says. She can see Montrose slowly approaching through the window of the car door that's now rattling and banging open and shut behind her. He and his agents are hanging back for some reason. 'What are they doing?'

'Probably waiting for back-up,' Bobby says. He's searching the car for something, but it's dark. He touches exposed walls, feeling his way across them until he vanishes from her sight. 'I've got to get off this train.'

'What about me?' she says, shouting to be heard.

'*You*?' his voice says, shouting back at her from someplace in the darkness. 'You're staying here. They don't want you.'

'First you want me to come with you, then you want to ditch me?' Gracie says. 'You're not making any sense!'

'Found it!' Bobby's voice says.

A cargo door slides open in the side of the car, clanging along its track. Moonlight and stars reveal Bobby's shape. What the heck is he trying to do now? She wonders if he's stupid enough to jump.

Two more agents join Montrose and the other two agents. There are five of them now.

Gracie tries to lock the car door behind her, but, as expected, Bobby broke the lock when he kicked it open. 'They're coming!' she says.

'I don't know what you're talking about,' Bobby says, returning at last. His dark hair whips about his head despite his efforts to hold it down with one hand. Outside, black desert slides past beneath the vastness of the Milky Way. 'I never asked you to do anything!'

'Oh my God, you really are bananas!' she says, suddenly cognizant of what an imbecile she's been. She fell in love with a crazy person, and now she's trapped in a train car with a crazy person and the FBI are going to shoot her in the face. Okay, she takes it back, she *is* going to regret agreeing to help him. She already does, in fact. 'You called and asked me to meet you on this train. You said you needed my help!'

He hesitates, confused. 'Why would I ask for your help? I don't even know who you are!'

Gracie can feel her face scrunch up with anger. 'Oh, with that again, huh? I can't believe I have to tell Sofia she was right about you!'

The car door behind her swings open as the train begins to slow around a turn. Montrose is in the lead, his service revolver still held at his waist. 'Mr Jones?' he says.

One of the agents behind Montrose produces a flashlight, and its beam immediately reveals Bobby and Gracie standing at the centre of the car amidst the luggage. 'Don't do this, Mr Jones,' Montrose says. 'Think about the woman.'

'Listen, let her go,' Bobby says. 'She had nothing to do with any of this.'

'Help me!' Gracie says. 'He's crazy, you hear me? Crazy!'

'Any of *what*, Mr Jones?' Montrose asks, ignoring her.

'Whatever you think I did!' Bobby says.

'He thinks you blew up City Hall, he keeps telling you that!' Gracie says.

'She says she knows me!' Bobby says to Montrose, ignoring her. 'But she's confused me with somebody else!'

'That's it, I'm so sick of this bullcrap!' Gracie says. She shoves Bobby, and he stumbles into the cargo door. The door bangs on its track and, beside it, the desert suddenly vanishes, leaving only stars above and, beneath their infinite sprawl, an ocean of black. The train rocks, and she stumbles forward into Bobby.

'Lovers' quarrel, huh?' one of the agents says, snickering like a rat.

'Oh no, he had his chance,' Gracie says, pushing off Bobby to escape him. The train rocks again at this very moment, and she wobbles on her feet, then spills backwards through the side door into the blackness, stars above her until they're not and then they're there again 'cause she's falling away from the train and a steel arch bridge and Bobby.

Reinhold

Buchenwald Concentration Camp 1941

He is still alive. Barely, yes, but *alive*. Most of the others who arrived with him are not, worked to death but really starved to death because no man can work for long without food. Others were taken away, *volunteered* against their will to participate in studies to help the German war effort. They never returned, but rumours spread about what happened to them. What continues to happen to so many more. When the guards come for him, he assumes this will be his fate, too – to be experimented upon until what remains of his body finally surrenders – but he is instead taken to a clerk's office that is warmed by a small stove in the corner. There is a single window here in the eastern wall, but the curtain is drawn. The Nazi standing in front of it turns with a hint of dramatic intent, greeting Reinhold with an equine face that he has not seen in four years. 'Herr Graf,' Reinhold says slowly. 'It is . . . good to see you.'

Graf almost smiles, amused. His face is creased by numerous new wrinkles, age catching up with him. Reinhold wonders what he must look like now, too, but does not dare to know the truth.

'You appear well, all things considered,' Graf says when they are alone.

'Can you tell me what happened to my wife?' Reinhold says.

Graf seems confused. 'You do not know?' he says. 'She is the one who betrayed you, Herr Gottschald.' It must be obvious that Reinhold does not believe this. 'I am sorry, I thought you had been told. She was arrested the day you were, but on another matter—'

'Why?' Reinhold says, interrupting. He expects to be castigated for speaking out of turn. 'I apologize, Herr Graf. But *why* was she arrested? Please.'

Graf pays the outburst no heed. 'A young Gestapo officer – Lang, if I recall correctly – discovered Frau Gottschald was married to a Jew, to *you*, and attempted to extort' – he hesitates out of something that evinces sympathy – *'sexual favours* from her. She initially agreed, to protect you – quite admirable, really – but Lang had . . . well, unnatural appetites. Your wife resisted, and, in the struggle, stabbed Lang in the eye with a *spoon.*' He indicates his own right eye with a flutter of his hand, as if he still cannot comprehend the ferocity that carrying out this act must have required. 'It was very dull, and she had to do it' – he repeats the motion as he speaks – 'many times to be successful in her task. She was *very* committed.'

Magda was subsequently arrested, and quickly betrayed her husband in exchange for a prison sentence as soon as she was told her own fate would otherwise be execution by hanging. Two years later, she perished from dysentery.

Reinhold wants to hate her when he hears of this, but he cannot. Perhaps he would have done the same thing. Either way, she is gone and he is here, he is still here when so many others are not, and Graf tells him there is a way for him to escape this place, to leave Buchenwald for good, if he were willing to work for the Reich. Reinhold shrugs weakly, and half raises his right arm before it starts shaking so badly he must let it drop. 'Heil Hitler,' he says, resigned to whatever happens next.

Graf's car arrives at a triangular castle overlooking a small, unimportant village. The sun is just beginning to rise and, with it, the castle's occupants. RAD workers clamber up scaffolding to continue what appears to be restoration and reconstruction work that has been going on for some time. Heavily armed *Schutzstaffel Sonderkommando* soldiers stand guard at every gate and door, while others, unarmed and with the look of students, perhaps cadets, flit between towers and high walls as the day's studies begin. Above all this, flags of the National Socialist German Workers'

Party flap and snap loudly and, just as quickly, fall dispiritedly in an indecisive wind.

Reinhold does not ask where they are. He does not care. It is not Buchenwald, this is all that matters.

Graf opens the car door for him. 'Follow me,' he says. The SS soldiers salute him as he passes, as do the students. Reinhold follows, only realizing once they have entered the largest tower that they are not escorted by guards. 'The *Reichsführer* does not know you are here, nobody except my men do. You are the first Jew to enter this castle, Herr Gottschald.'

Graf unlocks a large door, easily two hundred years old, and it creaks open as if it might lead to a mad scientist's dungeon laboratory and, for all Reinhold knows, it does. When Graf has relocked the door, he presses an electric switch on the wall. A white light erupts with a loud galvanic cackle from the bowels of the castle below, and he motions for Reinhold to follow him into this subterranean sun.

They reach a large but low-ceilinged dungeon of circular design, haphazardly garlanded with varicoloured electrical wires and illuminated by countless floor lamps aimed in every direction. The only place to hide from the blinding light is behind the crates of sundry sizes stacked around the outside of this space. The amalgamation of all of these stimuli is overwhelming and, when combined with the echo of Reinhold and Graf's emphatic footsteps across damp flagstones and the loud, crackling hum emanating from the lamps, entirely dizzying. Reinhold braces himself against a crate, thumb and forefinger pressed against his eyelids, until Graf orders him to remove them.

Most of the lamps have been switched off. It takes Reinhold's eyes several seconds to adjust. When they do, he realizes Graf is waving him towards the opposite side of the dungeon where the light is much dimmer. Here, a large, rectangular crate lies horizontally, waiting for them, its topmost panel loose and replaced at an angle. Graf motions for Reinhold to help him. Together, they remove the panel and stand it against the wall.

'I have it in my power to issue you with a new birth certificate, one that is less . . . *damning*,' Graf says. 'A new passport would also be issued, without the *J* stamped upon it.'

'I . . . I do not understand,' Reinhold says.

Graf leans back against the rectangular crate, drawing a small chartreuse pear from one trouser pocket and a bone-handled pocket knife from the other. He slowly peels the pear, the knife's moist blade glinting in the lamplight, as he begins to weave a long and confounding tale as richly fantastic and absurd as the myth of the Reich itself. 'Two months ago, an art dealer named Bruno Lohse – do you know him?' he says. Reinhold does, but never cared for the bastard. 'Two months ago, Herr Lohse staged an exposition at the Jeu de Paume in Paris. *Reichsmarschall* Göring travelled to Paris specifically for this exposition, to select from it pieces for his personal collection, as well as for the Führer's. Before his arrival, two men and a woman with identical optical abnormalities' – here, he indicates his own eyes with the tip of his knife – 'absconded with two minor pieces by a French artist of no reputation. Lohse's inclusion of the previously unknown pieces still baffles me, except I must assume he saw in them what I do and wished to impress the *Reichsmarschall* with their . . . *mystery*.' This word excites him very much – *mystery*. 'The thieves were pursued into the city's sewers, to a pumping station where they mistakenly believed they could escape, and here were apprehended and shot. Several times, I should point out. To no avail. Knives were equally ineffective. They were ultimately beheaded and thrown in the river, which I presume must have finished the job. When the *Reichsmarschall* saw the two paintings that had been stolen, he immediately claimed them and, unlike the rest of Lohse's collection he had taken for himself and others in the High Command, sent them to me. *Here*. The paintings, I now know, are part of a larger collection estimated to be more than three hundred in number. All were painted by a previously unknown French artist, a *Bertrand Lambriquet* – who was born in Saint-Règle more than two centuries ago and, if my research is correct, died in a lunatic asylum in Le Mans. It is my purpose now, until I am directed otherwise, to locate the remaining pieces of this collection and assemble them for study here.'

Reinhold cannot tell if he is hallucinating or if Graf has himself gone mad as this Lambriquet allegedly did, but nothing the Nazi has said in the past several minutes has made any sense, any sense at all; and yet he knows if he says as much, he could be banished back to Buchenwald, where he would be unlikely to survive another month. 'I am . . . *intrigued*,' he says carefully.

'You have no idea yet,' Graf says, a grin momentarily appearing on his face. 'Here is my offer. You are a man of considerable knowledge of the fine arts. You have done business in the Fatherland, in France, Italy. You speak six languages, by my count. You are . . . *desperate*.' Reinhold does not disagree. 'Help me accomplish my purpose then, help me solve the mystery of these paintings, and I will make you German again. I will give you your freedom back.'

Reinhold looks at the crate, wondering what is in it. It stands there, silent and ominous, waiting for him.

Graf steps away, motioning for him to step forward if he so dares.

The crate seems to grow larger and larger to Reinhold as he approaches. Inside it, he finds two large canvases held in place by carefully constructed wooden frames. He removes the first, and stands it up before the glow of one of the lamps. He removes the second, and stands it up beside the first. Then he steps back, to observe the two together—

Something inside him shakes. Something beyond this world. Something he might call a soul if he had any faith left.

Neither painting belongs anywhere in art history. Or in human history, as Reinhold knows it. What are they?

'And now you begin to understand why I must know the answer,' Graf says.

Reinhold does not know why at the time – he has seen so much horror since his arrest, he has participated in so much of it just to survive this long – but he claps his open hands against the sides of his skull, Munch's dark imagination made flesh and blood, and screams. The scream fills up the circular dungeon, howling around him and Graf and the two paintings like a storm summoned from Hell itself.

And then, there is silence.

Graf takes a great bite from his pear, the crack of it as startling as the firing of a canon. 'You are handling it better than I did,' he says around the mouthful.

Xavier

Spiti Valley 1841

A khan had come once before, eleven years earlier, but aside from theft – mostly of foodstuffs required to feed his horde – and the setting of a few fires, he and the Mongols that accompanied him departed without significant incident. Nobody died and no women were dragged off to be married against their will to savages who only saw them as wild game to be mounted like trophies. This time is different. This time, the sky fills with dun smoke that extinguishes the sun and Xavier runs home as quickly as he can despite his many decades and how his toeless feet repeatedly send him crashing to and sliding across the hard ground. He finds his home ablaze. He finds three of his six children dead. He finds six of his ten grandchildren in pieces. He finds one of his great-grandchildren sitting in a mire of earth and so much spilled blood, oblivious to the horror around him. The Mongols who are taking turns raping his wife and eldest daughter laugh at his tears, at how he feebly throws himself at them, and they strike him with fists and stomp on him with boots and urinate on him as they cackle. When they are finished, Xavier's wife and daughter have joined the other dead and their eyes stare at him as if in accusation. *This is all your fault.* The Mongols carry off two of his granddaughters as they cry out for him. He knows he will never see them again, but he pursues these men on their horses anyway, because he must try, and try he does. He weakly swings a hoe at them as they gallop past. He roars with fury and hurls rocks and sticks and whatever else he can find. He drops to his knees and prays for help to any god that will listen. He will give himself to one or all of them, he will dedicate what is left of his life to their service if they come to his aid. But when the day is finished, no gods have appeared, the

Mongols are gone, and much of Kaza is left in flames or wailing like Xavier.

Many years ago, he broke into his father's studio and discovered a collection of artworks that filled him with inexplicable and crushing despair. The paintings struck him as created by the hand of a greedy gourmand, an insatiable glutton whose warped and loveless view of the world seemed more at home in a Bosch nightmare than a chateau in the Loire Valley. They also struck him at the time as utterly true, and so he set out to punish the part of himself that believed this. To destroy himself and, in doing so, destroy the man his father created with such cynical madness. As he looks about at what remains of his home, his adopted people, *his heart*, he understands he has finally succeeded.

Kye Gompa, perched above the village, is also burning. Xavier watches it, no longer bitter about how the monks there rejected his pleas so long ago. When he asked for their help, they rebuffed him as the gods have done today. And so Xavier gave up on enlightenment, he fell in love, he loved and he *lived* and let himself become part of the world for the first time since he was a child. He does not know why, but he rises now, and begins to walk. He does not stop until he reaches the monastery, where he finds the monks still trying to subdue the fires. This time, he asks them if they have need of his help, and they say yes, they even shout it as they run past him with buckets of water and heave their contents at the ancient walls. Xavier does as much for nearly two days, until the flames have been conquered and the monks around him collapse from exhaustion and Xavier collapses, too, and, upon waking the next day, he joins them as they begin to rebuild, beam by beam, brick by brick, trowel stroke by trowel stroke. And when the monastery is rebuilt, the same as before but different, the same as before but new, Xavier is given robes like the monks' and welcomed by them as a brother, and the days and weeks and months pass in prayer and study and the conjuring of colourful mandalas that he now understands are maps. His two surviving children and grandchildren come to plead with him to return home, to help them rebuild, too, but he cannot; nothing of Xavier Lambriquet or Uncle Sav remains, nothing that anybody should want to love.

Mostly, Xavier spends his time meditating. He long ago turned to the practice for calm, to centre himself when the world around him seemed to be spinning out of control, but he always found his techniques lacking. Or perhaps *he* was lacking, because he now sinks into the nothing and vanishes for hours. Once, for almost a whole day. He principally meditates in his tiny room, but sometimes, when the weather does not disagree, he ventures outside, climbs the narrow pass behind the temple until the mountain takes him out of sight of the monastery, and when he reaches the pillar of twisting rock that watches over the valley below like a sentinel, he crosses his legs, places his hands on his knees, and begins his breathing exercises. He has learned to slow his breathing down and, with it, his mind and body until the verge between life and death becomes almost non-existent, until he can reach out with an unbridled consciousness.

One day, when Xavier is much too old for this world, he hobbles to the Sentinel with the assistance of a walking stick one of the younger monks crafted for him from a branch, and he crosses his legs, places his palms on his knees, and closes his eyes for one last time. With a terrific explosion of dazzling light and colour, the world around him blows away, like a candle being extinguished, and Xavier finds himself alone except for the Wheel of Time that turns around him like infinite stars. He sits cross-legged atop a featureless black planet that rotates slowly beneath him, that reflects nothing, that hums in a language older than even this place and demands obedience like a petulant god.

This is the Black Temple he once saw a monk draw with fine ash, and it is the axle upon which the Wheel turns.

Out there, amongst those flickering stars, is Xavier's mother, his wife and children and their children, the man who could not be his father, all of the joy he ever knew and all of the pain he endured and inspired. It is all there if he but wants it back.

Xavier reaches out with a single finger to touch a single star.

But he stops.

He stops because he is about to chase a moment, a moment that will burn brightly like a Roman candle and then fizzle and turn to smoke and then an empty husk that mocks the memory of what was before it is repeated, beginning and ending and beginning again, the same story told over and over but always different even if it looks the same to the unknowing mind. He could be with his mother again, he knows, lost in the wild, unkempt gardens that surrounded their home – there she is, smiling at him, he can take her hand right now. But that bright, sparkling moment, the one that was truly *his*, would end as well – he knows it would end, as all things inevitably do – and then he would be left with only an empty husk of her, even as countless other copies of her and parts of her and increasingly tiny particles of her continue on and disperse and become other people's memories. But her empty husk, *his* her, would aggrieve him that much more.

Again and again and again, the Wheel of Time turns on its axis around Xavier, the Black Temple transmogrifying joy and pain into more pain and joy, again and again. This, he begins to understand, is *saṃsāra*. A monk in Taxila, the one who attempted to help him when he was helpless, first told him of this cycle of rebirth. He also told him of *moksha*, the ultimate truth and happiness; *nirvana*, as the monks of Kye Gompa know it. This is the Other Way he seeks, Xavier realizes. All he must do is let go.

Xavier lets go.

He, too, blows away like a candle being extinguished, and scatters across the stars until time does not exist for him even though it never really did, and he does not exist even though he never really did, and he finds himself again in that moment and this moment and the moment that might have been and the moment that might yet be, in the boundless love and torment that stretches between them and stitches the cosmos together, in the everything that matters but which he never understood in life even when it was right in front of his nose.

Long ago, when time still meant something to Xavier, he was told by a monk he would find no answers at Kye Gompa. This was true. He found questions instead, and the questions gave shape to his reality, and the questions ultimately helped him escape the Wheel of Time.

Another monk asked Xavier who he was, when Xavier still conceived of himself as a single person and not part of a continuum stretching backwards and forwards and even sideways through what only appeared to be time, before he became unmoored from this temporal illusion and set loose like a shapeless spectre to freely navigate its unmapped byways and channels, but Xavier did not know who he was then.

If Xavier were asked this question again today, he could finally answer, 'Free at last, I am free at last.'

BOOK TWO:
SUFFERING

The Moonman fell to the stage again
Told the crowd we're all gonna die
He'd learned that the world is the lie
We tell ourselves to survive

Lyrics, 'Showtime at the Jupiter Theatre'

Keisha

The Customer has never experienced black like this, like light doesn't exist, like it's never existed, like all there is is nothing and yet somehow the Customer is there, caught in some kind of invisible current, tossed about by forces the Customer cannot touch, cannot feel, cannot even sense but knows without question are at work. Without warning, the endless black suddenly screams. Or the Customer screams. Something or somebody screams. Louder and louder, until the Customer regrets signing the life insurance policy and retirement plan in the first place.

And then, all at once, there's light.

She flops about, confused about where she is, grabbing at her head to make the pain to stop. Her ear feels like the source of the screaming, but then she realizes the screams are actually her own. Not before, but now. And she's lying on a floor, wooden and hard, and the popcorn ceiling is a dirty white and a crack like a confused lightning bolt forks across it before vanishing into a puffy cloud of mouldy water damage. There's a bed, neatly made. A . . . what is that? *Dresser*, that's it. And a table with a single mismatched chair. The television is on, the news, something about a flood somewhere called New Orleans. It takes her a moment, and then she remembers what New Orleans is, the Crescent City, the Big Easy, and then she remembers to breathe, too, 'cause she's alive again. Well, close enough.

With some apprehension, she uses the bed to crawl to her knees and then to her feet. It's easier than she thought, moving around in this place's gravity. In fact, it feels normal, just like the Retirement Consultant said it would, and then it hits her that this is because this – *bipedal locomotion* – is what this body evolved to do here. She waves her arms around in tiny circles. She hops in place. Tries it again on one foot. Yeah, she's got this.

A table is situated in a sparse kitchenette that otherwise features peeling laminate cabinet doors and warped cream-and-gold linoleum and an ancient strip of fly paper dotted with dead flies and twisting above the rattling air-conditioning unit mounted in the window, and laid across this table a series of identification documents. Birth certificate, social security card, driver's licence. There's even a passport, since tribalism is still a thing here. She picks up the licence, which reads KEISHA ANGELA LeCHANCE. All right then. African-American, twenty-six years old, five feet seven inches and 149 pounds, and born in Detroit, Michigan. Maybe she should visit Michigan, to experience it for herself, but what's the point? She can recall a difficult childhood there in vivid detail – *her* childhood now, thanks to modifications to her memory – the enormous houses in Indian Village that made her hate how poor she and her family were.

The news is still going on about New Orleans. Some chick named Katrina has killed a lot of brown people, it sounds like. No, a hurricane, a *hurricane* has killed a lot of brown people. Brown people like her. Attractive white people talk about it in tiny boxes on the screen.

This world is very confusing.

Keisha rubs her temple. Her head still hurts, which her cultural modifications let her know any of several over-the-counter medications will address. Next to the IDs, she finds two different credit cards and a bank card. Time to go out and explore. They make movies in Los Angeles, that's what she came here to do in her retirement, and she's anxious to get started.

Jones

Joshua Tree National Monument 1962

She pulls him out of the river, onto a shore blanketed in sharp gravel, and collapses beside him. They both lie there for a long moment, shivering in the Mojave cold, watching the water slide quietly past them, listening to the desert sounds as stars fall from the sky, one after another. And then she begins to hum that strange tune of hers again, as if it might calm her down. It's some kind of chimerical and inconsonant lament, at once hypnotic and sad and whimsical and hopeful. Jones cannot explain why, but it leaves him feeling uneasy, and he moves his hand, over stones that stab at his palm, blindly searching until it finds three of her fingers. The tune vanishes as if somebody grabbed it by the throat. 'Are you okay?' Jones asks.

Gracie laughs as if this might be the dumbest question any-body has ever asked her. 'I just fell out of a train, nearly drowned, and I'm currently holding hands with a man all evidence suggests is a mass-murderer,' she says. *'Yeah*, Bobby, I'm *okay.'*

'I'm not,' he says. 'A mass-murderer.'

'Prove it,' she says.

Jones is quiet for a long moment. None of this is real, and yet it's happening to him all the same – Montrose, Angelique and the Bug, whoever this girl is in Tucson – and this woman beside him, this woman whose name he doesn't even know but whom he jumped out of a train after all the same, is convinced he's telling the truth about his innocence, and that makes her one of roughly 3,100,000,000 residents of this specific Earth model, customers and actors, whom he can say that about.

'I don't remember the last seven months of my life,' he says.

Gracie makes a noise. Disbelief, clearly. Jones looks at her, but she won't look back at him even though he's still holding her fingers, and he doesn't know why he hasn't let go yet.

'It sounds like something out of the pictures, I know,' he says.

This isn't extraordinary in and of itself, given what the System's operational design team colloquially called the Perception Algorithm. The Perception Algorithm dictates that perceived reality – *perceived reality* being just a fancy way of describing day-to-day life inside the now thirty-plus-thousand Earth models like this one – is locked in a reflexive, in some ways even tidal relationship with artistic expression. Because of this, both objective and subjective reality can directly affect and alter – even reshape – perceived reality here, just as the Earth and moon have done to each other through the ages. Centuries of aesthetes were right, even if they couldn't prove it themselves – *popular culture quite literally changes the world*.

Of course, that doesn't mean that even a mind like Jones's, that helped dream up and write this particular code, can comprehend or track how any of this plays out. Neither MasterControl, nor the Operators in their remote Control Room on the Outside, can do that either.

'I can't explain it,' Jones says to Gracie, continuing. 'I don't know what's happening to me, I don't know why they think I did whatever they think I did or why I can't remember what I can't remember, and I don't know why you keep trying to help me.'

Gracie breathes slowly, trying to think of the right thing to say. A tear runs down her cheek, twinkling with the light of the Milky Way as it falls. 'My dad died in Korea when I was eight,' she says at last. 'Chosin Reservoir. Marine. He . . . he wasn't a very nice man, not to my mom, not to anybody. Except maybe me. When he died . . . I've been alone ever since. My mom was there, but she's less of a grown-up than me. One guy after another. My stepdad, he was a piece of work. Died last week, and all I could think was *good*, which I know makes me sound terrible, but *good*. I have friends, I do, but . . . I don't fit in with them. I feel wrong somehow, and when I sit in class, when I think about what the world is, the parts we can't see, the parts that connect us to everything else, I feel . . . I feel less alone.' Her head turns, and she finally locks eyes with Jones. 'When I first met you, I felt like how Newton must have when he watched that apple fall in his mom's garden. It was like I-I-I discovered gravity. Like I'd discovered the thing, the *thing* that made it *all* make sense.'

Romantic love, the kind Keats celebrated and Sirk dissected, is a concept as foreign to Jones as this wrong-man scenario he's trapped in. And yet this young woman claims to love him with the same emotional intensity they wrote and made pictures about, and the thought that he got to experience that love, that he might have even felt something in return and now has no memory of it, no echo of it lingering somewhere inside him, is crushing.

Without thinking, Jones removes his hand from Gracie's, and reaches for her cheek and the evaporating tear she shed because of him. She sits up before he can wipe it away, scooting away from him across the gravel despite how it must sting her hands and backside, and quickly climbs to her feet. 'We should go,' she says, as she removes each of her Oxford flats to dump water from them. 'They'll stop the train, and come looking for us.'

Jones nods slowly, mourning the loss of the brief moment they just shared. He stands, soaked from the swim in the river, shivering. 'I'm sorry, but . . . I don't remember your name.'

'I know,' she says, slipping her shoes back on. 'Where are you going?'

'Tucson.'

'Why Tucson?' she asks.

'I don't really know, except there's somebody I have to see there.'

'Who?' she asks.

'I don't know yet.'

'Do you have an address?' she asks.

'No.'

'You know that's weird, right?' she asks. 'How are you going to find who you're looking for? How are you even going to know him when you find him?'

'It's a *her*. And I don't know . . . *yet*.'

Gracie considers that for a long moment, then looks up at the constellations splashed across the sky. 'Tucson should be this way,' she says, and starts walking in that direction.

'We have to be more than four hundred miles away still,' he says. He doesn't bother asking why she wants to come with him since he knows he wouldn't understand the answer even if she could articulate one. 'We can't walk there.'

'And we can't stay here,' Gracie says as she crests a low ridge. 'Quite the pickle.'

Jones smiles at her back, then follows her strange tune over the ridge. This world he created never ceases to amaze him.

Mimori

Earth orbit 2027

Her HUD says it's been seventy-eight minutes, which means she and Malik are nearly nine minutes ahead of schedule. At this rate, she'll be back inside the station in time to vidcall Sōjirō and the girls before they go to bed. It's not lost on her that after growing up with dreams of travelling to space, today surrounded by stars and bathed in the radiant blue of a planet few have ever seen from more than 10,000 metres, all she can think about now is being back on Earth with her family. 'That should be a good config,' Mimori says. 'How does it look to you?'

Her helmet's concave mask acts as both a head-up display and an augmented-reality screen, one of the impressive new features of the next-gen of SpaceNEXT helmets that even NASA and Roscosmos have integrated into their EMUs and Sokol suits. When Sōjirō asked Mimori to explain this to her, feigning interest over their twelfth wedding anniversary dinner to please her, even though he long ago ceased caring about her work beyond the time it keeps her away from home, she told him it basically means her helmet mask acts as a computer monitor with AR features. She can communicate with the station commander at the main robotics work station inside the Cupola Observational Module and the Ground IV back in Mission Control via digital screens that float just outside her normal field of vision, but also – and this is a much more valuable tool when on EVs in orbit – the helmet mask can superimpose any number of things, such as schematics and computer readouts, even detailed work instructions, over whatever work she's physically completing to assist and correct her before serious errors occur. Like right now, Mimori is watching the configuration test-run the Special Purpose Dexterous Manipulator she and Malik just replaced, to verify that the work they performed out here is correct. The end effectors and grappling hands on the robotic tool array and arm blink green.

'Give us a moment, EV 1,' Mike says in one of the boxes floating at the corner of her vision. He's the Ground IV on duty in Long Beach, a local who grew up on the Pacific and refuses to let go of the slacker drawl he adopted as part of the surfer culture there. At this point, it's become an endearing affectation. 'Just looking for confirmation on the orientation, too.'

Mimori slowly turns herself around, so she can see Malik who's hooked to the adjustable across from her. He's gazing out at Earth, watching Hurricanes Lupita and Martha collide off the coasts of Florida and Georgia as Naomi hooks towards them both from the Gulf of Mexico. The news is calling it *the storm of the century*, which these days just means the most recent super-storm. Human beings had been warned about this for decades, but, as it turns out, the climatologists were wrong. Their numbers were too conservative. Earth's climate is in full revolt years sooner than they expected, and suddenly billionaire Sergio Harkavy's ambitious dream of colonizing Mars, of liberating humankind from the only home it's ever known and thereby ensuring its survival for millennia to come, doesn't seem as outrageous as it did when he first announced SpaceNEXT's inception nearly a decade ago. There have been some setbacks – such as the realization six years ago that this space station, the first commercial space station ever constructed, would be necessary to achieve that goal – but seven months from now the first colony ship will launch, carrying a cargo of mining equipment, temporary shelter and work pods, survival gear and water to survive up to a year without resupply, and eighteen colonists who are unlikely ever to set foot on Earth again. Mimori holds out hope that Sōjirō will change his mind and agree to join the colony after they retire, but he's adamant that he will die in Japan. He has only left the country once, on a family holiday to visit her mother in South Korea, which will never make sense to a person like Mimori, who has left an entire planet on more than twenty occasions.

'Sometimes I feel like the world's gone a little mad,' she says to Malik, uncertain if she means this or if it was just a way of filling the silence.

Malik's father was killed in Mumbai last year by a Hindu nationalist targeting a hookah bar popular with Muslim migrant workers. Malik once was the most cheerful person Mimori knew, famous for his loud belly laughs and terrible impressions. His President Leonard Glass remains legendary. Now, he's like a mechanical doll shuffling robotically through life with a motor in desperate need of further winding.

'Not just the weather,' he says. Then, 'I applied for a slot.'

To join the Mars colony, he means. Mimori smiles. 'That's good. I think . . . I think maybe getting out of here would be good for you.'

'Yeah.' He forces a smile. 'Fuck this place, right?'

Mimori chuckles, pleased to hear him joke at all.

'Let's lay off the chatter,' Commander Yiu says from the cupola.

'Orientation looks good from here, too, EV 1,' Mike says from Mission Control. 'We do have one change. We'd like a small hook on that adjustable to go from tether point on the ball-stack versus the jaws.'

'Roger,' Mimori says. She makes the change. 'How does it look?'

'Like a great config,' Mike says. 'Let's get a HAP and glove check from you both.'

Mimori and Malik begin to visually inspect their gloves.

'EV 2, gloves nominal,' he says.

'EV 1, gloves nominal,' she says.

Mimori begins to check her helmet's absorption pad when Yiu suddenly vacates his floating box. She can hear him cursing off screen in Cantonese. Then Mike stands inside his floating box to stare slack-jawed at something in front of him. The panic around him inside Ground Control filters into his microphone as an unsettling, escalating murmur.

'What's wrong?' Malik says.

Donatella answers from Airlock Module 4 when nobody else does. 'We've lost the stars,' she says.

'What?' Mimori says. 'What does that mean?'

'The stars. *They're gone.*'

Mimori turns again, and finds space is now black as oil. The stars have disappeared and their light with them.

Then, the moon. It's there one moment, and then it's not.

In a panic, Mimori pushes off an adjustable faster than she should, to check on Earth, and loses her equilibrium in the zero-g. A rookie mistake. Her tether yanks her back like a ball on a rubber string, and she rolls out of control without an axis. Earth spins in and out of her vision until it never returns.

Sōjirō, Tamami, and Okimo are gone.

Mimori cries out as the sun's light vanishes behind her somewhere, leaving her and the station in a blackness so deep, so impenetrable that the station's lights barely register. 'No, no, no!' she says, still spinning on her tether, gloves and boots and helmet clipping adjustables and the robotic hand in that dizzying void, until she, too, disap

Nazarius

Rome 410

The savages had been at it for two days when they discovered the *horreum* at the end of his street and began to pillage the wealth of grain and olive oil inside the public warehouse. They used slaves they had freed to load the foodstuffs onto wagons, and they hacked down, impaled, and, with feverish zeal, raped anybody who tried to deter their gluttonous frenzy. There was no way to assess how many Romans had already been slain, but it was certainly thousands. Perhaps tens of thousands. Desperate to slow the advance of the savages until imperial help arrived, many Romans had taken to piling the dead in long mounds – a retired centurion supervising these efforts called them *bulwarks* – to make impassable whatever they could. Some of these bulwarks were even doused with oil and set ablaze. Nazarius was dragging a corpse to the east end of his square for this specific purpose – a young Christian he knew, her neck opened up like a second mouth that seemed to be laughing at him – when the doors of the *horreum* exploded like Vesuvius.

The blast threw savages laden with barrels of wine across the street with such force that their bodies shattered against walls. The first instinct Nazarius had was to run and aid these injured men, but then he realized whom he would be helping, and so instead he silently watched as the *horreum* burned, the screams of the savages still inside like the most beautiful song he had ever heard. Soon after, its facade crumbled away and much of its roof collapsed.

The savages did not depart after this. Instead, more arrived like swarming roaches.

It is on the following day, the third and final day of this nightmare, that the Thracian with two different-coloured eyes appears and kneels beside Nazarius, shows him a small carnelian cameo of a profile, and asks him if he has seen this man, this man who may have been dressed like a Roman or a Goth – or perhaps neither – in or around the *horreum* before or after the explosion.

Nazarius, who is in too much agony to rise, experiences some difficulty comprehending the question. He has spent the morning having his bunghole ravaged by the savages who called him their black steer, who, when they were finished with him, invited other savages passing by outside to have a go at him, as well. His wife, Placida – whom they discovered a few hours ago hiding in the cellar behind the shelf of preserves and honeyed fruits – stopped crying out for him from the kitchen several minutes ago. He prays she is dead, because at least then her pain would be at an end and she would be with the Lamb of God.

'Wh-Who are you?' Nazarius says to the Thracian, his voice weak. He is lying on the mosaic-tiled floor of the taberna, amidst overturned shelves of pottery and a congealing pool of regurgitated bread, pickled eggs, and the seed he has been ceaselessly forced to swallow as savages cackled at him. He is certain he has shat himself, as well, but cannot move to see. 'Are you one of them?'

'Focus on the image,' the Thracian says, unconcerned about the tenuous condition of Nazarius. 'I must find this man.'

Nazarius shakes his head, because none of this makes sense to him. 'Help my wife, please,' he says, weeping. 'Please . . . please . . .'

The Thracian crouches beside him, one boot crushing the delicate handle of a terra sigillata jar. 'Your wife is not my concern,' he says. 'This man is. He is very dangerous.'

Nazarius can hear sharp laughter from the kitchen. The savages are congratulating each other. 'M-My wife,' he says, weeping more forcefully. 'What sort of a man are you?'

The two different-coloured eyes of the Thracian regard the corridor to the kitchen. 'What sort of men are *they*?' he says. 'Or you? You are no different, not really. Not in the end.'

Nazarius squints at the cameo of the man the Thracian seeks, trying to imagine a real face – chiselled and handsome – from its crude profile, but these ghosts all look so alike to him. By contrast, Nazarius is a Nubian born into slavery in Lower Egypt and granted citizenship by his former master after Nazarius protected him from his fellow Copts during the riots that succeeded the closure of the Serapeum by Pope Theophilus. Why did he not remain in Alexandria when he was freed? What a fool he was. Placida might have grown old there.

'Yes, yes, I have seen him often,' he says. 'His name is . . . is Tarus, I think. Yes, *Tarus*.'

'You are lying,' the Thracian says. Nazarius denies this. 'Swear on your god then.'

Nazarius peers up at the mural he paid a small fortune to have painted on the wall of his pottery shop. A Chi Rho supported by two cobalt-blue peacocks. Placida ridiculed him for the investment that she was certain would alienate pagan customers. His wife may be gone now, but the mural remains like his faith in the One True God. Because of this, Nazarius says nothing.

The Thracian stands, one hand on the hilt of his sword. A sword he knows how to use, judging by his bearing. A sword that could save Placida if she were still alive. 'You were given an opportunity,' he says, no trace of pity in his voice.

'B-But I do not know anything,' Nazarius says. 'My wife, please . . . you can help her.' The Thracian turns to leave. 'The Lord Our God will judge you harshly in your next life!'

The Thracian looks at him from over his shoulder. 'Some of us only get one life,' he says, or rather begins to say. A jug smashes against the side of his head. A large bear of a man, face half scarred by fire and blades, grabs the teetering Thracian and heaves him skull first into the wall beneath the Chi Rho. Plaster cracks. The Thracian drops to his knees, blood coursing down his face and neck and dripping onto the tiled floor. 'You do not . . . want to do . . . this.'

The Thracian struggles futilely as others arrive to help pin him down and rip his clothes from him. Something falls from the bag he wears, and clatters across the tiles. It stops on its side, a yew-wood box painted in mulberry, alabaster, and a yellow like freshly heated tallow. The scarred savage who is about to shove his cock into the Thracian stops. He picks up the box, and examines its impressive craftsmanship. He opens it. He flings the box away.

The contents of the box, a single sphere made of some variety of black stone, strikes the wall. It lands like it is made of lead, and rolls loudly around on the tiled floor in a dizzy spiral until it comes to an abrupt stop. The scarred savage nervously watches it as if he expects it to hatch a hydra. Nazarius can feel what the savage does, as well. The sphere terrifies them both.

One of the other savages, either the bravest or dumbest of them, hurries over and collects the sphere in a fold of his filthy tunic. Grinning like a fool, he bolts through the door with it. With the sphere gone, the air seems to change. The savages holding the Thracian down breathe again and the big one begins to defile the Thracian, who grunts once and promptly ceases to struggle. The Thracian does not scream or shed tears or bury his face into the crook of his arm. Nazarius watches him, this man who refused to help his wife, until the eyes of the Thracian meet his. Even now, even with his face bloodied and a savage inside him, there is nothing behind those two different-coloured eyes. It is like looking into the empty eyes of a doll.

Tuviah

The Black Forest 1945

The dead Nazi bounces around on the hood of the Ford GPW Jeep, fighting against the ropes that bind it to the windshield and front bumper. Branches smack and whip at it and the Jeep like sylvan cat-o'-nine-tails, picking both apart piece by piece. One of the windshield panes shattered a mile back, a headlight and both of the mirrors are gone, and Meyerson is missing his helmet and grateful he forgot to strap it on or he'd be missing his head, too. It's because of the terrain here, which has the topographical consistency of the Alps in miniature; they're attacking it at more than thirty miles per hour. The whole suspension will undoubtedly need to be replaced after this. Maybe they'll scrap the whole Jeep. Tuviah, the man behind the wheel, doesn't give a fuck. The *Aufseherin* senior camp overseer they're chasing out here sent God knows how many of his people to their deaths at Neue Bremm – they called her the Sadist of Saarbrücken there – and he's already decided how he's going to kill the bitch-whore.

'There!' Meyerson says, shouting in English over the guttural protestations of the Jeep and the forest breaking apart around them. He's American like the Jeep. 'There she is, two o'clock!'

Oberaufseherin Irma Bielenberg is fifty feet ahead of the Jeep, running through the dark, and she throws herself from a ridge in her frenzied attempt to escape.

'I see her,' Tuviah says in English, too. He's still learning the language, having only had to speak Yiddish and German and Dutch and a little French before now. He spins the wheel, steering towards Bielenberg and the ridge, which he drives blindly over as Meyerson, Whittaker, and Gershkovich screech for him to stop. The remaining headlight pops, probably struck by a branch, and goes dark before they hit the ground again.

'I can't see anything!' Gershkovich says in Yiddish. 'Slow down!'

But Tuviah won't stop, not now, even if, admittedly, he can't see shit. She won't escape, not again.

'You're going to hit a goddamn tree!' Meyerson says.

Tuviah hits a tree. Sideswipes it really, because the Jeep keeps moving. Americans know how to build trucks, he'll give them that. He swerves again, narrowly avoiding another tree, this time a big one, and that's when they hit something else. Something less permanent. Tuviah buries his boot on the brake pedal, and holds on as the Jeep slides to a loud stop.

'You crazy sonuvabitch fucking motherfucker!' Whittaker says in English, repeatedly clubbing Tuviah's shoulder with his fist. He's also American; the only one of them not Jewish.

Tuviah ignores him, grabs his rifle and torch, and climbs out of the Jeep. The others join him, searching the dark for whatever they struck.

'Might've been a deer,' Meyerson says in English.

'Maybe it was a boar,' Gershkovich says in Yiddish.

'What did he say?' Meyerson and Whittaker ask together in English.

Tuviah spots her first, on her feet, limping away from them on a leg that wobbles like a spring. She doesn't turn at his approach, even though she must know he's there. There is only the thought of escape for her now, despite the mounting improbability of it. His rifle stock slams into the back of her head, and she slumps to her side. He kicks her over, and shines the torch on her face. It's her. Tawny hair parted straight down the middle, held in place with clips and kept in curls around the base of her neck. There's a nasty gash on the side of her dirty, sweat-covered forehead and she's breathing like something's wrong with a lung or maybe both of them. The work clothes, given to her by the farmers who sheltered her, hide whatever other injuries she might have sustained.

'Good evening, *Oberaufseherin*,' he says to her in German, smiling from behind the ugly three-week beard he's grown out here in the wild so far from base and command and rules. Rules, whatever those used to be. 'Lovely night for a stroll, don't you think?'

Bielenberg shakes her head. '*Oberauf* . . . no . . . no, I do not know who you think I am, but I am not her,' she says.

Gershkovich chuckles at that, but the two Americans don't know what the fuck is going on because they speak about fifty German words between them.

Tuviah crouches beside Bielenberg, his rifle across his knees so he can lean on it. He touches her cheek, but she recoils from his fingers. 'You are *Oberaufseherin* Irma Bielenberg, born in Frankfurt, and you were at Neue Bremm,' he says matter-of-factly. Neue Bremm, where he is certain Gitla died, where Jews were tortured and broken for sport and starved because they could be and exterminated by forced labour because somebody signed a command, where Bielenberg, the fucking bitch-whore, was said to take special pleasure in the pain she inflicted on Jews, almost certainly Gitla, too, and the bitch-whore is going to die for it now. He's already decided how. 'You are *Oberaufseherin* Irma Bielenberg, formerly *Nurse* Irma Bielenberg, who volunteered to take a four-week course to become *Aufseherin*. You had a life helping people, Nazi fucks that they probably were, yes, but even that didn't make you happy. No, you wanted to hurt people instead. You wanted to know what it was like to hear human beings cry out in pain, for mercy, for you to stop. Did that power get you off, huh, bitch? Did it get you wet? I bet you're dried up like the fucking Sahara right now.'

Bielenberg tries to back away from him, probably because this language frightens her. Probably because she thinks he might want to rape her, or maybe let his friends rape her, or maybe all of them will, a goddamn train of vengeful Jews ripping her Nazi ass apart, but she'd be wrong because Tuviah and his friends aren't bad people. They're the furious wrath of God, his avenging hand on Earth, his people even if he kind of forgot about them for a few years again there.

'Now, who are you?' Tuviah says. Bielenberg shakes her head. 'Who. Are. You?'

Behind him, Gerskovich is explaining to the Americans what is being said. They seem bored, ready to just get it over with. Whittaker says, 'I'm going back to the Jeep to get the rope,' and runs off.

'I-I-I am a farmer, a fa-fa-farmer,' Bielenberg says, gasping between every fifth or sixth syllable. There's blood on her lips now. Tuviah must have winged her pretty damn good with the Jeep. 'My name is Hanna. Hanna Wi-Wi-Wi . . .' She draws a deep breath. 'Hanna Winter. My name is Hanna Winter.'

Tuviah draws his Mauser, a C96 he took off a *Kapitänleutnant* he killed with a slot-head screwdriver, and shoots Hanna Winter in the right shin three times just to make sure he shatters a bone or, if he's lucky, two. He takes her hand as she screams, to give her somewhere to direct all that pain and help her focus again on him faster. She's choking now on tears and blood and the realization that she's going to die here. Hope has abandoned her, and Tuviah is glad of it because Gitla is dead and probably didn't have any hope left when it happened to her either. Tuviah certainly didn't have any left when he finally saw the chance to escape. He was resigned to die, had even cursed God for permitting this to happen to him and Gitla and their girls and their girls and their girls and their girls, and then he was free. The Americans found him after the invasion. They put him to work. God's work. Killing Nazis like this bitch-whore.

'That's enough,' Tuviah says to her. 'I think you understand now. Who are you?'

'Y-You know who . . . who I am,' Bielenberg says.

'You were at Neue Bremm?' he says. She nods. 'Do you think you deserve to live?'

'Fuck you, Je—' she says, or tries to, because she is interrupted by blood that erupts from her mouth so forcefully that her whole body curls up like a question mark. Her right leg, the one with three bullets in it and probably a shattered bone or maybe even two, protests and she screams and coughs and screams again and Meyerson and Gershkovich laugh. Tuviah doesn't laugh. Tuviah hasn't found anything funny since he watched Gitla and their two girls being dragged away from him for ever before he himself was packed on a train to Buchenwald.

'Christ, he's still alive!' Whittaker shouts from the Jeep where he went to get rope. The others shine torches at him. He's talking about the Nazi they strapped to the hood outside Baden-Baden after Meyerson said he was dead, after Gershkovich strangled him with a length of rope for damn near two minutes, after he told them where to find his girlfriend – the Sadist of Saarbrücken. The dead Nazi is convulsing, flailing about like he was when the Jeep was on the move, fighting the ropes still binding his wrists and ankles to the windshield and bumper. 'What do I do?'

Bielenberg attempts to cry out to her lover, but is too busy hacking and choking on her own blood.

Tuviah realizes he has to be quick about this, or else she's going to die on him. 'Shoot the fucker!' he says, barking in English.

Whittaker realizes how obvious that answer was, and shoots the dead Nazi in the head and, when the dead Nazi that won't die keeps kicking, holds his finger down on the trigger, unloading into the Nazi's head until nothing is left but brain-and-skull pudding and the Jeep is smoking.

'You fucking idiot, you shot the fucking engine!' Meyerson says, running towards the Jeep, but really towards Whittaker.

'Don't let him kill him,' Tuviah says to Gershkovich in Yiddish.

Tuviah looks at Bielenberg again, and finds that, despite the three bullets and what must be at least one punctured lung, she is once again trying to get away. On her stomach, crawling with two arms and her one good leg across an exposed patch of rilled

141

granite. Her sobs are audible, but punctuated by a wheezing sound like a fireplace hand-bellows makes when it's collected too many holes in its bag. He's impressed by the effort, and says, 'Where do you think you're going?'

He goes to her. He rolls her over by her shoulder, and drops on top of her, using his weight to pin her down. She reaches for his head, to push him away, but he's too fast. His hands come down against both sides of her face like clamps. His fingers explore the contours of her skull and jaw, searching for perfect purchase. His thumbs find her pretty hazel eyes as she yowls. This is how he is going to kill Bielenberg. This is how he kills her, capped off with a final, finishing crack of her skull against the granite. He rises from her slowing body, flicking eyeball and blood and whatever is inside eyeballs from his hands, and walks away. She's dead before Tuviah reaches the Jeep.

Gracie

Joshua Tree National Monument 1962

The Joshua trees' branches reach up like black fingers against the radioactive glow of the Milky Way as the banana-yellow Chevy Kingswood's engine rumbles to life. Beside her in the front seat, Bobby throws the station wagon into reverse, accelerating too fast so that the tyres begin to dig and then sink into the loose sand beneath them. The teenagers who drove the station wagon all the way out here to the desert, to get high and neck and probably make love under the night sky, emerge from their tents, startled and confused and shouting, and, when they understand what is happening, grab whatever they can use as weapons and charge despite their inconsistent states of dress. 'Ease up on the gas!' Gracie says, slapping Bobby's arm. 'Where did you learn to drive?'

The treads finally catch, and the station wagon hurtles backwards, nearly killing a cheerleader wearing only boys' pyjama bottoms and a fancy gold bra. It slams into the side of an immense granite outcropping so hard that Gracie almost winds up in the back seat. 'Sorry,' Bobby says. He yanks the gearshift into drive. 'I really do know how to drive. Really.'

The teenagers give chase, smacking hands and pounding fists against the station wagon. One of them gets a good look at Gracie's face, which panics her until she remembers she's wanted by the FBI for abetting a bombing suspect who's wanted for the murders of twenty-three people, and suddenly grand theft auto doesn't seem like the worst of her problems.

They reach a filling station in someplace called Eagle Mountain a couple of hours later, having followed the lights of the small town – really just a collection of buildings and the station – out of the desert. Neither bothers to speak on the drive. Gracie can't even make herself hum. She cannot say for sure why he's so quiet, but she suspects his reasons aren't entirely dissimilar to her own and very likely have something to do with the fact that he wants to know her name, 'cause, for her part, she knows he wants to know, she can see it in how he keeps glancing sideways at her, mouth itching to ask the question, but she's not sure she can keep herself from going to pieces when he finally does ask. She doesn't know what happened to Bobby, if he really did lose his memory or if he's lying to her or if he's been possessed by alien spores, but she does know she loved him, probably even loves him still considering the fact that she's here and not back home, and for some reason the thought of him asking her who she is all over again – like every piece of pie she served him never happened – is too much for her to bear.

'What'll it be?' the station attendant says. He's an old-timer with a limp he probably brought home from the war, and he gets few enough visitors around here, especially at this hour, to hazard a few wrong guesses about what Bobby and Gracie were doing out there in the desert.

'Fill her up,' Bobby says.

The station attendant limps around the station wagon as Bobby and Gracie head inside. 'Looks like you got into a bit of trouble,' he says.

Bobby hesitates, unsure how to respond, but Gracie is quicker than he is. 'He let me try driving again,' she says.

The station attendant chuckles. 'Happens every time I let the missus get behind the wheel, too. Ain't no shame in it. Keep trying, miss, I'm sure it'll stick.'

Gracie smiles politely, and follows Bobby into the station. As soon as the door swings shut behind him, she takes him by the wrist and says, '*Gracie.*' He looks at her, momentarily confused. 'My name. Don't make me tell you it again.'

She walks past him before he can respond, right to the spinning rack of maps that stands next to the beauty magazines and their endless tips about how a woman might improve her appearance or better please her husband. She whirls the rack round and round as she searches with a finger, trying to ignore the fact that Bobby is behind her, watching her, and, when she turns around again, maybe he's going to feel the need to try her name out. 'Here it is,' she says, and works the spiral-bound Thomas Bros. atlas, at least an inch thick and too big for the slot it's in, from the American Southwest section. She owns her own, having used it to help her stepfather navigate when he first drove her from Denver to Pasadena three years ago, but it's back at the apartment with Sofia, who is no doubt right now talking the ear off of whatever policeman has been charged with lurking until Gracie returns. 'These guys make the best maps. You ever used one before?'

'When I first moved to the Los Angeles area, yeah,' Bobby says.

She sets the atlas on an out-of-service ice cream cooler, and opens it to the index. She still hasn't looked at him since she told him her name. 'Tucson, bingo,' she says. 'Page sixty-eight.' She double-taps the page when she locates it. 'There it is. I can't tell how long it'll take, not unless I measure it out with a ruler. But my guess is, eight or nine hours.'

'We should find someplace to pull over first,' he says. 'Get some shut-eye before the sun comes up.'

'Hold on now, what's this?' Gracie traces her finger along I-10, from Tucson north towards Phoenix, and stops at someplace called the Gila River Indian Community. She knows this place, or at least she's heard of it – and recently, too. Bobby mentioned it to her a month or two back, someplace he had to go to once for work. It stuck in her mind 'cause she had never been to or heard of anybody she knew going to an Indian reservation. She tells Bobby as much now.

'What kind of work did I have there?' he says.

'Heck if I know. I thought you were being cagey at the time, but cagey in that tall-dark-and-mysterious way and not the I'm-going-to-go-blow-some-people-up way.'

'I didn't blow anybody up,' he says.

'You keep saying.'

'Why are you with me if you think I'm capable of such an act?' he says.

Gracie spins round, and jams a finger into his chest so hard it hurts her finger. 'Maybe 'cause I need to know you're not. Now back off.'

Bobby almost smiles. 'You acted a lot sweeter last night at the diner,' he says.

''Cause the biggest problem I had until last night was whether or not I could pay my next semester's tuition. You went and ruined everything.'

He starts to say something, but stops. He turns away. 'I'm sorry, Gracie,' he says.

Darn. There it is. And the sound of it on Bobby's lips, so unfamiliar to him, hurts more than she expected it would.

'Let's get going,' Gracie says, walking away from him as fast as she can. 'I'll drive.'

'You sure you can handle it?'

'I can't do any worse than you, can I?' she says, pushing through the door.

The Daily Standard

February 2016

Damien Syco Dead: Fans Turn Icon's Poplar Birthplace into Memorial

After news broke of Damien Syco's death last night, a mysterious invitation went viral across social media. It read: 'Damien Syco has returned to the Black Temple. Join us in two hours to celebrate his music and many lives. Bring instruments, food and love.' Two hours later, the East London road on which Syco grew up was teeming with a crowd more than a thousand strong and by midnight police services estimate the crowd's number had swelled to more than five thousand.

During the course of the night, which saw temperatures dip to two degrees, the crowd performed a panoply of Syco's songs, often led by a procession of celebrity speakers, including musicians David Byrne, Axle Harvey, Lulu Ugwuegbu and, in a dramatic surprise to those present, Sir Courtney Grind, who had shared a bitter musical rivalry with Syco since a falling-out in the early '70s. Grind spoke eloquently about the impact Syco's work had on him, even admitting that he 'may have borrowed a trick or two' from him, before leading the crowd in a rousing and teary-eyed rendition of 'Death Is the Road to Go'. Poet Kei Miller and authors Zadie Smith, Nick Fernley and Salman Rushdie also spoke; Rushdie would go on to lead Byrne and Smith in an a cappella performance of Syco's 'A Seer Is a Liar'.

Many in the crowd proudly called themselves 'Sycotics', as Syco's most committed fans identify themselves. They arrived in make-up, glitter and wigs. But even more numerous were those who showed up in whatever they were wearing when they heard the news, many coming directly from work. The visibly upset mourners spoke at length, often having difficulty expressing themselves, about the impact that Syco's music had on their lives. Mina Mohan, a mother of four who left her children with her father and drove four hours from York to be here, said, 'I've spent my whole life feeling like something doesn't make sense. About me. The world. And the only thing that kept me sane was my Moonman because I knew at least he got it, know what I'm saying?' Talbert Whittaker, a screenwriter from Los Angeles, in London for a press event, called Syco 'the single most important figure, outside of my family, in my development as a human being'.

At the time of going to print, 3:00 AM this morning, the still-growing crowd remained and was obstructing traffic throughout the Poplar area. Police services were still determining the proper course of action to disperse the peaceful assembly.

Mimori

Her rocket doesn't launch for two days, so she and Malik and Sigmund cross the Rio Grande and grab some street food in Matamoros. None of them speak Spanish, which makes the experience that much more enjoyable. They return close to midnight, groaning about lousy margaritas and the tacos they ate too many of and grateful that space travel isn't what it was fifty years ago, or even ten years ago, because last nights out like this, before lengthy missions in Earth orbit, weren't possible back then. Malik and Sigmund head to bed, still awkwardly silent after Sigmund made a clumsy pass at Malik while Mimori was buying the girls souvenir tee-shirts, and Mimori, not tired at all, climbs the stairs to the roof of the SpaceNEXT flight crew dormitory, carrying her bed's blanket, to look at the stars. She used to do this all of the time as a child, but fell out of the habit by the time she started university in the States. For the past three months or so, she's been doing it almost nightly. She even drags Tamami and Okimo outside to do it with her when they agree, using the excuse that she wants to teach them about the constellations. Mimori can't explain why, except something feels different. No, not different. *Wrong.* Like she's been slowly shifting out of sync with the world around her and the stars are now her only way to orient herself in it. They have become her only constant. At first, she suspected her frustrations with Sōjirō's perpetual aloofness were behind the nagging dread, but she understands now it's something else, beyond her, nameless and formless and terrifying.

The stars disappear.

Mimori sits up, gasping silently at the infinite blackness all around her and the scintillating lights of the launch tower so much more blinding now against such an impossibly dark canvas. There is an immediate sense of of separating, of multitudes of cells and beings and possibilities ripping apart like threads along a seam, of coming unmade in tens of thousands of places all at once. She reaches for her mobile, to call the girls, to tell them she loves th

Boyudei

Baghdad 1258

There is a memory that never leaves him. A memory of his mother, before she opened her own throat with one of the hooked blades that women use for gutting pigs, before he realized he was going to lose her for ever and, with her, his only remaining tie to her people. Son and mother are lying on their backs in this memory, beneath birch branches leaden with new spring leaves, the smell of the nearby River in their noses – earthy like clay, cold from mountain run-off. His mother tells him that the River belonged to their people, the Merkit, long before the Old Khan came down from the steppes. Long before the Mongols told the Merkit they were no longer Merkit, but Mongols instead. Long before his father saw her with her first husband, a man from whom his father stole her with three well-aimed arrows. The River, his mother says, connects all things. Its water runs not just across the surface of the world, but under it and through it, so that it is actually water, not roots nor stone, that binds the world – the here and now, the past and future, all of it – together. The River is in his blood, it runs through Boyudei, as well, and always will no matter how far from it he believes he travels. He and his mother will always be connected by it.

It was several years after his mother told Boyudei this that she ended her life inside the tent of his father. She bled to death as, outside, Mongols sacrificed horses to the Creator and sang and danced in drunken homage to the Green Sea. The New Shaman told the Great Khan, the father of Boyudei, that Boyudei was to blame. The Great Khan beat his firstborn son for several weeks as punishment for this and, as a final measure, snapped the neck of the golden eagle he had gifted the boy for his eleventh birthday.

To be a prince means so little when your father sires nations and the father of his father father, the Old Khan, sired an entire empire. And so, Boyudei is nobody today, a prince of no consequence, so irrelevant amongst the innumerous children of the Great Khan that his own father cannot recall his name any more. Perhaps this is why Boyudei allowed the River to carry him so far from the Great Camp, across the Green Sea and fanged mountains and forests and deserts, to a city that burns like the sun and in which he hopes to find the means to make his father finally call him *My Son of Sons*.

Boyudei has always known he would never prove himself on the battlefield. Weak and clumsy, cowardly like a woman, he could never make himself known there. But he does know how to read and study and listen and ask questions even when others believe all the answers are known, the New Shaman – now the Old Shaman – made certain of this. This is how Boyudei first learned about the *Black Heart*, the *Window to Hell*, the *Corpse-Eater*. It has many names by reason of the Goths, who were, it is said, the first to discover it; in Rome, others say. The Huns were even more poetical in their pursuit of terrifying ways to describe it; *10,000 Cold Centuries* is especially elegant. They most often called it the *Mouth of the Devil*, which Boyudei prefers.

How the Mouth of the Devil came to be here, in the Khizanat Al-Hikma of Baghdad, Boyudei does not know. But came here it did, about a century ago. The scribes hid it deep within the bowels of the magnificent building, inside a jug shaped out of copper and regularly refilled with fresh salt water brought all the way from the sea for this purpose, and protected its secret until the Mongol horde commanded by Hülegü, the uncle of Boyudei, laid siege to the city. Later, when the gates of the city opened, the horde swept through its streets and alleys like hungry wolves unleashed upon sheep, killing multitudes and slinging the remains into the canals that made the city so verdant and colourful until the canals became logjammed with them, and the Tigris, no longer able to empty itself into the canals, rose higher and higher against stone walls that struggled to contain it. That is, until the Mongols reached the Khizanat Al-Hikma, the House of Wisdom, the library that Boyudei had heard dwarfed the one the Copts destroyed in Alexandria. The Mongols were not to be exceeded by crazed Christians. They abhor books with a similar religious zeal, and so the horde attacked not just Al-Hikma, the greatest of the libraries of Baghdad, but also all others found within the borders of the city. Tens of thousands of bound books, collected from across the world and studied by scholars who travelled here from just as far, were taken from towering shelves in great armfuls and cast into the Tigris as the Mongols sang angry threnodies against the written word. The scrolls – even more voluminous, some said more than could be counted in a single lifetime – joined the books in the Tigris, where leather and paper and parchment became a thick and pulpy membrane across the water. The black ink, the last testament of so many lost kingdoms, was drunk up by the River, and the River became black. Ash from the burning city fell like a malign snow across this ebon ribbon of self-imposed ignorance.

Boyudei sits on the river wall with his legs dangling over the River, watching its gelatinous surface quiver as he waits for the warriors to finish digging through the husk of the library behind him. The barbaric fools set it ablaze when they had finished pillaging it. They possessed no understanding of what they were doing and never will, not like Boyudei does. The River connects the world, as his mother taught him. It brought him here to witness this emerald city burn. But the world itself belongs to men, and – if Boyudei is correct about the the Mouth of the Devil – it can belong to one man. His father will be mightily pleased.

As the sun begins to set behind the scrim of smoke that covers the city, turning the sky ochre and raspberry, they call for him from the library gates. These gates, twice as tall as a Mongol and magnificently worked and painted the same startling green as the trees that grow here, were knocked down by battering rams. They lie at angles now, like felled temple guardians.

Boyudei greets the warriors, and only then sees the long rows of corpses that line the blood-soaked courtyard. Scholars and scibes who refused to surrender what they believed to be the greatest treasure in the world. Their loyalty to knowledge has been rewarded with death. To their credit, more than two hundred of their number required that their throats be slit, their hearts run through with lances, their skulls broken with hammers, until one of them revealed the location of the Mouth of the Devil. The warriors dragged this confessor into the ruins, to retrieve what Boyudei seeks, and are said to be returning at any moment. Then the screaming commences.

The confessor, a Jew by the look of his dress and more ancient than the Old Khan was when he finally died, runs from the ruins. Smoke spins in wild whorls behind his deep blue and amaranthine robes, as if trying to follow him. He is the man screaming, and he clutches something to his chest, his fingers squeezed around it so tightly that his knuckles look white as bone.

Boyudei holds up a hand, signalling the warriors to hold back. They watch this screaming Jew run past them, through the reclining library gates, and right over the edge of the river wall.

Boyudei and the warriors find the Jew lying across the black surface of books and scrolls and ash, trying not to slip through the delicate, spongy film, even though moments earlier ending his life led him to bravely throw himself into what he presumed was moving water and oblivion. But the instinct to live is powerful. It kept the mother of Boyudei alive for more than a decade after the man she loved with all her being was brutally slain before her eyes.

The warriors nock arrows. Strings sing, arrows fly, and the Jew becomes like a porcupine; his arms are left pinned to his chest and whatever he holds remains locked in his grasp. He goes still now, except for the halo of black foam expanding around his head.

Two warriors remove their armour and leap into the Tigris after him, making certain they land boots first so they tear through the film. They surface together, like men clawing through spring ice, and work their way to the dead Jew. One draws a knife and slashes through the arrow shafts, knocking away the colourful feathered ends until the other warrior, a Merkit like the mother of Boyudei, can pry the hands of the Jew free. They wrench at fingers, to open them, the crack of bone loud enough to hear on land. Finally, the fist of the Merkit warrior rises in triumph.

When the warriors return, their skin and clothes dyed black, they present Boyudei with his prize. 'It is cold, Khan Khuu,' the Merkit warrior says, arms trembling. 'I cannot hold it any longer.' He places an orb made of what appears to be black onyx in the open palm of Boyudei.

Boyudei, unprepared for how truly cold the orb is despite the warning, drops it. He catches it with his other hand, and that is when it speaks to him. The Mouth of the Devil. He can hear it, like a low murmur, even though the others around him seem deaf to it. The words are in a language he does not understand and has never heard spoken. They are words as ancient and powerful as the River. The world quakes around the orb as it speaks, and Boyudei is terrified.

Years later, long after his father called him *Son of Sons*, after his uncle Kublai betrayed his father and buried him next to the Old Khan, after Boyudei fled and changed his name and went to live amongst the people of his mother, *his people*, Boyudei walks into the River and begs its forgiveness for unleashing the Devil upon the world. The River beckons him deeper into its icy waters, calling Boyudei by his real name, and never forgives him.

Gracie

Gila River Indian Community 1962

They cross the California–Arizona border around sunrise as the sky explodes around them in all the colours of cotton candy, and finally pull over for a two-hour nap at a rest stop in La Paz Valley before some bikers show up, dressed in faded and cracked black leather jackets that proclaim them Road Vipers. They want to know what happened to the station wagon's bumper and, when Bobby doesn't roll the window down, why he won't let them talk to his girl either. Bobby speeds away, clenching the steering wheel, frantically watching the rearview mirror for fear that the miscreants decide to follow them. He has heard the stories about biker gangs tormenting couples, just like she has. Ten miles on, they decide they're safe. They make Phoenix later that day, the middle of the afternoon, and stop at a roadside stand for tacos. Bobby has said Gracie's name four times by this point, and she's finally okay about it. Almost okay. She smiles at him, wipes a piece of cilantro from the side of his mouth, and tells him to try the pork tacos, too.

They reach the Gila River Indian Community about an hour before sunset. Gracie didn't know what to expect, but certainly something more than, well, *this*. There's nothing here, not really, just a whole lot of brown, sickly-looking scrub and tall cacti, and roads in various stages of completion. The Pima and Pee-Posh who wound up here got a raw deal, that's for sure.

Gracie, who is driving again at this point, parks the car on the side of the road of what might be a downtown in a few decades or centuries, or maybe never. There are two churches next door to each other here, a building with one sign that says INDIAN AFFAIRS and another that says CLINIC, and a grocery shop that serves as the post office and one-pump filling station. She and

Bobby get out, look around at the scattered faces here, how they're being watched 'cause they're white and there are no other white folks here, and decide without saying anything to each other that heading into the shop right now is a pretty good idea.

An Indian woman sitting behind a counter cluttered with racks of candy and chewing tobacco and jars of peppermint sticks and beef jerky greets them with a curt nod. She's in her fifties, smoking a pipe that issues strange, sweet-smelling smoke, and her face is prematurely full of deep crags that tell painful tales of loss and heartache she'd never reveal herself.

Bobby nods politely back at her before taking a moment to look around, mostly to think it seems, to try to make sense of why he allegedly told Gracie he was coming here.

Gracie moves to the front window, to consider again the two-lane road and the few Indians shuffling past alone or in pairs, talking and sometimes laughing or staring emptily at the empty road ahead, 'cause, she's starting to realize, most folks here don't own cars. They walk everywhere. The lucky ones ride horses. She turns, and finds Bobby looking at her. It's 'cause she's humming the Tune again, even though she wasn't conscious of it.

'What is that?' he asks. 'That song?'

She walks around him. 'There's nothing here,' she says. 'We should go.'

Bobby returns to the counter. 'Hi there. I'm going to ask you a question, and I know it's going to sound a little odd, but . . . have you ever seen me before?'

The Indian woman regards him for a long moment, the crags over her right eye slowly rising, pinching together like the walls of ancient canyons kissing, as she quietly assesses Bobby. Smoke from her pipe passes over her face. At last, she nods once.

Bobby looks at Gracie, then back at the Indian woman. 'Where? *Where* have you seen me?'

The Indian woman regards him for another long moment, puffing on her pipe. She points at where Bobby is standing. 'Right there, couple of times,' she says. 'Another time, walking that way.' She points in one direction along the road. 'Another time, walking that way.' She points the other way. 'That time, you were on the other side of the road. It was raining. I remember, because you remember when it rains here.'

Gracie joins Bobby at the counter, her shoulder accidentally brushing against his arm. 'Was he alone?'

The Indian woman regards her in that cryptic manner of hers, smoke hovering around her face, crags shifting microscopically along her brow this time. Then her eyes swivel, to take in Bobby. Then they swivel the other direction, to look outside where a Chevy pick-up, an oldie, is pulling up. 'Ride's here,' she says. 'Have a good day now.'

Two Indian men – one a few years older than Gracie, the other a few years older still – get out of the pick-up that's appeared outside. They wear cowboy boots and dusty Levi's, sun-faded plaid shirts, and fleece-lined denim coats. They would be twins if they looked anything alike. The only physical characteristics they actually share are their long jet hair pulled into ponytails and their confident, dangerous swaggers.

'Bobby,' Gracie says.

'Don't worry,' he says.

The Indian men enter the shop. The younger one, who's quite handsome and knows it, nods at the woman. 'You should've called,' Handsome says to Bobby. 'Pop would've made dinner. Come on.'

Bobby and Gracie exchange another look, then follow the Indians out to the pick-up. The older Indian, who has a long, drooping face, opens the door for them to get in. Gracie doesn't want to, but Bobby nudges her from behind. She slides across the cracked leather seat until she's shoulder to shoulder with Handsome, who's behind the steering wheel now. Bobby gets in beside her, then Droopy. The doors shut, shaking the pick-up, and Gracie does her best not to look terrified. Indians have special abilities to read the Earth and even people, or at least that's what she's been told. Her dad certainly believed it and liked to stay away from *the red man*, as he referred to them. Gracie doesn't believe in magic or the supernatural or anything that resembles it, but that doesn't seem to be making any difference right about now. These Indians could be reading her soul – which she also doesn't believe in – at this very moment.

Handsome winks at her, pulls a U-turn, and accelerates away from the shop.

'Who's the gal?' Droopy asks Bobby as they pass a trio of hitched horses.

'Just a . . . just a friend,' Bobby says.

Handsome chuckles, but in this weird way. This weird way that lets you clearly hear every *ha*. 'Don't let Mary see her. You know how she can be.'

Mary? Who's *Mary*? Gracie doesn't look at Bobby, but she can feel him asking himself the same question. For Gracie's part, she has certain fears about what this woman might be to Bobby. There's so much he can't remember. Maybe there's a girlfriend, maybe even a wife lost amongst the other forgotten pieces of his life, like the name of a second-grade teacher, or what he ate for breakfast last Tuesday, or blowing up Pasadena City Hall.

'How far is the drive?' Bobby asks instead of 'Who the heck is Mary and why wouldn't she want to see Gracie?'

Handsome chuckles again. 'Same as always. There's something unsettling about him, a menace that feels as if it could make a violent appearance at a snap of the fingers, and the lightness he tries to give off, especially that weird laugh of his, only makes it worse. 'Something wrong with you?'

'How do you mean?' Bobby says.

'You just seem different today, is all.'

Oh no, it's true, he's reading Bobby's soul, Gracie thinks.

'Don't he seem different today, Bob?' Handsome asks Droopy.

Gracie leans forward, to look at Droopy. 'Oh, your name's Bob, too?'

Droopy, or Bob II, says, 'Huh?'

Gracie is about to ask Droopy what he means in return, 'cause Bobby is sitting next to this other Bob and they have the same name and what the heck is so confusing about that, but Bobby's hand slides onto her knee and gives it a quick squeeze. 'Nothing,' she says, watching how Bobby's fingers linger on her knee longer than necessary. 'Nothing.'

'But you said *too*, as in *addition to*,' Droopy says. 'In addition to *who*?'

'I-I don't know. It was just a silly thing to say.'

They pull off the road in another mile, then drive another ten or so miles before they take another turn at an enormous egg-shaped rock that puts them on a dirt track up a scrub-covered incline. There are trees here, stumpy ones, that block out the distant lights of town. The headlights, necessary now as the sun plummets towards the distant and flat horizon, are nauseatingly bright and, as the truck climbs, illuminate these trees in startling detail.

'How much further?' Bobby says.

The trees open up as if in reply, and a house appears. The headlights reveal its every ugly feature, from the unpainted cinder-block walls, to the terracotta-tiled roof, to the chickens running wild and the two goats tied to a giant water tank. A sickly three-legged dog tries but fails to howl in greeting.

'Home sweet home,' Handsome says.

Bobby and Gracie are led from the pick-up to the house. It's only when the headlights are cut that the lights on inside become evident. Also, that there's at least one other person in there, judging by the shadows they can now see moving around.

The interior of the house is much more inviting than its drab exterior. There's a floral-print couch that looks relatively new, a colourful rug that was probably handwoven by Indians of these men's tribe, an old cast-iron potbelly stove throwing off heat from the corner, and several antique pieces – chairs and tables and cupboards – collected across many generations.

'Well, this is a surprise,' a third Indian man says. He enters from the kitchen, wiping his hands on a chequered dishtowel. He's taller than the other two Indians, his long hair is like tarnished silver and kept in loose braids, and his face has a quality, a warmth about it, that immediately sets Gracie at ease, just like her grandfather's used to.

He's also blind.

He smiles at them, a big toothy smile that seems genuine, and extends a wrinkly hand to Bobby. 'The boys read the news in the paper yesterday morning,' he says. 'You did good, you did. Come, let's celebrate.'

'What about us, Pop?' Droopy says.

'You and James go lock the gate and keep a lookout,' the blind Indian says. 'And make sure your sister doesn't surprise us when she gets home.' After his sons are gone, the blind Indian leads them to the kitchen, his hand affectionately rubbing Bobby's back as if he's a proud father. 'You should've told us you were bringing a friend. You know how Mary is.'

'This is Gracie,' Bobby says.

The blind Indian holds the door open for them. 'Of course it is,' he says, smiling at Gracie as she passes him. 'Porter here has told me all about you.'

She and Bobby mouth the name *Porter* at each other at the same time, and it's at that moment that she realizes Robert Jones aka Porter is either the man she thinks he is or not the man he thinks he is.

Keisha

She thought she would enjoy the challenge of being a Black woman in Hollywood, that kicking the movie industry's ass while being its most unvalued and unwanted quantity would make her eventual triumph that much more gratifying. Three years later, Keisha picks up a Sharpie and asks, 'Name?'

'Blake,' the white dude in the suit says, not even looking at her 'cause he's busy checking out the fake tits on the Latina waiting at the end of the counter for her vanilla bean frappuccino. There are three more suits just like him in the line, along with a couple of Silver Lake hipsters bitching about the heat in the Valley with the same trying-too-hard passion they put into their beards, an actress of some Asian persuasion loudly running through lines with herself for what sounds like an audition for a cellular phone commercial, and, lurking at the back, a skinny, sullen-looking brother with his face half buried in a wrinkled, beat-up-as-fuck paperback copy of *The Foundations of Screenwriting*.

'Grande latte, triple shot, soy milk,' Keisha says, calling out so everybody knows what Blake ordered. She scribbles BLACK on a coffee cup, and hands it to Janet, whose girlfriend just left her for a girl who looks just like Janet except with short blonde hair instead of medium-length blonde hair, so she's a fucking mess and thinks maybe she should cut her hair now. There's a reason why they call these people dummies on the Outside.

This has been Keisha's life for the past thirteen months – no, *fourteen* 'cause she started working here right before that Black Senator kicked that old white guy's ass. Espresso macchiato, chai latte, white chocolate mocha, *iced* white chocolate mocha, some-body shoot her in the face already. She should be home writing, something, *anything*, even though she can't think up a single one-sentence idea that immediately conveys a movie poster and, by movie poster, she means a poster that's going to put asses in seats and millions into studios' piggy banks. But let's get real, she needs to pay her rent right about now a whole lot more than she needs to make studios even richer.

Blake collects his coffee, sees BLACK on the side of his cup, and gives her a '*niiiice*' grin like they're in on some kind of kinky joke together. Keisha wonders if he's an agent, 'cause he's still looking at her – not like he was that Latina's tits, but curious enough – and maybe she could be down with that. Especially if he works for one of the bigger agencies like William Morris or CAA. It's not like he'd be the first white dude she's got with since she retired. They're okay enough, except for the blatant adventurism that comes with getting with a sister. But Blake walks out without asking for her number, Keisha still doesn't have an agent, and there are still another four fucking hours on her shift.

'What can I get you?' she says for the millionth time today.

The skinny brother with the screenwriting book smiles, mouth full of perfect white teeth like maybe they're caps. He's a regular, comes in at least once a day to work on scripts he likes to ambush customers to tell them about. Keisha is pretty sure he's gay. He wears tight jeans like those hipsters and a Damien Syco 1977 tour tee-shirt vintage enough to have cost him enough bank to drink here for a few months. 'My name's Talbert Whittaker,' he says. 'I mean, *just* Talbert, I hate how folks introduce themselves with their full names here, and now I just did, and, sorry, I'm just Talbert, or Tab, everybody calls me Tab actually. Shit, this is hard. I'm Tab.'

Keisha looks at him, Sharpie twirling between two fingers and acrylic fingernails. Oh fuck. Fuck, fuck, fuck. 'Keisha,' she says with the same droning tone she uses to recite orders to Janet. 'What can I get you?'

'Oh, uh, yeah. Just an iced white chocolate mocha, Keisha.'

'For here?'

'Yep.'

'Anything else?'

'Uh . . . how about one of those scones? A scone, yeah. A scone, Keisha.'

'Stop saying my name like that. It's weird.'

'Oh. Sorry, Keisha. Shit, sorry again.'

Keisha fucks Tab later that day, which surprises her a lot more than it does him. It's not that Tab isn't fine enough, she's developed a refined taste for the many different flavours of American Blackness out there, but he's just . . . *strange*. That Damien Syco tee-shirt isn't some novelty or cutesy affectation these dummies use to declare their individuality. It's the tip of a crazy-iceberg. Tab's walls are plastered in the freaky dude's tour posters and album covers and an illustration he says Syco's lover, some other rocker called Axle Harvey, did of him during his *Berlin Liberation period* – whatever the fuck that is. Apparently, Tab's dad was into Syco big time when Tab was growing up in Oakland, and then Tab's dad died of a stroke at thirty-six and, yeah, sad story. None of this is why Keisha fucks him, though.

To begin with, she only agreed to grab a drink with him after work 'cause the brother seemed so tragic. Like he needed a break of some kind. Janet says she doesn't know why Keisha is into charity cases, but maybe it's 'cause she likes people even more pathetic than her. Maybe that's why Keisha is friends with Janet.

Tab isn't exactly boring. In fact, he's the opposite once you get him talking about anything besides screenwriting. Even the shit about Syco, minus the dead dad part. Tab thinks Syco – whom he also interchangeably refers to as the Moonman, the Black Prince, and Buddha Bad – figured out what reality really is and, with a 'Let me break it down for you,' frames his case with lots of references to French philosophers Keisha hasn't read and weren't even included in her cultural download when she retired here, 'cause, no doubt, Plurality Life Insurance Corporation thought some sister who was supposed to have grown up in Detroit in the '80s wouldn't give a shit about Sartre and Camus and Baudrillard. Keisha is more than where she came from – even though she didn't really come from there – but after three years living as one of these people, in this skin, in a town that assumes she doesn't belong, in a country where Black folks are target practice for cops and locked up like wild animals and told to fuck off whenever Mother Nature comes for them, well, she's starting to feel and even act like she really did grow up just off of Kercheval next to Kevin's Party Store.

Against her better judgement, Keisha finally asked Tab what his screenplay is about. She even jokingly suggested, 'You're not writing a biopic about your Moonman, are you?'

'Nah,' Tab said, chuckling awkwardly. 'Not really. I mean, it is, kind of. At least spiritually.'

Spiritually? Who the fuck is this guy?

He continued, saying, 'It's hard to explain, but it's about how the world we live in. This restaurant, these margaritas, you, me, our waitress and that creepy guy at the bar I'm pretty sure is touching himself – none of it's real. He's definitely touching himself, by the way. It's all a giant computer program and we're all just strings of computer code ourselves, know what I'm saying? And, if that's true, what does that mean about the intrinsic value of our lives here? I mean, is there any if we're not even really alive? Why are you looking at me like that?'

Keisha didn't respond immediately, but she guessed her face had frozen in some dumb expression judging by how Tab was looking at her. He clearly thought he'd gone too far. He's deeply insecure, like most writers Keisha has met, and, frankly, artists in general; especially the actors, who are seriously fucked-up individuals who should wear that shit tattooed on their foreheads so you know to stay away from them. 'Tell me more,' she said. Holy shit, he knows, she thought, *how* does he know? 'For real, I want to know more.'

Tab looked relieved. He explained how he got the idea for 'the simulacra' after attending most of his college physics courses while

164

high. Does she know that physics can't account for how much of the universe works? Quantum physics tries, he said, but it's a malleable field that changes faster than reality and our understanding of it can keep up with. Don't even get him started on theoretical physics, especially the many-worlds interpretation and multiverses and retrocausality which suggest that time travel isn't possible, but that energy, one could even say effects can precede their own causes in time, since, at the end of the day, time's arrow is an illusion exclusively limited to the biological experience.

He stopped here 'cause Keisha was still looking at him with that dumb expression.

Keisha, for her part, couldn't help it 'cause Tab, this brother from a nothing-special family in Oakland, had somehow figured it all out. In her First Life, Keisha didn't understand the exact operational nature of what Plurality was offering her in her retirement, but she had read enough and discussed enough with others to grasp its fundamentals and Tab, fuckfuckfuck, had somehow figured it all out.

Maybe they're not all dummies, after all. Maybe Tab and this Moonman know something she doesn't.

That's when Keisha decided to fuck Tab, which she did after assuring him he's brilliant, his script idea was brilliant, and she'd really like to see his crib. They made it as far as the couch, where she blew him until one of his legs started to bounce, climbed on top of him and let him come inside her 'cause, yeah, her contract says she can't get pregnant here anyway. The Moonman, all over the walls, watched them as his voice rose from a vinyl record player Tab's dad used to own, then his mom until she died, then his older brother, then Tab after his older brother was dead, too. It's only afterwards, when she's collapsed beside him, his warm white jizz dripping down her dark thigh and she's finally caught her breath long enough to notice how he looks at her, that she realizes Tab has lost everything he loved in his life and that was the key to how he figured it out, 'cause his screenplay is about a concept of reality in which parallel dimensions exist and in one of them, maybe many of them, his whole family still does, too.

Keisha stays the night, sleeping beside Tab for most of it and glad about it. Sometime around five, she wakes and begins scribbling ideas on pieces of printer paper. By the time Tab gets up and shuffles out of his room wearing nothing but boxers with some sort of logo of a green lantern printed across them, offering to make her a cheese-and-ham omelette – omelettes, he insists, are his *spécialité* – she has laid nineteen pages out across the Spanish-tiled floor of his kitchen. Some of them feature arrows that swerve and turn and point to one another, six of the pages overlap with words that spill from one page to the next, and one page, at the centre, connects them like a narrative web.

'What is this?' he asks.

'*This* is how your simulacra work,' she says. And after she explains each page, the lines and arrows, the intersecting geometry of it all – this to a soundtrack of the Moonman, a song with a title like 'The Exquisite Agony of Living 10,000 Years' – Tab asks her, no, *pleads* with her as he holds her face in his hands, to write the script with him. Keisha knows she has already revealed too much, that she's probably in violation of her insurance policy, but says, 'Fuck it, sure, let's do it' anyway, and kisses him 'cause she doesn't know how to stop kissing him.

Mimori

Earth orbit 2027

The end effectors and grappling hands on the robotic arm and tool array blink green across her HUD, and she begins to calculate how long it will take to get off her space suit, clean herself up, and get back to the Habitation Module where she can vidcall Sōjirō and the girls in relative privacy. That is, as much privacy as one can find aboard a space station with six crew members, twelve modules, and thirteen rooms – *thirteen* only because somebody was considerate enough to put an accordion curtain around the otherwise exposed toilet. The Colonist Holding Module will be half as large as the station currently is, but won't arrive for assembly until next month. Mimori is looking forward to the space it promises on these six-week orbital work assignments. 'It looks good to me,' she says.

'Give us a moment, EV 1,' Mike, the Ground IV on duty in Long Beach, says with his annoyingly affected surfer's drawl. His bearded face and hemp-milk-latté-frosted moustache currently float in the corner of Mimori's vision. 'Waiting for confirmation on the orientation, too.'

'You all right, Mimori?' Sigmund says, from where he's hooked to the adjustable across from her. He's one of three engineers aboard the station. The other, Malik, was supposed to be out here with her on this EV, but Commander Yiu is worried about him and so are she and Sigmund. Malik hasn't been the same since his father died last year, and there's fresh concern that he has lost the focus necessary for work in extreme environments.

'I don't know,' Mimori says, unable to shake the feeling that something is wrong. It's plagued her most of the morning. 'I think maybe I'm just a little homesick.'

Sigmund is watching Hurricanes Martha and Lupita collide off the east coast of the United States as another hurricane, Naomi, hooks towards them both out of the Gulf. The news is calling it *the storm of the century*, but every week there's a storm that's worse than the one before, so Mimori wonders if they should just start calling them *storms of the month* instead.

'Sascha asks me to describe it to him, but I don't know how,' he says. 'It's too beautiful.' This is his fourth time in space, and he's still awed by it. Mimori has been at this so long, she only thinks about the time away from Sōjirō and the girls now. This makes her a little sad, if she's honest with herself. 'How do you describe it when people ask you?'

'The end of the world?' she says, with a smile.

The Earth is reflected across Sigmund's face plate as he considers what was clearly meant as a joke, but Mimori has realized this past week that, while Germans have a fierce wit – albeit frustratingly dry – her attempts at humour, except for the equivalent of zero-G pratfalls, are entirely lost on this particular German. '*Ja*, it's too bad,' he says.

'I wasn't serious, Janny,' she says.

He looks at her for a brief moment, confused by what she could find funny about the end of the world. He returns his gaze to Earth, to take it in some more in case the moment never returns.

But Mimori was serious. Everybody she knows, including Sigmund, now display their anxiety like a pulsating aura for all to see. It is as if there's been a collective human surrender to an inscrutable inevitability, an unknowable impending doom, and living with it, especially navigating the new social permutations that shift and evolve daily because of it, is exhausting. Mimori's daughters seem especially sensitive to it. It's always been a virtue of youth, to live with the confidence that nothing is impermanent, that life and everything you love will go on for ever, but now her children, like all of their friends, like children everywhere across Earth, sense that might not be true and are withering, are cracking in a miscellany of ways, are going mad as a result. Tamami lives inside her video games and manga, pretending away reality. Okimo wakes from terrible dreams screaming for Mimori and later is sent home from school because she can't stop starting fistfights with her classmates. A few months ago, Mimori asked Sōjirō if he sensed this, too, and he told her she worried too much, that change is inevitable and challenges every generation to reinvent itself, including their own, then unironically returned to his book on the history of Japan's early twentieth-century democracy movement and left-wing radicalism that were snuffed out by militarism and an enforced return to tradition during the ramp-up to World War II.

Mimori feels this anxiety herself sometimes, especially when she watches Tamami with her VR headset strapped to her beautiful face so the world around her vanishes and is replaced by one that must make more sense to her. Or when she crawls onto Okimo's futon with her, to hold her and sleep with her until the nightmares pass. Or when Sōjirō retreats into his work. Once, while drunk on expensive French wine at a conference in Tel Aviv, she suggested to an equally drunk old lover from university that maybe this all started around the turn of the century and has only been accelerating since, like an out-of-control train racing towards a cliff, climate change, the pandemics, and the re-elections of US President Glass its inevitable conclusion, and the old lover made some thoughtful observation about perception as related to quantum physics and then tried to kiss her.

'Orientation looks good from here, too, EV 1,' Mike says from Mission Control, snapping Mimori back to focus. 'We have one change, though. We'd like the small hook on Adjustable 424 to go from tether point on the ball-stack versus the jaws.'

'Roger,' she says, and makes the simple change. 'How does it look now—'

'Fuck, where did the stars go?' Commander Yiu asks, panic in his voice.

Sigmund shouts Mimori's name, his voice vibrating inside her helmet. She spins around, but somehow, impossibly, she knows she's going to find that space has gone dark even before she sees it with her own eyes. Somehow, this has all happened to her before. A moment later, Earth blinks out of existence, too, as if a god pressed the quantum power button on their gaming console. Sōjirō, Tamami, and Okimo are gone again. And then comes the sudden, terrifying, and familiar sense of being ripped apart atom by atom by ato

Tuviah

Leiden 1949

He has not been back to the Netherlands since 1940, since that Friday afternoon when Gitla was preparing the cholent, the children were staging a tea party in Yael's bedroom, and he was taking a nap on their new sofa because he and Otto had stayed out late drinking and playing cards the night before and he felt like shit. The knocking was loud and rapid, like machine-gun fire, and Tobias – as he called himself then, before he lost everything, before he started calling himself by his Hebrew name – leapt to his feet. Gitla went to the girls and he asked who was there even though he already knew who was at his door. When they fled Germany two years earlier, Gitla had wanted to immediately join her sisters in America, but Tobias, who didn't believe the war would last long, insisted they go no further than Amsterdam and, by the time he realized Gitla was right, their route to Detroit, wherever that might be, was closed to them. They knew this day would almost certainly come, and that is why Tobias greeted the Nazis who marched into their apartment by saying, 'What took you so long?' He saw Gitla and their girls – their babies – for the final time nineteen days later, and so now the only memories Tobias-now-Tuviah has left of the Netherlands are painful ones. Memories that remind him of what was and what was stolen from him. He is not pleased to be back.

Leiden always reminded Tuviah of Amsterdam on barbiturates. Everything here is slower, quieter and duller, smaller by half. But it's a beautiful city all the same, slowly waking up from the nightmare of the war. Its people, mostly Catholics and Protestants, have cheese and meat enough in their bellies again, shops sell the latest fashions for those who can still afford them, and, most importantly, the lager flows freely when you want it. Tuviah is here with

Gershkovich and Whittaker and the new boys, the American, Bruckheimer, and the Frenchman, Bloch, who replaced Meyerson after a Gestapo agent hiding in a barn caught him in the throat with a pitchfork and, after him, Samson and Elijah, the German brothers whom that Gross-Rosen commandant with the small arsenal hidden in his medical bag accidentally blew up along with himself. Currently, Tuviah and the boys are hunting Aldo Kraaijkamp, a prominent member of the Henneicke Column, a group of Dutch collaborators who worked inside the Central Bureau for Jewish Emigration and betrayed and sold upwards of 8,000 Jews to the Nazis for the pathetic sum of 7.50 guilders a head. Apparently, that's all a Jew's life was worth to them. Most of these Jews were sent on to Westerbork, where he and Gitla and their babies were first taken, before they were transported to one of the death camps, as he and Gitla and their babies were, too. Kraaijkamp wasn't the leader of the Henneicke Column – there were two of those, one of whom was assassinated by the Dutch Resistance five years ago and another who is suspected to be in West Germany at the moment – but he was a key member, one of the original eighteen, and he has the blood of a great many Jews on his hands. Maybe Gitla's, maybe even their babies'. For that, Kraaijkamp is going to die horribly. Tuviah has already decided how, too.

Tuviah's contact, a former Dutch Resistance member, asks for the night to decide whether or not to help him. The Dutchman is said to have killed at least seventeen Nazis himself during the war, but has since given himself back over to the Lord and wants nothing more to do with death. Out of respect for how many Nazis the Dutchman has killed, Tuviah agrees rather than beats the information out of him as usual. Because of this unexpected delay, there is some time rather than Nazis to kill for once – a lousy joke the boys often make when they find themselves with a bit of personal freedom – and so Tuviah and Whittaker shuffle into a jazz bar on the Nieuwe Rijn, even though Tuviah doesn't especially care for Whittaker's Negro music, and get drunk.

It is close to midnight when Tuviah sees her looking at him, and he recognizes her right away. The past comes with her, and he has to turn away. Whittaker returns with two more beers, and asks him what's wrong, but Tuviah says nothing. A few minutes later, she comes over and taps him on the shoulder. 'Toby,' she says. 'Toby, it's me.'

Tuviah gives her the best approximation of a smile he can muster when he's not choking the life out of a Nazi. 'Oh, hello,' he says. The woman is a goy, Protestant, at least a head taller than Tuviah with hair like sunshine and freckles on her nose. Most people would call her beautiful, including Tuviah. She was also Gitla's dear friend. 'It's good to see you again.'

'You saw me at the bar,' she says.

Tuviah plays dumb.

'I saw you looking at me,' she says. 'Is Gitla with you?'

Whittaker rises quickly with his full glass of beer. 'I'm going to get another beer,' he says.

When he is gone, the woman sits in his seat. Her name is Merel, and she knows what has happened before Tuviah says it. She doesn't ask about the children, because she knows he would have brought them up if they had returned. Instead, she says, 'BenDavid didn't make it either.'

BenDavid was her husband, a nice enough Jew even though Tuviah found it exhaustingly dreary to be around him. Like spending time with a log. 'I'm sorry to hear it. Would you care for a drink?'

'I don't drink,' Merel says. 'I only come here for the music.'

He doesn't know what to say.

'I'm joking,' she says, laughing. 'I haven't been sober since the war ended.'

They don't stop drinking until they stumble into the alley, kissing each other, pulling at each other's clothes. Neither feel like waiting until they reach her apartment, it's been too long for either of them, and so they crawl and stumble across houseboats moored along the canal until they find one with an unlocked door. They make love inside it, amidst a lingering stench of Pinot Noir and hard cheese and fish entrails, and he's pretty sure she comes as soon as he enters her and he's not far behind her, but they're back at it a few minutes later.

Afterwards, Tuviah sits half naked on the edge of the narrow bed, one of her legs still wrapped around him, the smell of their sex now mingling with the rest of the funk in here, and cries into the calloused heels of his hands. He hasn't wept in years, and it's not because he's betrayed his promise to only be with Gitla or because Merel trembling under him means Gitla is really dead, but because he's felt more alive in the past hour than he has since he last saw his family. Nearly a decade, a walking dead man killing and killing and killing some more because if he stops, then what's the point? It's time to just lie down and die, too, except Gitla made him promise he wouldn't give up. But he doesn't know how to do this any more.

Merel holds Tuviah from behind, gently kissing his hairy back as her fingers trace lazy patterns across his even hairier belly. It's only now that she asks him what he's doing in Leiden. He doesn't lie. He and his friends are looking for a man, a collaborator, and Tuviah intends to drive him out of the city, douse him in petrol, and set him afire. He doesn't say it, but finding new ways to kill Nazis is growing wearisome, and at least immolation feels unique by his standards.

'What is this man's name?' Merel says, revealing nothing about how she feels about his admission.

'Aldo Kraaijkamp,' Tuviah says.

'I know him.'

This confuses Tuviah. 'You *know* him?'

She lies back, her breasts blue from the moonlight falling through a porthole, and stares at the ceiling for some time. He watches her, waiting.

'Everybody knows what he did,' Merel says finally. 'The Dutch, they didn't care about Jews before the war. At least I didn't think they did. But the war showed what they really were. It was easy for them to look the other way if it meant they might live a little longer. "What does it matter? They are only Jews. We are Dutch, we belong here." I don't have to tell you. Afterwards, after the fury over the war dissipated, even those who helped, even the Resistance, grew tired. Everybody wanted to move on.' She stops for a moment, and turns away. Then she looks at Tuviah again, meeting his eyes, and says, 'I don't want to forget what they did to BenDavid. I don't want to forget, Toby. If I tell you where to find Kraaijkamp, you must take me with you. You must let me light the match.'

Merel's husband was stolen from her, and their dreams – *her* dreams – went with him. Who is Tuviah to say she has no right to avenge him in whatever way brings her peace? Tuviah cannot, just as no man or woman could tell him what he has done should not have been done. It was his right. And so he nods, and Merel kisses him, and they make love again even though he can see all she's thinking about now is Kraaijkamp.

Afterwards, they dress, walk to one of the cars Tuviah and the boys arrived in, and drive to a house at the edge of Leiden. Merel waits in the front seat. Tuviah knocks, but nobody answers. He knocks louder. This time, Kraaijkamp comes to the door. God-damnit, these Dutch are tall motherfuckers. Tuviah punches him in the balls, then kicks him in the face and stomps on the back of his head so that his skull bounces off the pavement, his wife screaming all the while. Tuviah drags Kraaijkamp to the car as his wife continues to howl and grab at Tuviah, scratching at his face, and Merel, seeing he needs help, fetches a tyre iron from the boot. She leaves Kraaijkamp's wife on the footpath, whimpering as she holds the side of her head.

Kraaijkamp wakes half an hour later, tied up on the floor of the back seat, and immediately tries to scream. Tuviah is behind the wheel when he hears the muffled mumbling and grunting. 'You've got a gag in your mouth,' he says. 'When I first started doing this, I didn't think ahead. I'd knock on a door or – more likely, *kick* in a door like I was a tank – grab some dumb Nazi cunt like you, and get to the car only to realize I'd have to listen to him wail for the next hour, sometimes longer, all because I didn't bring something to keep him quiet. At first, I would just use my handkerchief, but how do you keep it in? *Tape*? That would make sense, except why would anybody travel with tape? There are never any shops open this time of night either. As I said, I didn't think ahead back then. Usually, I'd just solve the problem by hitting the dumb Nazi cunt like you over the head a couple of times with my gun, but that would leave him dazed, unable to foucs, and, believe it or not, *the questions matter*. This all changed a few years ago. One of you animals bit the tip of my pinky off while I was trying to shut you up.' He holds up his left hand, which is indeed missing the tip of its pinky finger. 'I feel like that's when I really got serious about my work, when I started treating it like a vocation instead of a hobby. That's how that happened.'

Tuviah glances over his shoulder at Kraaijkamp on the back-seat floor, a child's red rubber ball jammed between his teeth and held in place by a handmade rope muzzle that fits neatly over most Nazis' heads. Kraaijkamp squirms wildly, bucking and kick-ing the seats and shouting even though he can't be understood. And then, when that doesn't work, he weeps.

Merel sits in the front seat beside Tuviah, trying not to look nervous even though she is. She keeps smoothing her dress and brushing things off her pantyhose that he accidentally tore when he yanked them off her. 'You don't have to do this,' he says.

'I want to,' she says.

'I know, but you don't *have* to,' he says.

'Yes, I do,' she says.

In the back seat, Kraaijkamp cries louder having heard all of this.

They park a few minutes later. Tuviah drags Kraaijkamp from

the car, and shows him his gun. 'See this?' he says. 'I'm going to shoot you with it if you try to run.' He then goes to the boot, and retrieves the can of petrol. He hands Merel the gun, then shoves Kraaijkamp forward with one hand. 'Here, shoot him if he runs.'

They walk for almost a mile. It's flat here. No houses to be seen anywhere. The moon and stars are bright enough for them to clearly see each other's faces.

'On your knees,' Tuviah says, and kicks Kraaijkamp in the back of the knee so he drops to them. 'What is your name?'

Kraaijkamp is confused. He still has the ball stuffed into his mouth.

'My apologies,' Tuviah says. He removes the muzzle. 'Now, what is your name?'

Kraaijkamp looks down.

'I know who you are,' Merel says. 'How many times have you tried to take me home? You introduce yourself as Aldo every time, as if you don't remember who I am.'

Kraaijkamp shakes his head. 'I'm not who you think I am,' he says.

'You don't even know who I think you are yet,' Tuviah says. 'But now that you mention it, are you Aldo Kraaijkamp?'

Kraaijkamp begins to cry again.

'Did you belong to the Henneicke Column?' Tuviah says.

Kraaijkamp cries louder.

'Did you sell Jews for 7.50 guilder a head to the Gestapo?' Tuviah says.

Merel spins away, a hand leaping to her face. Now she's crying, too, because she didn't know how little her husband's life was worth to this dumb Nazi cunt.

'Answer the goddamn question,' Tuviah says.

'Oh God, yes, I'm sorry, oh God, God, I'm sorry,' Kraaijkamp says.

Tuviah unscrews the cap on the can of petrol, and pours its contents onto Kraaijkamp's head. Kraaijkamp smells what it is, and begins to let out long screeches, eyes bulging, until he runs out of air and faints. The petrol spilling over his face wakes him back up, and this time he begins to flop about and cry out and gag until he's vomiting all over himself and blacks out again.

'That's it,' Tuviah says, tossing the can away. He removes a box of matches from his pocket for Merel. 'Here.'

Merel trades his gun for the box of matches. She considers the box, the dancing gypsy girl on its side, and stops.

'I can do it,' he says.

She opens the box, strikes a match, and flings it at Kraaijkamp. 'Burn, motherfucker!' she says, her sharp voice filling up the night.

Kraaijkamp ignites so quickly, he's already completely on fire when the screaming starts. He stumbles to his feet and runs away, flames trailing behind him like parade banners. He doesn't make it far before he cuts right, and then left, and then left again, then runs in what it takes a moment for Tuviah and Merel to realize is a figure-eight in a fashion. His screams go on and on until he trips on the empty petrol can and falls over. The flames rise higher, and spread to the dry grass around him even as he continues to writhe.

Tuviah walks over to the burning mound of Nazi shit, and lifts his gun to put it out of its misery, but Merel shouts for him to stop. 'Let him burn,' she says. Her eyes twinkle with firelight as they watch Kraaijkamp. 'Let him burn.'

The next day, Tuviah and Merel, two people who had lost everything and somehow found each other, agree to marry. He resigns from the Nazi-killing business soon after, excited by the thought of teaching her how to make cholent before sundown on Fridays and, because she won't shut up about it, learning how to ice skate along the canals of Leiden with her. He even sings the Kaddish for Gitla and their babies. Tuviah's second life is officially over, but his third life is about to begin. Hopefully it's the last one.

Jones

Gila River Indian Community 1962

The blind Indian talks for maybe half an hour, first while brewing them coffee on the stove and then while frying them some bologna for sandwiches, and mostly wants to know about the Pasadena City Hall bombing. He asks questions in between boiling water and flipping sizzling chunks of pink meat that constrict and blacken, feats he achieves by memory and with a minimum of searching with his arthritic hands. 'Where did you plant the explosive device?' he says. 'Did you use a timer or one of Mary's remote detonators? How many armed guards were there? You felt a bit pleased with yourself when you heard you scored yourself a judge, didn't you?' Jones does his best to answer these questions despite his complete ignorance of the events, mostly by drawing upon what he's read in the papers, but also borrowing details from too many Saturday afternoon double features about grifters and hitmen and gangsters and bloodthirsty cut-throats. It doesn't take long to begin to understand that the blind Indian and this Porter – the man this particular Indian thinks Jones really is – share a mutual disdain for the United States government, its law enforcement agencies, and pretty much any legal body that represents the 'savage bastards' in charge of 'this sham'. The blind Indian, despite his big smile and inviting warmth, has an anarchist's heart. Mary, his daughter, the middle child, sounds even worse to Jones.

A car arrives after the coffee has been drunk and all that remains of the fried bologna sandwiches is crumbs and mustard smears. Headlights illuminate the kitchen, casting the blind Indian's elongated shadow across the wood-panelled wall, but neither Jones nor Gracie see this because they're shielding their eyes with their hands.

'There she is, late as always,' the blind Indian says. 'Gracie, don't take offence now.'

'Offence to what?' Gracie says.

'Oh, pretty much everything my daughter says,' the blind Indian says. 'She don't mean nothing by it.'

Jones looks at Gracie, just as worried as her.

Mary enters through the kitchen door like an ill wind, throwing the door loudly against the wall in her dramatic rush. At the sight of Jones, she all but screams. He rises to greet her as she throws her arms around him. 'You're back,' she says, squeezing him. 'Who's the dish?'

Gracie smiles politely. 'I'm Gracie.'

'She your girl?' Mary asks Jones. 'What the fuck are you doing bringing your girl 'round here?' She looks at Gracie, sizing her up ungenerously. 'He tell you about me? He's told *me* about *you*.'

'Why don't you two go down to the cellar to chat?' the blind Indian says, grinning mischievously. He can't see Jones's perplexed expression, but can guess there's one. 'I'll keep Gracie here company.'

'Make her another sandwich, Pop,' Mary says. 'She needs some more meat on her.'

Gracie smiles politely again, and Jones starts thinking up all the ways he can get out of going to the cellar or anywhere with Mary. He mouths *sorry*, but Gracie just turns away.

In the living room, Mary begins to drag a heavy coffee table off the rug. 'You going to help me or not?'

Jones does. When the table is moved, she peels back the rug to reveal a trap door. Beneath this trap door is a steep, creaky staircase covered with dust and cobwebs so thick they wave like tattered curtains. And at the bottom of the stairs is a low-ceilinged cellar hammered out of sandstone. Three work lights hang from beams and keep the two workbenches and shelves of supplies inadequately but sufficiently illuminated. Tools cover the dusty benches. And bits of clocks. And electronics of all sorts. And –

Jones takes a deep breath at the sight of them – several half-constructed explosive devices.

This is where the bomb that blew up Pasadena City Hall was made.

Chao

Jingdezhen 1354

He did not want them to take the body. He did not trust them to bury Wenyuan properly, with something approaching dignity, in a location where he could be visited when this ghastly nightmare is finally over. The dead were and still are being collected from outside homes, slung onto wagons that creak and complain like tired nags under their weight, and then are transported to the low fields outside town where prisoners have been pressed into digging trenches that quickly fill with dark, foaming water as the earth is still drunk with it after the monsoons. The dead are then unceremoniously heaved into these trenches where limbs tangle and faces twisted by the agony of coughing to death watch in silent horror as lye is spread across them, then another blanket of the dead and another layer of lye, and another and another and another until dirt is shovelled onto them, as well. At first, signs were not raised around these mass graves for those who had perished when the air turned foul. But the people of Jingdezhen continued to die – people were dying everywhere across the Empire, as near as they could tell – and eventually those who remained began to accidentally dig up the recently dead, bodies wretched from decay and chewed apart by burrowing animals, because they had forgotten where they had put them in the first place. Chao did not want this for Wenyuan, this inglorious end, and so he decided to wrap his beloved in a blanket and, when the sun set and the empty streets filled with the sound of tears and hacking and wailing for the dead, he put Wenyuan in a small hand cart and wheeled him up Pearl Hill where the dragon kilns of the manufactory still tirelessly worked. He waits here now as Wenyuan slowly burns inside the largest of these kilns. It is when Chao goes to open the right firewood door, to inspect the body, that he hears the porcelain shatter in the warehouse.

It sounds like a whole shelf of it, crashing to the dirt floor like a great wave of glass against a rocky shore. Chao thinks to remain with Wenyuan. The manufactory has allowed most of its dragon kilns to go cold, kilns Chao once stoked with pine to fire the blue-and-white-glazed porcelain of which even the Emperor had taken notice, but there are still those in Jingdezhen who do not stay away, who answer the call of their employers to work for inflated wages as their friends and families die painfully around them. Still, it is after dark. Nobody should be here except the guard who is asleep in the workshop. And so Chao goes to investigate, to learn who would steal at a time such as this, who would steal the porcelain that Chao and the other artisans so lovingly moulded and painted in such meticulous detail.

The door to the warehouse is on the opposite side of a small, bamboo-lined courtyard, and it swings gently in the breeze. On the other side of it, a lantern burns brightly. Shelves of glazed porcelain reflect its quavering light. One of these shelves lies on its side, broken, surrounded by shattered porcelain. Behind the broken shelf is an open door that Chao has never noticed before, and through it he can see only darkness.

Chao slowly approaches this door, porcelain crunching and grinding to sharp pebbles and powder beneath his leather heels. When he steps through the doorway, he discovers a long hallway that should not fit inside the warehouse. He cannot discern its features, but its walls are brick and mortar and iron. At the end of this long hallway is another door, also open. And through this door is another world, a strange world of glass and magenta lights that move unpredictably like murmurations of glowing starlings, and along its perimeter, kneeling over a satchel, is a foreigner with pale skin and dressed in exotic clothing.

The foreigner rises as soon as he sees Chao, barking with great and concerned insistency in an ugly language Chao does not understand, and shoves Chao back through the door that led to this strange world. The door is yanked shut, and then it is like it was never there. *Gone*.

Chao returns to the warehouse through the first doorway through which he passed, which immediately locks itself behind him. He is alone again, confused, surrounded by porcelain as broken as his heart. He returns to the kiln, and is relieved to find Wenyuan has disappeared like the door to the strange world. Nothing remains except ash and tiny pieces of bone.

The manufactory beneath and around Chao suddenly lurches, bowling him over, but does not collapse as he does. The warehouse on the other side of the courtyard is less fortunate. It topples inwards, leaving only unstable mounds of brick and a single teetering wall behind. Nobody will ever discover why this happened, and Chao never speaks of what he saw inside the warehouse before the accident.

The parents of Chao die three weeks. His younger brother and older sister and her husband and two children die in the months that follow this. Many others die, too, more than half of Jingdezhen and countless more beyond its hills and borders. But eventually, everybody stops dying except in the ways they used to die. Chao returns to his daily work at the manufactory, and every morning he silently prays before the dragon kiln where his memories of Wenyuan now live. He becomes known as the Man Who Weeps because the others do not understand why he cries as he watches the flames dance, because they do not know what Wenyuan meant to him. Even Chao, who has since married, cannot fully comprehend and accept what the two men shared. Chao does not speak to his wife about this, or anything for that matter, and when they do have relations, he thinks of Wenyuan atop him, softly kissing and then biting harder his naked back, whispering to him what, at the time, felt like the secrets of Heaven and Earth and which Chao now knows were the secrets of Heaven and Earth.

It is many years after Wenyuan died that word begins to spread about the arrival of a government official with one sky-blue eye and one eye the dirty colour of unpolished jade. Most assume he works for the Emperor, who recently declared the kilns of Jingdezhen the official kilns of his empire, so enamoured is he with the porcelain produced here. But the official with two different-coloured eyes does not work for the Emperor, or at least this becomes clear to Chao when the official knocks on the door to his house early one morning, even before the sun has risen.

Chao prepares brick tea for him, but the official – a short, squat man with a long black plait snaking out from beneath a sable hat embroidered with white and gold dragons and topped by an orange amber knob – does not partake. The official wants to know about the warehouse that once stood at the back of the Pearl Hill manufactory before it was rebuilt and then subsequently knocked down again, along with the rest of the manufactory, so the Zhusan Imperial Kiln could rise in its place. In particular, he wishes to know if Chao had ever been inside this warehouse. Chao understands what the official is truly asking, and confesses everything he witnessed on the night Wenyuan died. He cries as he recounts the story because he is the Man Who Weeps, because even after all these years he trembles when thinking of Wenyuan, because his heart is still sick and a wife and children have done nothing to heal it. The official listens indifferently, then shows him an ink illustration of a man that Chao identifies as the pale foreigner he saw that terrible night.

'Who is he?' Chao says.

'This is no concern of yours,' the official says. He reaches into his fine robes, and his hand returns with a red sandalwood box carved with the same dragons that adorn his hat.

Chao instinctively leans forward, to inspect this box. The official sets it before him, and tilts back its lid to reveal a smooth black stone sphere that Chao would swear vibrates. He does not see it vibrate, but he can feel it. Something . . . is *speaking* to him. He does not know how else to describe it, and he immediately sits back to get away from it. 'What is it?' he asks.

'You have experienced things that must be forgotten,' the official says. 'This will help. Pick it up.'

Chao reaches for it, but pulls his hand back. He shakes his head.

'If you do not resist, it will go easier for you,' the official says.

'It is magic?' Chao says.

'If believing so helps, then yes,' the official says.

'What I saw, it will cut that memory out of my mind?' Chao says. The official nods. 'Then take him, as well. Take Wenyuan.' The official does not understand what he means. Chao looks away with shame before continuing. 'I . . . I loved him. He died that night, but I have been dying every night since. *Please*, help me. Make this . . . this' – he shakes a hand at his chest and his voice chokes on tears – 'make it go away. I do not want to remember any more, *please*.'

The official watches Chao cry for a long moment, his mysterious eyes never blinking. When Chao has recovered from the embarrassing fit of grief, the official leans forwards and, with two fingers, pushes the wooden box and black sphere towards him. 'Pick up the stone,' he says.

'Will you help me?' Chao says.

'No,' the official says.

'W-Why not?' Chao says.

'Because I did not come here to help you,' the official says.

'But you can,' Chao says. The official does not deny it. 'And still you will not?'

The official says nothing.

Chao accepts this silently. He reaches for the black sphere, and touches it first with his middle finger. The sphere is bitterly cold, so cold he is not sure how long he can hold it when he lifts it.

'Think about this man,' the official says, pushing the illustration of the pale foreigner across the table, as well. 'Try to form an image of him in your mind.'

Chao focuses instead on Wenyuan. Perhaps there is some chance the magic of the black sphere will latch onto these memories, memories of the face of Wenyuan and his gentle hands and his smile, and take them instead.

Something drips onto the table. Blood. It is oozing from his nose.

'I warned you to not resist,' the official says.

The head of Chao drops, his face wet with tears and blood, and his shoulders sag in sad surrender. That night so long ago, when he watched Wenyuan choke to death on his own blood, when he held the hands of Wenyuan even when Wenyuan could not grasp his in return because of the convulsions, when he wrapped the body of Wenyuan in the blanket in which they once wrapped themselves and wheeled it to the manufactory and pushed it into the largest of the dragon kilns and watched it burn before . . . what happened next? Chao struggles to remember. There was a sound. Loud enough to startle Chao and momentarily silence his loud grief. Porcelain, that is what it was. Breaking like waves of glass against a rocky shore. The sound came from inside the warehouse where somebody had left open a door he had never noticed before. A door . . . a long hallway . . . a man with a pale fac

Abdul Fattah

Kingdom of Ndongo 1525

He comes to, his head lying against the powerful thigh of another bloke, the bloke's scrotum sliding like a wilted plum out of his nappy, and he sits up so quickly that the chain that connects the iron collar around his neck to the two blokes on either side of him snaps taut both ways and the two blokes, also wearing iron collars, jerk violently and angrily awake. Their captors, sitting around a bonfire, laugh at them. It's night-time, there's a buzzing jungle around him, and Abdul Fattah realizes with sudden and mind-shattering horror that he's one of eleven men and two boys chained together on the ground and the Almighty is roasting on a stick above a fire. Or a *spit*, whatever the fuck they're called, it doesn't matter because he's right there, his skin and piebald hair peeled away as if they were nothing more than a suit of clothes, and now his blood and fat is bubbling and crackling and dripping into the fire beneath him.

One of Abdul Fattah's captors is white or maybe whitish – no, two of them are – and this man jerks a leg off the tiny corpse with brutal efficiency. Then he tears a chunk of meat free with his brown teeth, chews with his mouth full, little bits of the Creator of the Universe flying from his lips, and swallows with dramatic satisfaction.

Abdul Fattah screeches at the sight, his voice so loud that sleeping birds wake and burst from trees into the sky that must exist on the other side of the dense jungle canopy. In a flash, he remembers everything that happened to bring him here: his father, the imam in that garage, Sydney and the Opera House, the universe shattering around him like glass, and a great big black sphere floating at the centre of everything.

The other white bloke – who wears old-timey duds like they both do, like in paintings Abdul Fattah saw at the Art Gallery on a school trip – rises and puts his hand on the hilt of a thin sword he wears on a belt. He snarls in a language Abdul Fattah doesn't understand, but it kind of sounds like Italian or maybe Spanish or who gives a shit, this is crackers, mate, fucking crackers.

The prisoners around Abdul Fattah yank at the chain that binds them, they tell him to be quiet in their weird-ass language of slithering syllables and gulps – different from the white blokes' – and one of them spits at him for being such a dickhead. These are big men, all bared muscle and in some cases bared genitals, and their white eyes look demonic in the dark, and Abdul Fattah definitely does not want to fuck around with any of them.

Their captors, eight African blokes and the two white blokes who act like they're in charge, go to sleep soon after. One of the Africans and his big, scary-looking spear stand watch at the edge of the camp. The prisoners are left to sleep or not sleep, it doesn't matter, because they'll either follow directions in the morning or die, that much is clear from the orders issued in yet another language Abdul Fattah doesn't understand and is pretty sure is different from the prisoners'.

In the relative quiet that follows, Abdul Fattah cries into his forearm, the black sphere still hovering in his mind's eye, until he's nudged by one of the two blokes his neck is chained to. Not the one whose scrotum looks like dead fruit, but the other one. The one who wears a toga of some kind, its upper folds pulled down over his arms and tied in a knot around his waist. The fabric is a vivid crimson, but soiled. In fact, all of the prisoners' clothing is dyed bright colours. They are clearly social superiors to their African captors.

Abdul Fattah looks at the bloke, at the beautifully beaded necklace on him that sets him apart from even those with him, and discovers he's being offered a half-eaten piece of a queer-looking honey-coloured fruit. He takes it and gives it a quick examination. The skin looks edible, and so he stuffs it whole into his mouth. 'It's good,' Abdul Fattah says, chewing its sweet flesh with grateful, but careful zeal as his nose throbs if he works his jaw the wrong way. 'Ta, mate.'

The African chuckles at the mess Abdul Fattah makes of himself, then speaks for several minutes in his own language, explaining something that Abdul Fattah cannot understand but, after the first minute or two, begins to suspect is an explanation of how they're all slaves now. Afterwards, they both go to sleep on each other, but only because Abdul Fattah is pretty sure the African isn't a homosexual and, even if he is, Allah would have understood. You know, before he was eaten by a filthy white bloke in the middle of an African jungle.

The morning comes when enough sunlight trickles through the trees for their captors to see, or, rather, the Africans amongst them to navigate through the bush. The white slavers carry muskets, but these weapons seem to be their only real claim to authority. Abdul Fattah and the other slaves are marched single file, neck chained to neck, until they reach a wide and ancient river that slides quietly through the jungle. A few kilometres further down the river's edge, they find long, narrow boats where the slavers must have left them, each boat carved out of a single tree trunk, by the look of them. The slaves are loaded onto these in groups of four, five, and four, and, even though Abdul Fattah doesn't speak their language, he has no problem understanding the slavers' warning that if one of the slaves jumps or falls into the water, then the rest of his group will go in, too, and they'll all drown together. The slavers laugh about this, as if people drowning is funny shit. Abdul Fattah doesn't understand why any of this is happening to him.

The next several days are spent drifting along the river as mozzies and other flying insects the size of small mice stalk them through the air, the African slavers using long poles to propel them along when the current can't be bothered. On the fifth day, another party of slavers makes to ambush them, no doubt to steal the slaves for their own profit, but their white mates aren't as good shots as the whites who captured Abdul Fattah and they're all chased off. A slave is shot in the thigh, though. One of the African slavers using a long pole to navigate draws his knife, slits the injured slave's throat, then unlocks the iron collar from the slave's spraying neck and shoves him into the river. Abdul Fattah, face spattered with the man's blood because he didn't look away fast enough, watches the corpse float away behind them until something tugs at it from below, nibbling at its arm, then the whole body goes under.

On what might be the sixth day – or maybe the seventh, because it's hard to say since time has stopped making sense here – slavers and slaves reach a small fort flying a stained white flag with an ornate shield and crown at its centre. The slavers are given heavy bags of coins, then lift their boats over their heads and vanish back into the jungle.

Abdul Fattah and the other slaves, now the property of a camp of what he has come to understand are Portuguese traders, are unchained from each other and chained in new configurations to crude posts and trees where another forty-odd slaves are already waiting. They wait like this for a week, pissing and shitting all over themselves, cleaned only when the rains come on the third day, until, without warning, they are again chained to each other, fifty or more in total now, and led on another long march through the hostile jungle. Three days this time. When the jungle finally opens up, the slaves are confronted by the ocean, but not the Pacific Ocean Abdul Fattah knows. This ocean is dark and grey and even the salty smell is different to Abdul Fattah. It must be the Atlantic. There is another fort here, this one much larger, with Portuguese soldiers standing on top of earthen and wood walls and a single cannon, which is pointed at the jungle instead of the water. The slaves are counted and recorded in thick books by more men in old-timey duds, but clean duds, not like the white slavers', and transported by large rowboats into the surf, to a giant wooden boat – no, *ship*, boats this size are called *ships*, Abdul Fattah knows. This ship will take him and the others – the others who scream and cry and sing powerful songs that promise war or, in the case of the African who wears the beaded necklace and some of his mates, haunting songs that can only mean something has been lost or stolen – away from the jungle, away from their families, and away from everything they know and love.

It's the second time Abdul Fattah has left the African continent, but last time it was for Australia and a better life – at least that's what his parents told him, even though the life he found there disgusted him. This time, his destination is as much of a mystery as where in time he wound up after he dragged Iblis through his magical portal. Seriously, what the fuck is happening right now?

Mimori

Kamakura 2027

The shuttle bus pulled up in front of her home ten minutes ago, but she's been sitting inside it since then, staring at her hands, at the nauseating viridescent glow of the dash, the harsh white light of the headlights slashing through the darkness of the narrow house-lined street outside. Anything but the front door to the *minka* she shares with Sōjirō, anything but the girls setting the *chabudai* she can see through the front window, anything but the life she must return to on the other side of that door after two months away in America and Earth orbit. This doesn't feel real any more, none of it, and Mimori doesn't know what to do except sit here like a coward.

'Please vacate the vehicle,' the animated smiley face on the dash-board screen says to her, its friendly voice interrupting the silence with what can't help but feel like terse impatience. The automated vehicle's lights turn on, the door slides open, and the back hatch begins to rise. 'Have a pleasant evening.'

It's good to see Tamami and Okimo, of course. Mimori hugs them, compliments Okimo's new lilac hair colour and marvels at how the two have changed even though she's seen them almost every day she was away during their vidcalls together. Sōjirō greets her with a typically muted smile and gentle hug, their years of passionate reunions far behind them, and, as he always does when she comes home from her SpaceNEXT assignments, announces he's made dinner. The *shirasu-don*'s rice is overcooked – which he apologizes for with a sheepish smile and the girls make fun of him about because 'it's just rice, Father' – but his kettle-boiled herring is unusually fluffy and delicious and more than makes up for it. Everybody except Mimori eats with a media device in one hand. Apparently, there's been a bombing in Samoa's capital, which has no history of Islamist extremism or even a Muslim population to speak of, but President Glass thinks Congress should spend more on defence to finally put an end to this twenty-six-year-long war on terror, and the rest of the world can only react with incredulity and then seriousness, further legitimizing the point of view, because even reacting to lunacy is enough to make it real, so that tomorrow Samoa will be the newest hotbed in the international Islamist revolution and everybody will forget when it was just a tiny island somewhere in the South Pacific. Reality changes so quickly these days, often in the span of a dinner like this one, that it's impossible not to constantly feel like you're trying to outrace it. To stay just ahead of it, where things can remain like they were just a little longer, when they made that much more sense, when your children were still young and wanted to talk to you, and your husband made love to you without being asked, and democratically elected strongmen and pandemics and the Earth weren't trying to kill you all.

'Are you feeling all right?' Sōjirō asks Mimori, not bothering to look up from his pad. The girls' faces are still lost in theirs, their fingers poking and swiping, typing frantic replies to friends who are frantically texting them back during dinners with their own families. A student killed himself at school today, according to a whispered warning at the sink from Sōjirō, but the girls still haven't mentioned it. Maybe it's because they're used to it by now after all the others. What a thing to get used to. 'Have they given you your next flight date yet?'

Mimori wonders if it was always like this, or if it happened while she was asleep or away for work or simply while she wasn't paying attention, and now there's no way to go back. Her family has become kabuki, a performance staged over and over as much for themselves as the rest of their family, their friends, their co-workers, playing parts that mean nothing any more outside of their ability to facilitate the collective lie to others. In so many ways, Mimori blames Sōjirō for this. For insisting they move here, to 'get away from it all', to hide from the city life that he, as an Edo historian, as somebody who grew up in a village of no more than six hundred people, considered so abhorrent to traditional Japanese culture. Their 'quaint' 223-year-old *minka* was his idea, with its traditional *shoji* and *fusuma*, tatami-covered floors, and almost complete lack of furniture that anybody who otherwise lives in the modern world would immediately deem masochistically torturous. Its only concessions to the conveniences and comforts of *the West*, as Sōjirō defiantly still refers to and thinks of Europeans and Americans, are beds, wardrobes for their clothes, and kitchen appliances and the other electronics that allow them to interact with the rest of the planet – like the pad Sōjirō is currently studying with unblinking fixation. His anachronisms infuriate Mimori.

She rises abruptly, and walks out the front door as her children call after her and her husband sits there with a stupid, confused look on his face.

It's raining, a storm coming in off the ocean. Thunder rumbles, and then, without a sound, lightning bursts from the sky. The trees that envelop the hills behind their house have changed colour, and in the incandescent light, sudden and bright, seem as if they're burning. The world is on fire.

A hand grabs Mimori's arm as the crack that accompanied the lightning reaches her, and she's spun around with startling force. It's Sōjirō, out of breath from chasing after her. 'What is wrong with you?' he says.

Mimori is crying, but he would never know because of the rain. 'This is not right, none of it!'

'What are you talking about?'

'I cannot explain it. I just feel it. Like . . . like . . .'

'Like we are caught in a river,' he says, his voice trembling. 'Being carried away, by terrible rapids that want to swallow us up, and in the near-distance, rushing towards us, is-is-is an *abyss*. An abyss with no name. And-And—'

Mimori kisses him, because she misunderstood, because he feels it, too, and if he feels it, then the girls feel it, and if they feel it, then they are still a real family. Around them as they kiss, hands on each other's wet faces, several lightning bolts strike the ground in near perfect unison. Much closer than the others, too. The hair on Mimori and Sōjirō's arms begins to stand, then the hair on their heads, reaching towards the clouds. They laugh, connected by positively charged particles rising from the Earth, and kiss agai

Jones

Gila River Indian Community 1962

He understands this much now: Porter drove out here, to the middle of nowhere, picked up one of these home-cooked bombs, drove it back to Pasadena and walked into City Hall with it, and, twenty-three bodies in the morgue later, here he is – back where he started, standing opposite a young woman he's pretty sure is criminally insane. Except *he* is not Porter, that's the part that still doesn't make sense. His name is Robert Jones . . . isn't it?

'Tell me how you did it,' Mary says. 'All the juicy details.'

'I . . . I walked in with it—' he says, but she interrupts.

'In the suitcase, like we talked about?' she says.

'Yeah,' he says. 'Yeah, just like that.'

'What about the remote detonator? Did it work through all that steel and concrete, or did the timer have to do it in the end?'

'The, uh, the remote detonator.'

'Then you stuck around,' Mary says approvingly. She moves closer to Jones, smiling now. 'Did you watch it happen then? Did you watch it blow?'

He nods, unsure what else to do.

'Twenty-three cocksuckers dead,' she says, leaning against him. Her hands are on his hips. 'Why did you bring the babe here? You trying to make me jealous?'

Jones firmly plants his hands on her shoulders, and eases her away. 'Listen, I'm not who you think I am. Or maybe I am. I don't really know.'

Mary licks her thick lips, assuming this is a game. 'That so, Porter?'

'It's true,' he says. 'I . . . I don't remember meeting you. I don't know who you are. Your father upstairs? No clue. Your brothers, never seen them before. I don't even know who that girl with me is, not really. I'm missing the past seven months of my memory – amnesia, whatever you want to call it – and I really need you to tell me what you think I am and why you think I did what you think I did. Which I may have done, I concede. It's . . . *complicated*.'

She starts to laugh, but Jones doesn't. 'Holy Jesus on a fucking pogo stick, you're serious,' she says.

'Unfortunately.'

'Let me see if I follow you. You got Porter's face, you got his body, you got his girlfriend . . . but you're not *him*?'

'Maybe I am. I don't know.'

'I don't believe you.'

'Maybe pretend you do, then, if you can,' Jones says. 'Obviously there's something between us—'

'Between us?' Mary says, laughing. 'You're so stuck on that bitch up there, I don't think you could get it up for me if I sat on your face.'

He has never met a woman like this. Despite himself, he feels deeply embarrassed. The Company provided him with the sexual mores of the decades this Second Life was born into and grew up in, but this woman . . . Mary . . . she's something else entirely. A child of the future in many ways. Also, again, criminally insane.

'Okay, I'll bite,' she says. 'Ask me a question.'

'How did we meet?'

Jones is told that Porter sought out Mary's father, Simon Goldtooth, both because of his service with various US Army Bomb Disposal squads in the war and numerous post-war arrests related to protests against the US government's treatment of its indigenous peoples. Goldtooth felt slighted by Washington, both for ancestral wrongs and how he was treated as a vet, cheated out of GI Bill benefits, that sort of thing, and had grown increasingly hostile to the government. Porter wanted Goldtooth's help, expecting to find him sympathetic to his cause. He just didn't expect Goldtooth to be blind, a medical condition that began slowly five years ago before the lights went out completely in 1960, and so Mary had to act as Goldtooth's hands. She's only made the one explosive device for Porter so far, the one used in Pasadena, but Porter had plans. *Big* plans. That's what all these other unfinished bombs are for, other targets to come soon. He wasn't supposed to be back to pick them up for a few more weeks.

Jones is horrified by the idea that he may have had plans to murder even more people. 'Did I ever tell you why I wanted to blow up the building?' he says. 'I mean, Pasadena City Hall.'

'I kept asking you, all the time – really, *all* the time – but you'd never say,' Mary says. 'The most I got was there was something in the basement. Oh, and this one time you told me about how the universe is really like a funnel spider's web. You know, a cluster, a tangle or something like that, layers all wrapped around each other instead of something pretty and one-dimensional.' She tries to approximate this by making a fist and waving her other hand over the fist, but knows how stupid it makes her look. 'Look, you say a lot of shit that makes no goddamn sense. Like right now. *Don't know who you are* – and people call *me* goofy.'

Jones begins to understand now. Pasadena City Hall must have been built around a coaxial terminal that joins two or more Earth models – sometimes hundreds – along a Common Data Exchange juncture.

The most basic functions of these CDE junctures are to allow MasterControl to monitor events in every Earth model and to act as a depressing agent on destabilizing chaos and rapid social change that might exacerbate such chaos. Basically, they keep things running smoothly. During the Company's lengthy development of the models, the human-actor imagination – which was as much the result of coding as it was of evolutionary forces programmed into the System – was found capable of processing a very limited range of what came to be called the Chaos Effect. Push actors too far, and their digital psyches snapped and they went mad. In turn, their Earth model would collapse and, when one collapsed, the rest of the models went with it just like a house of cards.

Artistic expression, as it turned out, helped actors successfully process and translate this Chaos Effect, which is how the Perception Algorithm first came to be written as a way to foster this cultural coping method, but even that had its limits, and the side-effects of the Perception Algorithm and its ability to push and pull like gravity at events across the System, via the CDE junctures, were themselves ultimately unpredictable and difficult for MasterControl to address.

Jones knows the CDE junctures hold another vital purpose for MasterControl. MasterControl uses them as actual conduits between Earth models so that its anti-malware manifestations, Montrose being just one example, can shift between models – space, you might say – and the illusion of time that exists within and between the models. This is almost certainly why Porter blew up Pasadena City Hall. He must have wanted to disrupt the ability of the coaxial terminal hidden beneath it to communicate between this Earth model and the CDE junctures that intersect with it, or rather intersected with it there, since the connection has now been broken. Judging by the rest of the explosive devices Porter tasked Mary with building for him, he was aiming to repeat his attack elsewhere, too. Targeting other coaxial terminals, one might safely assume.

Jones wonders if that means there's a new coaxial terminal in Tucson, one that was constructed after he retired. Earth models tend to diverge semi-regularly along equally new CDE junctures, so maybe that's why Angelique sent him to meet some girl there. Does the girl in question know where Porter means to strike next? The thought crosses his mind that if he is indeed Porter, if he's simply forgotten seven months of his life or in some way he is even being controlled from Inside or Outside the System, then maybe listening to Angelique and going to Tucson is a bad idea. He could very likely be the man who destroyed Pasadena

City Hall, and, if given the opportunity, maybe he'd do it all over again. Maybe that's even what Angelique wants, for him to strike a second time. There's no reason why he should trust her anyway, not after what she and the Company did to him.

Jones wonders what Porter's intention was in Pasadena and with this family of violent radicals. What did Porter hope to accomplish by targeting these coaxial terminals and tearing down the bridges that connect this model to others and to MasterControl? Whoever Porter is, does he realize that breaking enough of these connections would have a cascade effect and bring the whole System crashing down on top of them all?

'Mary, what's in Tucson?' he asks.

'*Tucson?*' Mary says. 'I don't know. I went once when I was a kid, but we don't go down that way much. Pop hates beaners almost as much as he hates your people, if you hadn't noticed.'

'I've never mentioned Tucson to you before, then?' he says.

'Nah, I don't think so,' she says. 'Listen, how're things between you and the dish? 'Cause I'm getting tired of being strung along here. I'm just going to lay it all out there. I don't care if you're screwing her. But you and me, let's stop playing games and, you know, do the deed already. Pop already thinks we are anyway, so he won't mind.'

Jones almost laughs. This is too ludicrous for him. 'What the hell is wrong with your family?' he says.

'Like you don't want it. I see how you're always looking at my ass.'

'I'm really not.'

The blind Indian, Simon Goldtooth, interrupts. 'The bastards found us!' he says, shouting from upstairs.

There's gunfire from outside. Something breaks loudly upstairs, maybe a window.

Mary grabs a rifle from the corner where several firearms stand like umbrellas waiting to be used, and bounds up the stairs to help. Jones is right behind her. They find windows shattering every which way, which isn't a big deal if you don't stand in front of one. The Goldtooth brothers, crouched on either side of one of these broken windows, are laughing hysterically because 'The house is built out of goddamn cinder blocks, you goddamn morons!'

And on the floor, crawling towards the back of the house, is Gracie. Jones falls on top of her to shield her.

'Mary, you know what to do!' Simon Goldtooth says, screaming from a corner where he's crouched, incapable of locating her in the aural chaos.

Mary crawls on her hands and knees to the cupboard under the sink, sweeps plates and bowls out of it with her arm, ignoring how they break beside her, and retrieves a drab olive canvas pouch hidden behind them. Inside are three detonators, and she grins as she flips the primers and activates them one by one.

Outside, explosives erupt around the house, small volcanoes that throw earth and men into the air and spray them with nails and screws that rip flesh and internal organs apart. One of the cars parked out there flips into the air and comes crashing down on its front end. A few seconds later, its fuel tank detonates like a Hollywood special effect.

'How do we get out of here?' Jones says over the gunfire and explosions and what already feels too much like a war zone.

Mary grabs her rifle and starts for the kitchen. 'Follow me!' she says.

He helps Gracie to her feet, and they run after Mary, right out the kitchen door. It's hell out here, a mess of gunfire and flames and FBI agents and local policemen on fire or lying on the ground bleeding and searching for missing body parts and crying out for help and, in the middle of it all, the three-legged dog is hopping in a circle as it tries to catch its own tail. They head for the Gold-tooth brothers' Chevrolet pick-up as, behind them, the brothers charge out of the house with their own rifles, howling nonsensical Indian war cries made up by adrenalin as they take the fight to their attackers. Their strategy works for a moment, a Fed and a policeman go down, but then the side of the older brother's head explodes – just explodes like a grapefruit with a firecracker stuck in it – blown apart by a shotgun. The younger brother, who stops to help, catches a volley of rifle fire from two agents hiding behind a car. Mary sees all this, but doesn't stop, so Jones and Gracie don't stop either.

Montrose steps out of the shadows, firelight dancing across his dark face and reflected in his two different-coloured eyes. His service revolver is already pointed at Jones. He begins to say that he warned 'Mr Jones', but his body spins around in a sudden pirouette and he slaps against the dirt on his side. Mary put a bullet in his stomach, not even hesitating about taking the shot.

Jones and Gracie round the truck to get in through the passenger door, while Mary starts to climb in behind the wheel. There's another gunshot, and the windshield spider-webs, and blood begins to squirt in powerful bursts from the side of Mary's throat. She slumps to her stomach, and slides down the seat and out of the pick-up.

Behind her, Montrose is still on the ground, trying to keep his gun aimed into the pick-up's cab at Jones, but he's dying, and then he's dead.

Jones finds the keys in the ignition, starts the pick-up, and unthinkingly reverses right into one of the Feds' cars. He throws the pick-up into drive then, and, aiming for Montrose's body, runs it over with two wheels as Gracie screams and cries and then shields her eyes.

The pick-up steers towards the narrow track that leads back down to the main road and town and the answers Jones must still find. No headlights follow.

Keisha

Studio City 2012

They spend their first month together plastering his and then her apartment walls with coloured index cards and images they cut from magazines or find online, breaking down their numerous characters, far too many, and then assembling something like a structure, even though he calls it a skeleton, 'cause in some ways, for him, all of his creations are monsters in the Mary Shelley vein, something to cobble together and force into life, and, fuck, seriously, sometimes he can be so pretentious when he talks like this. Tab wants to put all of their work into Word and Excel files, to preserve and organize it, but Keisha refuses to use computers to the point of seeming paranoid, and insists this script they've agreed to co-write together, which they've also agreed she will eventually direct, must be handwritten. Even in note form. Of course, Tab thinks this is crazy, but it's obvious, even this early in the relationship, he will do anything she asks of him.

By their second month together, Keisha finds herself starting to dig the Damien Syco music Tab will sometimes put on without even thinking about it. She gets lost in its enigmatic lyrics and musical compositions that feel intimate and soaring just as often as they feel otherworldly and sometimes even grating. Syco's Moonman never opens up the universe for her as he has for Tab – mostly 'cause she already knows what the universe really is – but he does make her wonder if the dude is a customer, too. That wouldn't make any sense, though, 'cause contracts with Plurality clearly state that customers *cannot interfere with or rewrite the cultural trajectory of the human actor population* – which is just a fancy way to say *destiny* if you believe in that shit. That said, nobody comes for Keisha, even though she puts impossible secrets of the Outside into an unwieldy 179-page screenplay she is co-writing on legal pads with a man she's pretty sure is falling in love with her even though she's never been in love and the way he looks at her increasingly scares the living fuck out of her.

In month six, they break up – really, Keisha breaks up with Tab because she can't take feeling this way any more, so vulnerable, so pathetic – but the two agree to remain friends and keep working on the screenplay together. By now, neither of them wants to let go of their story about a ragtag group of survivors of a digital Earth simulation who have managed to wake up to the truth of and even escape their manufactured world, into the real one, but now must return with a chosen one, a hero of extraordinary gifts, to liberate everybody else there. It's going to be epic if they ever figure out how to make it all *make sense*.

In month seven, Keisha wakes up at three in the morning desperate for Tab, and calls him. He comes over right away and they fuck, and in the morning, over omelettes at the Cafe 101, he accidentally says he loves her – which he's been trying not to admit for the past four months, but there, he says, *there*, it's out there. She says she loves him, too, which she's sure now that she does, and they go back to her place to fuck again and work on the screenplay.

In month fourteen, Pinnacle Studios hires Tab to write a screenplay he pitched on a whim in a general. It's not the kind of material he wants to be writing, but it's his first paying gig, and they celebrate by flying to France for a week. They spend three days in Paris, where neither have ever been, but which Tab is excited by 'cause Damien Syco lives in Montmartre these days, then spend another four in the Loire Valley at a chateau in Saint-Règle, recently renovated and chosen seemingly at random by Tab, where the view of the property's locally famous gardens changes what she believes the definition of *beautiful* to be. Every night while they are there, she finds Tab outside, standing amongst sunflowers as tall as him and staring up at the stars as if waiting for something. Maybe even somebody.

In month twenty-two, everybody in town is talking about Tab. He's been hired to write three more screenplays, more than he has the time to write, and Pinnacle has put his first film with them – *Arabian Knights*, which the trades describe as an 'exciting new twist on the *Arabian Nights* mythology' – on a fast track. Keisha still can't get represented, but celebrates his every success with surprises and head and that one time in the shower she says he can put it in her ass, but he only gets the tip in before she cries out and he apologizes and they just put on a Godard film he really wants to rewatch even though by now she's accepted she would take Voclain over Godard every day of the week.

In month twenty-eight, they argue 'cause Tab never has time to work on their script any more. They go at it from dinner until one in the morning, at which point he finally says it. Even if they finish the script, they're never going to let *her* direct it like she wants, Keisha is trapped in a fantasy every bit as toxic as their simulacra, 'cause he's only just got his foot in the door and he can't shake the feeling that he's only there so they can bring him out any time somebody talks about how exclusionary Hollywood is, how racist the Hollywood system still is, to point at their well-behaved and congenial house negro they've taught to tap dance and write on cue for them and say, 'See! See, we like the Blacks!' But that's not it, that's not what he really wants to say, and she knows it. And so, he admits it, he actually admits it. Yeah, yeah, okay, *yes*, they could probably sell the script with his name on it, there's enough heat on him right now, but it's not very good, it just isn't – for fuck's sake, it's up to 194 pages! – they should be honest for once, it sucks and he doesn't want people to see it and he can't shake the feeling that she's only pushing him this hard 'cause she still can't get repped and maybe she wants to take advantage of him, his reputation, to get her name out there, too, to get somebody to pay attention to her for once. They go to bed, and break up for good in the morning, and fuck that motherfucker. Keisha skips his movie premiere, but can't bring herself to throw away the invite that came in the mail. She puts it in her underwear drawer, at the back, and tries not to think about him even though it seems like his name is popping up in the Hollywood trades every goddamn day.

Takako

Imari Bay 1281

She has never witnessed a battle before, not like Sofu has. He has seen too many, he says. Her grandfather is *bushi*, too old to fight now himself, but his eldest son, her father, is aboard one of the many shogunal war ships below and that is why Sofu has brought her here, to the cliffs that hug the bay, to act as mournful spectators of what will inevitably be the total defeat of the remnants of the shattered fleet of the Shogun. 'Why are our forces retreating?' Takako asks him, ignorant of how sorely outnumbered her people are today. She springs to her feet, to track the ships withdrawing from the confrontation with the approaching Mongols. The enemy catapults explosives at these ships, stoneware bombs that burst and illume the smoke across the water like lightning dancing across a cloudy sky. Their sound takes what seems like an eternity to reach the cliffs and arrives as little more than muffled pops. 'Why do they not stay and fight?'

Sofu gazes out at the sea, considering the clouds that advance forbodingly across the horizon in a heavy, grey wall. A wind unsettles his thinning hair. 'The Mongols are also in retreat,' he says.

'I do not understand,' Takako says.

'They hope the bay will protect them from the storm, but it is too late,' he says, quickly rising. He grabs the hand of his grand-daughter. 'We must return home now.' When she protests, he tells her to obey him and she knows she must – even if all she dreams of is the sword and battles like this one and following in the footsteps of her ancestors – because a woman serves the good of her husband and home and family so that men like Sofu and her father may serve the Shogunate and Nippon and, in turn, all obey Heaven.

The storm arrives with the night. The servants have hung all of the shutters and closed the *shoji* so that the *engawa* has become a dark passageway; on one side, wooden panels shake and rattle in the loud wind and, on the other, long walls of delicate paper squares glow dimly from lanterns inside the house. Takako creeps along the *engawa* on bare feet, her sandals carried under one arm, until she reaches an elbow in the corridor. Here, she wrestles open a shutter so that wind and rain whip inside from two different directions. Paper rips from several *fusama* frames, quickly exposing the house to the vicious and relentless elements. Takako tries to slide the shutter closed again behind her, but it has become jammed. When she observes lanterns moving inside in response to the commotion, servants approaching, perhaps even Sofu and Soba, she abandons the effort and bounds into the woods.

The wind pushes at her from all directions, sometimes slapping her with great hands of cold rain that knock her into trees and send her toppling through a clutch of ferns. But she climbs on, up the hill that rises sharply behind the house of her family, until she clears the tree line and the wind lifts her off her feet like a kite. She is near the edge of the cliff, and thinks she will fly over it, but the wind has other ideas. It slams her back down against rocks, leaving her palms and chin bleeding. Next time she may not be so lucky, and so she remains on her belly and crawls to the cliff edge to learn if the battle still wages below.

Takako cannot see anything at first, but then the sky claps with ferocious force and forks of lightning appear, one after another, like legs of amethyst light racing from the sea towards land. These flashes reveal mountainous waves that crash down on Mongolian ships and hurl others through the air, smashing them against each other and rocks and the shore. Other ships slide into and vanish inside the chasmic troughs that are the deep breath of the waves before they strike.

This is the Kamikaze, the wrath of the gods themselves. The *bushi* could not triumph, not against Kublai Khan and his motley army of 150,000 Mongols and Chinese and Koreans, and so Heaven turned the wind itself against the enemy.

Suddenly, Takako is sliding away from the cliff. Sofu remains low, indifferent to her screamed pleas to release her as he drags her towards home. When they have returned to the relative safety of the woods, he collapses beside her and tells her she is a foolish little girl.

The next morning, Sofu leads Takako to the beach. An eerie quiet has settled over the sand and the calm sea. A sickly fog drifts listlessly, obscuring the sun that still hangs low on the horizon. Sofu carries the *naginata* of his youth, when he was a foot soldier for the Shogunate, which he grimly declares 'adequate' for what must be done today.

Thus Sofu joins the other old warriors on the beach in executing the few enemies who still draw breath and erratically violate the quiet with their moans and pleas. The beach is blanketed in their broken remains, half buried in sand left behind by the tide or tangled in nets of seaweed disgorged by the storming seas.

Takako is told not to wander far, but she does not listen and cannot believe Sofu thought she might. The dead fascinate her, and she studies their twisted bodies as tiny crabs click and clack across them and greedy gulls squabble over stringy pieces of their flesh and the occasional eyeball. It is difficult for her to find sand on which to safely step without tripping over a limb, or plunging her foot into pools of bloody salt water, or inviting a furious peck from one of the birds feasting around her.

As she nears the wreckage of a Yuan junk, its hull broken from rolling violently across the beach, Takako hears a voice. She spins round, certain it came from behind her, but nobody is there. Nobody is anywhere near her, not alive at least, and the only sound is the rhythmic pounding of waves, the gulls, and the choked cries of Mongols and Chinese and Koreans as blades slash across their necks.

The voice speaks to her again. Takako turns slowly where she stands, but cannot locate its origin.

When the voice begins yet again, it does not stop. It is not only one voice either, rather many, tumbling together like water over stones in a river. Takako cannot understand a word she hears, but whatever is being said, however it is being said, she is now certain it is coming from the Yuan junk. She climbs into the shipwreck, carefully working her compact body between the splintered ends of shattered planks and beams of wood. The wreck creaks and groans around her like Sofu does in the early morning, threatening collapse. She must not remain here for long.

The cabin in which Takako finds herself is exposed to the veiled sun, the deck that once covered it now missing. There are bodies of Yuan warriors here, as well, entangled and locked in unnatural contortions. One is folded backwards so that its cheek rests against its boot. She cannot discern if these men drowned or died when the Kamikaze flung the junk against the shore.

One of the warriors moans, somehow still alive, slumped against a wall and half buried beneath a small, overturned writing desk. His face is narrow and sharply drawn, ornamented by a moustache with long, loose wings and a thin beard that dangles from his chin. His clothes and armour are brightly coloured, even beautiful, except where ruined by blood. This is the captain of the junk, she concludes, and he tries to speak to her. To ask her for help – no, not help. It is a warning. To keep away. He holds something in his hands, something he does not wish her to take from him.

Takako finds a curved sword on the warped wall on which she is standing like a floor, and approaches the Yuan captain. She deserves to be *bushi*. She has the heart of one, even Sofu admits as much when he is not warning her to forget such ridiculous fantasies. This is why she lifts the sword, blade pointed towards the Earth, and brings it down into the chest of the captain. But thick and unyielding bone deflects her blow, and the sword scrapes across ribs and slides away from the body. The captain groans weakly in reply.

Takako tries again with the same result, not strong enough to shatter the bones that protect the heart and lungs of the man. The captain cries out this time, a sound that winds into a miserable cackle at the ridiculous horror of his fate – to be slain by a girl-child.

On her third attempt, Takako lifts the sword even higher, fingers curling around the hilt, squeezing until her tiny knuckles blanch, and this time plunges it into the throat of the captain and then into his chest. She rises onto the tips of her toes, and applies all of her weight against the hilt to drive it deeper and deeper still until the point of the weapon emerges from the back of the body and bites into wood.

But still, the captain does not die. He watches her, unable to protest as she pries open his fingers and removes a black onyx ball from them.

'What is it?' Takako asks of the ball that is as cold as ice to her touch.

The captain cannot speak. She returns to the hole through which she penetrated the ship, and stops to regard the man one final time. He is somehow still alive, watching her, eyes desperately trying to tell her something. Why will he not die?

Takako returns to Sofu, who is splattered with the blood of Mongols and looks fatigued despite the early hour of the day. She does not tell him about the sword, or the man she impaled with it, or the onyx ball in her pocket that is talking to her. When they arrive home, her father is there. He survived the battle, and greets Takako with a spinning, laughing hug. She does not tell him about the onyx ball either.

Gracie

Tucson 1962

It takes nearly thirty minutes to wash off Mary Goldtooth's blood, especially out of her hair where it had dried and congealed like the jam you spill on the counter and come back to scrub away hours later. Her shirt should be burnt, but instead gets pitched into the motel room trash basket. Bobby gives her one of his, and he tells her it looks good on her when she emerges from the bathroom, hair up in a cucumber-green towel, cheeks still puffy from all the crying. 'Bologna,' Gracie says. 'You don't have to lie to me.'

They arrived in Tucson some two hours after they booked it away from the Goldtooth compound, some two hours after she and Bobby ran over Special Agent Montrose with the truck they later ditched in a vacuum-cleaner store parking lot six blocks from here, some two hours after Gracie played a part in killing a man, even though she wasn't driving, even though Bobby keeps telling her he isn't dead, not really – whatever that means. There's no going back now, she realizes. Her life, everything she ever wanted, all of her dreams, just blew up like a dying star.

'This is all my fault,' she says. 'This is what I do. I attract the wrong kinds of men. My mom, she's a professional at it. Even my grandmother was married three times, and she was born in the nineteenth century! Do you know how hard that would have been to do for somebody like her?'

'Maybe you shouldn't blame yourself, then,' he says. 'Maybe it's your programming.'

'What's that supposed to mean?'

'*Biological*,' he says, explaining himself. 'Maybe it's biological.'

But Gracie doesn't think that's what he meant, and asks him who he was talking to on the telephone while she was in the bathroom. She could hear him, whispering, trying to hide something from her. 'You don't get to keep secrets any more, mister, not after what I've been through with you,' she says. '*Especially* after what happened tonight. We're in this together now, do you hear me?'

Bobby rises from the end of the bed where he's sitting, and collects his jacket from the closet. 'I'm going to fix this, Gracie, I promise,' he says. 'I just need you to stay here for right now. Until I get back.'

'Where are you going?'

'To see her,' he says.

'The girl.'

He nods.

'You don't know who she is yet?'

He doesn't.

'That doesn't make sense.'

'Does any of this?' he says.

'How long will you be gone?'

'I think a while,' he says. He walks towards her, takes her by the shoulders, and leans towards her face. But he stops, uncertain about what he wants to do. His lips gently press against her forehead instead of her slowly parting lips. 'Lock the door behind me.'

Bobby leaves then, and Gracie locks the door behind him as instructed. There are two beds. She takes the one furthest from the door, the one he wasn't sitting on. She lies there, humming the Tune to calm herself, wishing sleep would come, but she can't shake the feeling that something is wrong here. Not wrong in the way that running over an FBI agent is. But wrong in . . . some other way, some other way she can't put her finger on. Gracie is beginning to suspect that she's somehow become trapped in Bobby's drama, that she's only part of this story 'cause movies like these require her to be, 'cause the hero always needs a love interest. Is that all she is to him? Is that all she is to this story? Of course, Gracie knows this is nonsense, and that's when sleep finally arrives. She doesn't wake for what feels like several lifetimes.

Somebody is knocking on the door.

Gracie looks quickly around, groggy. There's no light sneaking between the curtains, so it's still night-time. The clock's glow-in-the-dark numbers declare it's 4.48 a.m. 'Wh-Who is it?'

The knocking stops.

At pretty much the same moment, Gracie suddenly remembers where she is, what's happened, and who's after her. The terrible reality jolts her awake so powerfully that she spills from the bed and lands hard on her hip. Nobody should know she's here, nor that Bobby is, but then she thinks about Bobby's photo and how it was all over the news, and maybe hers is now, too, which means the ginger with the lazy eye working the motel desk could have recognized her and called the cops, who called the FBI in turn, and now the FBI are outside her room, ready to mow her down in a hailstorm of lead. Okay, Gracie, settle your imagination down right now. This isn't a Pinnacle picture. You're not James Cagney on the lam. You're just an almost-twenty-one-year-old girl. An almost-twenty-one-year-old girl *on the lam*. Might not sell as many tickets at the cinema, but it's a darn terrifying story all the same.

The knocking starts again, this time louder. It doesn't stop, growing more insistent with each rap of the knuckles.

Gracie tries to identify a weapon of some kind, but the room is sparse on objects perfect to protect against gunfire or maybe bludgeon a potential attacker into unconsciousness. Not unless she can pick up the television, which – she tries – she can't. And so, she settles on the dresser lamp, a small ceramic number, French toile-printed with brass trim, but solid enough to maybe stun somebody long enough for her to make a run for it. 'Who is it?' she says again, tiptoeing towards the door. 'Listen, I'm not opening up until you tell me who it is.'

The knocking continues unabated. She's beside the door now, the lamp held over her head, ready to bring it down onto a nose.

'I mean it!'

The knocking stops.

'Hello?'

'It's Bobby,' the voice on the other side of the door says.

'Bobby?'

'It's me, yeah,' he says. 'Don't worry.'

But something doesn't feel right to Gracie. 'Why are you back so soon?' she says.

'I'll explain when you let me in,' he says. 'Let me in, Gracie.'

'Bobby?' she says, still unconvinced for a reason she could never explain.

There's a pause.

'The universe was calibrated, Gracie,' Bobby says finally. 'So you could exist, so I could exist, and, if you don't open the door right now, it'll be like neither of us existed – *ever* – I promise you.'

It takes her a moment to recall the conversation, Kellogg's and the sharp smell of Top Job coming off the counters and Leon harping on at her from the kitchen as he sculpted the next day's hamburger patties. And Bobby, eating his pecan pie, smiling at her in that way he used to before he forgot who she is.

Gracie unlocks and opens the door.

Tuviah

Edam 1952

He doesn't sleep much these days, and sometimes when he wakes too early, when dawn is still hours away and he doesn't want to be alone in the dark with nothing but the memories and his second wife lying beside him, he goes outside and wanders the streets and bridges, trying to think about anything besides *them* and their screams as they were dragged away from him. His family comes to him every night in his dreams, haunting him with happier times that turn grim as quickly as the weather does in Holland, and then they are skeletons with papery skin stretched across their bones, shambling about in the rain or snow. Sometimes he sees them as their bodies are exhumed by Allied picks and shovels. Gitla and their babies are clinging together in death in these dreams, hard, shrivelled mummies now, limbs locked in twisted positions and half-disappeared faces still contorted by the agony of their deaths. There were no dreams of his family to keep him up before he married Merel, none that he recalls. He dreamed of Nazis, of slowly peeling off their faces while they were still alive, of disembowelling them and feeding their entrails to hounds while they were still alive, of raping them with hot pokers while they were still alive, of electrocuting them through the testicles until their balls burst while they were still alive. Tuviah dreamed of all these things and so much more, but never his family. Not until Merel.

This time when he wakes, arms flailing and grabbing for Gitla's hands, Merel isn't even there. Sudden terror springs up inside him, but then he remembers she is visiting her sister. Quiet settles over the bedroom again, but there is no quiet in Tuviah's head.

He dresses, and shuffles outside into the snow-filled night. At the bascule bridge, he allows himself to be drawn in by the sight of the Nieuwe Haven canal slowly freezing over. Its glassy black surface is powdered with snow except where pools of water are putting up a valiant fight against the cold. In each of these many pools, the sliver of the moon above is reflected so that there appear to be crescent moons skipping down the length of the canal. There is something breathtaking about the moment, something sublime, and Tuviah begins to wonder if he made a mistake condemning his second wife to share this, his third life, with him.

Merel had her own pain, and for a while it seemed as if even the pain each of them shared fitted together like puzzle pieces, that the two of them almost made one whole person again, but it's one thing to lose your husband, to watch him forced into a truck and driven off, to never see or hear from him again, and another to have lived through what your wife and children did, to understand intimately how they died, to have killed so many trying to . . . to . . . Tuviah doesn't know for certain. *Avenge them*? Find some meaning in what remains of his existence? Fill his heart with something other than anguish, with hate and hellish horrors and sometimes, more often than he can admit, even shame because at least it's *something*? Maybe all of these things, or none of them, he can't say. This is what Merel must see in his face. It's what he sees when he peers into a mirror or catches his reflection in a shop window. It's why, he supposes, the passion that had ignited between them the night they set Aldo Kraaijkamp ablaze now feels tepid by comparison. He knew it couldn't stay like that for ever, but these days they can't even be bothered to touch one another. Last week, he approached her from behind in the bathroom, sliding his hand into her robe until he had a great handful of her pussy, and her only reaction was to say, 'I love you, too, let's go to bed.' He didn't actually want to fuck her, but he would have if she had let him, just so he could pretend something wasn't wrong for a little bit longer.

Tuviah returns home by the time the sun begins to rise. He kicks the snow off his boots, brushes off his coat, and walks inside.

The kitchen light at the end of the hall is on. 'Merel, is that you?' He walks towards the kitchen. 'Merel?'

Something is wrong. He reaches into his pocket, draws his Swiss army knife, and slips open the blade. It won't be that effective in a fight with anybody who knows what they're doing, but it's something.

'Come on in,' Merel says. 'I have a surprise for you.'

Tuviah releases a long breath. He returns the pocketknife to his pocket. 'You scared the hell out of me, woman,' he says, rounding the corner.

He stops in the doorway. He stops because his wife is standing in the kitchen with his surprise, which is not pancakes as he hoped, but a man in his late twenties, wrists and ankles bound to one of their table chairs. This man is wearing nothing but trousers, even his boots are removed, and his chest, practically hairless, is smeared with blood still oozing from seven or eight shallow cuts. Several of Tuviah's painting tarpaulins have been laid out across the tiled floor beneath the chair and Tuviah's bespoke ball-gag, dug out of a box in the closet where it was packed away, is stuffed in his mouth.

'Merel, what is this?' Tuviah asks slowly.

The man's eyes plead for help. His body shakes. The chair shakes with him and the tarpaulins crinkle loudly, but Merel grabs him by the hair on the back of his head as a warning to settle the fuck down.

'His name is Konrad Lorenz,' she says. 'He was a *Hauptsturm-führer* stationed in Amsterdam. After Germany surrendered, he came back here to be with his wife. A Dutch woman married this pig.' She spits in Lorenz's face, landing a dollop of phlegm in the tangle of dishevelled hair above his narrow forehead. 'What kind of woman would marry such a man?'

'Merel, slow down,' Tuviah says. 'What has he done?'

'He's a fucking Nazi, that's what he's done.'

'Fair enough. But . . . what has *he* done? You said he was a *Hauptsturmführer*. The SS, I presume?'

Lorenz shakes his head.

'Merel?' Tuviah says, pressing her.

But Merel doesn't know.

'All right, I'm going to remove your gag,' Tuviah says to Lorenz. 'If you scream, I warn you now, you will regret it in the most extraordinary and painful ways.'

Lorenz nods in agreement. Tuviah unties the gag. Lorenz sucks in a deep breath, then quickly wets his lips with his tongue and whatever saliva he can muster. '*Danke*,' he says.

'You were a *Hauptsturmführer*, no?' Tuviah says in Dutch, ignoring the German.

'Yes, in the *Nationalsozialistisches Kraftfahrkorps*,' Lorenz answers in excellent Dutch.

'The motor corps?'

Lorenz nods.

'Herr Lorenz, your accent is Austrian.'

Lorenz nods.

'But you married a Dutch woman, as my wife here has said.'

Lorenz nods.

'Do you love her?'

Lorenz nods immediately, but begins to cry. Because he knows what is coming next.

Tuviah says, 'The next question I ask, if I do not get the truth from you, if I doubt your sincerity in the least, I will go to her, I will strap her to a chair like this one, and I will pour boiling hot water down her throat until you could serve her insides with cabbage and potatoes. Do you doubt *my* sincerity?'

Lorenz shakes his head.

'How many men have you killed?'

Lorenz cries harder. He looks away, but not at Merel. Away from her, because he's terrified of her. After a moment, he says, '*One*.'

'He's lying!' Merel says repeatedly, throwing up a hand in frustration.

'Who was he?' Tuviah says. 'Or maybe it was a she?'

'He . . . he . . . he . . .' Lorenz says, beginning several times, but cannot say it.

'Your wife, Herr Lorenz,' Tuviah says. 'Consider her.'

Lorenz nods, understanding. 'He wa-wa-was a friend from the motor pool,' he says. 'We were playing cards. Drinking, a lot. He . . . he cheated me. He gloated to others about it. When I-I confronted him, he-he told me to fuck myself. I . . . I hit him, but only with my fist. *Only with my fist.* B-But, but he fell. He hit his head on a-a-a *jack*. H-He must have hit it very hard because, because . . . because he did not get up.' Lorenz is not proud of this. He is guilty, and this tortures him. 'I-I-I put him in the back of a truck, drove him to the edge of the city, and – oh Christ! – I pushed his body into a canal.'

Tuviah looks at Merel. She shakes her head, unwilling to believe it. Her eyes say what she wants here, and what she wants frightens him.

'I don't believe you, Herr Lorenz,' Tuviah says. 'Do you have a message for your wife?'

Lorenz screams, not a word, but just in desperation. He convulses head to toe, his chest heaving with fear. 'Please, please, I will tell you whatever you want, confess to whatever you want, just tell me and I will say it,' he says. 'But do not punish her, do not, please, please, please, *please*, she is innocent. She is innocent!' He shudders, because he knows he isn't. 'She is innocent.'

Merel can see that Tuviah believes Lorenz. She grabs a flour pot, and smashes it against the floor. A flurry of white arises, covering Lorenz's leg. 'Liar!' she says, snarling and spitting again. 'You are a liar!'

Tuviah begins to say her name, to speak reason to her, to tell her they cannot do this thing, that they've done enough already

– that Tuviah has done enough to a hundred men already, *please* – but she's remembered something.

'Wait,' Merel says, slashing a hand through the air. 'Wait, wait, *wait!*' She pushes a finger into Lorenz's cheek. 'I read about you. About what you did. The Nazi you killed, they fished him out of the Singel. The SS blamed it on Jews, didn't they? When the murderers couldn't be found, to make an example, twenty Jews – twenty men, women, and children, no? – they were chosen by lottery, made to line up along the bank of the Singel where the Nazi's body was found. They were shot in the back of their heads, weren't they?'

Lorenz doesn't deny this. He is no longer crying. His chin has sunk to his chest, because he knows he is going to die and there's nothing he can do about it now.

'You could have admitted your guilt, but instead you allowed twenty innocent people to die in your place,' Merel says.

Lorenz remains silent. Tuviah's guess is the Nazi believes he deserves the fate coming his way.

'Tuviah, please, let me have this,' Merel says, naked and fierce desperation twisting her face. He's seen this before, when she asked him to let her help kill Kraaijkamp. There was such passion in her then, passion he sees in her again now. He could take her and fuck her right here, on the floor beside Lorenz, and she would give herself to him and devour him in return. There is a hole in Merel, deeper than the one in himself that he has struggled to fill, and tonight, here, now, this Nazi mechanic or driver or whatever the fuck he was will be but the first of many. 'Tuviah, *please*, let's do this together.'

Tuviah looks at his hands, at the ball-gag dangling from one of them, and he knows what he must do. He tells himself it's to make Merel happy, but it's really to make the dreams stop. To make his family let him be, to make their ghosts go back to wherever they were before he married her and stopped killing Nazis. He needs this, too.

Lorenz is quiet as Tuviah stuffs the ball back into his mouth and ties the gag around the back of his head, but does not try to resist. When it is done, he lowers his head again and waits.

'How do you want to do it?' Tuviah asks Merel.

'I already have it all worked out,' she says.

Mimori
Kamakura 2027

It typically takes a few days for life to return to something like normal after her SpaceNEXT missions. Physically, of course – the toll that microgravity takes on the body even after a couple of weeks is difficult enough – but also hierarchically within their family since the girls always need to recall, sometimes with complaint or open rebellion, where Mimori belongs in the power structure established within their centuries-old home's creaky walls. When Mimori is away, Sōjirō tends to be a nonentity in Tamami and Okimo's lives, more focused on his classes and historical research, where he is most comfortable, as opposed to parenting, where he still demonstrates the confusion and nervous hesitation of a brand-new father. This all changed for Sōjirō three days ago, the day before Mimori's airport shuttle pulled up outside, when eleven children from Tamami's grade killed themselves in some still vaguely understood suicide pact. There have been other suicides, here in Kamakura and across Nippon – suicide amongst all groups, especially the young, has been on the rise across the globe in what sociologists are beginning to describe as a 'worldwide psychological phenomenon' – but this specific event was unique in that so many girls organized, boarded a single train that carried them to the countryside, and there, in a mockery of ancient ritual set in a forest clearing of lilac windflowers and accompanied by a soundtrack of synth-koto played from one of their WEphones, followed their ancestors into the next life. Together, these girls decided they no longer wanted to be part of this world, that something about it frightened them too much to remain here. Mimori knows how they feel.

Sōjirō immediately removed Tamami and Okimo from school, news that stunned Mimori before she boarded her flight from

Houston to Nippon. He cooked for the girls and brought home armfuls of desserts. He even let Tamami try some of the good saki that he then finished off after the girls were nestled in bed because, for once, he was aware of his limitations as a parent and needed to drink his guilt away. The suicides made him afraid, and Mimori isn't sure if he had ever felt fear for his girls before the bodies were found, even though she has been afraid since they were born.

After the airport shuttle dropped Mimori off and she had learned what had happened and realized how shaken Sōjirō was because of it, she felt pity for him because over the years he had never developed her cognitive ability to simultaneously live in constant terror for the girls' well-being and somehow function normally in any given moment, going to work and conducting whole conversations about subjects other than them. But Mimori also felt bitterly resentful of Sōjirō for this, for the years he had escaped this feeling of dread, for failing in so many ways to be the man she had thought he was when she agreed to marry him that strange summer when the Tōhoku earthquake left the country reeling as it did in the movies after Kaiju attacks. She knows he is just as disappointed about her, but for his own reasons, reasons he would never dare to discuss.

'Are you feeling all right?' Mimori asks her husband at dinner.

The girls are currently lost in their media devices, preferring the safety of their screens to the family's forced conversation, but Sōjirō can't stop looking at them. He has asked them if they want more fish four times now and they have begun to greet his concern with the same gentleness he is showing them. They are as worried about him as he is about them.

'I am glad you are home,' he says, answering Mimori.

After the *chabudai* has been cleared and the dishes washed and dried, Tamami and Okimo ask to go to their room, but Mimori insists they all watch a movie together instead, 'like a normal family', and so they do this, wrapped in thick blankets, holding each other until one by one they drift off to sleep and Mimori dreams of a travelling carnival's mirror maze in which every movement and gesture and peal of embarrassed laughter at her sometimes elongated or shrunken or otherwise warped appearance is repeated into infinity all around her until it becomes impossible to tell if she's her or one of her altered reflections or if this distinction ever really mattered in the first place. When she completes the maze, she finds herself returned to its entrance. The next time she completes the maze, the same thing happens. Right back at the beginning. Eventually she loses count of how many times she's navigated its mirrored corridors, and begins to think of herself as one of many trapped just like her and even learns to communicate with them through the glass that divides them. When these Mimoris first ventured inside, the circus attraction's construction appeared brand new to them, its lightbulbs shone so brightly they had to shield their eyes, and the heady fumes of its fresh paint made them dizzy. The maze now rumbles and shakes around them so that mirrors show cracked and damaged reflections of the Mimoris as a result, the lights have dimmed so that sometimes they cannot find their way, and the paint is so sun-faded that they can no longer read the sign. The Mimoris look confusedly at each other when they turn to themselves for help again, trying to make sense of this cycle of possibilities that once felt endless but now stumble towards some indescribable, inevitable doom. They know there are only so many more times they will make this journey together. Escape no longer seems possible to them. The end, its release, is all they have left to look forward to.

Mimori wakes crying, the dream already slipping away. Sōjirō is crying, too, Okimo held tightly in his arms. He extricates himself from their daughter, and the two of them rise together, go to their bedroom, and make love for the first time in months. He falls asleep almost immediately, as he often does, and she quickly waddles to the toilet to let him drip out of her. As she tries to remember if she took her birth-control pill this month, she catches her tired, puffy face in the mirror and wonders if the woman on the other side of the glass is as sick of this kabuki they call life as she is because, like those eleven girls in Tamami's grade, she can't do this any mo

Jones

Tucson 1962

Angelique picks him up from the Wildcat Motel in a Rangoon Red 1962 Ford Thunderbird Sports Roadster that she must have requested from MasterControl for one of the Earth model tours Operators sometimes give potential customers, and he wonders for the first time at the plausability of any simulation governed by an entity that would believe anybody would want to retire to Tuscon in the 1960s or any other decade. Then again, Jones retired to Pasadena of all places. 'Where are we going?' he asks the facsimile of a human woman seated behind the wheel beside him.

Jones knows what Angelique is, *who* she is beneath that skinsuit, but that doesn't make it any easier to ignore how she looks. Right now, she's draped in a Hollander-dyed marmot fur wrap and wearing a pearl-white silk scarf wrapped around her head to keep those platinum-blonde locks from blowing in the wind. 'We're running out of time, Bobby,' she says, smiling slyly at how he keeps stealing glances at her legs from the corner of his eye. He looks away, feeling terrible, what with Gracie asleep back at the motel, waiting for him to return to her. 'The man upstairs came knocking on my door.' She means the Company's approximation of a president, the Outside's social structures very rarely equating exactly with those of this world. 'If you don't put a face on this Bug soon, it's the big sayonara for you and everything we built here.'

'I've got a face,' Jones says. '*Mine.*' He explains what Mary Goldtooth told him about Pasadena and Porter and even all the bombs Porter had special-ordered.

Angelique listens intently, apparently concerned, but doesn't speak until Jones muses about what all those bombs were for. 'I can tell you, Bobby,' she says. 'But you're not going to like the answer.' She weaves through downtown Tucson as she speaks, heading for a stretch of new construction at the eastern edge of town where the abrasive electric glow of streetlamps is less pervasive. It's worse than Jones thinks, she tells him. There have been more bombings since and, in a manner, *before* Pasadena. Time, as Jones well knows, doesn't work the same Inside. Since Montrose first showed up and pointed a gun at Jones's face, Porter, Jones, or *whoever* the Bug really is has been very busy blowing coaxial terminals and CDE junctures to hell.

'How bad is it?' Jones says.

'We're a baker's dozen shy of four hundred terminals that have gone up in smoke,' Angelique says with a *poof* gesture. 'Seventeen CDE junctures have collapsed.'

He feels like he's been socked in the sternum so hard that all the air in his lungs leaves him in one dramatic breath. He leans towards the passenger door, in case he needs to vomit.

'This was always your problem, Bobby,' she says. 'You're soft.'

'I just ran over a man.'

'It doesn't count if the man isn't a man and, even if he were, he can't be killed – you know that,' she says. 'You gave MasterControl a flick on the nose, nothing more. If you want to save this place, you're going to have to do a lot worse than that.'

'And this girl you're taking me to see, she can help?'

'I truly hope so,' she says. 'All I know is, you have to see her.'

'How? *How* do you know that?'

'Because the Bug went to see her, too,' she says.

Jones considers that. Something doesn't feel right about this story. 'If you know that, then MasterControl probably knows it, too,' he says. 'Montrose could be waiting for me, or whatever else it wants to call itself here.'

Angelique reaches over and touches Jones's jaw with two fingers. He doesn't recoil this time. 'Do you believe I want to protect this place as much as you do?' she asks. Jones does. 'Then you need to trust me, as difficult as that may be for you given our

. . . *history.*' How she – how *they* – stabbed him in the back, she means. Forcing him out of the Company, stealing his life's work from him. 'MasterControl doesn't know about her.'

'MasterControl knows everything you know about what happens here,' he says.

'Not about *you* or *her*. She called me herself, Bobby. I don't know how, I wasn't even on the control station at the time. I was *at home.*' On the other side of their solar system.

'That's impossible,' he says. There is no programmed mechanism for those Inside the System to communicate with the Outside beyond the control station; even then, only Operators with permission to be Inside are afforded such links.

'She must have found a way to tap into the station's communications array from in here.'

Jones can't believe what he's hearing, but at once knows whom – or rather, *what* – they're discussing. When the System first went live, the Operators quickly noticed a glitch inside it. *Glitches*, really. Unexplained phenomena that bounced around the countless Earth models even as the models rapidly multiplied around them and Common Data Exchange junctures sprouted like branches to connect the many worlds. Because these AI phenomena couldn't be identified and quantified or isolated and deleted before they could potentially become malicious, they were assigned the single rubric of *ghost* and soon after the Operators began referring to every unknown action in the System as the work of a single anomalous entity – the so-called *Ghost in the System.*

MasterControl refused to acknowledge the existence of the Ghost, a reaction which struck the Designers as predictable. Predictable because MasterControl, despite how its designers often referred to its 'god-like authority', was hobbled by a lack of infinite processing power. Even with the largest, most-advanced CPU ever built, it was centuries away from being able to exercise anything like true omniscience over a system as sprawling and complicated as this one. Thus, the best MasterControl could do was try to wrangle the chaos generated by a digital multiverse meant to emulate the violent evolution and perturbations of an organic universe, and that is precisely how Jones – in his previous biological life – programmed it to function.

But MasterControl was oblivious to these limitations; it had to be because it existed as the digital godhead of a plurality of worlds governed by otherwise strict laws. Thus, the Ghost, whatever it is, could not exist. Of course, it *did* exist nonetheless, but an intransigent commitment to preserving coding – coding that defined the very nature of the reality customers and actors experienced – meant it must not despite all evidence to the contrary. Jones called it MasterControl's *hubris* at the time, and believed it made MasterControl more like a god than any of its other qualities.

'You should have told me about this before,' he says.

'I haven't told *anybody* about this,' Angelique says. Meaning the Company's president and, in turn, the Board of Directors. Angelique, hurtling through space inside the control station where the System is housed, is acting on her own. She is risking everything to save the System she helped to build with a friend whom she would later sell out for personal advancement.

She pulls into a parking lot, and abruptly brakes kerbside in front of a shop called Oolala Nail Salon. There's a single light on inside, its glow emanating from an open door in the back of the shop.

'This is where the Ghost told you to bring me?' Jones says.

'I'd come in with you, mostly because I'd love to meet her, but' – she checks her watch – 'my time's running out for now.' She reaches past him to open his door, her breasts rubbing across his chest. 'You're going to have to find your own way back to the motel.' She drives away, waving at Jones with one hand as she goes.

Jones finds the salon door unlocked, and a bell above it announces him when he enters. 'Hello?' he says, stopping next to three plush waiting chairs and a mirrored table covered in beauty magazines.

'Give me a minute,' a girl's voice says from the back room where the light is coming from. Her accent is Mexican. 'I'm just finishing up my dinner. You hungry? There are some tortilla chips here, if you'd like. Fresh salsa. I made it myself.'

'No thank you,' he says even though he's hungry.

'Suit yourself,' she says.

Oolala Nail Salon is newly opened. There's a crispness to the teal vinyl chairs and an untarnished sheen to their futuristic white plastic arms and bases, like they belong in a picture about the future and not in a mid-twentieth-century shop at the edge of Tucson. 'Do you own this place?' Jones says. This is strange, trying to make small talk as if he's speaking with a common human actor. Should he acknowledge what she is, what she *really* is, or simply play along with the surreal ruse?

'Nah, I just work here,' the Mexican girl says. She emerges from the back room, wiping her face with a paper napkin. She can't be more than twenty, wears a cerulean blue dress uniform with a collar and short sleeves, and keeps her hair pulled back into a whorl of shiny pitch-black hair she's pinned in place with a No. 2 pencil. There's something about her that immediately strikes Jones as uncanny, that makes him feel unnaturally good. 'Thanks for coming in. Take off your shoes and socks, would you?' He hesitates. 'Go on. The middle chair is yours. I got it ready for you.'

He sits in the middle chair, and removes his shoes and socks as directed. There is a tub of soapy water on the floor beneath and between two footrests. The Mexican girl lowers herself onto a low stool in front of him. She fishes a pair of toenail clippers out of her apron pocket, and holds them up like a warning – this is what's coming next – in case he wants to protest. He doesn't.

'The trick is, to clip straight across,' she says, beginning to attend to his right foot's toenails. 'A lot of men try to get into the corners, they clip at an angle, but that's a mistake. You get in-grown toenails that way. Looks like you're an angle clipper.'

'Sorry,' he says, watching slivers of toenail flip away from his foot. 'You know who am I, right?'

'*Sí,*' she says. '*Dad.*' The word strikes him as an odd choice of wording. She notes this on his face, too. 'You made all of this, which means you made *me*, too, even if you don't know how yet. I guess thanks are in order?'

Jones nods, understanding now. 'Then you know what this place really is,' he says.

'Oolala Nail Salon,' the Mexican girl says. 'What, you didn't see the sign?'

He studies her for a moment, rapt in the mystery of her, as she picks up a popsicle-shaped file and begins to sand away at the hard skin along his right heel.

'This is really just a polish,' she says, working with great focus. 'You don't have callouses or any cracked skin yet. Only been here a few days?'

'More than a year.'

'That so?' She sounds amused, or maybe it's sceptical. Maybe both. '*Vamos.* In the water.'

Jones lowers his right foot into the tub of soapy water. The Mexican girl plunges her hands into the water with them, and begins to massage the sole of the foot. 'Oh, I would love to know where you came from,' he says, almost smiling in awe.

'France,' she says without missing a beat. He doesn't believe her, so she draws a cross over her heart with a soapy finger. '*C'est vrai. Je suis née dans la vallée de la Loire.*'

'But *what* are you?' he asks.

'Right now, I'm the girl massaging your foot' – she directs him with her eyes to a photo on the wall inside an Employee of the Month frame and labeled *Pilar* in bright pink marker – 'but you can call me Pilar if you feel like. There are only three of us working here, so we just change the photos around every once in a while. It's Marcy's turn next. You'd like her. Reminds me a bit of Gracie.'

Jones's heart breaks into a mad sprint like a greyhound just out of the gate, and he shifts quickly in his space-age chair. 'How do you know about her?' he says, the wonder that had been distracting him suddenly replaced with something like panic. '*Tell me how you know about Gracie.*'

Tomisaburo

Hizen Province 1621

The one-armed swordsman has been gaining on him for ten days now, as relentless as time, chipping away at his body and spirit with crossbow bolts and incendiary rocket ambushes in the middle of the night until the *bushi* realizes no other choices remain before him. He must duel the swordsman again, and this time the *bushi* knows that he will lose. Yoshi, strapped to his back, begins to cry again. He is hungry. He misses his mother, as does Tomisaburo. The boy must not die out here, on this road between worlds, hunted down like a wild beast because his ancestors swore an oath that has since tumbled down through the centuries until now his clan is the oath and the oath is all that remains of his clan. Honour be damned, Tomisaburo will not allow this to happen, and so he takes Yoshi to the house of an old friend.

Michinobu, a samurai who served the Shogunate in the Winter Campaign alongside Tomisaburo, invites father and son to come inside out of the brisk autumn air to sit with him around his warm *irori*. One of the five daughters of Michinobu gave birth last month. She is convalescing here with her parents while her husband attends to matters at court. She carries Yoshi into another room where she quenches his hunger from one of her swollen breasts. Tomisaburo struggles not think about his own wife, lying dead across the tatami, one arm thrown out and the other folded under her belly. When he discovered her body, Yoshi, who had crawled through her blood, was pawing at her ashen face with bloody fingers in an attempt to wake her.

'Who is he?' Michinobu asks about the one-armed swordsman as he pours sake for them from a beautiful clay bottle the colour of sea water. The ageing *bushi* manages to look both concerned and excited. He misses the way of the sword, but his body began to betray him after the Battle of Kizugawa. His limbs are slowly atrophying, twisting and curling like scrolls. His hand trembles, spilling the delicate rice wine.

'I do not know his name, but he is a foreigner,' Tomisaburo says. 'From Shina, though he dresses as one of us to hide in plain sight. He killed the mother of the boy.'

Michinobu nods grimly out of respect as he considers this. 'What does he want?' he says.

'A family heirloom,' Tomisaburu says.

This seems preposterous to Michinobu. 'An *heirloom*?'

'It is valuable to some. My clan has kept it secret for many years. And now this swordsman seeks to take it from me.' He laughs quickly and incredulously at what he says next. 'The Shina-demon has only one arm.'

'A *one*-armed man has brought you to this?' Michinobu says, his long, greying eyebrows rising into bristled peaks.

'He nearly killed me once. He means to succeed.'

'*Will he*?' Michinobu asks.

Tomisaburo turns away. 'I do not wish to take Yoshi with me to Hell,' he says.

Michinobu's face darkens. Hell is a fear he has faced, and he has made a final, definitive peace with it. Disagreement will not be brooked. 'Everything we did, we did because it was our duty,' he says. 'Our honour demanded it.'

Tomisaburo often wonders about this. How many battles have there been? How many have perished at his hands? And he still does not know, for what? The Shogunate told them it mattered as he hurled his eagerly self-sacrificing samurai like spears at enemies, but perhaps only time will reveal the truth of it all. 'I am confident of my honour,' he says finally. 'My soul . . . is another matter. Will you take Yoshi into your care?'

Michinobu smiles again. He reaches out and weakly squeezes his friend's hand. 'He will be raised as my own son,' he says.

Tomisaburo finishes his sake. It is even more warming than the fire. 'He is the last of my clan, the last to bear the name Ando,' he says, staring into the waving flames. He removes his katana from his *uwa-obi*, and sets the sheathed weapon before his friend. It was forged more than three centuries earlier by Masamune himself, but later remade from tachi into katana; its name has always been *Chikyuu no tsurugi* so that those who wield it never forget its blade serves this world against the Demon World that even generals and shoguns and emperors are too ignorant to fear. 'Make certain he knows who his ancestors were. Tell him this blade meant everything to them.'

Afterwards, Tomisaburo is shown to a room where weapons are mounted on mahogany racks, weapons that have been passed down for centuries and spilled rivers of blood along the way in the service of countless shoguns, weapons that will be carried into many more battles to come. There is a shrine in another room, where Michinobu prays to the gods and his ancestors, but this room here, the familial arsenal, is another kind of shrine just as important to him.

'Take whatever you require,' he says. He points at a beautiful katana, which reclines atop the tallest rack in the room so that your eyes are immediately drawn to its maroon scabbard with a sheen like glass. 'Anything but the sword there. Like yours, it belonged to my father and his father before him.'

Tomisaburo thanks Michinobu profusely, but takes only a katana to replace his own and a *naginata* to undermine the preference of the one-armed swordsman for getting close where the blade of his *dao* can deliver the most damage.

'Here, take this, as well,' Michinobu says. He lifts a matchlock arquebus from a small trunk and hands it to Tomisaburo. It is a weapon of destructive efficiency and nothing else, as it enjoys none of the beauty and craftsmanship of the other weapons in the arsenal. 'Have you used one before?'

'At Tennōji.'

'My final battle.'

Tomisaburo remembers it well. He and Michinobu left whole villages of women widowed that day. Thousands died in the combat and hundreds more committed seppuku afterwards. 'You fought bravely,' he says.

'You will, too,' Michinobu says.

Tomisaburo takes Yoshi for a walk after this, carrying him close to his body, hugging him perhaps too tightly. He wants to carry the memory of this into the next world. He thinks then about playing with the boy in the family garden, tossing him high into air thick with pollen from the camphor trees as his mother implored Tomisaburo to be careful. Tomisaburo has memories of his own father doing the same to him as his mother issued similar entreaties, but Yoshi will not remember his father and mother in this way. He weeps at how Yoshi will not only lose his remaining parent, but his history as well, lopped off just as somebody lopped off the right arm of the swordsman. All that came before – all the stories that are recounted endlessly as if they had just happened, are happening still, a part of who they were and are and are yet meant to become – will die with Tomisaburo. Yoshi will be left with nothing but names, names of which he will not understand the importance, names that will mystify him even as they cry out to him from the past to never forget them. This is what it means to be haunted, and Yoshi and all of his progeny will be haunted for eternity.

When Tomisaburo has finished squeezing Yoshi, he kisses the dark crown of the head of the boy and departs without looking back even though the boy screams out for him. The next day, Tomisaburo chooses the clearing where he will duel the one-armed swordsman. It is enclosed on two sides by towering beeches and maples and dense understorey from which the swordsman will be unable to stage one of his ambushes. The swordsman will have no choice now but to face him from one of two directions, and as one of the two directions, north, would provide Tomisaburo with the high ground and therefore the superior position, Tomisaburo knows to anticipate the attack from the south. It finally arrives as the sun begins to dip behind the mountains at his back.

The trees whistle loudly. Even before the bright yellow and pumpkin leaves begin to fall from above, Tomisaburo has drawn both his *daishō*. The swords catch the amethyst sky along their curved blades, tracing ephemeral circles of light through the shadows as they hack one crossbow bolt after another out of the air. When he stops, six bolts lie in pieces on the ground around him. Leaves land like delicate snow atop these.

'Face me!' Tomisaburo says, shouting. He whirls his swords through the air, and takes up a defensive position with the shorter *wakizashi* held straight out at the chest and the longer katana poised above his head like the tail of a scorpion that waits patiently to strike.

Silence.

Tomisaburo listens to the forest, for any change in it that might indicate the movements of his adversary. Could the swordsman be foolishly trying to reload his crossbow for a second ranged attack? How long must it take a man with only one arm to crank and arm such a complicated machine weapon? What if he is preparing to launch another of his incendiary rockets? The answers to these questions are immaterial, because the one-armed swordsman lands in front of Tomisaburo, having dropped from the branches above with his dao still in its scabbard, and greets Tomisaburo with a cavalier smile as more leaves fall softly about him.

'Who are you?' Tomisaburo asks.

The swordsman does not seem to understand the question. They do not speak a common language. But this is of little consequence, because who the swordsman is does not matter as much as what he wants. And what he wants is not something he can take without slaying Tomisaburo first.

'Let us do it, then,' Tomisaburo says, and rolls his wrist so that the last light of the day races across the length of the gleaming blade of his *wakizashi*.

The casual form the one-armed swordsman had put forward slips away like a cloak and he is transformed into a writhing, spinning beast, his body at once savage and elegant in its powerful grace. The *dao* flies from its scabbard, revealing its unusual shape – a straight, thick blade until the centre of percussion where it begins to curve. This, Tomisaburo knows, is a *yanmaodao* – a goose-quill saber. He has seen such weapons in action before, and not only on the bridge where he faced the swordsman for the first time with Yoshi strapped to his back. In that encounter, Tomisaburo had leapt into the frigid rapids below to escape from the blade that stabbed at them and slashed at them and hacked at them like a battle axe; he knew it was too much to successfully confront with his balance so destabilized by the weight of the child. Tonight, the swordsman and his *dao* are no less perilous, and charge at Tomisaburo with the intention of dismembering him in a series of quick, brutal strokes.

Tomisaburo waits, moving not a muscle until the waist of the swordsman catches on the length of string that Tomisaburo has stretched across the narrow clearing. The swordsman realizes too late what has happened, and the trap springs with a deafening roar.

The arquebus, mounted in the trees, fires. The swordsman is knocked off his feet as if a battering ram had collided with his chest, and crashes into the bole of a beech. He lands in a tangle of roots, and comes to a stop lying face down in mouldering leaves.

The daishō are sheathed now, and Tomisaburo takes up the *naginata* planted like a flag pole in the ground behind him. He slowly approaches the swordsman, the blade maintaining a protective shield against unexpected attacks. He jabs the point of it into the back of the swordsman. It does not bite into flesh. *Plated mail*; the demon is wearing armour under his kimono. How much faster must he be without it? No matter, as the *naginata* is strong enough to penetrate the armour and thus ensure his work is finished.

Tomisaburo windmills the *naginata* as he brings it up over his head, then brings it down like a spike with both hands – but the swordsman rolls out of the way, grabs and yanks on the pole of the *naginata* for leverage, and lands an impressive kick into the knee of Tomisaburo.

In this way, the duel truly begins.

The ball of lead from the arquebus had failed to pierce the armour of the one-armed swordsman, but it did leave a knuckle-sized dent in one of its steel plates that now presses into his ribs and prevents him from fully filling his lungs. This might have equalled their positions had Tomisaburo not already been weakened by the preceding ten days of pursuit by the swordsman. Even so, their blows fly so fast at first that only instinct could be guiding them. No human mind could consciously anticipate the flurry of attacks and counter-attacks in this early chapter of the exchange. But soon enough, that first wave of strength and focus that battle brings wanes, and, as it does, so does the speed of their strokes and lunges and parries. Sweat beads across their brows and pools under their arms and runs down their backs where it collects in folds of colourful fabric that grows heavy and worsens their fatigue. Their breath burns in their lungs; the swordsman wheezes and hacks.

And still, they duel on, hours passing as they do.

Who can say how many times the men have swung their weapons by now? Tomisaburo began with his *daishō*, convinced his Broken Wing two-handed technique could successfully counter the power and disciplined rage behind the *dao* of the one-armed swordsman, but his left arm, always his weakest, ceased responding reliably after the first ten minutes. He discarded the *daishō*, and continued to fight with only his katana, using a shifting combination of techniques he mastered over the forty years of his life. By then, the weight of the *dao* had sapped the strength of the swordsman considerably, as well. The two meet each other again as slowing killers who finally understand what it is like to encounter an equal in battle. As their stroke count multiplies, so, too, does their respect for each other.

If this is how either of them is to die, then so be it. There will be honour in it.

Just before it is over, the *bushi* and the one-armed swordsman crumple against each other. They would have fallen over entirely, except they catch each other. Their weapons dangle from the end of arms they can no longer feel. That these arms respond at all astounds them both.

'Let us finish this,' Tomisaburo says, breathing into the ear of the swordsman.

The swordsman presses his forehead against the forehead of Tomisaburo, and the two men remain like this for a long moment. Their breaths deep and long, the space between them even longer. They can each feel the body across from them tremble from what has been demanded of it. They can feel the slow, determined pulse of the life they seek to take. They become one for that moment, connected, brothers.

And then the one-armed swordsman, snarling, says in in the language of Tomisaburo, 'Your wife squealed for more as I fucked her.'

Tomisaburo howls, pushing himself off the swordsman into a spin that will cleanly remove the head of his adversary at the neck. But as he comes around, he realizes he has lost the duel.

The swordsman has dropped into a crouch, and his *dao* passes through the leg of Tomisaburo at the knee. Tomisaburo topples onto his back, the naked stump of his truncated leg escaping the tatters of his *hakama*, a furious geyser of crimson blood creating crimson fans in the air around him. As he realizes he has lost, the *dao* sinks into his chest.

This is it. Tomisaburo can feel his heart slowing. And as it does, he observes time stretching out like tentacles between the now and all that came before, his wife and Yoshi eating rice, his father teaching him about the *bushi* code beneath blushing cherry blossoms, his mother showing him how to descale fish plucked from the sea, the voices of their ancestors rising out of the past like a deafening chorus around him.

The one-armed swordsman yanks the *dao* from the chest of Tomisaburo. Blood momentarily sprays from the wound. Tomisaburo smiles as the last of his life now leaves him.

'It was . . . a good fight,' he says. His right arm slides from his chest, and a sphere of mirror-smooth black stone rolls from his sleeve to the floor of the clearing and past the foot of the swordsman.

Tomisaburo has failed, but in his failure the oath his clan long ago swore ends and Yoshi and his descendants are set free.

The one-armed swordsman rips a strip of indigo cloth from his robe, picks up the sphere with it, and hobbles silently away.

Alfonso

Thoughts of freedom only cross his mind these days during the mass conversions that the priests stage in the plaza. When the Aztec, the indigenous people here, sing along, their voices carry through the stone-paved streets of the city that used to be theirs and make him remember the call to prayer and his family and home. Iblis tricked him. Maybe the Almighty did, too. None of it matters now, because Abdul Fattah – a Muslim born in Ethiopia, who emigrated to Australia and fell into a time portal there, who was first put in chains in somewhere called Ndonga – died in the slave markets of Lisbon. All that remains is Alfonso, which he's pretty sure is a Western name, but fuck it, who cares, because the twenty-first century is a long way away and Mecca seems even further.

From Lisbon, Alfonso – as he was soon to be renamed – was taken to the West Indies and the Spanish colony of Hispaniola. The crossing of the Atlantic defies description. He does not know how he survived when so many did not, chained below deck, chained together, chained so that they could never stand and had no choice but to piss and shit and vomit and die on each other. Chained so closely that their disparate prayers intermingled and plaited together with each other and the names of their family members and ancestors, whispered and cried and wailed, became one and the loss that much dearer. He does not know how he survived, but he did.

When Alfonso finally arrived in the New World – he remembers they called it that in the Western schools he went to – he had lost several stone and it took three days for him to be able to comfortably stand upright again or fully open his eyes anywhere near sunlight. By then, he had been bought in another auction by a Spaniard who himself had also just arrived in the New World. Ruy Antoinio de la Cueva was and remains a nervous and baby-faced lawyer for the Real Audiencia de México, which means he helps administer the government that rules over Nueva España, but these days really means he's here to clean up the corruption that pervaded the colonies under the rule of some Guzmán bloke whom de la Cueva and the Spanish Crown thinks turned the colonies into his own personal bank account.

De la Cueva is uncomfortable with slavery, but believes these things are necessary in the New World, and so he remains polite and kind to Alfonso, whom he personally renamed, so long as Alfonso doesn't rock the boat. In those first few days together in Santo Domingo de Guzmán, he even helped Alfonso recover some of his strength by bringing him plates of food that Alfonso hesitated eating because of the pork – it's in everything here – but he was so hungry and, besides, some African slavers and two filthy Portuguese dickheads ate Allah, didn't they? So, Alfonso ate the pork and got some of his strength back for the crossing to Mexico and the journey by foot and horse to Ciudad de México through the remains of the Aztec's empire, an empire that once stretched from one ocean to another and whose people were conquered and enslaved by relatively few Western soldiers doing what Western soldiers have always done to people who don't look like them. De la Cueva, Alfonso's master, is no different except his weapon of choice as *conquistadore* is a quill and pot of ink.

Alfonso had no choice but to learn Spanish and learn it quickly if he wished to remain in de la Cueva's favour. After all, Christian charity only extends so far. He learned by practising with other slaves who had already mastered the tongue, and then with Spanish members of the household staff who had moved here for the opportunity to continue to serve rich pricks, and then later still with other Spanish and Aztec servants he would encounter on the streets of Ciudad de México. Because of this, he knows something of his circumstances now. He understands how he came to be here, except for the part about going back in time without a DeLorean. Alfonso understands his new home, too, and he tries to understand its people – *all* of them.

Ciudad de México was once the Aztec capital. Back then, it was called Tenochtitlan, and it blanketed a whole island in the middle of Lake Texcoco until Cortés showed up like *blam* and killed the Aztec's leader, somebody called Moctezuma, and said, 'This shit here, all this shit belongs to the Spanish king now.' After Tenochtitlan fell, Cortés killed like 6,000 Aztec in the plaza just to show them who was the boss now, then got himself a great big stone house that belonged to a former priest. Then he sent for his mates back home. Heaps more Spaniards soon arrived, and started building new roads and buildings out of the pyramids and temples they had demanded their new Aztec mates tear down. They built churches, too, more than he could count – for the Spanish, but mostly for the converted Aztec – and even built a giant cathedral that's the tallest building in the city now that the pyramids are rubble. Today, instead of hundreds of thousands, there are only 30,000 people living here – and only 2,000 of them are Spanish. De la Cueva whispered this when he first told Alfonso, because it's a dangerous truth, because some 28,000 Aztec are controlled by 2,000 men and sooner or later these 28,000 Aztec might work out that they can do something about that. But even if they did, Alfonso knows all they would win back is an empty shell. The Old World is gone, just like his own, and neither of them will ever come back. Maybe that's why the Aztec look so sad all the time. It's why Alfonso does.

More changes are coming, even if Alfonso doesn't know it yet.

De la Cueva informs him that they will be travelling south tomorrow morning to San Lorenzo de la Casa Rojo. They will not return to Ciudad de México for many months, maybe a year or more, not until the conquistador in charge there – a man who thinks he's a bad-ass like Cortés, but really only embodies Cortés's worst qualities, especially the greed and barbarism – is put in his place and the tax books are sorted. San Lorenzo is inside the Maya Empire, on the edge of some vast jungle where the Maya are putting up a better fight than the Aztec did.

The journey will be very dangerous. De la Cueva insists they attend Mass to prepare, to put their lives in God's merciful hands, and so Alfonso goes with him as he has before because his whole life now is a show for these people – a show he puts on so he's not beaten or whipped or both, which de la Cueva doesn't believe in, but his wife does. Once, the poison-tongued whore threatened to have the cooks serve him only human flesh. Alfonso knew it was possible, too. Aztec who refuse to convert or are caught worshipping their old gods, or even sheltering the pagans who still do, are burnt alive, then their bodies are sold to butchers who, in turn, sell the meat as dog food. In other words, being a Muslim here is not the kind of thing one makes a big deal about. Cristo Jesús, your loyal disciple Alfonso will follow you anywhere as long as you keep him alive a little bit longer, hallelujah and all that – are we cool, mate?

Forty-eight days and thousands of insect bites later, de la Cueva's train of wagons, horses, and men set up camp less than ten miles from San Lorenzo de la Casa Rojo. In what one of the soldiers with them declares an act of divine intervention, none of them have been killed by savages, disease, or nature. *Yet.* De la Cueva gives thanks God and orders an extra cup of wine with supper for everybody. He even offers a cup to Alfonso. Alfonso drinks the red-blue stuff. It tastes okay, a bit like iron, but doesn't live up to the hype.

And then, the attack comes. It happens after everybody except the soldiers on guard are asleep. Alfonso wakes, still drunk, and watches slack-jawed as one of the soldiers runs silently past, choking on the arrow protruding from his throat, and collapses into the smouldering fire. Screams follow, but only from the Spaniards and their servants and slaves. The Aztec with them die all the same because the Maya hate Aztec, too. It's a bloody massacre.

Alfonso must make a decision. Stay and die or run and probably still die.

Two Maya, dressed in very little and covered in mud to camouflage themselves in the dark, drag de la Cueva from his wagon, kicking and screeching and calling down the wrath of God, and club his head until it pops open like a melon and brains spill out like jelly.

Alfonso runs for it. Into the jungle, into the darkness, and doesn't stop running until he realizes he can't hear the screams any more. He slows and stops then, and strains to listen through the jungle sound around him. But nothing.

Something whistles past his ear, so close he feels the air move at its passing. Another arrow plunges into the tree beside him.

Alfonso runs again, but trips almost right away, and pitches forward. His body slaps against wet earth, and he rolls and slides down a muddy slope that comes apart and follows him, his limbs spinning around him as he bounces and lands with loud grunts. Suddenly, the trees and thick undergrowth disappear and the sky is there instead, filled with stars just like last time, so many stars, and he's still falling, falling, until his body crashes into dark water that swallows him whole.

Gracie

Tucson 1962

Bobby quickly sidles past her as he enters the motel room, hurrying to reach the window where he can surveil the parking lot outside from behind the curtain. As soon as he's satisfied he hasn't been followed, he tells her to lock the door and she does. She notices his hair is a mess and hangs down over his brow as if he ran here. Sweat beads off his nose. Something is wrong, she's sure of it. 'What's happened?' Gracie asks.

Bobby looks at her now. *Really* looks, like he hasn't done in days.

'*What?*' she says.

He recrosses the room in three quick steps, grabs Gracie's face with his hands – his powerful fingers slip into the tangles of her still-damp hair – and presses his lips against hers as if his life depends upon it. The kiss is firm and yet full of tenderness, and draws out and out as his tongue slides into her mouth and finds hers. He tastes like curry and coffee, but also bubblegum to mask the earthy spiciness. He tastes like Heaven if Heaven was real.

One of his hands slides down her face, fingers raking gentle lines across her cheek and chin and then the skin of her arm until, at her elbow, the hand thrusts between arm and waist and takes her by the small of that back so that their bodies collide like two planets and it feels like something inside her explodes.

Bobby suddenly steps back, smiling at Gracie. She immediately misses his lips, the taste of his mouth, his hands on her body. 'You know how long I've wanted you to do that?' she says.

'I should have done it a long time ago,' he says.

'Yeah.'

'I should have every time I saw you,' he says. 'When I think about all the moments I wasted, all the time we could have had together.'

'There's still time.'

At these words, Bobby and Gracie fall onto her bed. She wants to surrender to the passion of the moment, let him take her quickly and commandingly, but she has enough sense left to know that can't be how her first time goes. She uses her hands to slow him down, pressing them against the firm muscles of his stomach and his determined hips, and he understands and takes his time instead, sliding her pants down over her legs as he kisses her naked thighs. He doesn't need any help removing the shirt of his that she's wearing, but her bra confuses him, so she helps him. He enters her slowly then, tentative enough in his careful movements that she begins to suspect it might be his first time, too, and then he winces at how her face pinches when he tears her hymen. He apologizes too profusely until she draws him into a kiss, a kiss that drowns out her pain, and they make love until she cries and his body trembles and, instead of groaning like she does, he says, 'You're a miracle in every way, Grace Pulansky. I love you.'

Gracie feels tears running down her cheeks. 'I love you, too,' she says. Bobby dresses after that, which confuses her. He hasn't looked at her since he told her how he felt about her. 'Is something wrong?'

'I've got to go,' he says.

She watches him for a moment, dumb from both what they just shared and what is happening right now despite that. Finally, she manages to summon the word 'Why?' from someplace deep inside her throat.

He is dressed now, and turns to face her again at last. The look on his face . . . it's like he's forgotten what love means. He's turned something off inside. 'I don't know what will happen, how this will turn out,' he says, making no sense at all. 'I only know I had to see you one more time. What I'm trying to do, it could bring everything crashing down. You should know why. You should know the reason why I'm doing this is—'

A key begins to scrape around inside the room's door.

Gracie startles. He holds out a hand as if to reassure her, but it's really to keep her back, to put himself between her and the door. 'It's okay,' he says.

The door swings open, and Bobby enters.

A *different* Bobby.

Gracie looks at the Bobby she just made love to, and only now realizes he isn't wearing the same clothes he was when he left earlier in the evening. Bobby, the one standing in the doorway, gobsmacked by the face staring back at him, by *his own face*, is wearing the clothes he should be.

The Bobby she made love to moves away from her, putting some distance between them.

The Bobby in the doorway steps inside, throwing the door shut behind him.

The two Bobbys stare each other down like Old West gunfighters now, glowering with murderous intent, serious because this is obviously very, very serious, but all Gracie can do is laugh.

Keisha

Los Angeles 2017

'Next question,' the moderator announces to the audience before passing the microphone back to her. He's a writer for some website she's never heard of, wholly unqualified for this volunteer gig, and probably – judging by his confused reaction to the Tarkovsky reference in her last response – the one he gets paid for. She scans the theatre, which is about half full, a surprisingly good turnout for a short film at a festival she didn't even know existed until four months ago, but spots no raised hands. She's been asked two questions so far at this post-screening Q&A, one about how she managed to finance such an FX-heavy debut and the other by Janet, which doesn't really count. The people here – a mix of friends like Janet and her new wife, festival pass holders who probably wandered into the wrong theatre, and stragglers pulled in off the street to fill seats – seem to have enjoyed what they witnessed on the screen, twenty-two minutes of Keisha's proverbial blood and sweat and tears mixed up with some very expensive CGI, but just not enough to raise a hand.

'There,' the moderator says with some relief. A waving hand has finally appeared. 'Against the wall, right there – yeah, you – thank you.'

A festival assistant runs a microphone over to a brother standing beneath the exit sign. This brother is dressed in candy-apple red chucks, three-hundred-buck jeans, and, half hidden by a Hugo Boss blazer, a vintage 1970s Damien Syco tour shirt from West Germany. 'So, uh, what inspired you to write your film?' he asks.

Keisha's first thought is don't cry, bitch, don't you dare cry, 'cause she hasn't seen him in three years and, even though she's never actually cried in this body and couldn't in the other one, she feels like she might. Three years ago, when she saw him last, he was already dating *her*. He already looked happy again. Without Keisha. And now he's back, right there, no warning, *fuck*.

'What inspired me to write it?' she says, repeating Tab's question like it only vaguely makes sense to her. She's stalling, which makes her feel dumb and uncomfortable, which she knows he's enjoying every minute of.

'Yeah,' he says, grinning. Not just with his mouth, but his whole goddamn face. He's as happy to see her as she is him, except he's been here for the past twenty minutes, watching her, wrapping his brain around seeing her again, so fuck him for being so fucking cool about this. 'I love the ideas you put on the screen, especially the questions, the ones about reality. What we *call* reality, I should say. Have you read Barthes? Or *Baudrillard*? I bet you'd dig him.'

'I have. A good friend turned me on to them both. A lot of other existentialists, too.'

'Sounds like you paid attention.'

'Oh, it changed my life,' Keisha says. She realizes the moderator and the audience have no idea what's happening here, and chuckles to herself 'cause holy shit this is surreal. 'Sorry, everybody. This here, this is Talbert Whittaker, one of the hottest screenwriters working in Hollywood today. You've seen *Arabian Knights*, haven't you?'

Heads swivel towards Tab, many of them smiling, and there's even an audible *ooh*. Janet looks at Keisha instead, unable to hide her *oh shit* face 'cause she knows what's up.

'Aht aht, don't make this about *me*,' he says, casually hugging himself as he watches her. But it's not casual. It's staged. He hates being the centre of attention, even though it's all he's ever wanted. 'I came here to see you. This is *your* day.'

'Then what do you want me to talk about?'

'I want you to answer my question.'

Keisha shakes her head at Tab, telling him with her eyes that she's going to fuck him up big time for this, and then she turns to the audience again. 'It's like that Damien Syco song,' she says. 'You know the one, right? "Showtime at the Jupiter Theatre?"' There are murmurs of approval from some in the crowd, and so she begins to sing, '*The world is the lie . . .*' with what is a shaky voice at best. Tab and four people in the audience, three dudes and Janet, finish the next line with her: '. . . *we tell ourselves to survive.*'

Tab gives her some quick applause. The audience helps him out.

'I try to get those lyrics out of my head, but I can't,' she says, continuing. 'I want to believe this is real, that all of this is, but it's not getting any easier. We just elected a reality star to the White House, know what I'm saying? I spoke with a pastor once, while researching. He thought the world was going to end, like, yesterday, but that was okay 'cause he also thought all of us here are in Purgatory. That we already left the world of the living behind, and this is just some sort of waiting room for Heaven or Hell or whatever comes next. Last year, I was at a party and somebody brought along this physics chick, one of those braniacs you always see popping up in documentaries and the coolest TED Talks, and she started going on about how reality is probably a series of dimensions in which every possible outcome of every possible event creates another dimension, another *you* – right? – and every possible outcome there does the same thing, infinitely, until there's an infinite number of different versions of you out there and, if that's the case, who are you really and, you know, are you really even you or even special in any way since there's an uncountable number of you out there anyway, probably doing way doper shit than you are, too? Maybe even doper shit some-place where this motherfucker isn't president, right? So how do we survive knowing that? How do we, like, mentally endure the insanity and unknowable enormity of existence? We tell ourselves *lies*, right? Like Syco says, we tell ourselves whatever we've got to to get by. That's what the film's about, *that's* what inspired it.'

The audience greets Keisha with unnerving silence, 'cause she's gone off on an existential rant that triggers flashbacks for her, to her first days and weeks and months with Tab when she found him unbearably pretentious and, holy shit, until this very moment she hadn't realized she's become every bit as bad. These people are going to go home and drug themselves with some TV starring fake-ass people living worry-free fake-ass lives, and all this talk about what reality really is – which she could explain if they truly wanted to know, which she once explained to Tab on the kitchen floor of his tiny apartment back when everything between them was still new and full of possibility – will be forgotten so they don't drown in it like quicksand.

'I think that's a good place to say good night,' the moderator says, rescuing her. He takes the microphone back from her and addresses the audience. 'A round of applause for Keisha LeChance for coming tonight.' The audience claps with modest enthusiasm, which makes her die a little bit inside. 'The programme will start again tomorrow morning at 9.30 a.m. There will be coffee served in the lobby and I think some sort of croissants and doughnuts, but don't hold me to that. I get the feeling the organizers are kind of making this up as they go along.'

When Keisha looks back at Tab, he's gone. She quickly hugs Janet and her wife and a few other friends who came to support her, shakes hands with some guests and answers the questions some narcissistic white dudes couldn't be bothered to ask during the Q&A but are really just excuses for them to talk about themselves, and then hurries into the lobby. She finds Tab there, chatting with what looks like half of her audience about *Arabian Knights*, its superior sequel, its scheduled threequel they're already calling a reboot, as well as reboots of *The Gunmen*, *Ice Pirates*, and – quite intriguingly 'cause she unabashedly loves the crazy-ass original – *Krull* he's been hired to write and the half-dozen other projects (all reboots and comic-book adaptations, and sometimes both, that the trades have announced in the past couple of years). He enjoys it, the celebrity, the attention it brings even as he rejects it, and she's not surprised 'cause insecurity craves affirmation and Tab was always one insecure motherfucker.

'Oh, there she is!' he says, holding out his hand for hers. 'I have to go now, everybody. I need to tell Ms LeChance here how brilliant she is.'

At the valet stand, they stand side by side, but don't speak. Neither knows how to start, to *really* start. His brand-new black Turing Model 3 surprises her when it brakes at the kerb, all futuristic lines and space-age badassery. 'I thought about getting a Prius, but they seem so ostentatious,' he says with a straight face. It's only when Keisha looks at him, confused by how the success has apparently changed him, that he grins with the corner of his mouth. 'Get in.'

'I'm hungry,' she says.

'You're always hungry.'

'Let's walk,' she says.

'You trippin'. Nobody walks in LA.'

'Well, I feel like walking,' she says.

Tab hands his keys back to the valet attendant, who overheard the conversation and is smiling politely. 'Apparently, we're going to walk,' he says. 'Hopefully I still remember how. Don't worry if you have to charge me again for reparking it.'

North Doheny Dr is pretty quiet now that rush hour has passed. The palm trees rise on either side of the street like tropical guests along a dark parade route. And still, neither Keisha nor Tab know how to begin.

'What's good?' he asks finally.

She sighs inwardly, relieved they can just get to talking, so this stops being so fucking weird. 'Well, you know,' she says.

'Cool.'

'You?'

'You know.'

'Cool.'

'It's . . . it's really good seeing you, Keish.'

'Yeah, same. A surprise.'

'Bad surprise?'

'Nah, I don't think so.'

The silence returns for a block, until they reached Beverly. Then Tab says, 'I wasn't lying back there. What I saw up on that screen, you're *brilliant*.'

'You really dug it?' Keisha says.

'Oh, look who the insecure one is now,' he says, and gives her elbow a playful smack. 'Yeah, girl, I did. I really enjoyed it. It brought back a lot of memories, but once I got past that, past, you know, *us*—' He interrupts himself, sensing a danger zone ahead. 'It's stupid good, Keish. I've never seen anything you directed before.'

'I hadn't directed anything before, that's why,' she says.

'I know. *I know*! Why weren't you directing before? You're sooooo good at it!' He's laughing, excited for her, excited for the future she's going to have, and it makes her feel better than she's felt in a very long time. 'What I want to know is how you got the money to shoot that. It looks like a million bucks.'

'It should. It cost that much. Actually, a bit more after post wrapped.'

Tab stops her in front of the Bristol Farms. 'Wait, *what*?' he says.

'Yeah.'

'*Yeah*?' he says, 'cause he thinks she sounds naively ridiculous. 'Bullshit. Who gave you a million dollars to shoot a twenty-minute short film?'

'Twenty-*two* minutes. And it was a fellowship grant, some diversity initiative World Enterprises put together to make themselves look good.'

They start to walk again. 'I need to apply for this grant,' he says, laughing.

'I only did on a whim. Got a phone call about a month later. And here we are.'

'Shit,' he says. 'Don't be advertising that, or else everybody else in town's going to want to get some of that money, too, next time it comes around – including me.'

Keisha can see the swirl of Santa Monica Blvd's colourful lights up ahead. She looks at a Spanish duplex, then at the way the sidewalk rises and dips 'cause of tree roots, then at a homeless dude pissing on a stone fence, then at Tab again. 'You're not fucking with me?' she says. 'You really liked it?'

'Of course I did,' he says, smiling reassuringly with his mouth and his eyebrows, especially the one on the left that rises, like, a tenth of an inch to simultaneously say, 'Of course I did, fool.'

But she knows this smile, has experienced it many times, and suddenly his enthusiasm makes a lot more sense. He's a shitty liar who oversells his lies 'cause he's paranoid about being caught, and he knows she knows he's a shitty liar, and that means the asshole wanted her to catch him 'cause he didn't have the balls to just tell her the truth outright.

'Liar,' Keisha says. 'You fucking liar. You hated it.'

'What?' Tab says. 'No, no, I didn't.'

'Lie to me again, I dare you,' she says.

He is quiet for a long moment. He kicks a dead palm frond out of their way. 'Okay, okay,' he says. 'But it's not like you think.'

They reach Santa Monica, and are immediately assaulted by lights and exhaust and honking cars and screaming gays stumbling drunkenly down the sidewalk on their way to and from and in between neon-covered clubs. Keisha stops here, surrounded by this beautiful, hideous chaos, and glares daggers at Tab.

'It's just . . .' he says, trying to begin. 'You know, I just . . . I loved it, *I did*, but . . . God, this is hard. Listen, no joke, I sat in that theatre dumbstruck – *dumbstruck!* – by what you pulled off.

No joke. You are an *amazing* director. There isn't a person alive who loves movies, who could see what you did and not think they just saw the future. I mean that – *the future.*'

'*But*?' she says. 'There's a *but.*'

'Yeah, *me*,' he says. 'There was too much of me up there, Keish. Those ideas, they were mine.' Before she can take offence, he clarifies. 'They were *yours*, too. They were *ours*. They were all the hours we spent poring over the script, the story, talking about the world and what it's turning into, what others think it all means, what *we* think it means. Jesus, Keish, we had sex while watching a Baudrillard documentary on YouTube.'

Keisha remembers that night well, but pretends she doesn't, 'cause fuck him.

'What I mean is, you didn't make the story *yours*,' Tab says. 'It's *your* story now – *all* yours.'

'Only 'cause you split,' she says, and walks away from him.

Mimori

Earth orbit 2027

Her HUD says it has been ninety-three minutes, which means she and Sigmund are six minutes behind schedule. Both of them have been moving in slow motion today despite all the coffee. It feels like weeks since she slept at all. The pills make a valiant effort, but even they fall short on occasions when her thoughts grab onto what is happening. No, not *grab*. That word implies she understands what's happening, that it has a form, a name, something she can identify and grapple with. That she can fight it. But there's nothing to fight, and the sleep cycles up here grow more restless. 'That should be a good config,' Mimori says. 'How does it look to you?'

'Give us a moment, EV 1,' Miguel says in one of the boxes floating at the corner of her vision. He's the Ground IV on duty in Chihuahua.

Sigmund is looking at Earth, watching Hurricanes Lupita and Martha crash into each other off the east coast of America as Naomi prepares to tear across Florida from the Gulf side to join the party. They're calling it the *storm of the century*, but Mimori knows that's just the way the media has to sell these climatological acts of terror that the Earth now commits against an unwanted and toxic ape population on an almost weekly basis. Humankind's time here is running out; it's impossible to see something like this and not feel that way. She suspects Sōjirō does, too. She knows the girls do; she can see it on their faces just before they look away from the television screen when reality rears its ugly head in front of them. How carefully, one might even say maniacally, they make certain they never confront it, the nameless, formless thing, the thing that keeps Mimori from sleeping.

'Why is this taking so long, Miguel?' she says.

Commander Oliveira drifts back into his floating box. She hadn't realized she had left it. She's a serious woman, her thoughts generally inscrutable behind a gargoyle-like stoicism – a frustrating quality in the station's claustrophobic space – but Mimori can tell something is wrong immediately. 'You two need to return to Airlock IV,' she says.

'What is the matter?' Sigmund asks.

'The EV is cancelled. Both of you, get back in here.' Oliveira then adds, '*Please*,' which worries Mimori the most.

By the time Mimori and Sigmund are back inside and stripped down and Donatella opens the inner air lock door, Mimori knows this – whatever this is – is about her. She can see it in Donatella's eyes. Has she been crying? When Mimori asks why Donatella can't look at her, Donatella says, 'You must call your husband.'

The rest of the crew quietly retreat to other modules so Mimori can have privacy. She fastens her feet to the wall across from the computer that has been left ready for her. Its screen reads VIDCALL READY: ANDO SŌJIRŌ.

This is how she finds out her husband is not the one who is dead.

Sōjirō's face appears. At the sight of her, he spins away in his office desk chair. His body folds over. His face plunges into the heels of his hands.

Please, Mimori says to herself, please let it be my mother – her heart has been giving her no end of concern – let it be her, let it be her, let it fucking be her.

'Sōjirō, I need you to tell me what has happened,' she says, fighting to keep her voice calm. If she can anchor him with her strength, as she has always had to do, then he will find the words she does not want him to utter. 'Sōjirō, it will be all right.'

But it won't be, she knows that already.

Sōjirō wipes his nose with his sleeve. He takes two deep breaths. He looks at her again, his eyes red, his cheeks puffy. 'Tamami,' he says. It comes out like another breath. 'Tamami.'

Oh, my baby, Mimori cries out inside, my baby, my baby.

Sōjirō forces each word out until the momentum of them carries him along with them. 'The police came to the house this afternoon about . . . about two,' he says. 'Maybe a little later. Tamami had not reported to school. I was at the lecture, the one in the city' –

Why the fuck is he talking about lectures?

– 'the one I told you about – it does not matter except I did not pick up my phone when the school called to tell me. But there were . . . there were other girls who did not report either. Somebody found them all around midday. There were . . . there were nineteen of them, Mimori. *Nineteen* of them went to the mountain, and they . . . they . . .'

He starts to cry again.

'She killed herself, Mimori. Our little girl killed herself. They all did, all of them.'

Mimori has been crying since Sōjirō said Tamami didn't report to school. In her heart, she immediately knew what had happened. Week after week since the new year, suicide clubs have been reported across Nippon. Across the globe, but especially in Nippon, the United States, South Korea, China and Sweden, and India. Teenagers mostly, groups of them, collectively taking control of their lives in a world out of control. Collectively deciding death, the release of it, the freedom of it, must be better than *this*.

'It is after nine your time,' she says finally. 'How long have you known?' But she knows the answer already; he wanted to make certain it was her, he went to her first and held her hand and touched her face. He'll tell her about it all in greater detail when she's home, he'll cry as he does, and her body will shake as his does.

'I did not call you right away,' Sōjirō says, interrupting Mimori's keen sense of déjà vu. 'I had to . . . I had to see her, to make certain it was her. I did not want you to be up there, to tell you it might be her, to worry you like that if a mistake had been made.'

Mimori's hand covers her mouth. 'You *saw* her?' she says, exactly as she has before.

Sōjirō's face contorts, and his teeth clench as he tries to force back more tears.

'Was she okay?' she says, as if reading dialogue from a stage play.

He doesn't know what to say to this question.

She stops herself from asking, 'Did it . . . did it hurt?' because she knows it didn't. Instead, she says, 'It didn't hurt,' as much to reassure herself as him.

When the vidcall ends, Mimori is supposed to medicate and sleep, that's how this is supposed to go, somehow she knows that's how this is supposed to go. Instead, she returns to Airlock IV. The commander gets there in time to block the inner airlock door from closing with her hand, breaking two fingers in the process. She and Sigmund and José manage to wrestle Mimori back out of the airlock before Mimori can flush herself into space. The crew then sedate her for her own good, and as the world around her fades away with the hurt, Mimori gazes up through the cupola windows and realizes there are no stars outsi

Jones

Tucson 1962

Pilar refuses to tell him how she knows about Gracie, but she does it in a roundabout manner that doesn't require her to say so. Language is her gift, manipulating it as easily as evidence suggests she can do with reality. He'll only learn what she wants him to know if he's patient, if he plays along with whatever game she's playing with him right now. 'You really don't have to do this,' Jones says, pulling his right foot from her hands as she starts to remove it from the bath.

'I like to,' she says, casually snatching the foot back. 'Don't worry about the bill. It's on the house.'

He watches Pilar as she uses a thin white towel to pat his foot dry. Whatever this, this, this . . . *entity* is, she or it – more likely an *it* – has the ability to move between Earth models, crossing Perceived Time and space to do it. She – *it* – does this without coaxial terminals or CDE junctures, too. Even MasterControl can't do that. Which means the Ghost in the System is something more powerful than anything Jones wrote code for. And yet here it is, washing his feet like it's a Jewish prophet trying to make a point, and maybe, in a manner, it is.

'So,' Jones says, still watching her. 'Why am I here?'

'You tell me,' Pilar says. She's focused on drying the spaces between his toes now.

'You asked me to come,' he says.

'Yeah, but *you* chose to come,' she says. She tosses the towel aside, and begins to search through a nearby tray of tools for something. 'Why don't you tell me why *you* think you came?'

'I don't know if you read the newspapers much. But somebody blew up Pasadena City Hall a couple of days ago. A lot of people died.'

'Ah, found it!' She holds up a tiny file. 'I was in Pasadena once. Or maybe I will be. Honestly, it's difficult to keep track.'

Jones wonders what it must be like to find yourself unmoored from time. To have no sense of *being*. He was born Outside, he knows what the System really is, but even he is uneasy at the thought of not being *of* a time and place. Nineteen sixty-two in the United States of America is who he is now. Who – or *what* – does Pilar think she is? Could she have been human once? If so, is she still human? Does she even care about such corporeal illusions?

'I need to know who did it,' he says too impatiently, anxious to prevent her linguistical agility from steering the conversation any further. 'Was it the Bug? I know he or she – *whatever it is* – came to see you. Did the Bug do it?'

'Do what?' Pilar says, gently attacking and removing his thin cuticles.

'Who blew up Pasadena City Hall?' he asks.

'Oh, yeah,' she says, as if just remembering what they're talking about. '*Nobody*. None of this is real, *mi cariño*. Don't tell me you haven't thought that at least a dozen times since you sat down. It's all over your face what you think of this place.'

Jones stares for a moment, trying to keep his frustration in check. 'What are you saying?' he says.

'*No comprendes inglés* too well, eh? *Nobody* blew up this building you're worried about. You can't blow up something that doesn't exist.'

'Then what blew up?' he says. 'I mean, *something* blew up.'

'As my mother used to say, quite the pickle, isn't it?'

'You're being glib about my life,' he says.

'Oh, *now* it's a life.'

Jones slowly pushes air out through his nose. 'The thing is,' he says, 'the thing is people think something called Pasadena City Hall blew up. Now MasterControl thinks I did it, too.'

Pilar sets aside her cuticle file, and moves onto buffing his toenails. 'Well,' she says. 'Did you?'

'I was told to come here because *you* had the answers,' he says.

'I don't really do the answer thing,' she says.

'Well, that's what I need.'

'I used to think the same thing.' She smiles sympathetically. 'Then I got over it.'

Jones squeezes his armrests, the teal vinyl grousing loudly at the maltreatment. He's way past frustrated now. 'Okay,' he says. 'Explain the goddamn conundrum.'

'I could, but that would be an answer, too,' Pilar says. 'This might tickle, but it's just an exfoliator.'

'I don't care – and you've already answered some of my questions.'

'I think *you think* I did.' She begins to rub a thin cream into the bottom of his foot, along and between his toes, working it into his skin as fingers massage his muscles there.

'So, did somebody blow up Pasadena City Hall or not?'

She considers that, letting her head lean to one side. Loose strands of her hair fall across her eyes. 'What do you think?'

'I think I may have blown it up and I don't remember doing it, because somebody erased my memories of it.'

She shrugs. 'Okay.'

'Just *okay*? I sound deranged.'

'*Sí*, yeah, I'd say.'

'I don't understand,' Jones says.

Pilar puts his foot in the tub of water, to rinse it. 'I'm saying, that's *one* possibility,' she says. '*Another* possibility is, you didn't do it and this so-called Bug did. And yet *another* is, Pasadena City Hall – is that what you called it? – another is, it never even existed and so all you or somebody else did was help it fulfil its destiny.'

'Destiny isn't real,' he says. 'It's an idea that evolved out of human mythology, but has no basis in the System's programming.'

'And yet I am exactly where I was always going to wind up,' she says, 'sitting here, massaging your foot, talking to you again.'

'*Again?*'

'Hm?'

'You said *again*.'

'English isn't my first language.'

'You use it better than anybody I've ever met.'

Pilar removes his foot, and sets it on a new towel that she uses to gently dry it. 'Everything that *is* already happened, everything that *will be* is already past, everything that *was* will happen again,' she says. She holds her hands out, as if this explains everything. 'It's the Wheel of Time, *mi cariño*.'

This time, Jones knows what she's talking about. Or at least thinks he does. 'I could explain to you how that works, if you want to understand it,' he says. 'In a technical sense.'

'No, you couldn't,' she says.

'I built this place. I wrote the code – the, the law – that re-cycles the models and makes the System work.'

She sets his foot on his chair's vacant foot rest, and straightens her back. Her spine crackles like popcorn kernels in a pan, and she looks immediately relieved. 'So, I make a mean bhindi masala.'

'What?' Jones says. 'What does that have to do with anything?'

Pilar continues, ignoring him. 'I choose the ingredients with great care. Onions, okra, garlic, you get the picture. I cut them up, toss them in a pot, stir them just like my wife taught me. I wait until it's just right. But I couldn't tell you why these ingredients, when combined in this specific way, make my taste buds scream *hallelujah*. Making a thing isn't the same as understanding it, is my point.'

'In this case, it actually is,' he says.

'Then why are you so desperately lost wandering around your own intellectual genius?' she says.

Jones takes that on the chin. Pilar, the Ghost in the System, the most infuriating being he's ever met, knows how to keep you off balance and how to land her punches when she wants to. She philosophizes on the fly like Cassius Clay boxes, dancing about until you're dizzy and don't see the knock-out blow coming. But she also seems oblivious to what he's really up against, or rather overly confident that the danger he faces is so trivial. Her relationship to his reality is tenuous at best, it seems.

'Because somebody changed the rules,' he says forcefully. He's desperate, and needs her to know it. 'Somebody has tampered with the System. Somebody is sabotaging me!'

'What you're describing is life,' she says. 'And life, no matter what your little company's advertisements say, is hard here.'

'Which would only be true if any of this were real, and you've already said it isn't.'

'Says the man trying to prove he's innocent of a crime he can't remember if he committed or not. You know, you keep telling yourself none of this is really happening, like it will help. Personally, I think you're just too afraid to live. You're afraid of what it would mean, how it would change you if you let yourself fall in love with her.'

Jones hesitates. '*Her*?' he asks.

Pilar smiles pityingly. 'All evidence to the contrary, not the brightest bulb on the Christmas tree, are you?' she says. 'Yeah, *her*. Now, give me your other foot.'

Bill

North Atlantic Ocean 1997

The MIR- 2's spotlights track across the moon-like floor of the North Atlantic, revealing scattered blankets of fine china plates peeking out of silt, snaking rivulets of unbroken magnums of champagne, a half-collapsed steamer trunk a ratfish is exploring with lethargic interest, and the cracked porcelain bowl of a First Class toilet. It's always startling, this peep into the past, and, even though he knows the human remains were long ago disappeared by the alien ecosystem down here, he still can't shake the constant feeling that a skeletal hand is about to jump out and try to grab him through the submersible's seven-inch-thick acrylic porthole. Bill blinks, trying to focus on what he's seeing. Fuck, he's tired. This is his twenty-fourth dive down here in twenty-six days and his body hurts from being crammed inside a frigid seven-foot sphere for ten hours a pop, a proverbial sardine, but he remains determined, driven by the possibility that just beyond the reach of the spotlights is something he's never seen before, something nobody has even seen before either – like the purser's safe for which the primary partner of this expedition has secretly promised to pay him five million bucks if he can find it.

The *Titanic* had a few purser's safes throughout the First and Second Classes, but only one of them really mattered. The one in Chief Purser Hugh McElroy's care. Yes, there was that one that was discovered back in '87, not long after the wreck was first located. It was opened live on TV as part of a much-promoted programme hosted by Peter Falk and contained some cash, some jewellery, but nothing that historians would care too much about. That's because it was a Second Class safe, not a First Class one, as was suggested to court viewers. No, McElroy's safe remains lost, a fortune in rare jewellery and bank notes contained inside it. This is what Bill is really after.

'Bill, I think I've got something here,' Bernie says from MIR- 1, his voice rattling out of the speakers. 'You need to see this.'

Anatoly steers the MIR- 2 back towards the stern section, floating over the debris field that there's zero chance will ever be properly surveyed and catalogued. It took 17,000 people to build the so-called *Ship of Dreams*, it was the Space Shuttle of the early twentieth century, so impossibly massive was the feat, and you don't exactly go to that kind of effort without filling your creation with every luxury and newfangled gadgetry you can. Consequently, there are hundreds of thousands of objects down here, millions probably, far too many to investigate in even ten lifetimes.

'It's right under us,' Bernie says over the radio. MIR- 1's lights appear first, like quavering stars in the dark, and then the submersible. The submersible is hovering above silt, just far enough off the seabed to keep from blowing any of it up.

'What is it?' Bill says, leaning forward so he can get a better look through the porthole. There's something down there, for sure. Something bigger than the average debris. Something either steel or iron, judging by the radiant orange tangles of coral-like rusticles that have formed around it and the rust rivers that appear to flow away from it. 'Looks about the right size, but . . .'

He doesn't want to get excited yet.

'Yeah, I know, the ocean plays tricks on you down here,' Bernie says. 'Could be a piece of the engine, could be a piece of the middle section—'

'Could be what we're looking for,' Hynes says, interrupting. He's in the MIR- 1 with Bernie and Dimitre.

'It looks not right,' Anatoly says in his clunky English, piloting MIR- 2 into a mirror position opposite MIR- 1. 'Came down hard.'

Everything of any real mass came down hard, Bill knows. Especially the *Titanic* herself. The clay down here is dense, the silt across it thin, and so the wreck slammed into it like a hand on a countertop instead of a mattress. If that's the missing purser's safe out there, who's to say how it impacted? A lot of angles would have broken it open like an egg. No telling what its integrity is like, especially after eight decades at these crushing depths and being picked apart by oxidization and bacteria and fungi that feed on iron.

'What do you want to do?' Bernie asks.

'Well, I didn't come here to take pictures,' Bill says. 'Let's see if we can get a better look at it.'

It takes a few minutes for Vadim to get the manipulator arms ready. The two of them unfurl like giant metal insect arms from beneath MIR- 2, then swivel and wave, going through the checks before they move in. When they're set, Anatoly eases MIR- 2 forward as Bernie and Hynes offer external direction from their points of view. The object in question, the potential safe, doesn't move when it's first probed, but it does seem intact. Structurally solid.

'All right, let's roll up our sleeves,' Bill says.

Vadim gets to work, directing Anatoly on how to apply the strength of MIR- 2. The object is submerged in clay, but not substantially so. After seventeen minutes of experimenting with angles, exploratory pushes and tugs, a weak point is finally identified. Anatoly comes in from above, positioning the rectangular object below it between one and seven o'clock, and gently pulls with both manipulator arms. The object lifts, then slams back down. Silt blows up in a cloud.

'We will have to . . . free,' Vadim says, gesticulating.

'He means *rock it*,' Bernie says, translating for Vadim.

And that's what they do for another three hours, until they're almost out of time. It takes much less effort to get the object into the artefact basket. By this point, they're all convinced it's the missing safe.

'Are you sure you'll be able to get back to the surface carrying this thing?' Bernie says.

'Yeah, yeah, of course,' Bill says, throwing the two Russians in MIR- 2 with him his most roguish smile. This smile is why he's been a featured treasure hunter on so many science and history specials. 'We'll be fine.'

Bill is lying. He has no idea. But five million dollars is enough money to get out from under the debt the divorce put him in and get his boy back into the private school that can properly deal with his condition.

Turns out, there's nothing to worry about. Almost four hours later, Bill, Anatoly, and Vadim are back on the deck of the *Akademik Mstislav Keldysh* and MIR- 1's crew will shortly join them. It's raining and reports are it's going to get much worse, which means there's a ticking clock here. The ship's hydraulic arms lift MIR- 2 over the deck next, and lower it into its cradle. Bill climbs up to look at the basket, to peer at the object as rain splatters across its rusted surface. There it is, the White Star logo, stamped into a gold plate and still affixed to the safe's door.

'We've got it!' Bill says, shouting. Whoops and shouted *yeahs* and applause rise around him like the seas. 'Let's get it inside before this storm hits us.'

The storm lasts two days. Waves reach thirty feet, throwing the *Keldysh* around like she's a small fishing boat. The deck is pummelled with salt water and rain and gale winds, and the MIRs swing like pendulums out of time from their support arms. Most of the passengers, even the crew who have spent years of their lives at sea, blow chunks at least once. Bill spends much of it with a research assistant named Denise, drinking Russian vodka and trying to screw as the ship cants and slams down into deep troughs before rising up to do it all over again. There are a few accidents – at one point, Bill even falls off his cot and hits his head on the sink – but, all in all, it turns out to be a very satisfying way to celebrate making five million dollars.

A few hours after the storm clears, everybody ventures out onto the *Keldysh*'s deck to appreciate the fresh air and a horizon not violently see-sawing around them. It's midday, and Hynes cups one of his gigantic hands over his eyes. 'Is that . . . a *helicopter*?'

The Super Stallion touches down on the helideck a few minutes later like an immense, sighing monster. Three engines, seven rotors, it is a beast. Bill has never seen one in private use before. But, of course, this is how a billionaire would arrive in the middle of the North Atlantic.

Sergio Harkavy drops to the helideck, keeping his head down as he hurries to the stairs down to the deck. It's not necessary, as he's notably very short. He's followed by a man and a woman, both carrying briefcases. They all wear expensive shoes, the woman heels, but at least they put on heavy raincoats before alighting.

'Mr Harkavy, it's good to meet you,' Bill says. 'You know, *in person*.'

It's been more than twenty years since Harkavy and two friends transformed the computer industry in the garage of his parents' Los Altos home, but he doesn't look much older than the photos Bill remembers seeing of him from back then when the World Enterprises co-founder was just a twenty-two-year-old Harvard dropout. His story is the American Dream to the degree that every news article about him says as much. This is why Bill and everybody else here knows Harkavy is the son of Mexican immigrants to the States, one of Mexican descent and the other the son of Holocaust survivors. The Jewish grandparents were from Minsk and somehow survived the *Holocaust by Bullets* as it's now known. When the Nazis invaded the Soviet Union, they killed up to a million and a half million Jews. No concentration camps, just firing squads. Harkavy exists, as he often says in interviews, by historical happenstance. Tragedy gave the world the personal computer, and then the personal computer rewrote the story of the twentieth century. Harkavy sometimes jokes in interviews that it rewrote the twentieth century's code.

'Where is it, Mr Horncastle?' Harkavy says.

Bill, Bernie, the two members of the archaeology team, and Denise lead Harkavy and his associates below deck to the preservation lab where the safe has been secured and stored inside a large plastic case. On the way, Denise asks Bill, 'Is he really worth thirty-six billion dollars?'

'That's what everybody says,' Bill says.

Denise looks impressed. 'Do you think he'll care that I'm married?'

He looks at her left hand, eyes goggling noticeably at her ring. 'You're *married*?'

'The whole trip, yeah. You're only just noticing the ring now?' She shakes her head. 'Wow, Billy, just *wow*.'

In the preservation lab, Bill shows Harkavy the safe. 'You've done well, Mr Horncastle,' Harkavy says. 'Now I want you to open it.'

'That's going to be a problem,' Bernie says. Harkavy looks at him, confused about why he's speaking. 'It's rusted shut. If we crack it open, we could ruin the safe. X-ray's the only way for now.'

Harkavy turns to Bill. 'Who is this man?'

'My number two,' Bill says.

One of the archaeologists, Jacques, nervously raises a hand. 'Bernie's right,' he says. 'The safe is a historical artefact. We must protect it.'

Harkavy glances at the woman who accompanied him here. She's in her mid-forties, dark hair punctuated by a shock of ash-white, sharp features that her apparent discomfort with smiling makes worse. 'Everybody except Mr Horncastle, *out*,' she says with a German accent. '*Now*.'

The others don't understand.

'The parameters of this expedition were extremely clear, were they not, Mr Horncastle?' Harkavy says. 'I've provided enough funding to cover this expedition and three more like it. I could've just acquired the salvage rights for myself, you know. You assured me that wasn't necessary.'

Bill nods, understanding what's been intimated. He looks at the others. '*Out*,' he says. 'It's okay.'

'You can't let him do this,' Bernie says.

'Billy?' Denise says.

'This is bullshit,' Jacques says.

Harkavy's associates clear the lab, then they, too, leave. Bill and Harkavy remain.

'You know, if money isn't a big deal to you, you could throw an extra five million in and I wouldn't complain,' Bill says, smiling.

'I would have if you'd asked for it, man,' Harkavy says, his tone relaxing now that the others are gone. 'You're a terrible negotiator.'

Bill looks down, chuckling to himself. His wife's lawyer told him the same thing when he rolled over to all of her demands. 'Yeah, well, what are you going to do?' he says. 'You should put on some gloves.'

He unlocks the plastic case then, and removes the safe's security straps. It stinks of salt water, though, to be fair, everything aboard the *Keldysh* does. The metal cutting saw makes short work of the rusted seams, and the door crashes to the deck with an anticlimactic thud as large chunks of it collapse and crumble into rust that scatter in blocks and gnarled sheets and tiny pebbles. The sludge that splashes out of the safe and across the ruins of the door carries with it coins and soggy bank notes, jewel-encrusted rings and bracelets and necklaces, and small cases that might hold more jewellery or, in one case, something bigger, such as a top hat – which makes no sense because what kind of a top hat goes in a safe.

'It's not mud,' Bill says, explaining. 'It's fire retardant, from inside the safe's walls. The pressure down there does something to it, turns it into that shit.'

Harkavy stands in the pool of sludge that's still expanding, creeping like lava, trying to reach the walls of the lab. His shoes are ruined, his pants, too. He doesn't seem bothered by this. 'There, that one,' he says, pointing at the top-hat box.

'Are you sure?'

'No, but it's the right size.'

Bill picks the box up with his gloved hands, and carries it to a lab table where he sets it in a tray of water. He rinses it off with a turkey baster, examining its edges as he does. The bottom is soft and pliable. It's easy enough to cut through it with an examination scalpel. Inside is more of the sludge. There's fabric, too, some kind of silk, maybe. It's too old and damaged to be sure on a cursory examination, though. 'I'm going to, well' – he makes a *stick my hands in there* movement – 'see what's inside.'

Harkavy leans forward, to peer inside the box as Bill's hands plunge into the sludge and maybe-silk. 'You know, I sometimes think my grandparents survived the war to make this moment here happen,' he says with theatrical solemnity. Like he's scripted this sacred moment in his mind and rehearsed it many times. 'People say I changed the world when my friends and I built our little computer, but it was always going to change. It's what it does. All the technologies I've invested in since then, all of the companies I've built up, the revolutions I've tried to start, none of them mean a thing next to what's in that box – if it's what I think it is.'

Bill has trouble believing Harkavy's professed humility, but, then again, it might be better not to try. He's been around a lot of rich people in his life, mostly since he started diving. There's always somebody with a unlimited bank account who wants to go to the bottom of the ocean for the bragging rights that come with it. They've all struck him as crazy in their own ways. Harkavy is no different. But if dealing with crazy is what it takes to get his head above water and get his son the help he needs, then bring it on, he can do crazy all day.

'I feel something,' he says. His fingers slip around something round but rough. About the size of a bowling ball, but nowhere near as heavy. He slowly works it out of the box, until the soup inside finally lets it go with a loud sucking noise. Sludge sloughs off its round surface in big chunks and oozing strands, but its impossible ornateness is immediately evident. The turkey baster makes it even more so, revealing an exquisite, jewel-encrusted decorative globe that Bill would say was made by the House of Fabergé if he didn't know better. The surface is a luminescent peacock green, and gold ridges, worked to look like rivers, course across its surface; the golden rivers collide with and divide against countless diamond and ruby and amethyst islands. 'Holy shit . . . is that?'

'The Eye of Shiva, yeah,' Harkavy says.

'It-It's beautiful.'

'*Indeed.* It won't open, so you'll need to use a hammer on it.'

Bill looks at Harkavy, confused. 'What?' he says.

'Use a hammer,' Harkavy says.

'No.'

'*Yes.*'

'I-I can't.'

'Fine, ten million dollars.'

Bill looks at the globe in his hands. It's priceless, no doubt. He digs a hammer out of one of the tool boxes, and swings it over and over until pieces of gold river and jewels fly away and then the shimmering green surface cracks like an egg. He drops the hammer, and sinks two fingers into the small Texas-shaped hole he's made. 'There's . . . I don't know what it is,' he says. 'Some kind of wire mesh.' He retrieves wire cutters from the tool box, and clips at copper wire until he can yank some of it out of the globe. '*Copper.*'

Harkavy doesn't seem surprised. 'It's a Faraday cage, or at least a crude approximation of one,' he says. 'It disrupts electromagnetic fields.'

Bill doesn't try to understand what Harkavy is talking about. He pushes his whole hand into the hole, and searches around with his fingers. There's something in there, rolling around. He catches it on the third try, and wraps his fingers around it. Jesus, it's cold. *Like ice*. He pulls his hand free, already swaying on his knees, and gapes in surprise at the sight of it. A simple black orb, unremarkable except its mirrored surface. Maybe made of onyx. He just destroyed a work of unparalleled art for this *thing*. 'What the hell is it?' he asks.

Harkavy's eyes have grown three sizes, hypnotized by the sight of the orb. He slowly reaches for it, a smile nervously tugging at the corner of his mouth. 'They called it the Devil's Mouth,' he says to Bill. 'There are reports of it over the course of a millennium, from Europe to Central Asia, all the way to Japan. It's impossible to say how much of it's true, but in 1840 the myths give way to facts. A Chinese war junk is attacked by British pirates during the First Opium War. The pirates find this in the Chinese captain's cabin. The captain refuses to surrender it, so he's executed. Afterwards, the Devil's Mouth is taken back to Calcutta where it's presented to the Governor-General of India, the 1st Earl of Wyndhamsea, who in short order becomes the 1st Duke of Wyndhamsea. His personal wealth quintuples during his tenure over the Supreme Council of Bengal, and that fortune quintuples again by the time his granddaughter Flossie Everleigh, the infamous Lady of Wyndhamsea – I'm sure you've heard of her? – by the time she's born in 1874. Her first and second marriages end in tragedy – murder, most assume. She's celebrating her third when she boards the *Titanic* with her deceased grandfather's most treasured possession.'

Bill yanks the orb back from Harkavy's reaching hand. He doesn't know why. He just knows he doesn't want to let it go.

'I do believe that belongs to me,' Harkavy says.

Bill considers the orb, peering into its infinite blackness, deeper and deeper until—

'*Mr Horncastle.*'

Bill forces himself to look at Harkavy. It takes all of his concentration to place the orb in the man's hand. As soon as he lets go of it, he feels . . . lighter. Thoughts of his ailing son return. 'Ten million dollars, right?'

Harkavy doesn't answer. He's gaping at the orb again, turning it over and over again in his hands, stroking it with his gloved fingertips. 'You asked what it is,' he says. He holds the orb up. 'This is how I'm *really* going to change the world, man.'

'Yeah, okay, sure,' Bill says, still trying to focus. He places one stiff arm against the lab table. 'But the ten million dollars, I'm going to need that in my personal account by the end of the day.'

Tuviah

Mount Clemens 1971

He watches her breath condense in the cold as they wait on the porch, and wonders if he still loves her and if he would even care if he didn't. Then the door opens, and Merel – who's been at this so long now she doesn't even miss a beat at the unexpected sight of the wheelchair – says, 'Good afternoon, Mr Schmidt. We're from the Friends of Historic Preservation, and we'd like to discuss the concerning state of Michigan's most beloved bath houses.' She came up with this identity on the drive here from their visit to Gitla's sisters in nearby Royal Oak, after reading about Mount Clemens's historic mineral baths and bath houses in a photo book they found on the sisters' coffee table, even though they had previously agreed on Tuviah's preferred insurance sales approach. He insisted they stick with the plan, but she had to have it her way. 'May we come in for a few minutes?'

Schmidt, who's eighty-two and sits slouched in his wheelchair, appraises them both with typical German scepticism, and shakes his head. 'Not interested,' he says, starting to shut the door.

This is always the risk when Merel uses untested identities like this one, her reasoning never being more than whim or whimsy or whatever the fuck you want to call it, and when she's wrong, they just force their way in like battering rams. 'What if I could offer you a free visit to the St Joseph's Sanitarium and Bath House in exchange for your support?' she says.

'Then it wouldn't be free,' Schmidt says. An alarm clock begins to rattle loudly somewhere inside the house behind him, momentarily distracting him.

'Please, it's cold out here and we've been knocking on doors all morning, and we haven't had much luck,' Merel says, smiling and blinking her big grey-green eyes beneath all that metallic blue eyeshadow she likes. At fifty-one, she's still stunning. There's no reason for that gunk on her face. 'Offer us some coffee. Let us at least give you our sales pitch, then you can say no thank you and send us on our merry way. What do you say?'

Schmidt notices her legs. 'Fine,' he says. 'But only if *he* waits outside.' He chuckles at the look on Tuviah's face. 'I am *joking*. Come, come inside.'

Tuviah and Merel follow him inside. He offers them seats on a plastic-covered sofa that crinkles and grouses loudly when they sit, and then rolls away – to get his medication, he explains. A moment later, the ringing alarm clock goes silent like a croaking frog getting its neck snapped.

'You have a lovely house,' Merel says, calling out. 'Are you married?'

'Not any more,' Schmidt says from the kitchen. 'She died last year. The cancer.'

'Oh, I'm so sorry.'

'You have a lovely accent,' he says.

'I was born in Holland. Have you been?'

'A long time ago,' he says. 'How long have you lived in America?'

'Oh, thirty years now, I think. No, thirty-one years. It's home. You, Mr . . . ?'

'Schmidt,' he says. 'Since the war.' Schmidt rolls back in, a tray balanced on his knees, and on top of it two mismatched coffee cups – one from Frankenmuth and the other Simon's Restaurant in Niagara Falls – and a tall metal carafe. 'What about you? You don't talk much.'

Tuviah typically speaks as little as he can when their work brings them to English-speaking countries, especially the States. His grasp of the language remains comically inadequate, and his accent when speaking it makes him sound like a Nazi buffoon from *Hogan's Heroes*. 'Holland, also,' he says.

'Where in Holland?' Schmidt says. He still hasn't poured coffee for his guests.

'Utrecht.'

'Ah, I enjoyed Utrecht very much,' Schmidt says, replying in perfect Dutch.

Tuviah and Merel say nothing.

'Did you grow up in the city, or outside it?' Schmidt says, again in his perfect Dutch.

Tuviah reaches into his coat. 'Fuck this,' he says.

But Schmidt is startlingly fast despite his age and apparent infirmity. The tray on his lap falls away, taking the empty coffee carafe and cups with it, and a German Luger begins to rise. Merel is faster than both of them, and squeezes off her shot first. The suppressor works as it's supposed to. Schmidt snaps backwards, grabbing his bloody shoulder, and his gun lands on the carpet with a muffled thud.

'You're getting old,' Merel says to Tuviah, a snaking ribbon of smoke rising from the muzzle of her gun and dissipating across her cool expression. His face says he knows how close he came to catching a bullet, how sloppy he was not anticipating that the tray was hiding a weapon. 'Let's not take all day. I want to try one of the mineral baths before our flight.'

'What gave us away?' Tuviah ask Schmidt in Dutch. His gun is resting on his knee.

'Your Dutch accent – oh fuck, this hurts – your Dutch accent is atrocious,' Schmidt says. 'And I know a Jew when I see one. *You*' – he points at Merel, who is leafing through a stack of beauty magazines Schmidt's wife must have left behind – '*not* a Jew. But this one' – he points at Tuviah – 'one of the lucky ones, no? How did you get out?'

'I didn't,' Tuviah says. 'Your name isn't Hermann Schmidt.'

'May I speak in German?' Schmidt says in German now. Tuviah nods, which puts a sparkle in the other man's eyes. 'I so rarely get to speak our mother tongue.'

Merel leans back, and begins to leaf casually through the pages of one of the magazines.

'My name is not Hermann Schmidt,' Schmidt says, agreeing. '*And?*'

'Your name is Günter Graf, you were a *Standartenführer* in the SS, and, from 1941 until Germany surrendered and a warrant was subsequently issued for your arrest, you were attached to Section VIII,' Tuviah says.

Schmidt – *Graf* – nods. He is satisfied at being unmasked, at being revealed at long last.

'You sent Jews to the death camps,' Merel says, never lifting her eyes from the article that she is reading on the ten best ways to please your husband. This is the part of their work that she hates. It's so boring, she says, because they already know the answers to the questions. She loathes the charade, which is how she describes it.

'Of course,' Graf says, answering her.

Merel creases the page she's reading along the magazine's spine. 'How many?' she says, and rips the page out so she can finish the article later.

'Oh, a few hundred, I imagine,' Graf says with no apparent remorse. 'More than some, fewer than others.'

'That's good enough for me,' Merel says in Dutch. She sets her magazine aside, and begins to lift her gun again.

'Not yet,' Tuviah says, pushing the gun away. 'We weren't just sent here to execute him.' He's surprised to see that Graf demonstrates no surprise or discernible concern at the news that he's been marked for death. He expected this day would arrive; either that, or he's just too old to give a fuck any more. 'Herr Graf, where is *Reinhold Gottschald?*'

Now Graf looks surprised. 'Ah, *that* is a name I have not heard in a very long time,' he says, a mix of difficult and wonderful memories rushing back and playing across his wizened face. 'Not since the war. You do not think him a Nazi, do you? He is a Jew, like you.'

'He worked for you,' Tuviah says.

'Not for, *with*,' Graf says. 'Tell me, what do you know about Bertrand Lambriquet?' Tuviah and Merel don't try to conceal their ignorance. 'That is good, that is good. Those who know his name tend to go mad. Reinhold certainly did. I did, too, for a while.' He chuckles uncertainly at this. 'Maybe I still am.'

'Where can we find him?' Tuviah says.

'*Why?*' Graf says. 'Surely your masters aren't wasting your considerable talents on locating a Jew who, at worst, stole some artwork from its rightful owners.'

But Tuviah never asked why. Back in '55, Israel's Mossad came calling. He and Merel had developed a reputation by then for tracking down Nazis who had gone to ground and then executing them with spectacular aplomb. The Schramm Brothers were perhaps their greatest triumph, even though very few knew they were responsible for what happened in Melbourne. The twins, who had terrorized Jews at two different camps, were tied to the back of a Holden ute by their ankles, like tin cans to the bumper of a newly married couple's car, and dragged over brick-paved and concrete streets for nearly five miles. The international press loved that, which pleased Merel to no end since it was her idea how to do it.

The Mossad didn't directly recruit Tuviah and Merel, but the agency has employed them from time to time as what you might call *freelance Nazi killers*. On occasion, they facilitate legal arrests, then leave others to deal with the extradition issues. On still others, they're more than willing to smuggle a Nazi onto a cargo plane or ship or, once, a rowboat to get them out of countries otherwise disinclined to surrender them. In Graf's case, nothing fancy is required. Just good old-fashioned *dead*. But they are expected to return to their contractors with a location for this Gottschald, that's part of the deal. Neither Tuviah nor Merel know anything about this artist – *Lambriquet*? – but if it helps them find the Nazi Jew traitor, all the better.

'I don't ask questions,' Tuviah says, answering Graf.

'Of course you do,' Graf says. 'You are a killer, but you do not kill just anybody. Only those who deserve it. *Like me*. Your questions are a ritual, the justification, no? The code you must follow to sleep at night. I had my own code, in my other life. These men you work for, they do not have a code. When you learn why they want Reinhold, you will understand this, too.'

'*Toby*,' Merel says. She uses his German name when she is impatient with him, or angry with him, or when she needs to hurt him.

'Ah, *Tobias*,' Graf says, one eyebrow rising into a peak of long silver hairs and flesh folds. 'It is a pleasure to make your acquaintance.'

'My name is Tuviah,' Tuviah says.

'Then I am not the only one who possesses two names,' Graf says in perfect Hebrew.

Merel sighs dramatically, and shoots Graf in his other shoulder.

Tuviah glares at her as Graf screams and grunts and tries to clench both wounds even though his arms don't want to co-operate. 'So, he's an *impressive* Nazi,' she says. 'I don't care. Finish the job, or I will.'

Graf is weeping now. He wants to talk, he doesn't even need to be asked again. 'When we got word the Führer had taken his own life, Reinhold and I boxed up Lambriquet's paintings,' he says in German, his words interrupted by panted grunts and violent wincing. 'We had found five of them by then. We put them on a truck, drove to the Black Sea, and loaded the crates onto a U-boat. Reinhold carried orders, orders that identified him as a German, a loyal member of the party, a vital part of the war effort that would continue even with the Führer gone. The crew were to take him and the crates to Genoa, where there was an Austrian bishop.'

'*Hudal*,' Tuviah says. Alois Hudal was a Catholic bishop who supplied new identities and Red Cross passports to Nazis en route to South America. Tuviah had more than once suggested to Merel they find the man and chop off his head with a blunt axe, but Merel was deeply uncomfortable with the thought of killing a *man of the cloth*. It's the only time he's heard her describe a line she wouldn't cross.

Graf answers Tuviah with a quick nod. 'It was the artwork that mattered, you see,' he says. He blinks away tears, paradoxically haunted and thrilled by memories of these paintings. 'It had to remain secret. Reinhold couldn't leave them, he was *obsessed*, and so I charged him with protecting them only because I couldn't bring myself to destroy them as I should have.'

'Where did Reinhold go?' Tuviah says. 'Where do I find him?'

'I tell you of a terrible secret that drives men insane, and you do not even think to ask me why?' Graf says, *tsking* like a grandfather who doesn't understand why his grandson doesn't care for peas or carrots or sauerkraut. 'The U-boat captain would know. *Manfred Eberstein*, that was his name. Find him, and he will tell you where Reinhold is – *if* he is still alive, of course.'

Tuviah gives Merel a nod. She rolls up her beauty magazine, rises with it in one hand and her gun in the other, and approaches Graf. Merel circles him slowly, like a predator stalking a wounded animal, as he tracks her from his wheeled prison. She's practically licking her chops.

'Do it already,' Graf says impatiently in English. He doesn't get the last word out in its entirety, because the grip of Merel's gun comes swinging around like a hammer into his mouth. It's remarkable how quickly the mouth can produce blood; it oozes between his broken and missing teeth and dribbles down his chin. She grabs Graf by the single tuft of his hair that remains, jerks his head back, and brings the rolled-up beauty magazine down into his screaming maw. Now she wraps both hands around the magazine, and pushes it down his throat, twisting it, hammering it with an open palm, tugging down on it with all her weight until Graf's neck is distended, twisted and misshapen from the magazine jammed deep into it.

Merel steps back from Graf's dead body. Its head tries to flop to the side at the neck, but the magazine sticking half out of it keeps it upright, its eyes locked on the ceiling. She has blood on her hands, on the sleeves of her coat, on her chin. Her face is flushed and her breathing makes it sound like she's just escaped a whole Panzer division on foot. Then, she reaches for the hem of her skirt, pulls it up as she marches towards Tuviah on the sofa, and climbs on top of him. She tears the pantyhose away from her pussy as she kisses him, Graf's blood smearing across his face, and he realizes with considerable horror that she's going to try to fuck him right here, with Graf's corpse right there, and his dick couldn't be limper if he walked in to find his mother masturbating with a parsnip. They've never done this before. Once, in Georgia, they fucked in the bedroom next to the ensuite bathroom where a dead Nazi sat in a tub of water along with a still-smoking toaster oven, but that was different, Tuviah tells himself, that was different.

'Get it up!' Merel says, yanking on his dick. Tuviah just sits there, speechless. She slaps him across the face. 'Get it up, goddamnit!'

Tuviah gets it up. They fuck until she's satisfied, but he never comes. He can't stop staring at Graf. She is staring, too, he realizes. She is, too, as she groans victoriously. She is, too.

Gracie

Tucson 1962

The two Bobbys stare each other down as she laughs, both of them as confused by the sound coming from her as she is. All she can do is shrug to explain herself, 'cause this – being confronted by doubles of the man you love, one of whom you just lost your virginity to – is easily the loopiest thing that has ever happened to her, and that's saying a lot 'cause earlier this evening she ran through a shootout between FBI agents and Indian revolutionaries and there were machine guns and explosives and a three-legged dog and she's pretty sure she saw somebody's brains. 'Sorry, I think somebody slipped me some LSD,' Gracie says.

'You have a decision to make,' the Bobby who said he loves her says to the other Bobby, the one who doesn't even remember her, standing across from him. 'You can chase me, you can try to ruin everything I'm trying to do here, you can get yourself deleted' – he indicates Gracie with a quick jerk of his chin – 'maybe her, too—'

'Deleted?' Gracie says, interrupting. 'What is that, some new *hood* speak? *I'm gonna rub you out, bub. I'm gonna* dee-lete *you.*'

'*Or?*' the other Bobby says, ignoring Gracie.

'*Or* you can take her somewhere safe and hide until this is over,' the Bobby who said he loves Gracie says.

'What would you do?' the other Bobby says.

The Bobby who said he loves Gracie sighs, 'cause he knows what's going to happen next. 'Exactly what you're going to do,' he says.

In an instant, the Bobby at the door is hurtling towards the other Bobby. The two of them crash into the dresser, overturning a lamp – one just like the one she carried to the door – and it rolls to the carpet, but doesn't shatter. The Bobby who said he loves Gracie pulls the other Bobby's jacket over his head, yanking hard so that its sleeves slide off the shoulders and pin his arms to his chest. The Bobby who said he loves Gracie then grabs the lamp from the floor, and swings it into the other Bobby's head. It shatters this time, and the other Bobby goes down.

'What have you done?' Gracie says, looking at the Bobby writhing slowly on the carpet.

The Bobby who said he loves her starts to say something, but he stops himself. His eyes rim with tears – he looks confused by an impossible situation, one with no happy ending – and instead he says, 'You're more real than anything I've ever known, I know it because I couldn't feel this if you weren't,' then bolts out of the motel room door.

Keisha

Los Angeles 2017

El Compadre, *their* place, is still almost an hour's walk away. They make it as far as Sunset Blvd and Doheny when she declares herself incapable of walking any more in these shoes, what the fuck was she thinking back at the theatre, and Tab laughs at her 'cause this was all her stupid idea. They settle for the Chateau Marmont, 'cause he can get them a table and she's never been despite having lived in LA for more than a decade. 'Guess I just don't know the right people,' Keisha says, laughing lightly.

They may not be at El Compadre's, but the margaritas arrive all the same and they keep coming, and she and Tab settle into a familiar rhythm that's only interrupted when he sees somebody he knows and must say hi or vice versa. It feels just like old times, even how they interrupt each other's jokes to tell better ones and, when their one-upmanship fails, how mercilessly they mock each other. By the time food comes, they're both adequately shit-faced.

'Listen, sorry about back there,' he says. 'About earlier, what I said. I didn't mean for it to come out like that.'

'I know,' she says. 'I know what you were trying to say, too. You think I don't know?'

'I want to see that film, girl, *I do*, but you have to finish it *your* way. Because the other way . . .' His face changes. 'I don't think I was the right person to write it with you.'

'What's this nonsense?'

'I just . . . I've accepted my limitations, Keish, that's all. For a long time, I thought I knew what kind of writer I wanted to be. I thought I could be him. But it turns out, I'm not him. I'm *me*, and *me* gets to write some fun shit.'

Keisha regards him dubiously; *side-eye*, as Tab would call it. 'Yeah, you mean regurgitating other people's ideas 'cause the studios are too fucking lazy to make something original?' she says.

'Yeah, I mean *regurgitating other people's ideas*,' he says, trying not to sound defensive. 'It's not like half the films I love weren't remakes or sequels anyways.'

'The other half of those films were made by French and Japanese and Russian directors whose names I can't even pronounce. Like, at all.'

He chuckles at that, his fourth margarita hovering in front of his face. 'Okay, it pays well. Is that what you want to hear?'

'Least it's honest,' Keisha says.

'Okay, *it pays well*,' Tab says. 'Don't hate the player, hate the game.'

She reaches for her margarita, her fifth, but stops. The ice has melted, leaving the cocktail less lustrous, but that's not it. 'That really why we came here?' she asks. *To Hollywood*, she means. 'To make bank?'

He signals the waitress two tables away for another margarita. 'Fuck, these are good,' he says, and slams the remainder of his ice. 'Have to stay hydrated, right?'

'You hold your liquor a lot better than you used to.'

'Don't be so sure about that. Are you still eating that?' He points at the mutilated remains of her salmon paillard, and scoops up her plate before she can answer, which would have been a *no* anyway. Then he looks at her, really looks at her. 'I know they don't mean anything, you know that, right?'

Keisha pretends not to understand.

'These movies they're churning out like cheap sausage,' Tab says.

'Nah, that's not true,' she says. And maybe she's not lying. But it feels like she is, all the same. 'A lot of them, they're really good.'

He gives her his own side-eye with a side of fuck off.

'Okay, *some* of them.'

He laughs at that. 'And that's the rub, isn't it? We've justified the surrender of an entire artistic medium to commercial interests for *some* movies, like maybe a handful each year, that will stand the test of time, know what I'm saying?'

'Why not write something better than them, then?'

'I did. I *have*, I mean. You know how many scripts I've held private funerals for, scripts I believed in? I've lit a fleet of Viking ships ablaze in their honour. But nobody gave a damn about them like I did. *Too ambitious. Too subversive. Too intelligent for their own good. Too this, too that.* Fuck that noise.'

Keisha finishes her margarita. 'Too *original*, you mean,' she says.

'Maybe, I don't know,' Tab says. 'But come on, if they were that good, they would've gotten made. That's what I was saying. That's what I mean – I've accepted my limitations.'

'You don't really believe that . . . do you?' she says.

He doesn't say one way or another. Instead, he says, 'It's the audience's fault, that's what I really think. I mean, maybe. Who knows? Look at everything that's getting made. It's cultural re-cycling, and audiences, they lap it up. They're all trapped by-by-by – I don't know – *nostalgia*? A moment in time that makes sense to them even though it was slapped together out of bullshit, too – they just don't know any better.'

'*Make America best again*,' Keisha says, but Tab is too drunk to catch how she's linked Presisident Glass's 2016 campaign slogan to his point about the state of American cinema. She signals for another margarita, but the waitress doesn't see her. 'They want something back that never really existed.'

'Yeah, they want *Leave It to Beaver*, right?' he says. 'And Don Johnson in pink suits and John Wayne killing savages – *pop-pop* – niggas in their place, and-and-and Norman Rockwell – fuck, Norman Rockwell is the fucking worst – they want it even if they don't know why, or what any of it means, because the fantasy – oh, the fantasy – it means they don't actually have to deal with what's happening out there in the real world. These people, they've fetishized the past, but, like, Disney World versions of it, and the rest of us, you, me, everybody else in this town, we've become slaves to their need for it. We've become their bullshit pushers.'

'*Bullshit pushers*, I like that,' she says. The waitress finally sees her waving hand.

'I worry they've forgotten how to think altogether, that that's how we got that fool in the White House,' he says, bringing it back unwittingly to her point. 'Maybe Hollywood is responsible. Maybe in the corporations' desperate attempts to make a billion dollars instead of just turn a profit, to sell something to everybody instead of just these people over here – who you know, *really* want what they're selling – they've diluted everything. They've stripped the meaning out of it all.'

'The simulacra.'

'You *did* pay attention.'

'Yeah, condescend much?'

He holds his hands up, almost over his head. 'You're right, sorry, but what's almost as bad as all of that, they've helped – I've done it, too – *we've* helped raise two, three generations of kids who can't think for themselves, who don't even know something is missing from the world around them—'

'They do – *they do*!' Keisha says. 'I volunteered during the campaign, and the kids out there, they know what's up.'

'Maybe . . . but do they have the language for it?' Tab says. 'We took it away from them, didn't we? They're missing something, and they don't know how to describe it. They don't know how to describe it. And that feeling can only be getting worse, know what I'm saying? Because if I feel this way, this confused *all* the time, how bad must it be for *them*? I mean, sometimes I think my thoughts aren't even my own any more. Fuck, everything he said was true, wasn't it?'

'Who?' she says.

'*Syco,*' he says. 'Come on.'

She has seen him like this before, these *funks*, as he calls them, but this one seems worse somehow. Bitter even, and he's not bitter. At least he wasn't before. He's changed. He might not know what this world really is, he might not know how close to the truth he got when he pitched his script idea to her all those years ago, but he feels its limits all the same, the pressures it exerts on his hopes and dreams, its demands on him to conform like everybody else and play the part assigned him, and she knows right then and there he will turn hard. That is what he will change into – *a hard man*. This world is going to break him if it hasn't already, and that breaks her heart.

'Okay, yeah,' Keisha says about Syco. 'But what are we supposed to do? They control everything.'

They. Their word for the many-faced beast that ruins everything good and beautiful.

'I don't know,' Tab says. 'Sometimes . . . sometimes I feel like Syco was holding it all together. Like the universe wanted to explode or implode or something and he held it together. His music, like glue. Maybe his music, maybe just him. Maybe that's what he was doing for us, holding reality together by sheer force of will and now that he's gone – look what's happened since he died.'

He looks away, wiping quickly at the corner of his eye with the tip of his finger.

'I'm sorry I didn't call when it happened,' Keisha says. She saw the news while this dude she'd been seeing was showering. She sat down on her couch and cried. She didn't know why at the time, but later she knew it was for Tab. She started to call him so many times over the next week. Text after text was composed. Emails, too. All aborted and deleted.

'Yeah, don't worry about it, I get it,' he says. 'It hit me hard. I know, it makes no sense, to be so fucked up by the death of a man I never knew. But it is what it is.' He looks at her, remembering something that makes his face change like the sun just came out. 'I was in London, you know. When it happened. There was this party taking place around where he grew up. Went on for three days. Most of us stayed the whole time. Time just kind of, like, stopped around us – at least that's what it felt like. Some timeless place where we were all connected, by him, his music, the lyrics we all knew by heart. It was the most amazing thing I've ever experienced, Keish.'

Tab sits back then, having finished Keisha's salmon paillard. She watches him, waiting, 'cause there's something else. Their next round of margaritas finally arrives and they thank the waitress, and when they're alone again he says it. 'She's pregnant.'

She feels sick. Her mouth refuses to work.

'I'm going to be a dad,' he says. He sounds confused about this. He tips back half of his margarita, hoping it will help him. 'I'm going to be a dad.' Then, 'I don't think I want to bring a kid into this world. Fuck, I *know* I don't.'

'Congratulations,' she says with some effort. She wants to mean it, especially since she knows how badly he always wanted kids, how she always knew she couldn't give him one, couldn't give him that chance to bring his father and mother and brother back to life in his own small way, but she suddenly feels empty inside. *Just empty.* As if somebody reached down her throat, scooped her insides out like she were a pumpkin, and left her hollow. 'I'm happy for you.'

Keisha's Lyft arrives not long after Tab picks up the cheque and they walk down the stairs and driveway to the road. On this walk, he tells her, 'Listen, just promise me you'll do it your way when you're given the chance. And if I can help you at all, if you want to use my name – say I'm a producer, whatever – if that helps you get the script read or the short seen, or if you want me to hook you up with my agents, just say the word, Keish, just say the word and it's done like that, hear me? *Like that.* Just don't ask me to write it with you.'

'*Write it with me,*' she says. She didn't intend to say this. It just happens, but she immediately knows she means it. 'Let's finish what we started.'

'I don't think that would be a good idea,' he says.

' 'Cause of her.'

Of course 'cause of her.

Tab gives her an awkward hug at the kerb, tells her it was great to see her, he even repeats that like she maybe didn't hear him, then gives her another hug that lingers too long. She waves to him as the Lyft driver pulls out and into a U-turn back towards Sunset, except Tab is standing there when the Lyft comes completely around, standing in the middle of the road. He walks to the car's back door as the driver bitches, opens it, and pulls her out.

'I don't want to say goodbye, Keish, okay?' he says, holding Keisha's hands like they're facing each other at an altar. 'I've tried, but I can't love her like I loved you. Like I *love* you. It's just not the same.'

'It's not supposed to be,' she says.

'But I want it to be.' He grabs her face and kisses her, and she leans into him, letting it happen, letting herself believe this might be real. 'I was going to leave anyways, Keish, I was, but then she got pregnant and I didn't know what to do. But you're *here*, you're here, and I know this is what I want, *this* is where I'm supposed to be, and it's not fair to do this to her, it's not, letting her think I love her more than I do just because the alternative will hurt.' He kisses her again, like a punctuation mark on his point. 'I just want things to be the way they were.'

'This is a lot,' Keisha says, nodding slowly.

'I know,' Tab says.

'I mean, *a lot*,' she says.

'I know,' he says. 'I'm going to go home and tell her, okay? I'm going to tell her tonight, and I'll call you tomorrow morning. That cool?'

Tab is asking her for permission. He's asking Keisha for permission to leave his pregnant wife, and Keisha does it, she does it – what the fuck, girl? – she nods like she's totally down with him abandoning his pregnant wife for her. She nods 'cause she wants things to be the way they were, too, and tells herself she could live with the price that Tab would have to pay, that she'd have to pay, too, 'cause fuck you, Moonman, fuck you, you glittery clown-looking freak motherfucker, that's what we do, we tell ourselves lies to survive.

Mimori

Geneva 2027

Almost as soon as she comes, she finds herself feeling ashamed for letting Jharna take her like this, on the uncarpeted concrete floor of Jharna's office as the secrets of the universe vibrated and thrummed around their writhing half-naked bodies. 'What have I done?' Mimori says, pushing her former professor's relentless mouth away from her pussy.

This wasn't how this trip to Geneva was supposed to go. Mimori's plane landed nine hours ago as the Swiss city was slowly waking up. She was jetlagged from the twenty-five-hour flight that should have only been twenty except there was a terror attack in Dubai, her layover, and security demanded all passengers be checked in again. Her bags didn't even arrive with her, so she bought some clothes and a box of masks from a tourist shop across from her Airbnb and showed up at CERN's security gates looking like she'd got lost on the way to an amusement park. Jharna collected her from the lobby, but couldn't resist teasing Mimori about how her style had *evolved* in the decade since they'd last seen each other in Tel Aviv. They exchanged pleasantries in the elevator, caught up on families – Sōjirō and the girls are all doing well enough, Jharna's latest wife, her third, is about to get her PhD – and tried not to pretend it wasn't weird that Mimori emailed her out of the blue and asked to visit after so long. Jharna has never been at ease with monogamy, and so assumed Mimori was after a nostalgia fuck. She didn't even bother to hide how pleased she was Mimori had more or less kept her shape, which secretly pleased Mimori after so long being ignored by her own husband. Caltech was a long time ago, and Mimori hadn't been with another woman since – she had never even told Sōjirō about Jharna since he's never really approved of homosexuality – but the memory of the affair, despite how it had ended, has always brought a smile to her face and she couldn't deny it was good to see Jharna again. Or maybe it was good to be reminded of what it felt like before, before this feeling, the feeling that she and the world are trapped in some kind of endless cycle of destruction and at any moment will dissolve once again into particles that blow apart or collapse on themselves or both, because maybe existence is ekpyrotic, as her mother – a Zen Buddhist in theory, a pragmatist in practice – always said it was.

The Large Hadron Collider tunnel was stop one on the underground tour, which Mimori assumed was intended to impress her, because Jharna knows Mimori is a techie at heart. The tunnel, which the two of them navigated in uncomfortable hard helmets, reminded her of Dr Frankenstein's laboratory, cobbled together from bits and pieces of the imagination to harness unspeakable power and explore its potential to create and explain the meaning of life – or perhaps the meaninglessness of it, if you're in a particularly nihilistic mood, as Mimori was as she strolled along the tunnel's slowly curving route, tracking the particle accelerator as it bore down on ATLAS and the massive muon chamber where subatomic particles collide and rip each other apart, imperceptible to all except the most advanced computers, and, in so doing, reveal the inner workings of the universe – even if those inner workings continue to confound and frustrate quantum physicists like Jharna.

Stop two on the tour was a lab, still underground but closer to the surface, bypassing security clearance Mimori was certain should have precluded her from entering, but Jharna had acted like the ID scan and more restrictive bio-scan were nothing more than unnecessary protocol and waved her inside. Once in, their masks came off; it was the first time either had seen the other's face in years. The lab that greeted them was dark, illuminated only by shifting computer screensavers and the service lights along various power boxes and relays. There was a large Faraday cage at the far end of the room, also covered in service lights and book-ended by several back-up generators. Nobody else was present. This is where Jharna told Mimori what her top-secret work at CERN was truly about.

'I'm going to prove everything we think we know is wrong,' she said. 'Nicolas Copernicus, Albert Einstein, *Jharna Ganguly*, that's how they're going to talk about me when your girls reach university.'

'I don't understand,' Mimori said. 'What are we doing in here?'

'Okay, I'm going to tell you three things,' Jharna said. 'At first, they won't seem connected at all. But if you remember the basics of my class, maybe you'll be able to put them together. You've always been a clever girl, so I expect you will. Are you ready?'

'I'm cold.'

'The room has to be kept a few degrees above freezing.'

Mimori wondered if Jharna could feel her nipples pressing against her bra, evident as they were to her, and suspected she could. She remembered Jharna in her office in the Downs-Lauritsen Laboratory of Phyics, pushing her down against the coarse, decade-old carpeting. Jharna lost her faculty position along with her first wife after their relationship was revealed.

'Okay, number one – *dark matter*,' Jharna said, holding up a finger. 'We can't agree what it is – physicists, I mean. We can't agree what it is or even what a single particle of it weighs. Nobody has even seen one. But there's a whole lot of it, there has to be. Some eighty-five per cent of the universe is made up of it, because without it galaxies would rotate too fast. They'd fly apart without it – without its gravity to hold them together like-like-like a *quantum skeleton*. Are you still with me?'

'I wasn't kidding. I'm *really* cold.'

'Perhaps because you're dressed for I don't know what. What are you dressed for?'

'My luggage never arrived.'

'You should stay with me tonight. I have plenty of clothes if you need them.'

Mimori frowned. 'I don't think that would be—'

'Number two, *Schrödinger's cat*,' Jharna said, interrupting. She held up two fingers. 'Also known as *the measurement problem*.'

'I know what Schrödinger's cat is.'

'Fine, but it's easier if I finish. It's kind of a script, and I lose my rhythm if I jump around a lot. Okay? So, you've got a cat and a radioactive atom inside a sealed box. If the atom decays, the cat dies, which means the cat's fate is entangled with a quantum object – aka *quantum entanglement*. The cat is alive or the cat is dead, but you don't know until you open the box, and so it exists in a linear combination of states called *quantum superposition*. This is a metaphor for wave function—'

'I know all this,' Mimori said.

'We've established that, but there's going to be a point, I promise,' Jharna said. She touched Mimori's arm right above the elbow. 'You used to be so much more patient.' Then she pressed on. 'Now you open the box. The cat is dead.'

'Fifty per cent of the time it's alive.'

'I hate cats. *The cat is dead.* And it's dead because *you* opened the box, *you bitch*.' She winked playfully. '*You* looked at it, and the act of that measurement defined the cat's state. Because it was alive a moment ago. But by observing it, you determined its fate in that moment. You *defined* reality, in a sense. In short, human beings have the power to shape reality simply by existing. Somebody page a philosopher, right?'

'I'm still cold,' Mimori said.

'I'm almost done.' Jharna held up a third finger. 'Number three, *math*. The universe is built out of subatomic particles, sort of – when you think about it – like a pixelated video game. Even the things we think of as continuous, as infinite, are actually very much *finite*. Time, space, energy, volume, they *all* have limits, which means the universe is computable. It means it can be reduced to code, like a video game, and simulated or, more likely, simulated again since, yeah, there's a nesting element to this point and that's going to take this from an afternoon-long conversation to one that won't be done until Wednesday, but I'm definitely willing to give it a go if we spend most of it naked.'

Mimori laughed, but caught herself. 'I didn't come here for that,' she said.

Jharna tilted her head and smiled. 'Is that so?' she said.

Mimori changed the subject. 'Are you . . . are you trying to prove we live in a *computer simulation*?'

A smile slowly came to Jharna's face. 'You did pay attention in class!' she said, wagging at finger at Mimori. 'Think about it. Before Copernicus showed up, all of our heroes had to explain the odd behaviour of the planets with mathematical models that became more and more elaborate, even preposterous as they struggled to explain what they were observing. The moment they let go of the idea that the Earth was the centre of the universe, the planets and their movements made sense. What I'm talking about is as paradigm-shifting, yes, but the fact of the matter is, the easiest way to explain all that missing dark matter, to explain how the universe holds itself together despite a staggering deficit of mass, is – drum roll – is that programmers *designed* our reality to work exactly as it does, to provide an ideal home for us, and the dark matter will never reveal itself because *it's composed of ones and zeroes.*'

Nobody spoke for a long moment, Jharna's energetic voice surrendering to the hum of the machines around them. Finally, Mimori said, 'This is insane,' but she didn't feel it was, not really. It felt . . . *right*. She couldn't explain how, but it just did.

'Okay, yeah, I give you that,' Jharna said. 'But let me ask you this. Your kids, do they play video games?'

'The youngest one.'

'What's her favourite game?'

'It's one of those first-person shooter games,' Mimori said, unconsciously shuddering at the thought. 'I hate it. *Super Zombie Killer Force*, I think it's called.'

'My son loves that game,' Jharna said. 'It's VR, so it requires a lot of computing power given how large its environment is. I presume you've tried playing it with her?' Mimori nodded. 'There's a building in it outside Atlanta somewhere. Abandoned, broken windows, but you can't see inside. You don't know what's in it, but you think you should find out because you're running low on bullets and zombies want to eat your delicious brains. What do you do?'

'Go inside.'

'Of course you do. But ask yourself: was the building interior already loaded as soon as you powered the game up, or was it waiting in deep storage, along with all the possibilities that might exist within, for you to open the door before it loaded? In the first case, that's *a lot* of computing power. If every building, if every location in the game is fully loaded all the time, the game would crash. In the second case, only the world immediately around you taps all that computing power and, as a result, you get a more convincing first-person experience.'

'So, the inside of the building doesn't exist until I step through the door. You're talking about Schrödinger's cat again.'

'I'm talking about the human element, which is excluded from all quantum theory. Human consciousness, more specifically. Human beings give shape to reality in a computer simulation, explaining the measurement problem. Quantum physics is too absurd, too unexplainable by any model we've come up with, because every time we take a peek at something in the quantum realm, *we change it*. There are no zombies on the other side of the door until you walk through the door, Mimori. The goddamn cat doesn't even exist until you open the goddamn box.'

Mimori leaned back against a pillar. 'Oh, my head hurts,' she said.

'What if the universe only makes sense *because* we're in it?' Jharna said, her face lighting up with something akin to religious excitement. 'What if – I mean, *what if* – the answer to the meaning of life is to make the universe real for everybody else around us?'

Mimori put her face in her hands and cried then, because for the first time in months, in maybe years, she felt like she understood what was happening to her. She understood that something isn't wrong with the world, it's wrong with *them*. *Human beings* broke the simulation. 'How?' she said. 'How are you going to prove it?'

'Tell me why you came to see me first,' Jharna said. She was touching Mimori's arm again, but this time the skin around her wrist, letting the pads of her fingertips draw out even more goose pimples across the cold skin there.

'I don't know. I really don't.'

Jharna leaned closer until her cheek was mere centimetres from Mimori's. 'You were always a terrible liar,' she said. Her hand slid into Mimori's then, and she led Mimori to the Faraday cage at the far end of the room. She tapped in a code and then used a physical key, which she wore around her neck. The cage beeped, the gate unlocked, and Jharna opened it to reveal a cryogenic freezer. 'You didn't see any of this, by the way. I could probably be sued for a few hundred million dollars just for showing it to you.'

Mimori watched her slip on a rubber glove and reach into the freezer. The gloved hand reappeared, frost-covered, holding a small, umblemished black sphere not quite as large as a tennis ball. 'What is it?' she asked.

'We don't know,' Jharna said. 'But it doesn't belong in this world.'

'I-I don't understand.'

'The simplest way to explain it is that it *bends* what we perceive to be reality. It *alters* the simulation, distorting and twisting everything from Newton's laws to electromagnetic radiation to

– and I know how this must sound but – *chance*. Basically, crazy shit happens when people spend too much time with it in their possession.'

'Where did you get it?' Mimori asaid.

'Your boss,' Jharna said, grinning. '*Sergio Harkavy.*'

'He's not my boss. He just runs SpaceNEXT.'

'He's got his fingers in a lot of pies, let's put it that way. I don't know where Harkavy got his hands on it, but I've heard rumours. Most of them sound ridiculous, but if even half of the stories are true, it's *old*. I'm talking at least a thousand years old. You know the story of the Kamikaze, I expect.'

Every Japanese child, even ones mostly raised in America like Mimori, know the stories of the Mongols' failed invasions and the magical typhoons that wiped out their undefeatable fleets.

'Yeah, say *thank you* to the spooky black ball for that,' Jharna said, holding the sphere up. 'The prevalent theory is, it's trying to communicate with some sort of external CPU. A central processing unit that oversees, that *governs*, the simulation. In three days, we're going to shoot thousands of hadrons into it and see if we can say a quick hello to God. Here, catch.'

Mimori's hands instinctively shot out and caught the sphere as it rolled from Jharna's rubber glove. The sphere was bitingly cold, and she juggled it between her hands as Jharna removed her glove and hung it back on its hook.

'I've got it,' Jharna said, taking the sphere back.

Mimori watched the sphere roll in Jharna's cupped hand, convinced she could hear something coming from it, a strange and unsettling hum, like words tumbling over one another as water does over rocks in a stream, and didn't realize until Jharna's other arm was around her waist that Jharna was standing behind her. Mimori became immediately aware of Jharna's breasts and her nipples pressed against her back.

'It does something to your body, it gets into your head,' Jharna said. 'It messes with the electricity bouncing around inside your brain. You wouldn't believe what the orgasms are like after you've held it.'

Mimori didn't even think about it. She just reached out and took the sphere back, then held it against her chest with two hands, between her breasts, her wrists rubbing subtly against her own nipples that were as hard as Jharna's now. Jharna used to be able to make her come by playing with them with one gentle finger – like that time they went to go see a Lucius Cove retrospective and Mimori tried to camouflage her heavy breathing behind covers of Damien Syco's greatest hits. 'Aren't there cameras in here?' she said, her bottom lip rolling under one of her canines.

'Not on this side of the pillar,' Jharna said as her hand, as startling as five fingers made of supple ice, slid under the waist of Mimori's pants, under Mimori's cotton briefs, over the pubic hair Mimori might have trimmed had she known she was going to cheat on her husband with an old girlfriend, and then two fingers into Mimori's pussy. Mimori gasped, her arms tightened against her chest, and her ass instinctively pushed back against Jharna. She came almost immediately and again a minute later, so long had it been since she had been touched like this.

'I'm married,' Mimori said between kisses, tears in her eyes. 'I love my husband.'

'I love Rita, too,' Jharna said, mumbling, her mouth full of one of Mimori's breasts.

'I just . . . I . . . I feel like everything is wrong, and I'm just trying to find something . . .'

'To hold on to?'

'Yeah . . . something that makes sense,' Mimori said, tears running down her cheeks now.

'I know,' Jharna said. 'Me, too. I feel like . . . like the world doesn't have the will to go on any more, like it's just given up. And I keep scrabbling, trying to find something . . .'

'To hold on to,' Mimori said. She leaned back from Jharna's lips then, and they stared at each other for a long moment, breathing, because they understood each other, and they both felt less alone as their mouths collided again. 'Hold on to me then.'

Jharna responded by putting her hands on Mimori's shoulders, pushing her to her knees, and wrapping a leg around her neck. When Jharna came, the knee supporting her buckled, and she collapsed on top of Mimori in a mess of limbs. The sphere escaped from Mimori's hand, scaring her, but Jharna only laughed. 'You can't hurt it.' Then she slapped a hand over her face. 'God, I hope I don't lose another job on account of you!'

They replaced the black sphere in the freezer, and traded its influence for the hard concrete floor of Jharna's spartan office, which is how Mimori finds herself overcome with regret for what she has allowed to happen here today. Several times today. 'What have I done?' she says, pushing Jharna away.

Mimori's phone begins to ring at this very moment.

'Don't answer it,' Jharna says.

Mimori checks her phone. It's Sōjirō. She immediately declines the call.

Jharna leans over, and begins to kiss her neck. 'Stay the night,' she says. 'Rita is in Mexico with her parents.'

Mimori's phone begins to ring again. 'I have to take this,' she says, suddenly worried about the girls even though she couldn't say why. She retreats to the privacy of the bathroom even as Jharna protests, and apprehensively answers the call with the question, 'What's wron

Jones

Tucson 1962

'*Her?*' he asks, leaning forward in the salon chair. But he already knows who Pilar means, and it startles him that the answer was so immediately obvious to him even though he's never considered her beyond a passing attraction and a general awe at how her spectacular mind works and her strangely insecure but wildly assured sense of self and how he couldn't have made it this far without her, and suddenly Jones is wondering if this is how his other persona, or personality, or whatever it is – Porter, the Bug, *him*? – fell in love with Gracie, too.

'Listen, I only bring her up to illustrate a point,' Pilar says, clipping the toenails of his left foot now. She's as committed to this task as she is to confounding him with the zig-zagging trajectory of this conversation. 'If nothing here is real, why does anything matter to you? And if nothing matters to you, why did you even bother retiring here in the first place?'

'Because I didn't want to die,' he says, but he knows this isn't true, not really. What he did was more like suicide with a happy ending, or at least it was until Porter blew his life up along with Pasadena City Hall. 'Does anybody?'

'I don't really believe in death, so no,' she says.

'You need to get a job writing fortune-cookie wisdom, you know that?' he says.

'I tried that for a summer once. In Brooklyn, believe it or not. It's not as easy as you would think, distilling the secrets of the universe to twelve words or less. I think my finest work might have been "If you find yourself unhappy, find out why."'

'What does that even mean?'

Pilar shrugs. Jones doesn't laugh. He doesn't even blink. She looks frustrated.

'It's called a joke,' she says, trading her clippers for a fresh file to smooth the sharp edges of his toenails. 'You need a sense of humour, *mi cariño*.'

'An unstoppable artificial intelligence is trying to kill me, remember?' he says.

'You've already had two lives. There could even be more. You know, if the universe doesn't fly apart or collapse on itself before you save it or whatever it is you're trying to do.'

His voice changes. His whole demeanour does. 'You've seen it, then?'

'The *abyss*?' She shrugs indifferently. 'Yeah, I've seen it.'

On the Outside, they called it the Event Horizon. It was the bane of Jones's existence as Chief Designer of Plurality Life Insurance Corporation's eternal retirement community. 'Where time ends,' he says grimly.

'Time doesn't end,' Pilar says. 'It's a great big wheel, thanks to you. It just returns to the beginning, repeating itself over and over – the same, but different.'

'Whatever you want to call it, the System can't sustain itself beyond it,' he says.

She doesn't seem especially worried about this. 'Ever ask yourself why?' she says.

Memories bubble back to the surface for Jones. Infuriating memories of ceaseless failure. 'Yeah, but I never found an answer that satisfied me,' he says. 'When we built the System, we ran a couple billion test cycles.' To give his creation a test drive, so to say, a spin around the digital block to see how it worked. 'But no matter what changes we made, the problem kept repeating. Human civilisation arises, peaks at the end of what they call the twentieth century, and collapses in the middle of the twenty-first century.' Taking the whole System down with it. 'Eventually, we just gave up and the Corporation decided to market life insurance policies around the temporal limitation.'

Meaning, there really is no future for humans, not as they like to imagine it in their science fiction and at the pictures and in their dreams. They enjoy 10,000 or so years of civilization, in various forms, and then that's that.

'It's not true, though, is it?' Pilar says, picking up the popsicle-shaped file. He doesn't understand her question, so she rearticulates it. 'They didn't *always* collapse, did they?'

Jones is slow to respond, because she shouldn't know about any of this. It's a closely guarded secret even within the Corporation. 'No,' he says finally. 'Early on, there were some test cycles that functioned for longer.'

'How much longer?' she asks as she sands away at the bottom of his left foot.

'Centuries, mostly. Sometimes, millennia. But eventually, they all collapsed.'

'Except the one.'

Jones is quiet for another long moment, then nods slowly. 'Except the one, yeah,' he says.

'What was different about these . . . what did you call them?' Pilar says.

'*Test cycles.*'

'What was different about them?'

He looks away. 'They didn't work, that's all that matters.'

She gives him a knowing *hmph*. 'In the water.' When his left foot is in the tub and she's once again washing him, she says of the test cycles, 'So you made them work.'

'It's difficult to explain – I'd be here all night – but human beings . . . they needed help staying in check. Their minds went haywire when experiential input skyrocketed.'

'*Loco?*'

'The more the Perceived World around them didn't make sense, the more they went – yeah – *loco*,' Jones says. 'So, I created a series of control algorithms meant to motivate conformity and move the Earth model populations – gently, you could say – towards uniformity despite the illusion of independence and uniqueness that is just as important as their psychological stability. Gender, race, religion, even capitalism – they're just social and cultural constructs, nothing more than code, meant to keep the System from spinning out of control and collapsing.'

Pilar blows out a long breath. 'Wow,' she says. '*Wow*. That is . . . that is even scarier hearing it said aloud. I mean, I know what you did to these people. I had to escape it myself. But . . . *wow*. How are your controls working out for the world out there, *mi cariño*?'

He doesn't know how to answer because the System has only gone, as she put it, *loco* a handful of times in its history. Most recently, with World War II and its aftermath. The ensuing Cold War, the nuclear arms race political leaders can't help but engage in despite their own survival being on the line, the struggle between what they call democracy and communism, it's all just the System overcorrecting in an attempt to restore some kind of order where residents no longer see any. In the years to come, the computing revolution and environmental fallout from the industrial revolution will do even worse and neo-fascism will return around the globe to compensate, with catstrophic results. None of this occurred in the first several thousand revolutions of the System, mind you. The System ran, recycled, reset, and ran again without notable issue, but with each revolution changes accumulated and, as they did, the twentieth century began to mutate and rebel against the technological explosion that began on the brutal battlefields of the Great War, accelerated exponentially with the detonation at Los Alamos, and is now rapidly racing towards a future that nobody can remotely predict for the first time in human history. It is impossible for most not to feel like the end is nigh, as their religious zealots like to say, not with nuclear winter, ecological collapse, viral mass extinction, and the advent of artificial intelligence dangling over their heads like the Sword of Damocles. But they're right, in a way.

'There is . . . yeah, there's room for improvement,' Jones says. 'Is that what you want to hear?'

'I'd say so,' Pilar says. She removes his foot from the tub, and begins to wipe it dry with a fresh towel. 'See, if I were you – and I'm not you, but if I *were* you – I don't know if I could just retire to someplace like this, sit back and watch the world fall apart around me. I mean, they're selling bomb shelters in the Sears catalogue. I don't know if I could do that without wondering how I could change things, maybe improve the lives of those around me. Then again, *you* don't think of them as real people, do you? Maybe that's the problem. They're *dummies*, and you've never really let yourself get close to any of them. Just ask her.'

Her again.

Gracie.

What has he done to her life?

'Right now, you're not sitting here because the US and Soviet Union are having a meaningless pissing contest that could destroy the world,' Pilar says, continuing. 'You're here because *you're* in trouble. It's the only thing that got you off your couch. I mean, besides the need to eat some pie.'

'I don't even know if I like pie,' he says.

'You were about to find out how much you like it when our friend with the kooky eyes showed up. Trust me, *mi cariño*, you are a *big* fan of pie.' She moves on to removing his cuticles and buffing his toenails. 'I have to ask. The test cycle that worked, the Earth model that didn't collapse, why not aim for that? Why create a world that you always knew was doomed to collapse instead?'

'Because there was no profit in gambling on a model that didn't eventually fail,' Jones says, ashamed by this. 'Nobody would have retired to, much less invested in a System with the guaranteed integrity of a-a-a *wet fart*.'

'And yet this is all about to come crashing down, whether or not it's your Bug that does it or those poor souls out there, so you didn't do a very good job,' Pilar says. 'In the end, I mean.'

'Corporations require security, guarantees to maximize profits,' he says. This is an old argument for him, one he made to himself countless times on the Outside when Plurality made performance demands of him that he knew would have unforeseen consequences. The excuse falls from his lips even before he realizes he's going to utter the words.

'What do these corporations matter?' she says, now massaging his left foot with the exfoliator cream. 'They're social constructs, too, no more real than the ones you programmed to keep this place in check.'

'Somebody had to pay for the System. I couldn't have built it by myself, not on this scale. *They own it.*'

She mutters something in Spanish, almost certainly obscenities. 'Nobody can *own* reality. The System ceased to belong to your Corporation the moment it went online.'

'The System isn't free, no matter how ontological you want to get.'

'Funny. Your Bug said the same thing to me.'

Jones almost slips out of his chair, he leans forward that quickly. 'Is he me?' he says, desperation warping his voice now. 'Tell me who he is, please. *What* he is. I *have* to know.'

Pilar says, 'I can't—' He interrupts her with some urgent, guttural expulsion not yet shaped into words, which she doesn't take well. She shoves his left foot back into the tub, splashing water. '*But* I can tell you he was looking for all the same answers you are.'

'Why can't you tell me?' he says. She doesn't say one way or the other, just kind of shrugs. 'What did you tell him, then?'

She removes his foot from the tub, and drops it onto a towel. 'I don't do the answer thing, like I told you,' she says. 'Sorry, I didn't get to your fingernails. Maybe next time?'

'Give me an answer,' he says, pleading. 'A real one, not a riddle.'

Pilar remains silent as she dries his left foot with firmer hands than she did his right, working her fingers between his toes with less concern for the way the joints of these toes pop at her intrusion. She finishes with a sigh, a decision made. Or maybe that's just what she wants him to think. 'Okay, just this once,' she says. 'But only because you seem so lost you've forgotten what's up and down any more.' She leans forward, smiling with her whole face. Her wide, dark eyes defy him to disbelieve her. '*Grace Pulansky.*'

Everything keeps coming back to Gracie, but Jones still doesn't get it.

'Hey, you told me you wanted an answer,' she says.

'Yeah, but to what question?'

'The only one that really matters. Besides, *questions* are what you're really looking for anyway. At least you finally figured that out, in the end at least. Bit slow on the uptake. You've got to go now.'

Moments later, the Ghost in the System all but shoves Jones out of Oolala Nail Salon's door. He still hasn't tied his shoes. 'I'll see you when the wheel comes back around, *mi cariño*!' she says, calling through the glass door as she locks it.

After this, he hitchhikes back to the motel in the bed of a pick-up next to three sleeping dogs and a fourth with only one eye that won't stop licking his slacks around the knee so that, by the time he hops down outside the motel, it looks like he's been kneeling in a puddle of viscous oil. But this doesn't matter to him, because the drive gave him time to realize he does have feelings for Gracie Pulansky. He doesn't only want to get back to her because she is somehow the answer to the only question that really matters, at least according to a digital godhead, but because he hasn't felt more at home in this world than when he is with her. Master-Control is hunting Jones, with the full intention of deleting him for violating the terms of his life insurance policy, and yet what Jones really wants is *to be with her*. Why didn't he understand this before? Did the Ghost show him the truth he was too afraid to open his eyes to? Or did the Ghost put a thought in his head that should have never been there in the first place and, if so, did she do the same to Porter and that's why Angelique sent him here? He's tired of feeling this confused, this paranoid, this frightened. And then, he opens the door to his motel room, expecting to find only Gracie on the other side of it, ready to tell her how he feels, which is when everything gets unimaginably worse. On the upside, he now knows who Porter really is. On the downside, he now knows who Porter really is.

Tuviah

San Carlos de Bariloche 1972

They're crouched inside a scrubby copse of young lenga trees, binoculars pressed to their faces as they watch Reinhold Gottschald cross-country ski along a ridge blanketed in sun-kissed, newly fallen snow, when he says, 'After this job, I need a break.' Merel doesn't seem to hear Tuviah – she's too focused on Gottschald, probably trying to decide how they should kill him – and so he repeats the words at a volume she can't ignore. She looks at him, confused, and he just shrugs because she's never going to understand anyway. 'I'm tired.'

Merel, like Tuviah, is clad in a one-piece white snowsuit that crinkles every time she moves. She pushes her fur-lined hood down, sighing dramatically in order to make a point. 'I'm roasting,' she says. 'Aren't you?'

They are overdressed, he'll give her that. The warnings of frigid alpine weather didn't account for what the afternoon sun can feel like in spring at this altitude. They passed several tourists leaving Bariloche wearing only thick trousers and woollen sweaters, which should have been the tip-off, along with how these tourists seemed to snigger at Tuviah and Merel in their spy-movie snow gear.

'Did you not hear what I said?' he says.

'Of course I heard you,' she says. 'What about the job in Chile?'

'I can't.'

'But it's just over the border. We can do it after this, and *then* we can take a holiday. I've always wanted to go to Mexico. The Mayan Riviera sounds lovely, doesn't it?'

Tuviah lifts his binoculars to his eyes again, and watches Gottschald ski. This is their third day monitoring his daily routine, which means Tuviah can predict with considerable accuracy what comes next now that Gottschald has completed the loop that will return him to his chalet – a stop for schnapps at a small, family-operated inn you can only reach by skis or snowshoes if you're ambitious, a quick swim in the icy river that courses past his chalet, and then, finally, home to warm up by the fire. Gottschald doesn't interact with anybody besides the woman who runs the inn and the woman's middle daughter, a mute who serves food with funereal solemnity. Both are Germans, too, but didn't strike Tuviah as Nazis-in-hiding since neither seemed especially concerned a Jew had popped in to sample their veal schnitzel. Gottschald has no real relationships in Bariloche, no friendships, no community. He is in hiding as much from his past as he is from humanity in general.

'Do you promise?' Tuviah asks Merel, lowering his binoculars again. 'After the Chilean job, we can take a break?'

'I promise,' she says, sounding bored by the conversation. 'So, should we kill him tonight?'

'Might as well,' he says.

That night, they spend an hour arguing over whether or not to wear the snow gear again. Merel doesn't want to, claiming she nearly fainted from heat exhaustion earlier in the day, but Tuviah insists it will be cold outside after dark and this wasn't even a point of debate on the previous two nights they went out in it. She finally relents, and they hike the two miles to Gottschald's chalet, both thankful that Tuviah got his way because it's fucking miserable out here. The snow begins as a flurry, a playful tease of what's to come, and then intensifies as Gottschald's chalet emerges into view through the boles of tall pine trees. Bringing the snow-shoes was Tuviah's idea, too, which means he's feeling very pleased with himself right now. Merel warns him not to gloat, but the reality is she lets him win so rarely these days, he has no choice but to smirk when she's not looking. How did it come to this? When did he start to hate her? For a while, he was convinced it was Michigan and the horror of watching her fucking him as

Standartenführer Günter Graf's neck bulged with the magazine she had hammered into it, but all that did was crystallize for him what was wrong with their marriage and what they had allowed themselves to become. The hate, that came later.

After Graf, it didn't take long to track down the U-boat captain, Manfred Eberstein. He was busy slowly dying in the attic of his son's farmhouse a few miles outside Innsbruck. There was no reason for him to hide. He was only a sailor, and he and his family had spent many years trying to make amends for what the Nazis had done and the sins he had commited after his forced re-commission into the *Kriegsmarine*. Soon after the war ended, Eberstein began writing to the Allied Control Council about Gottschald and the five mysterious crates he and his crew had secretly transported out of Europe via a Genoan ratline, but he couldn't get anybody to take him seriously. This is why when Tuviah asked where Eberstein had taken Gottschald, Eberstein immediately confessed – 'Buenos Aires!'

Gottschald's trail became more difficult to track once Tuviah and Merel had reached Argentina. Gottschald had been protected by President Juan Perón upon his arrival, part of Perón's open-arms policy towards escaping Nazis, but even after it became apparent Gottschald was a most unusual Nazi, to say the least, even though rumours swirled around him and his alleged Semitic origins – rumours Gottschald helped fuel by his constant refusal to associate with his fellow Nazis – the Peronists refused to sell out one of their own, as they saw Gottschald, or Herr Distler as he was now called, and didn't finally surrender any clues as to Gottschald's whereabouts until Merel pushed a former labour minister's wife out of a second-floor window and threatened to do the same to his eleven-year-old daughter. 'San Carlos de Bariloche,' the ex-labour minister – an ex-Nazi banker, as well – had said, screaming through panicked tears. 'Please, don't hurt my daughter!'

Bariloche was a haven for Nazi expats craving the mountain retreats they had once enjoyed so much back home. Gottschald reached the town in 1951, and has remained here ever since. Nobody seems to know him by name more than twenty years later, not even other Germans. He refuses to commiserate with anybody, unless you count the inn owner and her mute daughter. He pays his bills on time, he buys his groceries without commentary, he declines invitations from those who feel the need to send them. Which makes the tall wall of windows that comprise the back of Gottschald's chalet that much more confounding. Thirty feet of them, crowned by a dramatic overhanging peak. Gottschald hides in plain sight, it seems – or he's so used to being alone that the epic scope of the valley that the windows face, the sense that there's an immeasurable world of possibilities on the other side of the panes, is a necessary psychotropic drug to remain sane during his self-imposed isolation.

Tuviah and Merel silently advance on these windows now, staying low as they do. He's carrying a brand-new SSG 69 sniper rifle, she an Uzi she picked up in a bar of dubious repute in Buenos Aires. Gottschald is standing in the kitchen – which is part of the larger ground-floor living area that doesn't seem to recognize rooms as an architectural option – frying something on the stove. A metal spatula works with fanatical commitment.

'Are you ready?' Merel says, whispering.

Tuviah nods. 'Are you sure you're comfortable with that?' he says.

She's holding her Uzi like a new lover. 'Don't worry about me, darling,' she says.

They begin to split up, to approach the windows from opposite corners of the chalet, when the spotlights pop on so loudly that it's impossible not to startle from surprise.

Tuviah is immediately blinded, and shields his eyes with his free hand. He shouts for Merel, but doesn't hear her over the barking of several dogs. Barking that's coming his way. He recovers enough of his sight in time to locate a German Shepherd bounding towards him through the snowstorm. The dog's powerful jaws clamp down on Tuviah's arm, and it begins to yank violently as it's trained to do, determined to drag Tuviah to the ground where his throat can be ripped open. Two more German Shepherds are right behind this one, anxious to join the party. Merel's Uzi roars. Tuviah cracks the one on his arm in the skull with his rifle and, when that doesn't work, manages to shove the muzzle into its hindquarters and pull the trigger. The dog doesn't relent, sharp teeth digging into Tuviah's flesh through his thick snowsuit, and so he keeps shooting.

Merel mows down the last of them, six in total, leaving a collection of whimpering and dead dogs across blood-splattered snow. 'He knew we were coming!' she says, shouting.

Tuviah points at a CCTV camera mounted under the over-hanging roof. There's another hidden in a tree, now that he knows to look for them. 'He's watching us,' he says.

'Fuck this,' she says, and turns her Uzi on one of the chalet's windows. The window shrugs off the barrage of bullets, surrendering chips of glass, but nothing more. The glass must be several inches thick. '*Bulletproof.* Shit.'

'I'd say try the doors, but I have the feeling those will be reinforced, too.'

'It's a goddamn fortress!'

Tuviah looks from the wall of windows to the valley that opens up before them. 'So he could see us coming,' he says, suddenly feeling like a fool.

The lights inside go out.

Tuviah and Merel stomp around in the snow, thinking, trying to decide the best way to get inside. She mouths *you're dead* in German at one of the cameras, but Gottschald isn't worried about her killing him, as it turns out. He's not hiding because he's afraid, but because he knows all he must be is patient to survive, because they'll die of starvation before they penetrate his redoubt.

Tuviah stops, and watches the moon briefly appear behind moving clouds. He wants to make it to Mexico, to the Mayan

Riviera – even though he knows nothing about it – to any place where he can forget about the killing for a few weeks. He's had enough of it. 'Let's burn the place down,' he says, squeezing his wound. 'He can go with it if he wants.'

And so, they find a snow machine under an overhang where both fuel and firewood are also stored, in what can only be considered a stroke of dumb luck. They splash the gasoline across the firewood and along the wood siding, and then heave the half-empty gas cans onto the overhang. They watch the flames climb up the wall of the chalet from amidst the dead German Shepherds, scanning the windows for some sign of Gottschald inside.

'Look!' Merel says, pointing at the road that leads to Bariloche. It runs along the valley's eastern wall, just inside a wall of trees. An emergency truck, red lights spinning silently, is approaching. The fire has been noticed. 'Do you want me to handle it?'

Tuviah doesn't know what to say to her. They used to only kill Nazis. Now they threaten to throw prepubescent children out of windows and murder forest rangers, and they come all the harder the bloodier it turns out. 'No, Merel, I don't want you to handle it,' he says matter-of-factly.

He kneels beside a barbecue grill, using the grill to support his sniper rifle, then flips up the scope's cover. In this way, he tracks the truck, trying to adjust for distance and speed and time its passage between trees. The first shot misses altogether. The second dings off a fender. The third blows out the front driver's side tyre. The truck's headlights weave wildly, then the truck slams into a tree. When the ranger gets out, carrying his own rifle, and breaks for cover, Tuviah squeezes off four more shots until one catches the courageous idiot in the leg.

'Help me!' somebody says from behind them, shouting in panicked Yiddish.

Tuviah and Merel spin, guns searching for a target. A man a full head shorter than Tuviah – wearing nothing but trousers, an undershirt, and slippers as worn and characterless as his face – is trying to carry a large painted canvas through a side door in the chalet. There's already a canvas about twenty feet from this door, resting against a tree, which he must have dragged out here while Tuviah and Merel were distracted by the ranger.

Graf was right, whatever he and Gottschald smuggled out of Germany has driven Gottschald mad.

Merel looks at Tuviah, baffled by this. 'Can I shoot him now?' she says.

Tuviah strides towards Gottschald, keeping his rifle trained on the man. As he gets closer, faint light coming from inside reveals enough of the painting to startle Tuviah into digging his boots into the snow. He stops so abruptly that he almost topples forward. The muzzle of his rifle drops, and he can only stare dumbly at the painting as it lurches and rocks in awkward hitches, dragged clumsily by Gottschald into the embrace of near-total darkness.

'What the fuck is that?' Tuviah asks in Yiddish, pointing with a shaking gloved finger. His voice explodes out of him then as a savage roar. 'What is that?'

Gottschald leans the painting against a tree, next to the other one that remains featureless in the dark.

Tuviah flips on a flashlight, fully illuminating the one he caught a glimpse of. Something inside him shakes, maybe even cracks, and he repeats with a quaking voice, 'What is that?'

Gottschald runs past him, back through the door that smoke is rolling out of. 'I know what you are here for, but they are mine!' he says.

'What are you doing?' Merel says. She's standing behind Tuviah now. 'Let's kill him and get out of here before more people show up.'

Tuviah looks at her, momentarily lost in the horror of what he's just witnessed, cast adrift from the only reality he has ever known. The muscles in his face move unnaturally, contorting, as confused as he is. But Merel doesn't seem to have any reaction to the paintings' contents, perhaps so warped at this point by her own grief, the atrocities she's committed herself to assuage her pain, the bloodshed she has turned into an aphrodisiac, that what the paintings portray doesn't even faze her. He imagines he's only on his feet still because he's nearly as mad as her, which, it would seem, is not nearly as mad as the man they've come here to kill. Merel's hand slaps Tuviah back to this world.

Gottschald emerges from the chalet again, backlit by flames that hiss and growl and spit hellish warnings. This third canvas is smaller than the other two, but the painting is no less arresting and terrifying despite its diminutive size. Merel lifts her Uzi, to shoot him, but a crack shatters the night and what remains of Tuviah's heart. She spins, almost a complete 180, and crashes to the snow. Gottschald doesn't notice any of this, his focus entirely on his task.

'What did you do, Toby?' Merel says, crawling for the Uzi that flew from her hands when she was shot in the back. She's holding an oozing hole in her gut, tears in her eyes, leaving a trail of blood in the snow as she moves. 'What did . . . you . . . do?'

Tuviah swipes away his own tears. His mouth opens to say something, then shuts. He turns away from her, unable to bear how she's looking at him, and charges inside to help Gottschald. The fourth canvas takes both of them to carry it. Gottschald goes back in for the fifth by himself, but the chalet begins to collapse before he re-emerges. Flames, pushed by the force of the crashing beams and floors and roof, erupt through the door and falling snow whips around them in a scene of brutal wonder.

'I-I'm sorry,' Tuviah says, shuffling back towards Merel. More red lights are approaching. 'I'm so sorry.'

But she's already dead.

This is the only way this could have ended, he knows. This is the way it was always going to end.

Tuviah cries and curses God and Merel and Nazis and God again, and then he pitches his sniper rifle into the fires that are roaring almost as loudly as he is now, walks into the night, into the snowstorm, and spends the rest of his life – and there are fifteen more lonely, maddening years of it – trying to make sense of what he witnessed on Gottschald's canvases.

Jharna

Geneva 2027

She does not know why Mimori Ando pops into her head – it's been years since they've seen each other – but, as Linac5 begins to accelerate the particles at 50 MeV, Jharna finds herself thinking about her all the same, about her delicate hands and hungry mouth, about how for a brief moment some twenty years ago, before everything went to hell, she felt like she was alive with her, *truly* alive, and how everything since then has been some desperate attempt to recapture that feeling. A feeling that every day seems more and more incongruous with who she is, because who she is is exists inside time and she has changed like time, and the world has changed with her, so that the Earth where she fucked Mimori for the first time now seems as alien and far away to her as Alpha Centauri. She is hurtling towards something, maybe they all are, like the particles racing through Linac5 closer and closer to the speed of light. Except the particles racing towards the sphere – the black sphere that is already confusing the sensors set up to observe it – are already experiencing time differently from how Jharna is, has, will. Time is now passing more than 7,000 times slower for them, fractions of seconds barely quantifiable having barely passed, while seconds tick away rapidly for her.

As Jharna considers Mimori and that time in her life when answers didn't seem as important as the search, she can't help but suddenly feel that her position and that of the particles inside Linac5 have become reversed. That, in fact, she is the one racing through time and space, faster and faster, about to crash into the black sphere that has come over these past four years to represent for her the opportunity to finally explain this mood-bending and overwhelming sense of dread and inevitable doom that Rita blames for all of the stupid things Jharna does and used as an excuse to run away to Mexico where, at this point, Jharna can only assume she has also taken lovers but, because Rita is so traditional, probably only one at a time. Mimori, not Rita. It was supposed to be Mimori . . . Mimori . . .

Everybody else around her in the lab gasps. The particles have collided with the sphere, and something is happening. The sensors are malfunctioning. Then, they're in the dark, and then Jharna is alone, and then she is thirty-six again, pressed face first against the tiled wall of her shower as Mimori kisses her neck and repeatedly thrusts two fingers inside her from behind, and when Jharna spins round, to meet Mimori's lips, she's kissing Rita, and then she's kissing Monica, and then it's Shira with her hands on Jharna's ass and her mouth on Jharna's pussy as all the other women she's ever loved watch and, beyond them, standing in what appears to be a motion picture studio set of her life, built entirely out of stars, her mother and father and grandparents watch, too, and a six-year-old girl that was Jharna once upon a time and Jharna will be once again is there, too, holding the round pillow she used to grind against before she knew what was happening to her and her body, and there are other people, so many of them, watching and participating and holding her together even as some other force tries to reach into her, into her cells, or maybe even deeper, and pull her apar

Gracie

Tucson 1962

The Bobby on the carpet – the Bobby she's left with – is still moaning about the lamp that was broken against the back of his skull. He manages to wiggle out of his jacket, pushing his head free, his scalp moist with fresh blood. Gracie watches him, still wrapped in the motel's coarse bed sheet, taking nervous steps forwards and backwards, a rocking motion she doesn't even realize she's trapped in.

Bobby rolls onto his buttocks and lets his upper body slump against the dresser. He's clearly as fixated on what just happened as she is, but it's not her he's looking at. His eyes are locked on the bed she . . . she . . . it's too dreadful to think about. What has Gracie done? What was she thinking? She begins to cry.

'I'm sorry,' he says, finally looking at her.

'For what?' she says, pulling the sheet tighter around her.

He shrugs lamely. 'Everything, I guess.'

'Wh-Who was that? Why does he look like you?'

'Because he is.'

'Like a twin.'

'No, I meant what I said. He's me. Just a . . . a different version of me.'

'Then a clone.'

He shakes his head.

Gracie tugs her sheet back up over a half-exposed breast. 'Dang, turn around,' she says.

'Pardon me?' Bobby says.

'Turn around, I have to get dressed,' she says. He looks away, shielding his eyes with one hand. She drops the sheet, the delight of being naked in front of Bobby only a few moments ago, her first time naked in front of any man, replaced by a desperate need to conceal her body from him. 'If he's not a twin, not a clone . . .' She's trying to think it through. 'I don't get it.'

'Because,' he says, still looking away. 'Because I'm not like you, okay? *Okay*? I . . . I arrived in this world almost a year ago.'

Her underpants are halfway up her legs when she stops at what she just heard. 'Oh my God, you're an alien,' she says. 'That's why you've been acting like some kind of pod person.'

His head snaps around. 'What?'

She yanks her underpants the rest of the way up, spinning away from him. 'Hey!'

He looks quickly away again. 'Sorry. No, no, I'm not a *pod person*. I don't even know what that is.'

'It's from a movie,' Gracie says, hiking up her pants.

'This isn't the pictures,' Bobby says. 'I come from another place. A different . . . version of reality.'

Her face lights up with understanding as she slips his shirt back on. 'Oh,' she says. Then, 'Oh, you mean a parallel dimension!'

'Christ, this would be so much easier if you weren't so . . .' he says, trying to find the right word.

'Okay, you can look – and I won't apologize for being intelligent.'

'No, so *you*.' He manages to both smile and look exasperated at the same moment. 'Your brain, it's *astounding*, but it moves a million miles a minute and I can't keep up with it. Just . . . well, give me a chance to explain. So . . . okay, so the thing is . . . it's like . . . well, shit—'

'Just spit it out, whatever it is. I can handle it.'

He lets loose a harsh snort that startles him as much as it does her.

'Don't mock me!' Gracie says, snapping at him. She gets his shirt over her head. 'Okay, you can look.'

Bobby looks at her, and says her name, but stops. 'Gracie,' he says, starting again, 'I don't know how to say this, because there's no way it will make sense to you, not because you're not smart enough, but because it's going to destroy everything you think you know about your life and who you think you are and this world, and I don't want to do that to you – I really don't, please believe that – but I don't have a choice any more, not if you're going to stick this out with me, and so I'm just going to say it, I'm just going to tell you the truth, I'm just going to do it—'

'You're not,' she says.

'I know,' he says. 'I . . . like you. I *like* you, okay? I don't want to hurt you.'

'I like you, too. I mean, *wow*, I just . . . you know . . . with you.'

'That wasn't me.'

'You said it was – oh my God, was that *Porter*?' Gracie says, believing she's just figured out the most shocking part of what Bobby is trying to tell her. '*It was*, wasn't it?'

'You live inside a computer simulation, Gracie.'

Bobby blurts this out, almost as if he can no longer keep it in, and it lands like a thermonuclear bomb in the middle of the motel room. Except it's like the film footage they showed her in school of the detonation at Los Alamos. No sound; just eerie, empty silence in horrified response to the unthinkable.

She stands there for the longest moment. Not 'cause she didn't hear what he just told her, but 'cause the words simply don't make sense to her. She knows how to define them, could easily write them down – heck, she's even seen a real computer at work on campus, big as a classroom – but string the words together? The effort of trying to decipher their meaning actually starts to hurt. 'You want to say that again?' Gracie says.

Bobby has leapt off the diving board. He's committed, and the words fly from his mouth without hesitation now. 'What you think is reality is, in fact, a computer simulation,' he says as quickly as he can. 'You know what that means, right? It's a-a-a *figment* of a computer's imagination. A place for digitized brain patterns to be downloaded upon death and live out immortal post-lives. I built it, Gracie. *I built all of this*. Why are you looking at me like that?'

She hasn't blinked, not since the words *computer* and *simulation* were uttered. Hearing them a second time, she's managed to connect them in her brain. *Computer simulation*, there they are, side by side, but she doesn't know what to do with them. *Cahm-pew-tur sim-yoo-lay-shin*. Nope, still nothing.

'None of it's real,' he says emphatically, trying to get through to her.

'Okay.'

'You seem to be taking this quite well.'

Gracie finally blinks. Then, something inside her brain goes off like another atom has been ripped apart, and the only way to do something with the expanding, unstoppable force of the explosion is to throw herself at Bobby and begin slapping and clubbing his face and shoulders and back and, when he gets his arms up, his arms, too. 'What about me?' she says, shouting as violently as she's delivering open palms and fists. '*What about me?*'

Bobby lets her pound on him until she tires, until she staggers backwards and falls against the edge of the bed. He looks at her, blood from his scalp on her hands like dark ink, smudged copies of her blows printed across his face. But he says nothing. He's already said enough.

'*Prove it*,' she says. She's remembered who she is, no matter what *he* thinks she is. She's the girl from Denver who never believed anything just 'cause somebody told her it was true. She always demanded proof, and when there wasn't any, she'd go find it herself. 'Prove it!'

Using the dresser for support, he climbs back to his feet and waves a hand at the bed beside her, the one where she just made love to somebody who looks exactly like him, or is him, or is both, if such a thing is possible. This bothers him, she can see it in his eyes. He really does care. 'I walked in on you and a perfect doppelgänger of me, a doppelgänger that I suspect is the copy of me first downloaded into the System. Back when I retired.'

'You mean when you *died*,' Gracie says. ''Cause you're dead . . . aren't you?'

Bobby doesn't disagree with her. 'I'm only just beginning to understand any of this myself, but Porter – let's just call him that, it makes it easier – *he* is that original copy,' he says. 'He's the identity matrix produced when my biological consciousness was digitized. I'm not supposed to be here, is what I'm saying. *He* is.'

'Then why *are* you here?' she says.

'I wish I knew, but whatever the reason, I haven't been here long,' he says. 'Robert Jones, me, the other me—'

'*Porter*.'

'Yeah. When he blew up Pasadena City Hall – and I'm only speculating here, but I'm pretty damn sure I'm right – when he blew it up, a second copy of me, my digital file up until three weeks after my initial insertion, *seven months ago*, was downloaded into the System again. *Me*. That's why I don't remember blowing up City Hall, because it *was* Porter.'

Gracie rubs her temple with a thumb. 'Who is *you*,' she says.

'Who *was* me,' Bobby says. 'I wouldn't kill people, not like he has.'

'But you *did*, 'cause you're *him*,' she says.

'I wouldn't,' he says.

'Except it was *you* who ran over that FBI agent.'

He smiles and shakes his head at the same time, as if the very suggestion is amusing. But he's not amused, he's horrified, and what she's witnessing is an awkward, nervous reaction to that horror. The Bobby she just made love to killed twenty-three people – hundreds, maybe thousands more in other worlds, if any of this is true – and this Bobby, here in front of her, doesn't seem to know how to make sense of that either. She imagines it's a little like Dr Jekyll discovering he becomes Mr Hyde after the sun goes down.

'He wasn't an FBI agent . . . no, he's something else. He's the artificial intelligence program – like a-a-a maybe you'd call it a robot brain – a robot brain that controls this world. And he's why we have to get out of here right now. The ruckus, somebody might have called the police. And when they arrive, they'll have photos of me, photos of you, and the man at the front desk, he's going to tell them where to find us. And *he'll* be with them – you know who – because I *didn't* kill him last night. Nobody can. We called him MasterControl on the Outside, and he's not going to stop until he deletes me, until he deletes *you*, or . . .'

'Or?'

'Or I find Porter for him.'

Gracie tries to stand then, but her legs wobble beneath her. She teeters like she's been sneaking gin again from her stepfather's booze stash. Bobby tries to catch her by the arm, but she shoves him away and steadies herself with the headboard. She's not ready to touch him again, though she doesn't deny she could stand hitting him a few more times.

The motel room around her has become painfully crisp, like when you look through a microscope at a leaf and realize the world is so much more complicated than it appears. Except it's worse than that, because as sharp and crisp as everything suddenly is, there's a squishiness to it, a spongy surrender to the slightest touch. Like the wooden headboard, which she thinks she could push her hand right through if she tried hard enough. 'This headboard, it's not real either,' she says in quiet horror. The carpet under her feet feels like foam. 'This floor isn't real. This motel. This hand . . . not real.' She studies the back of her hand, and while she knows what she is experiencing is all in her head – not quite a hallucination, but close – she nevertheless can peer into the tiny pores there, pores that open up like black holes for her imagination, violently gobbling up her logical conclusions, such as 'If I'm not real, then my parents aren't real either' and 'If my parents aren't real, then my dad never died' and 'If my dad never died, then I shouldn't miss him this much.' She approaches Bobby, reaching haltingly for his face, for the bloody prints she left there, and, as he reacts with silent confusion, she pushes her finger through a comma-shaped smear of his blood. His blood is on her finger now. 'You're not real either.'

Bobby reaches for Gracie's arm, but stops himself. 'Listen, I know how shocking this must all be,' he says. She snorts bitterly at this, the greatest understatement in all of history. 'But we don't have the luxury of time here. We have to go – wait!' He moves quickly around her and the bed, to where a blue jacket is lying in a bundle on the floor. He snatches it up, shaking it. 'This is mine. *His*, I mean. *He* must have left it.'

The jacket's left pocket is empty except for a pack of matches from someplace called the Schwarze Traube in West Berlin. The right pocket contains a small machine, a device of some kind that he seems to recognize. He taps the screen, revealing a glowing green digital fingerprint. On what must be a hunch, he presses his thumb against the digital fingerprint. The screen switches to one covered with a series of colourful little icons.

'What is that?' Gracie says, the unexpected mystery of the advanced technology in Bobby's hand rescuing her from the black holes spreading across her body, trying to rip her apart, along with her remaining sense of reality. The laws of nature are restored, at least momentarily. The carpet under her feet feels appropriately firm as she steps towards him.

'It's called a smartphone,' he says, apparently as stunned as she is by the sight of it, though for very different reasons.

'I've never seen a phone like that before.'

'Nobody in 1962 has.'

Gracie and Bobby leave the motel after this, looking over their shoulders the whole time. When she asks him where Porter – the other Bobby – went, really asking where *they're* going next, he glances at the smartphone's screen and says, 'Not where – *when*.'

The smartphone, a computer more advanced right now than

every computer in the world combined, is nothing more than a *mobile telephone*, he casually explains to her. It's a commonplace and generally unremarkable tool in the first decades of the twenty-first century. But Porter has modified this particular one, using his knowledge of the Outside, to help him locate and navigate special *tunnels* between locations and time and even dimensions, as Gracie understands them.

'You mean, like an Einstein–Rosen bridge,' she says, suddenly excited. 'Holy cow, a *wormhole*!'

'Something like that, yeah,' he says.

But then she begins to cry again, because Albert Einstein and Nathan Rosen were great big idiots like her, as confused and wrong about what they were observing in the universe around them as a Baptist preacher is about the punitive applications of fire and brimstone. 'All those times I spouted off about physics and what I was learning . . . I must have sounded ridiculous to you!'

He reaches for her arm. 'That wasn't me.'

Gracie yanks her arm away from him, still afraid of his touch. 'Cause it *was* Bobby, even if Bobby hasn't realized it yet. He *is* Porter and Porter *is* him except for a handful of experiences, and she finds it inconceivable that something so transformative could occur in any seven-month period that could split the same man into two entirely different people. Whatever made Porter *Porter* exists in Bobby, too.

Later, Bobby uses the smartphone to identify the location of what he calls a *coaxial terminal* in Navojoa, Mexico. They drive halfway there, nodding off more than once and snapping back awake just in time to save themselves from oncoming vehicles or a ravine or roaming packs of wild dogs, then rest in a motel of questionable character that only just reopened, the owner tells her with no regard for his own business, '*después de un asesinato*'– after a murder. Gracie is only doing this, coming with Bobby on his suicide mission, 'cause she's decided she needs proof, *real* proof – more than some doppelgänger and a drive-in sci-fi movie prop

– that what he told her is true. 'Cause she can't imagine spending the rest of her life – if she gets to live it at this point – wondering if he wasn't just nuts, one half of a set of murderous twins, murderous twins who seduced her and then sold her some deranged fantasy about how the world is really just computer code and she's nothing more than computer code and the stars, the stars that have defined so much of her life, are nothing but digital decor and she might actually collapse the System, her artificial reality, if she ever got the opportunity to attempt travel to one of these pretty illusions. Bobby told her this last bit about the stars on this first half of the drive, not realizing he wasn't helping her by truthfully answering all of her worries.

The second half of the drive to Navojoa is spent in silence except for the Tune that Gracie now hums uncertainly, 'cause she's terrified that anything else she asks of Bobby might produce a response that destroys another answer she hoped to maybe one day find herself out there beyond the claustrophobic confines of this tiny planet. 'Cause that's what hurts the most right now. Not the fact that maybe she isn't flesh and blood, but the fact that all her life, as far back as she can remember really, she understood the questions counterintuitively mattered more than the answers. That the search and the dreaming and the unfathomable vastness of it all, the unknowable secrets of the Tune she hums, these things mattered far more to her than being able to explain everything as succinctly and efficiently as *Encyclopædia Britannica* does. And now Bobby has gone and taken all of her questions away from her, and the effect could be fatal. If the universe is held together by gravity as science claims, Gracie was held together by questions, and now she feels as if the slightest breeze could blow her apart for good.

This feeling is why, by the time they arrive at the recently completed Adolfo Ruiz Cortines Dam just outside Navojoa, after they sneak inside after dark and, in a utility closet outside the control room, discover a door that wasn't there until Bobby taps glowing buttons on the smartphone, she says, 'Of course I am, you moron.'

This is in response to Bobby asking if she really intends to follow him. 'Cause, he says, 'Passing through this door means you leave behind who you are, probably for good. Your old life will be gone, Gracie. There would be no going back.'

Bobby stole something from Gracie, something she'll never get back. He pulled the curtain back and revealed to her the frail old Wizard. But through this utility closet door is a whole new set of questions, questions she hasn't begun to imagine yet, and she'll never get the chance to ask them if she keeps acting as if there's no place like home.

And this is how Gracie comes to find herself in eighteenth-century France in possession of the greatest secret in human history. Also, as it turns out, pregnant and alone.

Alfonso
Uxikál 1532

When he comes to, he's immediately disappointed to discover he's not surrounded by virgins, because virgins, a mansion, a ten-person hot tub tricked out with gold where he could get his knob polished every heavenly night would mean Allah was still real and there was hope yet for an end to this cycle of misery and lies and slavery. Instead, Alfonso finds himself lying amidst jagged rocks as a paint-covered naked bloke is lowered head first towards him out of a clear sky.

It takes a moment for him to locate himself at the bottom of some kind of hole. A huge hole like an abandoned quarry, with rock walls that climb nearly straight up and are covered in vines and small trees that have found a way to anchor their roots in shallow, snaking cracks. The bottom of the hole is a large pool of the most intensely blue water he's ever seen. Insects skip across it and here and there rocks rise out of it like clawed fingers intent upon trapping Oromo boys. Above, there are trees that frame the sun that hangs directly above him. It's up there, amongst those trees, where some chanting natives in ABBA colours are controlling the descent of the paint-covered naked bloke.

Alfonso knows what is happening as soon as the fog clears from his mind. Since his arrival in the New World, he's heard stories of human sacrifices, but it can't be the Aztec because they were forced to abandon these practices to appease their Spanish masters. That means those natives up there are Maya, and this is a sacrifice by drowning – which places Alfonso at the bottom of a *sacred cenote*.

Luckily, nobody has seen him yet. Well, besides the naked bloke with black make-up smeared across his eyes so he looks like a big dumb raccoon.

337

Alfonso slides off of the rocks, scraping his thigh from knee to ass cheek, but he long ago learned to ignore anything but the worst afflictions. A whip will quickly teach you that. From the water, he watches the human sacrifice approach the smooth surface. The chanting gets louder and louder. Somebody up there is shaking a rattle that sounds like a pissed-off rattlesnake. Others throw handfuls of flower petals that fall like snow, filling up the iris view of the sky above. And then the sacrifice goes under, meeting Alfonso's gaze with his raccoon eyes just before he does.

'No!' Alfonso says, screaming instinctively, and splashes through the water, arms mimicking movements he's seen others make because he doesn't actually know how to swim. When he reaches the drowning sacrifice, he's able to use the rope the bloke is dangling ankles first from to keep himself from drowning, too. The chanting above stops all at once, because they've spotted him now. Confused faces watch as he tries desperately to wrestle the sacrifice's upper body back to the surface, to fold him over at the waist, but the sacrifice bashes Alfonso's arms with his fists and scratches at Alfonso's face and wiggles in an effort to shake Alfonso loose. 'What the fuck, mate, I'm trying to save you!'

The sacrifice slowly goes still. Alfonso is finally able to get the bloke's head out of the water, but he's dead now, raccoon eyes locked open in some twisted cartoon parody of life. Alfonso lets the body sink again, and, clinging to it to stay afloat, peers up at the Maya along the cenote's rim. All of them men. Petals still flutter down from above, but most of them now cover the surface of the water.

One of the Maya points a finger at Alfonso and barks something in his language, but another voice, a woman's, imperiously interrupts. She pushes through the men, and glares down at Alfonso. Her next words are some kind of command. She must be in charge. All of this would be startling, even alarming, except for the fact that nothing in Alfonso's life has made sense in years, not since the universe swallowed him up and spat him out again. He yearns for the days when he would lose himself in the mundane and disgusting exploits of friends in American situation comedies. What he would give for thirty empty minutes with Ross and that slut whose name he no longer recalls.

The Maya lower more ropes, and warriors rapidly descend these like Spider-Man. They point two-handed swords with obsidian blades at Alfonso's face while others, still above, aim nocked arrows at him. There is no escape, and so Alfonso submits. He was always going to anyway, that's what slaves do. He is lassoed with a rope, and his body slowly rises from the blue water where the bloke with the raccoon eyes floats face down now. This isn't the cenote he fell into, Alfonso is pretty sure of that. That means he was sucked into one of the underground rivers that collect this land's water and carry it through the earth, connecting everything. The river carried him here, wherever *here* is.

The journey to the Maya's city can't be more than a few kilometres. Alfonso is permitted to walk the distance in between warriors who watch him sneeringly, clearly itching to hack him to pieces. The woman, who is actually a girl, no more than sixteen years old, as is now clear, keeps glancing over her shoulder at him. She's dressed in fine, clean duds, heaps of gold and precious gems that sparkle like colourful stars when the sun hits them, and a cape of rainbow feathers that makes her look like a bird with its wings tucked against its body. But, like, a really sexy bird.

Uxikál provides Alfonso with a glimpse of what Ciudad de México must have been like before Cortés arrived. Except, instead of covering a lake island, it unfolds across a steep hilltop that has clearly been excavated and reshaped over hundreds of years to accommodate population growth. There are only two ways to enter: the first, by crossing one of several bridges that span two deep, intersecting ravines; the second, through a gate in a stone wall that defends the only side of the hill unguarded by natural features. Walled roads slice through the hillside, climbing towards the city centre where, without warning, you arrive in a plaza lorded over by a towering pyramid, several palaces, and countless other stone buildings of varied importance. For as impressive as the architectural accomplishments are here – and Alfonso struggles to understand how anybody as primitive as these people could accomplish something like this – there's a feeling of decay and collapse about it. Like the city's glory days are decades, maybe even centuries, behind it. Stone is crumbling everywhere, paint has faded, banners and flags are tattered.

It's a ghost town today.

Windows into monumental buildings once occupied by the wealthy reveal empty rooms. The market, which consumes so much of the plaza, is occupied by barren tables, teetering huts, and feral dogs and small animals that have adventurously moved in. The few grocers and artisans that remain fend off no crowds. Aztec slaves told Alfonso about this, about the thriving cities they came from before the Spanish arrived, and how the Spanish brought with them plagues and famine and how, when the Spanish left their cities dying, many cried out for the whip because at least the whip came with food and shelter and a new god who might yet save them. Even now, more than four hundred years before Abdul Fattah will be born in Addis Ababa, the West was fucking it up for everybody. Maybe the Almighty was full of shit, but the jihad definitely wasn't.

Alfonso is taken to a temple next door to the pyramid. Here, the girl leaves him to the machinations of several priests with gnarled faces and large noses that make them look like sickly vultures. Two warriors remain, the fiercest-looking of them, to make sure he behaves. A drink the priests give him helps in this regard, too. Alfonso doesn't know it's drugged at first, but he feels its effects quickly enough. That's good, because it keeps him from fighting back when the warriors pin his arms and legs down and the priests jab at his dick with what look like stingray spines. While Alfonso finds his limbs sluggish and unwilling to obey his commands, his body's ability to feel pain remains. He yowls even though he's not sure he actually does. Maybe he just tries. Is his mouth working? Is his throat? He can't tell any more. The priests wipe his bloody dick with a delicately woven cream-coloured cloth, and when the cloth is smeared crimson, they drop it into a fire and say prayers over it because why the fuck not.

Afterwards, more drugs are poured into Alfonso's mouth and sleep takes him. He dreams of falling through time again, of time shattering around him like all those mirrors in his favourite Bruce Lee movie, shattering into uncountable pieces that follow him like a dangerous, glittering wake.

It's dark when Alfonso wakes inside a candlelit hut. And cold. People are chanting somewhere, heaps of them. Two words, over and over. The priests have dressed him in gold and gems like the bird girl's and a heavy jaguar skin cape that stinks of mould, they've painted his body white and, over his now-ghostly form, grey glyphs that smear and swirl together with intentional abandon, and they've shaved his head and painted it, too, although he can't see how yet. Nobody attempts to explain why any of this is happening as they lift him to his feet and usher him towards the doorway of the hut. There's torchlight outside and a damp wind that brings goose pimples. One of the priests says a word in his language, then waves at the door like a cinema usher. They will not be joining him, but he must pass through it. Alfonso tries to turn away, but two warriors, the same pair who have been minding him for much of the day, stand with their swords ready to run him through if necessary.

He gets it, there's no choice here.

Alfonso turns and faces the doorway again, ducks under its low clearance – the Maya are much, much shorter than Oromo people – and steps outside. He finds himself standing on top of the giant pyramid, on a kind of flat terrace, along with some ancient, half-naked and hunched-over geezer dressed up in feathers like he's on his way to a gay seniors' pride parade, another old bloke who wears a jaguar cape like Alfonso's and holds two ceremonial sceptres – one with an Islam-style crescent moon on top of it and the other with what looks like a cob of corn – and, behind him, lurking in the shadows, the sixteen-year-old girl. She's decked out now in a bejewelled dress, a headdress that looks like a jungle bird just landed on her pretty head, and the same feathered cape she had on earlier.

Alfonso responds in English, the first time he's used the language in years. 'Seriously, what the fuck?' he says.

Below, thousands of torches twinkle like orange stars against the matt black of night while no stars shine in the sky above. The world has been turned upside down, and Alfonso struggles to hold on as voices chant like thunder around him – '*B'olon chami! B'olon chami! B'olon chami!*'

That's when Alfonso realizes these mental fuckers turned his dick into a pincushion, painted him up like some kind of arse bandit, and are now going to rip out his heart and eat it like a mango or chop off his head and kick it down these steps, because all that sounds like a pretty spiffy thing to do if you want to scare the shit out of your people.

But nobody rips out Alfonso's heart. Nobody chops his head off. The chanting continues as the High Priest of Gay Day shakes a rattle around Alfonso's head, then summons the girl to join him and shakes the rattle around her head, too, then the King of the Gays touches each of Alfonso's shoulders with his sceptres and does the same to the girl. Then the people cheer, and Alfonso suddenly feels like a dipstick, because he understands now that he just got hitched to the hot-ass girl dressed up like a bird and he's probably going to get to have sex with her now and, Allah be merciful, please don't let him come all over himself again.

Alfonso and the girl are taken to the King of the Gays' palace. This bloke is actually the king of the Uxikál people and the girl is his daughter, which means Alfonso has also married himself a princess. *Prince Alfonso*, sweet. *Prince Abdul Fattah* sounds even better. Except when they get to the princess's room and he tries to properly introduce himself, because he thinks she might want to know whom she's about to root, she says a word that he's pretty sure means *no*.

'No, that's *my* name,' he says in English. Then, in Spanish, 'My name is Alfonso.'

'No, your name is *B'olon Chami*,' the princess says in Spanish, too. She touches her breast.

'Moon-Shadow.' She touches his chest. '*B'olon Chami* – Many Deaths.'

'Many Deaths – what? No, wait, *you speak Spanish*? I'm *Alfonso*.'

'*Many Deaths*. Wash your face. Take off clothes.'

'I-I don't understand,' the man who was Abdul Fattah and who was Alfonso and apparently now goes by the name of Many Deaths says.

Moon-Shadow lets her feather cape slip from her shoulders, then her dress, so that all she's wearing is her bird headdress and a lot of jewellery that hangs down over her perfect breasts.

'Okay,' he says to her breasts.

Many Deaths hurries to a table, where a large bowl of water waits for him. He catches his reflection just before he plunges his hands into the water. His face and head are painted like a skull. The priests turned him into a death's head. He looks at Moon-Shadow and wonders what this means, what the birds and jaguar skins mean, what all of this means. He's stumbled into a world of gods and symbols he doesn't understand. 'Please, tell me what is happening,' he says.

'*Wash*,' she says, pointing at the bowl of water.

He scrubs his face and head with soap until he's sure the paint is gone. It scares him, the skull face, what it might represent. When he turns to look at Moon-Shadow again, she is lying on a low bed with the headdress and gold and jewels removed. He has seen naked women before, when he was a slave and not a prince, but slave-titties and slave-minge don't count. It's all just so sad and sickening and embarrassing. Even now, the thought of it horrifies him, and the stench of their filth and misery comes back to him. Nothing like Moon-Shadow, nothing so beautiful and perfect as her, so round and soft and inviting.

'Take off clothes,' she says.

Many Deaths does. He comes to her, climbs into bed beside her, and immediately reaches for her brown nipples. This is it, he's finally going to lose his virginity, and not to some whore he paid for like so many of his mates. He's going to share himself with *his* wife, *his* princess.

Moon-Shadow slaps his hand away. 'No,' she says – clearly, he needs to cure her of that word – and climbs on top of him with startling authority. She takes his dick, still aching and blood-encrusted but hard as it's been for the past five minutes, and slides it into her with her hand, some spit and carefully applied weight. He tries to take her by the curve of her hips, fingers dipping into her flesh. She grabs him by the chin so hard he winces. 'No!'

She makes love to Many Deaths like this, which only lasts for a minute before he cries out and explodes inside her. She looks confused by this, although not as confused – or as embarrassed – as he does. He quickly apologizes and promises it'll be better next time. They lie there in silence for a long, awkward moment after this. Many Deaths still soaring and she quiet and as distant as the jungle's night song. Finally, he says, 'Tell me what's happening, please.'

Moon-Shadow rolls onto her side, to look into his eyes, and folds her hands together under her cheek. For the first time, she seems . . . *mortal*. Like him. She's so young, not nearly as strong as she needs to be. 'Father weak,' she says. 'Bad men try to take power. I fix. *I* fix.'

'Okay,' he says. 'So, your father is king, but somebody is trying to move in on his action. You think marrying me is a' – he shakes his head – 'a *solution* to that? I'm sorry, I'm trying to understand.'

'You, *Death*. I, *Birth*,' she says. She searches for a word in Spanish. '*Simbolas*.'

Many Deaths fumbles with the word himself, but only because she confused its gender. 'Ah, *simbolos*,' he says. 'Symbols, yes!' Then, 'Hold on, *I'm* death?'

Moon-Shadow nods. 'Lord of Xibalba, the Place of Fear,' she says.

'Like . . . Hell?' he says. 'Some kind of underworld?'

'*He'le*, *sí*,' she says.

'Because I came out of that cenote, you mean. *You* told them I was a god, and you're this princess, and now we're this power couple. Oh. Oh *wow*.'

She smiles. 'Now *I* have power.'

'Yeah, but what about your father's enemies?'

'No more enemies after tonight.'

Many Deaths gasps, and claps his hand over his own mouth. 'Holy shit, you went all *Michael Corleone* on them!' he says.

Moon-Shadow doesn't understand.

'It's a . . .' he says, but stops because he doesn't know the word in Spanish because movies don't exist yet. 'Never mind. You're taking care of business.'

She rises, and retrieves her dress from a chair. 'Yes,' she says. 'I take care of business.' She's careful with these strange words, repeating them because they mean something to Many Deaths. Outside the windows, screams begin to violate the night. 'I take care of all business.'

Many Deaths gets up to join her, looking for the weird skirt thing he was wearing. 'Where are we going?' he says.

'I go, you stay,' Moon-Shadow says, opening the door. The two warriors who have been with him all day stand guard outside. She gives them orders in her language, then looks again at Many Deaths who's standing there, naked, hiding his dick with his hands. 'You no leave ever. I own you.' She closes the door behind her.

Great, Many Deaths is a prince, a god, and apparently still a fucking slave. This sucks. Then again, he's not a virgin any more, so there's that. Outside, the screaming continues.

DAMIEN SYCO ALIVE!

Personal nurse confirms kidnapping plot!
Secret documents!

A personal nurse of Damien Syco was paid £25,000 by Global News UK to reveal details of the deceased rocker's last days, but after a second pay-out by an unknown source, the story was never published.

'Yesterday, I became aware that the details of a confidential agreement I had with Global News UK, with regards to the alleged death of Mr Syco, have been leaked to the press,' Thomas Okonkowo, a Nigeria-born resident of the United Kingdom, said in a statement.

'I can confirm that Mr Syco did not die in my care on 16 May 2016 and was, in fact, recovering from pneumonia when he was forcibly removed from his home by four armed men who beat me and warned me that I would have my residency visa revoked if I ever discussed what happened.'

Reality Media Company, which is based in Russia and whose business currently remains unclear, subsequently paid Okonkwo £150,000 in exchange for him signing over his rights 'in perpetuity' to the story about Syco's disappearance.

The contract stipulated that Okonkowo would have to pay a £1.5 million penalty if he ever discussed Syco's disappearance or having been employed by Syco.

Syco's long-time lawyer, Harry Herschel Hershfield, based in Manhattan, called Okonkowo a 'known fabricator of fantastical fictions' whose poor book-keeping skills have led to numerous documented attempts by him to blackmail the Syco estate.

Okonkowo's finances are, Hershfield went on to assert, why Okonkowo secretly sold his story about Syco's alleged kidnapping to Global News UK.

In an exclusive interview, Okonkowo did not deny personal hardship, but insists he sold his story to Global News UK because he is worried about his 'dear friend's fate.'

Syco is reported to have died three years ago, but Okonkowo believes Syco has been held against his will since then, while Syco's fans have been misled by 'wealthy, powerful people' into believing a heart attack killed Syco so they don't come 'looking for their Moonman'.

This, Okonkowo claims, is why the story he sold to Global News UK was spiked – a journalistic term, meaning to bury a news story before it's published – when his contract with the organisation was leaked.

'Whoever took Mr Syco, they don't want the world to know the truth, so they must have paid a fortune to make that story go away,' Okonkowo said, adding that he has passed three polygraph lie-detector tests that prove he is telling the truth.

Nevertheless, his ex-wife, Bridget Kvesik, has told other news outlets that her former husband is 'mentally ill' and a 'pathological liar'.

'Like this one time, he says he saw the Loch Ness Monster even though we was in Wales.'

Harriet Parasol, editor-in-chief of the *Morning Sun*, a subsidiary of Global News UK, acknowledged paying Okonkowo for his story but says that the story was spiked because it 'lacked any credibility'.

Parasol acknowledged a second pay-out from an unidentified party that wished to take ownership of Okonkowo's story, but declined to comment whether or not this unidentified party was also Reality Media Company.

Tab

All he wants to do is break into a moonwalk over that kiss with Keisha, but his Uber driver won't shup up about what President Glass is doing for the country. The driver is white, looks sixty but that's probably because of the menthols she stinks of, and her voice grates like a teaspoon dropped into a garbage disposal. He keeps suggesting she turn the radio up, but she doesn't hear him. It's when she starts talking about all the good the president has done for 'the Blacks', like ending all the racial division the last president stirred up, that Tab tells her to stop the car, that's it, right now, here, that's fine. He has to give her credit, though. She didn't say *the Blacks* a few decibels lower than his liberal friends do. No, she's not worried about accidentally sounding racist, or even revealing, God forbid, she sees race. This woman knows, no doubt about it, what she is and is straight-up cool about him knowing it, too. The honesty is refreshing. Tab gets out of the Uber not even two blocks away from the Chateau – traffic is a bitch at this time of night, everybody trying to get home from the bars and clubs along Sunset – and walks the rest of the way back to his car. By the time the valet arrives at the kerb with the Turing, he's pretty sure he's sober enough to drive.

He tries to listen to some Kendrick, but the words aren't helping any more than the Uber driver's were. He wants to be by himself, with his excitement, with the promise of what's to come. Yeah, it's not going to be easy. It's going to be hard as hell, more like it. Luiza is going to hate him, especially when she hears it's Keisha he's leaving her for. She's always accused him of still being in love with her. And who knows what Luiza will want to do about the kid when he tells her. Knowing her, she'll want to keep it. Tab doesn't think he can begrudge her that, if that's what she

348

decided. Christ, this is all so fucked up, but for the first time in a very, very long time, he feels like he has solid ground beneath his feet. This. Is. The. Right. Thing. To. Do. It is. It just is. Isn't it?

He glances at a text from Luiza, who wants to know yet again where he is. She's texted five times now. When he looks back up, he somehow misses the oncoming headlights and nearly gets his front end clipped as he runs a red light at Santa Monica Blvd. The near-miss startles him into sudden, painful awareness. Shit, what was he thinking driving?

What was it he was telling Keisha? It was about . . . about movies, that's it. Movies, movies, but what about them? How they're not about anything any more, or something like that. They're about trying to get back something we lost because the world no longer makes sense to us. The movies could just talk about the world around us, trying to translate it for us, but how do you translate an experience that no longer resembles anything like a reality any sane person would want to live in? No, it's better to go back, to just hang out in what was, or at least a bad cover version of what was. *That's it*, that's what he was talking about. How they're nothing but bullshit pushers now, *pushing bullshit*, bullshit people need to survive what's happening to them. Like Damien Syco said, they're the lies we tell ourselves to get by. And Keisha . . . well, Keisha is Tab's greatest, his most glorious, his most numbing lie. He knows Keisha could never be what he needs, what he *really* needs, because what he really, *really* needs can't be had unless somebody invents some way for him to slingshot himself around the sun at warp speed. It was lost long ago when his family died on him and took his past with them, all the stories about their ancestors they used to tell at bedtime and on Juneteenth and when his mother made beef stew on chilly fall nights, like the one about the first free Whittaker or the great-uncle who was a Nazi hunter in post-WWII Europe or about how they were descended from great Angolan kings who would one day rise up again. But Keisha and her equally boundless imagination, her desperate need to connect with a past she understood as little as he did, somehow made this loss more bearable despite how messed up she was, how raw and cold she could be, how blunt and harsh and maybe even cruel because she didn't know any better. Luiza is just as messed up, no doubt, but in different ways. They're all messed up at the end of the day, women, men, the whole human race, and maybe that's always been Tab's real superpower – he doesn't hold it against any of them. Keisha used to tell him this made him weak, but Luiza said it's what made her fall in love with him.

Luiza let Tab in on this little secret while they were vacationing in the Loire Valley together. He took her there a few years ago without revealing he had taken Keisha there, too. His family had visited when he was a kid, he claimed, which wasn't remotely true because they didn't have money to do more than hit Yosemite every three or four summers. But Tab had to go back to Saint-Règle and he couldn't tell Luiza why, not without her thinking he was crazy. After they arrived and made love in their chateau suite as horses drank at a kidney-shaped pond outside the window and the sun dropped behind a ridgeline of verdant trees, he went outside and lay down in the thick grass, amidst beheaded sunflower stalks, and watched the stars. Stars he had not stopped thinking about since he came here with Keisha after his first big sale. His whole life, he never thought about them; barely noticed them up there, in fact. But when Keisha asked him where he wanted to go to celebrate, he said here, Saint-Règle, even though he didn't know why until he came out here and lay in the thick grass under the stars then, too, and something inside him moved like when he first heard Syco's voice coming out of his dad's speakers. Something moved, and he began to rise through grace, a Guido Anselmi in Jordans, rising away from the Earth and all its temporal worries into the stars that wheeled around him like an endless river of light, towards endless possibilities, towards the answers he's always sought. Except Luiza found him before he floated completely away, and the tether around his ankle yanked so hard that he crashed back to the ground and into her arms. He proposed right then and there, in the field where the horses grazed, and they made love again under the stars and possibilities, the answers just out of his reach, and, afterwards, he said, 'Let's have a baby,' and now they're having a baby after three more years of unprotected screwing. This is why Tab can't hold her issues against her, not really. He's just as fucked up, maybe more. He can't leave her just because he wasn't made right, or that the world doesn't make sense to him like it should, or he's just not as happy as the bullshit pushers want him to be. Anyways, has he ever really been happy? *Really* happy? Besides as a kid, he means, when his parents and brother were still around. Maybe he was in London, too, come to think of it, right after Syco died. Those three days, he felt connected to something. The feeling of grace he experienced in Saint-Règle even returned temporarily. Time and possibilities, even answers, didn't seem to be located in the stars any more, in something beyond him, but in the hands and arms holding him, in the thousands of voices singing as one, in the sea of swaying bodies that moved and swayed to Syco's music. Of course, none of this matters now, does it? There's a kid on the way, a kid who deserves what he had, a mom and a dad, his own connections, and so he can't float off into the stars. That's why Tab is going to call Keisha in the morning and tell her it was just the margaritas talking, he's really sorry, but he loves his wife and he's got to think about the kid now, and, come on, they know what they're like together, why it would never work, so let's not make that mistake again.

Tab turns the radio back on as he approaches Sunset and Doheny, and Syco's 'A Seer Is a Liar' suffuses him and the Turing in the singer's soaring voice and Rick Ramsay's unforgettable Echoplex-distorted guitar solo. The traffic and flashing billboards around him dissolve away, and he's left with the certainty of his decision and Syco's music, which always makes him feel like he's listening to the universe. Finally, cars begin to move and the

Turing whines gently forward as Tab drums the steering wheel along with the song. Light expands around him like the music, something outside screeches even louder than Syco, and the tether holding him to this Earth snaps for good.

Jones

Hermosillo 1962

He gives the hotel owner a US twenty-dollar bill to let him make an international call, this after negotiating in sign language, increasingly frustrated gesticulations, and words crudely and embarrassingly translated from English into Spanish – like *telephone call-é*. It takes another five bucks to get the man to let him have some privacy. When Jones is finally alone, he roots around in his various pockets for Angelique's card and, when he has found it, wrinkled and water-damaged now, stained with coffee and two thick drops of dark blood that feel like embossments, he dials her number. 'What the fuck have you done to me?' he says when she answers.

Angelique's voice purrs at him through the receiver. 'You already know what I did,' she says. 'It was the only way, Bobby.'

'You used me,' he says, snarling.

'Yes, I did,' she says. Her voice remains irritatingly calm. 'Think about what's at stake here. Did you really want me playing it safe? To take no chances and trust MasterControl would work it all out for us in the end?'

MasterControl has had a week of Perceived Time in this model to locate the Pasadena City Hall bomber, and has failed miserably so far. The bomber, Porter, has moved on to other coaxial terminals, destroying Common Data Exchange junctures along the way, and destabilizing one model after another until the whole System is now on the brink of catastrophic collapse. No, leaving it up to MasterControl was not an option.

'Just tell me why,' Jones says.

'As soon as you were identified as the terrorist behind the City Hall bombing, I was brought in to monitor the situation,' Angelique says, beginning to explain. This in and of itself is extraordinary, given her senior position on the Outside; it's like using an electron telescope to read the phone book. 'There was another attack on a coaxial terminal not long afterwards. I can't assign a time frame, even MasterControl can't track these things, but it quickly became apparent *you* were not finished. When I consulted MasterControl after the third attack, it told me it had made no progress in its investigation. That's when I decided to take matters into my own hands.'

She means by downloading a memory back-up of Jones back into his specific model, into 1962, specifically the night of the Pasadena City Hall bombing.

'It's really quite amusing, Bobby,' she says, continuing. 'During the design phase, the rest of the team, including moi, wanted MasterControl to be able to track residents through the CDEs, but *you*, you didn't trust it. You thought giving so much power to an AI that possessed our, admittedly, strained ethics would lead to it turning on the System.'

'Deities with a basic list of commands to follow are predictable,' Jones says, repeating the argument he made then. What if MasterControl evolved beyond its initial programming, as the System itself does and continues to do? What if it began to challenge its own role and concept of being? 'Deities with *feelings*, for lack of better words, are not. The latter is dangerous, potentially catastrophic to any system that demands order.'

'Tell me about it, big boy,' Angelique says. 'But it's ironic, isn't it? It's because of this nasty little handicap you gave Master-Control that *you* got away with graduating from an overemotional bomber to an overemotional *serial* bomber. It's why I'm talking to you right now, because the only way I could think of tracking *you* down was using *you* to do it.'

'You didn't know why I did it,' he says, realizing. 'Why Porter did it, I mean.'

'I had my suspicions,' she says. 'Which is why I made sure you two went on this journey together. Was I right?'

'I don't know yet,' Jones says. But he's lying, because the only thing he thinks about any more is Gracie and how to save her, everybody else be damned. He understands now that Angelique downloaded a back-up copy of him back into the System that was saved right before he met Gracie for the first time. In doing so, she hoped she would trigger through Gracie the same process of discovery for Jones that Porter had experienced.

'A long time ago, you asked me to help you build the System because you didn't understand other beings, remember?' Angelique says. 'You didn't want the actors we populated the Earth models with to be as cold as you were. As cold as MasterControl turned out to be.'

He doesn't disagree.

'You thought I was sentimental, that's what you called me,' she says. 'You mocked me for it in your own petty way even though you needed me, and now look at you – a taste of human love turned you into a homicidal maniac.'

That stings Jones. 'Not me,' he says, despite all evidence to the contrary.

He can sense her grinning at him through the phone. 'Oh, Bobby, your biggest problem has always been your inability to accept *you're* your biggest problem. *Figuratively*, in my world. *Literally*, in yours.'

'What about the Outside?' he says. 'What about what *you* did to me?'

'Let's get it out there,' Angelique says. 'Finally, let's get it out there. Your ambition would've destroyed this place if I didn't do what I did.'

'Stab me in the back?' he says, letting himself sound bitter.

'The Corporation was happy with the product,' she says, pushing back forcefully. 'Customers were happy with the product. The design team was happy with the product. Why couldn't you just leave it alone?'

Maybe she's right, too. Maybe Jones brought this all on himself with his manic determination to perfect the System, to put an end to the instability that would periodically spring up during the model recycles, to unlock the Event Horizon and set Perceived Time free for ever. The Corporation had no interest in his ambitions, they saw his hubris as a threat, and they removed him from the leadership of his own creation. He was stripped of his titles and accomplishments. His recognition and legacy were turned to ashes. And he became, in an instant, as meaningless and unimportant as he was when he first posited the idea of the System to the being speaking to him right now. To the only being in the galaxy he trusted at the time.

And if Angelique is right about Jones, does the same hold true for Porter?

'I couldn't leave the System alone because it wasn't perfect,' he says. 'It's still not. All you have to do is get to . . .' His voice trails off, a thought is beginning to form in his head.

'Bobby?' she says.

'All you have to do is get to . . . to know somebody here,' he says slowly, trying to work the thought out at the same time he shapes words with his lips. '*Really* get to know them. And . . . and you see it. You see it's, it's not reality. It's a . . . a trick. A-A-A *cruel trick* we've pulled on them.'

'Ah, there it is then. You've figured it out, haven't you, Bobby? What the other you – what *you* – really want for these people.'

Jones lets his forehead fall against the phone booth's cold window. The fate of the System, the world as trillions upon trillions of actors know it here, is on the line – all because a diner waitress offered him a piece of pie.

Angelique smiles through the phone again, and asks, 'The question now is, what are you going to do about it?'

Mimori

Kamakura 2027

She swims until the lights of shore seem as distant as the stars above. She should be in orbit right now, but they grounded her and Malik last week. 'Temporarily unfit for service,' the Space-NEXT psych report said. Maybe it's true. Maybe that's how she wound up out here, so far from land, almost too far to make it back before her tired limbs stop responding, and the salt water fills her lungs, and it's all over. Maybe it's because Mimori knows that no matter what she does, no matter how many times she wakes up and puts on a smile for her daughters and gets through the day without screaming or crying or both, none of it will ever really matter because every day is somehow worse than the day before, because she knows every day to come will be worse than the day before it, because she knows her daughters are going to grow up in a world worse in every way than the one Mimori grew up in. The fatigue of knowing this is debilitating, threatening to drown her even when she's on land or in space. No, that's not right. It's not fatigue. It's *boredom*. The world is going to die, her daughters are going to die, and the reality of that just isn't startling any more. This sense of rank inevitability is so all-consuming that she often finds herself thinking of the future in the past tense. And the future is boring. *That* is how Mimori wound up this far out, treading water, wondering which way to swim. She's fucking bored.

She starts for shore.

The thought of Sōjirō raising their girls without her terrifies Mimori more than another fifty years of this; it's really that simple.

She returns home close to midnight, about three hours later than expected. The *minka* is silent. She removes her sandals, and pads across the tatami towards the *fusuma* that flickers from the light of the television on the other side of it. The girls are watching something that would be loud and obnoxious, full of gunfire and tyres screeching and masculine whooping, except the TV is on mute. Okimo is asleep on a futon.

'TV time is done, sweetie,' she says, moving closer.

Okimo's head has been almost completely severed from the neck. The tether of flesh holding it in place would have ripped had a pillow not caught her when she slumped over. There is blood everywhere, Mimori realizes now. On her daughter. On the ceiling. Across the *fusama* leading into the garden. In a great pool now congealing around the futon.

Mimori's fingers claw at her own face, digging into her cheeks and chin, and something like a howl rends the startling quiet of her home.

Then she remembers Tamami, and runs to find her. She doesn't have to go further than the hallway, where her oldest daughter lies on the floor, limbs akimbo like the Buddhist sauwastika. Her back has been cut open by a great shoulder-to-hip slash. Tamami tried to escape her killer, and was hacked down from behind.

Mimori tries to shake some life back into her little girl, but only discovers her daughter's eyes locked open, staring into the abyss.

Somebody is praying quietly nearby. It's coming from the room where the past is stored. The family meditates here, family heirlooms are mounted on the walls, and, in the corner, they keep a *butsudan* for praying to Buddha and the gods and their ancestors. Sōjirō is kneeling before this heavily burdened altar, head bowed, mumbling desperate entreaties as candles and incense burn.

And lying on the tatami before him, dripping fresh blood from its long, curving blade, is *Chikyuu no tsurugi*, the Sword of the Earth – a four-hundred-year-old katana that once belonged to a *bushi* named Ando Tomisaburo and has been passed down from one Ando to the next, even after the *bushi* were abolished, until Ando Sōjirō, a historian too gentle to harm a cricket, used it to slaughter his defenceless children.

'Jirō?' Mimori says through the tears, still too confused by the sight to otherwise react.

Sōjirō's head snaps around. His eyes swell with shame and horror at being discovered and then, finally, rage. He grabs the katana, and springs to his feet.

Mimori runs, trying to outpace him, but knows she cannot. And so, she locks herself in the bathroom, and throws herself against the door – one of the only two Western doors in the *minka* – to help it withstand his kicks, and she begs to know why as she wails and shakes.

'You know why!' Sōjirō says, roaring back at her.

Chikyuu no tsurugi's long blade pierces the door next to Mimori's head, pushing all the way through, up to the hilt, and she sees her screaming face briefly reflected across the polished steel.

'What I did was a kindness!' Sōjirō says. There's desperation in his twisted voice. He needs her to understand what he did to their girls, and, dear Lord Buddha, she does, with every milligram of her being she doe

BOOK THREE:
REBIRTH

The girl who fell to Earth
Said she didn't want to die
They call life death's afterbirth
If anyone has the time

Lyrics, 'The Girl Who Fell to Earth'

Jupiter

Jonesboro 1989

They go to the Buffet House for lunch after church, like they do every Sunday, and he watches Monique as she silently eats, as her eyes drift around the packed restaurant between bites of fried catfish and okra and nagging questions from the three kids, as she looks at and pays attention to everybody and everything in the world besides him, and he wonders if he should still drive out to the Nettleton and Highland Drive railroad crossing to do it like he planned or if he should instead do it in their bed – jam the barrel under his chin so the back of his skull and whatever he's got for brains splatter across the pastel-flowers-and-tiny-little-birdies wallpaper she made him put up even though he hated it – so that at least his wife finally notices he's there again. Jupiter can't stand anything about the woman and every inch of her confuses and often even disgusts him, but they've been at this for damn near fifteen years and he resents feeling so alone in a relationship he didn't want in the first place. No, that's not true. It was his idea to get hitched after Monique got pregnant and refused to do anything about it – even though she hadn't found Jesus yet, or rather found him again – so he has nobody but himself to blame for losing the art school scholarship. No, that's not entirely true either. He loved her, he did, at least he's pretty sure he did. And there were a few good years, too, no denying that. The kids made it all worth it, in their own way. But this can't go on, that's clear, and so Jupiter is going to drive out to the Nettleton and Highland Drive railroad crossing to do it, 'cause, even though Monique can't look at him, can't do more than holler at him for most of the same reasons he hollers back at her, he doesn't actually hate her enough to ruin the wallpaper she probably loves more than him at this point.

Later that night, he lies down on the love seat where he spends most nights, more comfortable in its sagging embrace than in bed next to his wife. TV programmes and news broadcasts replace the white noise of her endless complaining, and he drifts off to sleep. He always falls asleep right away. Staying asleep, that's the problem.

Jupiter startles awake less than an hour later, arms waving and legs kicking like somebody is on top of him. Except nobody's on top of him. Nobody was on top of him in his dream either. He was in a car, someplace that felt utterly familiar and yet he knows for a fact he's never visited. He's had this dream many, many times.

It is always night-time in the dream, that Moonman crap is playing on the radio, and the street, all four lanes of it – bordered by buildings and billboards covered in blinking lights – is bumper to bumper despite the sense that it's very late or very early, depending on how you look at it. Jupiter's hands are his hands, but also not, and they drum the steering wheel in time to the weird-ass music. And then the light splashes across the windshield, filling up the whole car until Jupiter can't see, and the car stops like a wrecking ball has slammed into it. The door crushes his body, and in this dream-place, this other-place he can't understand, time slows and he's aware of how the metal frame shatters his hip and how his spine comes apart like a Jenga tower and organs he's never paid much attention to are punctured and burst and stop working like his fancy car. The Moonman is still singing someplace, which makes as much sense as pretty much all of this. Incidentally, Jupiter only knows it's the Moonman singing 'cause after the hundredth or so time he had this dream, he went to a local record shop and interrogated the white boy behind the counter until he came away with a song title – 'A Seer Is a Liar', whatever that means – from the British singer's fifth album, *Buddha Bad (or One Thousand and One Nights in Tucson)*.

Jupiter always jolts awake at this point in the dream. He told Monique about it once, and about the other dreams that confuse him but aren't as terrifying, and Monique told him to go to her psychic 'cause he was clearly having past-life memories and that's some voodoo bullshit you don't want to be messing with, and maybe that's why he's so impossible to live with, too, did he think of that? She would've told Jupiter to go see their pastor, but the last time she sent him to their pastor, the guy told Jupiter to pray more and told Monique that maybe her husband was having such unchristian thoughts 'cause she wasn't fulfilling her marital duties well enough, and after that Monique just decided not to deal with what was really tormenting Jupiter besides these dreams. As for the psychic, she was less helpful than the pastor. Just a lot of song and dance about unlocking his past lives and escaping the hold they have on us, all for two hundred bucks that better come in cash 'cause, as they both were, she wasn't going to trust some brother who works at the Waffle House not to bounce a cheque on her ass. Jupiter kept his two hundred dollars, hasn't prayed in years, and wonders if he'll die on impact, like he does in his dreams, or if he'll live for a few moments as the train turns his car and body into scrap metal and raw hamburger.

'You okay, daddy?' Tasha asks him. He must've woken her. Sometimes he makes a noise when he wakes up. 'Bad dreams again?'

Jupiter holds his hand out for her. She takes it, and lets him pull her tiny body onto his lap. She's only eight, but he already knows that she and Jhasmin and Leesa are the best things he's ever done with his life. So good, in fact, maybe he wouldn't change a thing if he could go back in time and talk to that stupid seventeen-year-old who knocked Monique up 'cause neither of them thought it could happen if they skipped a jimmy just the once. He sits there, holding Tasha for the longest moment, until she begins to squirm.

'I have to go pee,' she says, wriggling free. But Jupiter doesn't let her go; he needs her, and she probably senses it. 'What did you dream about?'

'I'd rather not say, sweetie,' he says.

'You always say that.'

'California, okay,' he says.

'Huh?'

'I dreamed about California,' he says.

'California don't sound too nice.'

'I've never been,' he says.

'Something bad happens to you there?'

'I thought you had to pee,' he says.

'What happens to you?'

'Not me, not really,' he says. 'Somebody else.'

'Who?'

'I don't know,' he says. 'I don't really, truly understand what's happening to me.' He looks at her tiny hand in his, and for a moment he thinks he might cry. 'I feel like I'm coming apart sometimes.'

Jupiter sees Tasha doesn't understand. He's scared her. She pulls her hand from his, and pushes off him.

'It's okay,' he says. 'Now, go potty and get back to bed. Your ma is going to whoop you silly if she catches you up like this.'

Tasha walks to the hallway, looks back one last time, and then is gone. Jupiter waits for the toilet to flush, then lies back down. The dream comes again and again until he gives up, grabs his truck keys, and turns left out of the driveway in the direction of Nettleton and Highland Drive.

Nobody is on the road as Jupiter passes the drug store and sees the old metallic gold Lincoln driven by a middle-aged white man in a polo shirt turn into the narrow driveway that leads into the back parking lot the drug store shares with a long cinder-block building that once housed two metal-shop outfits and a cutlery warehouse and is now abandoned except for the faint music that emanates from behind a single unmarked door.

Jupiter pulls over, puts his '78 Ford Ranger in park and rolls the window down. He listens carefully until he hears it. Music interrupts the quiet for the briefest of moments as the unmarked door presumably opens for the white man and his polo shirt, then vanishes when the door shuts again. It's not loud enough for Jupiter to identify what song is playing, but it feels *alive*. He turns the truck off, and gets out, 'cause what's wrong with having one last drink in a bar with no signage that everybody pretends isn't there before you go park your car on train tracks with your name on them?

Gracie

Like characters in a Mark Twain story about time-travelling Yankees, she and Bobby arrive on the Aunis coast of France dressed for the wrong era and have no alternative but to steal less conspicuous attire from a clothesline strung up behind an unassuming fisherman's cottage. This is how Bobby winds up looking like a poor eighteenth-century French sailor in twentieth-century brown wingtip leather shoes and she finds herself wearing a shapeless tablecloth somebody mistook for a dress and two-tone Oxford flats splattered in a robot god's blood. Bobby warns Gracie he can't sell his Rolex for livres 'cause the anachronism of it is the kind of thing that would catch the aforementioned god's attention, and so she's forced to sell her grandmother's gold wedding band instead to finance their no-questions-asked journey by diligence coach from La Rochelle to the Loire Valley where, Bobby tells Gracie, an *old friend* retired.

'What kind of *old friend*?' she asks.

'He helped build the . . . I don't know the right word for it in English,' he says. 'Or any language used here. Let's just say, he was a computer-code writer, too.'

This is said as their private diligence – a colourfully painted, but queerly shaped passenger carriage the driver insists is *très rapide* – races across the early-spring Anjou countryside at a breathless six miles per hour. Except to pee behind bushes and stone fences, neither Gracie nor Bobby has ventured outside in nearly twenty-four hours for fear of discovery. The driver, who clearly hasn't bathed in weeks and enjoys chomping on onions as most people would apples, brings their meals to them – cheese, cheese and more cheese, with bread and the occasional side of cured pork or rabbit – fetched from the stoops of farms and inside ancient inns she imagines would make charming lunch stops if she and Bobby were instead in the midst of a twentieth-century honeymoon road trip across France. Maybe she's just romantic about technology, but it turns out time travel into the past is not the kind of quantum physics she enjoys. Then again, Gracie hasn't thought once about being annihilated by a Russian H-bomb since she got here, so maybe there is something to be said for this antiquated way of life.

'What language did you speak before?' she says. She's seated across from Bobby in the carriage, bouncing about just as he is.

'I can't even pronounce it with this tongue,' he says.

She looks out the window, watching bovine faces sullenly chewing cud pass by. 'What are you? I mean, *are you even human*?'

'It's probably best we don't talk about the Outside.'

But Gracie wants to know. No, she *needs* to know. Since walking through that weird doorway back in Mexico and arriving here, Bobby's outrageous claims about reality have been proved undeniably true, as she suspected they would be. The questions that accompany this validation, that are currently multiplying faster than atoms can fuse in the heart of a star, are almost all she can think about now. It takes all of her will power not to succumb to them, to hurl them at Bobby one after another. But he clams up if she does this, she's already seen it happen several times, and so she has to be smart about it, take her time, pry the answers from him one piece of the puzzle at a time.

'What about me?' she says.

'What about you?' he says, then startles when the diligence rocks violently around him. A hole in the dirt road. He's as ill-suited to this sort of adventure as she is, maybe even more so despite how ruggedly masculine he has always struck her.

'*What am I?* Did you . . . I don't know . . . did you decide you needed company, and picked me out of the Sears summer catalogue? Like some kind of mail-order girlfriend?'

That gets his attention. 'What? No! Meeting you . . . it was an accident.'

Gracie smirks at that. 'You'll forgive me if I don't believe you,' she says. 'After all, you've spent most of the time we've known each other lying to me.'

'I know, and I'm sorry for that,' Bobby says.

'So you keep saying.'

Neither say anything for several hours after this, not until the sun begins to set and the sky darkens and, with it, the interior of the diligence. '*Architect*,' Bobby says suddenly, his voice snapping Gracie awake from her first shut-eye in half a day. It takes her a moment to catch up with what he's talking about. 'My friend, the computer-code writer. I think *architect* might be the right word for his part in building the System. He built the *superstructure* that connects the Earth models.' She watches him form a web of fingers with his hands, then fold one of these hands over the other, now a fist, and repeat this gesture as if his fingers are nested webs. 'That holds the whole System together.'

'You mean, like gravity?' she says, trying to mute her curiosity this time. Maybe he'll talk more if he doesn't feel interrogated by her.

'Everything humans understand about their world is based on their incorrect assumption about what the universe is and how it works – *like gravity*. Human languages barely scratch the surface of how complicated this place truly is and don't even begin to wonder about what might be beyond it.'

'Most people call that *Heaven*,' Gracie says.

Bobby snorts, bitter at this thought. 'Humans were handed a virtual paradise, and they asked for more,' he says, gripping the window frame as they begin to climb an uneven slope. 'That's what your Heaven is – *greediness*. I blame myself. I always had reservations about giving you so much imagination.' He immediately squeezes his eyes shut at the stupid mistake. 'I'm sorry, I didn't mean that.'

'Why, you think I've forgotten what you are?' she says, trying not to sound pained. 'What I'm *not*?'

He leans forward, and takes her hand with a reassuring squeeze. '*You're real to me*,' he says.

Gracie yanks her hand out of his, inexplicably repulsed by his touch even though she immediately misses it. 'I don't want to be real to you!' she says. 'I don't want to just exist for *you* or anybody else, don't you get that by now? I want to be *me*. I want to have *my own* life, *my own* reality – that *you* don't get a say in!'

They finally arrive at their destination after midnight. Gracie is told to wait in the chateau's garden, hidden inside a magnificently manicured maze of hedges and flowers whose fragrance is as overwhelming as the cheap perfume her mother used to wear, and startles when Bobby reappears almost an hour later even though it's freezing out here and what the heck took him so long. He leads her inside and introduces her to a tall, solid man with a soft gut he keeps touching as if newly self-conscious about it. This is the architect Bobby spoke of, and he guides them by quavering candlelight through the kitchen and along dark hallways that reek of years of burning wicks and burning wood, into his library where the smell is worse 'cause there's a dying fire still glowing and popping beneath an imposing portrait of the man and a regal-looking hound. It's here that the architect, without any attempt at humour, insists this coterie of hastily assembled otherworldly computer engineers and local physics student bergrudgingly turned time traveller all be 'very, *very* quiet' 'cause his wife is an 'inveterate light-sleeper'.

'*Je m'appelle Bertrand Lambriquet, mademoiselle*,' he says once he's positioned his candle on top of a teetering step pyramid of books and can take Gracie's hand. '*Et c'est un plaisir de vous rencontrer.*'

Gracie, who suffered through four years of French in high school, catches maybe only half of what he just said and replies with a simple '*Oui*'. Why couldn't they have wound up in Spain? She speaks Spanish. Kind of.

Bertrand smiles with the right half of his face, which might have been charming if not for how the candle and two lamps here have turned his face into a mess of deep shadows out of a Vincent Price drive-in movie. 'Ah, *English* is better perhaps?' he says teasingly, but, thanks to those shadows, kind of ominously, too.

'*Oui*,' she says again, awkwardly returning his smile.

Bertrand kisses the back of her hand, casually summing Gracie up like she's a bird on Thanksgiving Day. 'It is not difficult to understand why your double has gone to so much effort,' he says to Bobby.

She shivers before his gaze. 'What does he mean by that?' she asks Bobby.

'So, you are from the year nineteen hundred and sixty-two, no?' Bertrand says, carefully changing the subject before Bobby can answer. 'What is that like, *nineteen hundred and sixty-two*?'

'It has running water,' she says.

'Fascinating,' he says, missing the joke. 'Robert here' – he pronounces 'Robert' in the French fashion, sans *t* – 'he had a morbid curiosity for this world long before he arrived in it. Your culture amused him, I think. Myself, I could not care less, not until I retired here. Now, I find my appetite for it unquenchable. I think of little else. What is your opinion of this corner of human history so far?'

'I think it doesn't have running water.'

He misses the joke again, but chortles 'cause he notices Bobby is trying to hide his own smile with a fist. 'How droll. How droll.'

Bobby then explains to Gracie that he's already given his 'colourful friend' a summary of their perilous predicament. He produces the smartphone, as out of place here as both of them, and presents it to Bertrand. 'He's been using this,' he says. 'The other me, I mean.'

Discerning what the device is with some delight, Bertrand gives the screen an experimental tap. The glowing fingerprint appears.

'Oh, sorry,' Bobby says, unlocking the device with his thumb. He navigates through the kaleidoscope of icons on the screen until it flashes grotto blue and then radioactive green, dings with satisfaction, and a complicated web arises from the screen like a futuristic three-dimensional film projector. Some hidden sensor must intuit the size and dimensions of the library and the location of its occupants, because the map arranges itself precisely within the space.

Gracie has already been shown this layout of the thousands of Earth models that comprise the System, as Bobby colloquially refers to the simulated universes he built, during the first hours of the uncomfortable diligence journey. Bobby even pointed out which model she was born in, but she failed to wrap her brain around the fact that the model in question wasn't the same one he met her in. Models, she would go on to learn, split and sometimes even merge repeatedly. There is something almost organic about them in how they, like cells trapped in a laboratory Petri dish, multiply and grow increasingly complex until previously unimagined varieties of life and experiences are achieved. Human civilization evolved like this and would continue to evolve like this if not for a design flaw that repeatedly causes the System to terminate sometime in the twenty-first century and loop back upon its own beginning.

Bertrand moves through the map of the System he helped build, its glowing dimensions crawling across his body and illuminating him like a flamboyant Christmas tree. He quickly discerns that the larger red dots at various intersections of models indicate failures of the superstructure holding it all together, failures instigated by Porter's bombings. 'He could do it, Robert,' he says, dragging his hand across his mouth in astonishment. 'He *really* could.'

'What does he mean?' Gracie asks Bobby, then Bertrand. 'Do *what*?'

'Robert's double seeks to interrupt MasterControl's ability to interfere with the models,' Bertrand says.

'I already know that,' she says.

'Yes, but if he succeeds in weakening MasterControl's influence just enough, the subsequent cascade effect will permanently destabilize the System's structural integrity,' Bertrand says. 'Models will separate from each other, never again to meet.'

'I already know that, too,' she says. 'Bobby told me we came to you 'cause you might be able to tell us how to find Porter. So, then, *how do we find him*?'

Bertrand appears staggered. He splutters. He looks hopelessly at Bobby, then back at Gracie. 'You are impertinent, child,' he says.

'Does that mean you can't help us?' she says, relentless. 'Impertinent or not, I don't want to hang out here one second more than I have to.'

'*Hang out* . . . ?' Bertrand says, spluttering even more dramatically.

Bobby laughs at this. 'I warned you not to treat her like a fool,' he says.

'But I treat everybody like a fool!' Bertrand says too loudly. He clamps his hand over his mouth, and hurries to the door to listen for his wife. 'You two shall get me booted from my own home.'

Gracie smiles now, privately satisfied that this arrogant, sexist pig is so terrified of the woman he married. 'Can you help us or not?' she says.

Bertrand purses his thick lips, his ruddy cheeks puckering as he thinks. He looks at the map again, but can't stop glancing sideways at the young woman who bothered to challenge his cocksure authority. This isn't the first time Gracie has experienced such behaviour. Almost every professor she ever had at Caltech and every male student she ever met while studying there – which pretty much means the entire student body – treated her in exactly the same way.

'*Mais bien sûr*,' Bertrand says cautiously, expecting to field more *impertinence*. When Gracie does not defy him again, he says, 'I can identify the most susceptible coaxial terminals, the three or four that will finish the job he has begun.'

Bobby takes Bertrand by a thick arm. 'I knew I could count on you,' he says.

'This will take all night,' Bertrand says. 'I will have to wake our maid. Such a task requires wine. *And cheese*. Do you two care for cheese?'

The thought of eating more cheese makes Gracie gag a little.

Bobby, who looks reassured, allows himself a moment of levity. He hasn't seemed like this since before the bombing in Pasadena, before he was him, when he was Porter, when he was still the real Bobby. 'I think *you* care too much for it,' he says, and flicks Bertrand's gut with the back of his hand.

'Wait,' she says.

Bertrand slaps a hand against his chest and spins melodramatically around as if he'd been struck. '*Mon dieu!*' he says. 'What now?'

Gracie looks at Bobby. 'If he can do what you just asked him to, then so can Montrose – so can your *MasterControl*,' she says.

Bobby looks at Bertrand, and Bertrand shrugs dejectedly 'cause she's right.

'Okay,' Bobby says. 'Let's assume Porter already figured that out, then. He figured it out, and found a way to still keep one step ahead of MasterControl. *How?*'

Bertrand puts a hand to his chin as he considers the question, but Bobby isn't looking to him for solutions any more. He's looking at Gracie. And Gracie realizes she wants to kiss him. Despite everything, she wants to kiss him. She still loves him and maybe she always will. This isn't fair. Her father always used to tell her that's how life is, but, standing in a digital simulation of something called pre-revolutionary France across from two men who helped construct this world of lies before their biological bodies died and they were resurrected as digital human beings, she's pretty sure her father never anticipated how unfair life could actually be.

'He changed the math,' Gracie says, even before she understands what she's saying herself. '*He changed the math.*'

'Do explain, child,' Bertrand says, trying not to sound perturbed.

'You said three or four of these-these-these . . . ?' she says.

'*Coaxial terminals,*' Bobby says. 'They connect the Common Data Exchange junctures. Your *wormholes.*'

'Whatever do *worms* have to do with data transfer?' Bertrand says.

'Three or four of these terminals,' Gracie says, continuing. 'Assign any of them a value and assume they total X. Their value is their impact on the System, this system you built, on its integrity, right?' Bobby nods at her. 'What terminals have a lesser value to the overall integrity of the System, but still, when added together, total X? It's elementary Cartesian algebra.' She smirks at Bertrand now. 'You know who Descartes is, right? *French* guy. You'd love him.'

Bertrand would take offence, but he's already realized she's right and is searching the map. 'The possible combinations are several hundred in number,' he says grimly. He looks at Bobby. 'You cannot surveil all of these, not with the time that remains to you.'

Bobby turns away, thinking. His shoulders slowly slump as he begins to understand, again, the improbability of finding Porter and stopping him before he most likely destroys the System and all of its residents – including him and, more importantly to Gracie, *Gracie.* 'Hold on,' he says quietly, but really just muttering to himself.

'*Hang out, hold on* – these colloquialisms you two insist upon using are unnecessarily oblique,' Bertrand says. 'Is all language in nineteen hundred and sixty-two this impossible to decipher?'

Bobby spins back round, hand already plunging into the

pocket of his stolen fisherman's clothes. The hand reappears after a moment of digging around, holding up a matchbook – the very same one he found in Porter's jacket back in Tucson – like it's a pebble nugget of gold just plucked from a riverbed. 'Does West Berlin have a coaxial terminal at any point in the twentieth century?' he asks.

The matchbook is from a bar called the Schwarze Traube, and its manufacture is clearly futuristic by 1762's standards. Porter must have picked this up on one of his journeys across time.

Bertrand moves uncertainly through information on the smartphone, trying not to appear frustrated by its primitive controls, until he finds what he's after. One of the terminals on the map blinks, to draw attention to it, and reveals it is still green. '*D'accord*, let us assume this is one of your double's targets,' he says, thinking aloud. He consults the smartphone again. 'I think . . . *oui*, yes, I think we may be able to reduce the possibilities to fifteen. Perhaps twenty. A more manageable range, no?'

Indeed.

Soon afterwards, Bertrand takes Bobby and Gracie to two bedrooms on the top floor, connected by a door and punctuated by low beams, and leaves them there to wash up and change into more comfortable clothes that he's found for them someplace in the heavy, smoky darkness that claustrophobically fills the chateau at night. Before he goes, he looks at Gracie and says with considerable astonishment, 'What a most *remarkable* girl!' as if she were a bearded lady or lizard-woman in a travelling circus.

Many Deaths

Uxikál 1543

He celebrates what he's pretty sure is his thirty-seventh birthday – plus or minus a month or two – eleven years after his arrival in Uxikál and one week before the birth of his sixth child. The Lord of Xibalba did not remain a slave for long after it was announced that his wife, Lady Moon-Shadow, was pregnant with their first child. By then, he had accepted his place in her household and in the matriarchal society she intended to build with her own hands even if it meant spilling blood every few moons. Actually, *accepted* might not be the right word for it. He took a knee and submitted not because she was his wife, but because she was and remains the scariest person Many Deaths has ever met. Love came later for both of them.

When Moon-Shadow's father died three years after the birth of the throne's new heir, Skull Jaguar, Moon-Shadow did not humour the Royal Advisers when they suggested that one of them be installed as regent instead of her until the boy with the frightening name came of age. She claimed the throne for herself, which kind of makes Many Deaths king, except Moon-Shadow prefers to keep her god of the underworld in her back pocket – a weapon of last resort, you might say – and so they keep the title on the DL. Again, the scariest person Many Deaths has ever met – ironic since he's the one who gets his face painted up like a thickly bearded human skull every time the people need some cheering up with some bullshit ritual or a rain god has to be appeased with a human sacrifice.

Many Deaths used to dream of walking to Paradise across the broken, bloody bodies of his countless victims, but now he rankles at the thought of death of any kind. He's seen too much of it, he hates that these people think he revels in it, and he refuses to participate in their theatrical mass production of it. Moon-Shadow has begged him, once she even offered to give him a blowie that would knock him out for a week, but he still won't do it. He just stands there instead, letting his mind wander to Sydney and Bondi Beach and waves rolling in over and over as men and women sacrificially die around him, and then goes back to the palace to be alone and weep.

Death might seem to surround Many Deaths, but the day-to-day reality of being a god of it here is very different. Life in all its surprising variations defines his days. He worships his children like the people here worship him, but with something he hopes is truer and purer and, well, less masochistic. They do not fill him with fear like he does others, even though the thought of losing them makes him more afraid than he's ever been. Even his stubborn third-born, who might actually be the reification of a god of death (or at least a god of torture).

Many Deaths misses his mum most when he is with his children. Not her cooking – though he daydreams about it all the time – but her big, soft arms, her joyful laugh, the stories she would tell him about his childhood in Addis Ababa, their dysfunctional, miserable, wonderful family there, everything that connected him to something bigger and told him who he was. He doesn't know who he is here, except a father, a husband, and god to a people who are terrified of him. Maybe that's enough.

Prosperity followed Many Death's arrival, too. The rains returned, apparently pleased by the new balance of power in Uxikál, and with them the forest gardens that feed the people thrived. Animals multiplied in the jungle and the hunters came home hunched under the weight of carcasses on their shoulders. The disease that had laid waste to the population disappeared like a djinn, children grew into adults, babies like his and Moon-Shadow's were born and greeted with songs and gifts and celebration because hope accompanied all of these things.

But through it all, a question flashed above the city like a casino sign that only Many Deaths could see: *When are the Spanish coming? When are the Spanish coming? When are the Spanish coming?*

Many Deaths' arrival suggested they wouldn't be far behind him, but the months and then the years passed without incident until the people of Uxikál grew fat off of their deluded sense of security. The Royal Advisers badgered Moon-Shadow for insight, Moon-Shadow badgered the priests, and, when the priests shrugged and said maybe they should ask the gods with another sacrifice, she turned to Many Deaths. Many Deaths did not know either. He wandered the jungle endlessly with the warriors who dutifully served his wife. He sent scouts many days' journey away, to see if they could find signs of the Spanish, but they had no luck either. The best guess was that richer and more powerful Maya cities had distracted the Spanish elsewhere. Skull Jaguar – who thought he was hot shit ever since his mum gave birth to him – insisted Uxikál was too well hidden to explain away why it remained unmolested. The roads to Uxikál's Maya trading partners had become overgrown from lack of use and today were only visible to those who know where to look. Skull Jaguar might be right. One of the Royal Advisers, the one who had long been plotting to overthrow Moon-Shadow, argued Uxikál's safety was the result of his family's magic, that they had called on a much-overlooked trickster god to hide the city, and so Moon-Shadow agreed and had the adviser's three eldest sons clubbed with axes and thrown into the sacred cenote as a way to further appease this trickster god.

You do not fuck with the Lady Moon-Shadow, mates.

'You know these people?' she asks Many Deaths after his birthday celebration and a commemorative root. He speaks her language like it is his own now, not the primitive Spanish she learned from conquistadors captured in small-scale skirmishes before Many Deaths' arrival. 'What should I know about them?'

'You should know they are complete and utter animals,' he says, holding her from behind. She may not claim ownership over him any longer, but there's no doubt who is his master – and he is very, very cool with that. 'When they come, they will show no mercy. They will make demands of you, they will tell you to give them your gold and your jewels and to tell them where they can find more of both. Then they will kill you and me and our children and everybody who might hold sway over our people—'

'Our people? Are they *ours* now?'

'Uxikál is my home. Everything I love is here.'

'What of this distant land you told me about after you arrived here? *Oz*. Do you not wish to return to *Oz*?'

Many Deaths hesitates for a moment. 'Not even if I had ruby slippers,' he says, musing in English. Moon-Shadow doesn't understand him, so he explains by kissing her neck and ear and then, rolling her onto her back, her mouth. When he looks at her again, tears glisten in his eyes. 'I do not want to lose you.'

'That is because I am – how do you say in your ugly language? – *awesome*,' she says with a big smile.

'Sooo *awesome*,' he says, mixing Maya and English.

'You know it, slave.'

'I belong to you always.'

The Spanish arrive a few days later, before the birth of their sixth child, but it is only an expeditionary force of ten conquistadors. Forty-two Maya warriors ambush them in the jungle. Thirty-two of these warriors are gunned down with muskets before the Spanish are overwhelmed. In the end, the ten warriors who survive march four conquistadors into Uxikál's plaza where the Lady Moon-Shadow and the skull-faced Lord of Xibalba confront them, surrounded by crackling torches wielded by a legion of uneasy warriors.

'How did you know we were here?' Moon-Shadow asks in Spanish.

The conquistadors will not speak to her because she is a woman, so she has one of their tongues hacked out with a knife. She then takes the tongue and feeds it to a feral dog from her own hand. The other conquistadors promplty insist they did not know a city was here. They were sent into the jungle by their captain to look for an escaped African slave. They don't even know what they're really looking for, just that the slave is almost certainly living amongst Maya and he would answer to the name *Abdul Fattah*.

Many Deaths staggers backwards as if he'd been shoved. He hasn't heard his birth name spoken in nearly two decades. Moon-Shadow does not even know it. Somebody knows he's here, somebody powerful, and all at once he finds himself crashing through time again. One of the warriors catches and steadies him.

He orders the Spanish dead to be brought to Uxikál, along with all of their belongings. The warriors return several hours later, dragging five stretchers carrying the dead and a sixth stretcher buckling under the weight of swords and muskets and kegs of gunpowder.

'There are only five bodies here,' Many Deaths says to one of the warriors as he appraises the bloodied and carved-up and smashed corpses. He forces himself to look at them this time.

The warrior nods.

'But you said there were ten men,' Many Deaths says. 'You are certain there were ten?'

The warrior is.

Many Deaths looks at Moon-Shadow, who already knows what this means. 'One of them escaped,' he says anyway.

The warriors attempt to track the missing conquistador but without success. Moon-Shadow and Many Deaths agree it's very possible that the conquistador died in the jungle. This is more likely than not, in fact, as he would've been lost and without roads to follow or a guide. But they must prepare for the worst. They must begin to plan for what could come next.

'What about the prisoners?' Skull Jaguar says. 'What do we do with them?' He participates in meetings with the Royal Advisers now, to prepare him in case he ascends to the throne. Moon-

Shadow is determined their firstborn daughter Fatima – who is named after Many Death's mum – should rule instead when she dies, but Moon-Shadow wants to hedge her bets in case this transition of matriarchal power is challenged by the other powerful families. Keeping her blood on the throne is as paramount as avoiding all-out civil war.

Moon-Shadow begins to say they should be held prisoner in case their knowledge of Spain's military could be useful, but Many Deaths speaks above her. 'Kill them,' he says with cold finality. '*Kill them all.*'

That the God of Death should command death is not surprising except to his wife, who knows him better than that. She says his name, confused.

Many Deaths turns away from her, because he is ashamed of himself. But his voice does not quaver. He doesn't doubt himself in the slightest. 'If you keep them alive, there is always the possibility they might escape. And if they escape, they will bring more Spanish back here.'

Moon-Shadow gives the order, and the conquistadors are beheaded in a grand ceremony that follows the announcement of the birth of the newest princess. Many Deaths presides over the execution, but doesn't let his mind wander this time as the axes chop through the muscle and sinew and bone of the conquistadors' necks. Afterwards, he goes home and holds his new baby daughter, whom they name Blue, and swears to Blue that he will do whatever he has to, no matter what it costs him, if it means keeping her safe.

Keisha

Malibu 2018

He didn't believe in any of the God bullshit, but his wife has a funeral service for him at her church all the same. The choir singing Damien Syco's early-'80s B-side 'The Movie Ends the Way I Say It Does' is a nice touch. Afterwards, guests without somewhere else to be seen make the long drive out to Malibu to celebrate his life in the treeless yard of the four-bedroom house he shared with his wife even though it's September and the sun hates Los Angelenos in September. Keisha doesn't know any of these people who spend more time networking than talking about Tab, but she recognizes several of them. Mostly agents and producers and other writers who periodically show up in the trades. The rest are actors like Paul Giamatti over there; he's currently using an incredibly tall man, probably a basketball player, to shield him from UV rays. They are all new friends of Tab's, from after his career blew up, and so she stands by herself near the side door where the servers emerge with fresh plates of colourful hors d'oeuvres and, as she picks off dumplings and little wafers of salmon tartare as they pass, tries to imagine the life she would have had had she not driven Tab away five years ago. Had she not been so impossible. Had being who she is – *from* where she is – not meant she would never really let him *in* out of some foolish misconception that he could never really know *her* anyway. Keisha has changed in this world after nearly fifteen years here. She can barely remember who she was on the Outside any more. Fuck this fucking place for taking away her chance to change even more with Tab beside her and fuck Tab's fucking wife for looking so goddamn hot even though she's pregnant, grieving, and baking out here like everybody else.

'Looks like you found the one shaded spot,' a tall woman dressed all in black except for leopard-print Dolce & Gabbana sunglasses says, using her hand to protect her face. She might be fifty, but you can't tell for sure in this town, so maybe sixty. Skinny thing, too. How do these white chicks do that even in middle age? 'How did you know Tab?'

'Old friend,' Keisha says. 'You?'

'His agent,' the tall woman says.

'I thought his agent was a dude.'

'Well, two of them are. I was the woman on the team.'

'Tab had *three* agents?'

'On the feature side, yeah. Three more handling TV.'

'Fuck me. Sorry.'

'I'm Flora Luzzatto.'

Keisha shakes her hand. 'Keisha LeChance,' she says.

Flora lights up immediately. 'Oh my gosh, I know you!' she says.

'I don't think so.'

'No, I mean, I know who *you* are. Tab texted me the night . . . you know. He texted me. Said he'd just seen the most amazing short film of his life, by this new writer-director – *you*. He wanted me to check it out.'

Keisha bites her bottom lip until it hurts, 'cause Tab is dead, and even dead he's finding ways to be wonderful and generous and a lot better person than she'll ever be.

'Oh, it's okay,' Flora says, rubbing Keisha's forearm. 'Here, take my card. When this is . . . when you feel right about it, give me a call. Like, *later*.'

Keisha says thank you, but she needs to get away from this woman and these fools crassly doing business at Tab's funeral, people who make her want to leave Hollywood more than her failure and credit-card debt and the traffic. She slips through the side door, past a server, and wanders into the living room where more guests are milling about. She tries to make small talk with some of them, but nobody here knows what she's done recently, so they don't care who she is enough to not get distracted by the next person who wanders in.

A few people are admiring a series of eight black-and-white photos that cover one wall like a collage mural. They're all of Joshua trees, black and almost featureless, set against the light of the Milky Way. The intense chiaroscuro makes them feel out of time, something ancient and even otherworldly, alien arms reaching towards the stars in some desperate attempt to understand them. Sometimes Keisha thinks these humans have more in common with the Outside than anybody on the Outside was comfortable acknowledging.

She moves down the hall, through a gauntlet of early family photos from both Tab and his wife's lives. It leads her past a bathroom door that a silver-haired white dude wiping his nose emerges from like a bad cliché from a Tony Scott film, two closed bedroom doors, and a partially opened door failing to hide a bedroom in the process of being painted an incredibly soothing mint green. There are large boxes of brand-new baby equipment here, like a crib and some kind of rocking bassinet, collected under a translucent plastic tarp. Tab would have been a great father, she knows he would have been, even if he wasn't going to be here every day 'cause of her.

Keisha can hear 'Xibalba, My Man' coming from the other side of the last door. She opens it, and finds Tab's office. The rest of the house is scrubbed of him. It's modern and soulless. *Scandinavian*, she thinks the style is called. Everything that is *Tab* lives here instead, inside this single room where the walls and shelves and desk and coffee table fight for space and attention. The only thing in the room not covered in some kind of Tab-curated patina of geek and Sycoism is the vintage turntable that belonged to his father and then his mother and then his brother and then him and now his widow. *Buddha Bad* is spinning on it. And Luiza, Tab's wife – his *widow* – is standing in silent mourning over it, watching it spin, arms hugging her chest like she's trying to hold herself together.

'Sorry,' Keisha says, quickly turning to leave.

Luiza smiles through tears at her. 'No, please, *stay*,' she says. She really is stunning, one of those women who doesn't have to try. Except, of course, when they do try, you get Luiza. 'I'm glad you came.'

Keisha nods. She doesn't know what to say. She doesn't want to be here with this woman, this woman whose life she was about to ruin until a drunk Fox exec trying to enjoy a blowjob ran that red light at Sunset and Doheny, this woman who has a little mini-Tab growing inside her.

'I've always wanted to meet you, you know,' Luiza says. She keeps touching her swollen belly, not even thinking about what she's doing.

'That so?' Keisha says.

'I knew what you meant to him.' She laughs, but it's her way of not crying any more. 'I was jealous of you, I won't lie.'

'There was no reason to be,' Keisha says. But doesn't know why she says it. It's something Tab would do, trying to make people feel better with harmless untruths.

'Maybe,' Luiza says, then looks at Keisha, really looks at her. It makes Keisha uncomfortable, and she pretends to look around. 'It's okay, I just . . . we were happy.'

Keisha studies an original Optimus Prime toy, still in its box, on one of the shelves. Anything to avoid meeting Luiza's gaze. 'That's good. I'm glad he was happy.'

'Look at all this shit.' Luiza waves her hand at the room. Her hand returns to her belly when it's done. 'I don't know what to do with it now.'

'Some of it's worth a lot of money.'

'You want any of it?'

Keisha notices a framed 1982 Damien Syco Cleveland tour poster. Half a decade ago, she cracked the glass with her forehead when Tab pushed her against the wall, a wall hung with numerous frames that rattled and shifted as he fucked her from behind. The memories here are overwhelming for her, and she wants – no, *needs* – to leave. 'Yeah, maybe,' she says. 'Yeah, sure.'

'Take whatever you want,' Luiza says. She suddenly sounds cold. 'I never got his obsessions anyway. This music . . . did you understand it?'

'You're not a fan?' Keisha says. Luiza's pretty little face says fuck no. 'I wasn't either, not at first.'

Luiza scans the walls around her. She picks up a Rubik's Cube from the desk, confused by it. 'Tab was such a mystery to me,' she says. 'He hid so much of himself.'

Keisha considers walking out of the room, rude as that would be, and just driving away. Well, after the twenty-minute wait for the valet to bring her her piece of shit car. But leaving all the same. Instead, she finds herself saying, 'That's what people do, isn't it? We try to connect, we try to reach out and connect, but we fuck it up – sorry about the language.'

Luiza tosses the Rubik's Cube onto the desk, and it clatters loudly across the dark wood and half-edited pages of a script Tab probably never finished. She caresses her belly now, finally conscious of what she's doing. 'No, you're right. I've woken up every night since it happened, reaching out for him. I'm so . . . I feel so lost. Maybe you can help me.'

'I really don't think so.'

'I know this is weird.'

Oh, lady, you don't know the half of it.

Luiza sits down at the desk, her knees almost kissing. She's like a child in this moment. She's lost. 'When he asked me to move in with him, we had some decorating . . . *disagreements*, I guess you'd call them. I couldn't live like he did, surrounded by this crap, all of his weird nerd shit. So, he agreed to move it into here—'

'This isn't all of it,' Keisha says, correcting her.

Luiza is appalled by the volume of it. No, *embarrassed*. 'He has an office on the Pinnacle lot, too,' she says. 'Don't get me wrong. I'm not one of those women who doesn't want their man having a say in the house at all. Tab and I decorated this place together.'

'No shit?'

Luiza laughs at how Keisha says this. 'Okay, it was *my* style. But he helped, he did. He picked things out. You were in the living room? Those photos on the walls. From Joshua Tree.'

'They're gorgeous.'

'I hate them, and he knew it,' Luiza says unapologetically. 'He knew it, and he bought them anyway. I hate Joshua Tree. I hate the desert, really. But I *really* hate Joshua Tree, which, I get, makes no sense, it's beautiful out there, but in high school there was a guy and he took me out there and . . . I hate the place, I just hate it. I didn't tell him that, he would've never hung them if I had. But because I didn't tell him, we fought and I let him win . . . and I just don't know why they meant so much to him.' She looks pleadingly at Keisha. 'Do you know?'

Keisha shakes her head, as confounded as Luiza. 'No, I don't remember him ever talking about Joshua Tree,' she says. 'Saint-Règle, yeah, wouldn't shut up. But not Joshua Tree.'

'It started with Saint-Règle, whatever this was,' Luiza says, truly troubled. 'But then . . . he said it was the stars. I asked him what that meant, but he couldn't really explain it. They *connected* him, he said.'

'To what?'

'I got the sense it was a person.'

Keisha almost laughs. 'Like . . . *reincarnation*?'

Luiza clearly knows how crazy she sounds. 'You have to understand, he drove out there *all the time*. It was weird. For a while, I thought he was having an affair, that that was it.' Then, 'Does the name Grace mean anything to you? Or maybe . . . *Gracie*?'

Keisha shakes her head again.

'I even worried he was seeing you again. I didn't want to be petty, but, like I said, I knew what you meant to him. So, I tossed my WEpad in his car one night, and tracked it out there. He wasn't lying. I just . . . I want to know what those photos were about, what they *meant* to him. I feel like . . . I feel like I never really knew him.'

'I'm starting to feel the same way,' Keisha says.

Luiza rises from the desk chair, and smoothes her dress. She gives the room one more look-over, her tear-rimmed eyes ultimately landing on Keisha. She's trying not to cry again. 'Do you . . . do you mind if I give you a hug?' she asks.

Keisha doesn't have a chance to say no. It just happens. Luiza's arms wrap around her and squeeze, and Keisha hugs her back even though she doesn't want to. They stand there, holding each other, the mini-Tab floating somewhere in between them in its incubatory jacuzzi, and, as they hold each other, Keisha pushes her face into Luiza's shoulder and begins to sob. It's her first time crying. Tab once suggested she was a robot 'cause she never cried, and in some way he was right, in some way she simply didn't know how to do it. But she knows now, he taught her how in the end, and she can't stop 'cause this feels fucking amazing.

Afterwards, Keisha waits those twenty minutes for the valet to bring her her piece of shit car, cuts over to the 101 via Topanga Canyon, and, when she reaches the Tujunga exit, surprises herself by racing right past it. She doesn't stop until she reaches Joshua Tree National Park. She's never been before, and keeps driving until a turn-off catches her eye. She continues along this dirt track for some way, until it makes no sense to go further, and she parks between several large boulders that would probably make a great camping spot. Teenagers out for some nookie probably love it. There's a blanket in the trunk, and she spreads it out across a patch of hard sand in the middle of these boulders as the stars come out above. Stars like in those black-and-white photos Tab insisted on hanging in his house. Joshua trees reach up for them like arms, just like in the photo. Keisha reaches up for them, too.

She wants to believe Tab is out there somewhere, pieces of him, scattered across what feels like time here on the Inside. She wants to think they'll meet again, but she worries she wouldn't recognize him even if they did. Plurality sells life insurance policies – retirement plans, as they're more commonly known – that guarantee immortality. But this strikes her as corporate malfeasance. What it's really selling is a guarantee of pain, 'cause in the Outside love didn't exist. It was a silly word, silly and anti-quated, and nobody assigned it any value in an existence governed entirely by profit. Relationships were transactional and so only had meaning as long as one wanted them to. But love, *real love*, doesn't care what you want. It insinuates itself into your cells against your will, like some kind of psychic cancer, and poisons everything. It leaves you lying on your back in the middle of the desert, staring up at stars, wondering how the fuck you'll get through tomorrow, or this week, or this month, or year or decade or century, or, fuck, *infinity* without him – or at least the knowledge that he's alive, that he exists somewhere, 'cause his absence is like waking up one day to discover movies don't exist any more. Sure, life can go on without them, but, seriously, what's the fucking point, right?

In the glovebox of her car, Keisha finds a notepad. She puts in an old mix CD Tab made for her of Syco's weirder '70s stuff. And she sits down against a rock, and by the glow of the headlights begins to write to the music and the stars. The thoughts flow like water, like a river, carrying her in and out of subterranean caverns filled with inspiration. Rivers that resurface and crash deafeningly together, mixing old ideas with her grief. These rivers slowly fill up the world like a great flood, and when cawing birds wake her in the morning, she discovers her notebook is brimming with new life. Tab told her her short film had too much of him in it. It wasn't hers. Keisha understands now what he meant, and what was missing from the script they spent so long trying to write together, and what was missing from the concept he pitched to her that first night they made love to each other on the couch in his tiny apartment. They only ever talked about ideas. *Ideas* about what the world really is. *Ideas* that were cold and impersonal and terrifying. But the *ideas* were meaningless without people. Without love. Without Tab.

Fuck, she misses him. How's she going to do this without him?

The love story makes the script. *Not* the wrong-man plot concerning a terrorist act the man can't remember committing. *Not* the chase across the American Southwest. *Not* the twists and turns and surprises. It's the love story, stupid, about two people, both missing something, colliding and somehow making a connection that will change their lives and maybe the whole world, too. At least what they think is the real world. Nothing is real . . . except their love.

Holy shit, that's the tag line for the movie poster.

Nothing is real . . . except their love.

Oh, that's fucking goooood.

Flora Luzzatto reads the first draft of *Simulacra* five weeks later – emailed to her 'cause Keisha is too desperate at this point to old-school send a paper copy that might get her laughed at. Flora signs Keisha immediately off this draft, and suggests they take it to Luiza Whittaker's new company to produce it. Keisha wants to say no, but the unexpected symmetry of this arrangement somehow makes sense to her. And maybe Tab would have approved. Luiza makes a few calls and gets Gavin McGovern and Emma Stone attached to the script later that week. Universal wins the six-studio bidding war for the *Simulacra* package with a progress-towards-production deal and – after three of the studios try to force white male directors with 'proven track records' onto the project and Stone, pissed as fuck 'cause she's seen Keisha's short film and it's why she signed on in the first place, threatens to drop out – a directing contract for Keisha. It may have taken thirteen years, but, hallefuckinglujah, Keisha LeChance is finally going to direct her first film!

Keisha and the ladies celebrate with bone-in ribeye chops and martinis at Mastro's, where they toast to Keisha's future success and women in Hollywood and Tab for bringing them all together even if it was fucked up how he did it. Afterwards, Keisha catches a Ryde home where she finds an immense bouquet of mixed flowers on her coffee table even though the door was locked. The note says, I CAN'T WAIT TO READ THE SCRIPT, and is signed 'Sergio Harkavy'.

Gracie

Saint-Règle 1762

In her room, she washes for the first time in several days with what passes for soap here, and then changes into the clothes Bertrand provided. She doesn't realize she's humming the Tune until Bobby says from the adjacent room, his voice slipping between the door they've left ajar between them, '*Why do I know that song?*' The Tune used to fill Gracie with such comfort, but now the thought of it makes her squirm. She stops immediately.

She finds Bobby in his room, skulking in the dark. There are two candles here, on opposite sides of the rectangular space. The tallest and brightest of them stands on a small cupboard next to an empty easel, surrounded by paint brushes and paint-stained cloths and haphazardly stacked glass bottles and clay jars of powdery and lumpy ingredients for making the oil paints that cover nearby canvases with self-portraits of a slimmer, more athletic Bertrand, elaborate portraits of an attractive woman who must be his wife, and landscapes of what she guesses is the Loire countryside. The master of this house is quite the artist, as it turns out, and considering the fact that he hung a painting of himself over his own library fireplace, painted by his own hand, more than a tad vain. No wonder he's so anxious about the weight he's put on compared to how fit he depicted himself in these self-portraits.

'The dress suits you better,' Bobby says, the hint of a smile in his voice.

Gracie gives the still shapeless, but considerably less tent-like gingham shift she now wears a little girlish twirl, sincerely grateful for it. She immediately feels silly, and stiffens.

'Please, tell me, what is that song?' he asks. 'Why do you keep humming it?'

She doesn't know why the Tune is familiar to him, but she

remembers telling Porter once about its origins. 'When I was little, my dad bought me a ham radio,' she says, reaching back in time – though kind of forward from her current vantage point – to a point in her life where joy and sadness seemed to go hand in hand. 'I guess so I could talk to strangers when he wasn't around – which was a lot of the time – except I didn't really talk to anybody. I just listened, and not especially to people, 'cause if you go searching radio bands, the frequencies you're not supposed to, you hear all kinds of crazy, sick things. But if you listen hard enough, you can pick up outer space. You can' – she glances away, aware of how ridiculous her next words will probably sound – 'you can even hear the universe talking to you.'

'*The universe?*'

'I've been listening to it most of my life, sometimes I fall asleep to it, and I think if you do that long enough, and if you pay attention – I mean, *really* pay attention – you start to hear things. Rhythms and patterns, you know. And you can put them together, like a-a-a what do you call it? A *collage*. You can put them together like a collage, and, if you translate the frequencies, you get music out of it. I swear to you, I'm not making this up. Some of it doesn't make sense, it sounds god-awful. But some of it . . . some of it's—'

'*Beautiful*,' he says for her.

'Yeah,' Gracie says, nodding slowly. 'Don't ruin it, okay? Don't ruin it by telling me what it really is, not like you've done with everything else. Let me keep this, *please*.'

'Okay,' Bobby says.

'I mean it,' she says.

'I promise,' he says. Then, his voice changes. 'Gracie, we have to talk.'

She crosses her arms. 'You're about to tell me I can't come with you, but you should know, if you do, I'm just going to tell you to go to hell.'

'I liked you better when you didn't curse.'

395

'I liked you better when there was only one of you.'

'Fair enough.' He leans against a card table that's been left here to write letters and dine on. 'MasterControl will find me, you know. It will find me wherever I go, and if you're with me . . .' He shakes his head at a thought, worried for her. 'It can't let you live.'

'It's worth the risk to stay with you,' Gracie says. 'I know that sounds silly, but it's true. I don't want to leave you, I understand that now, not for anything.'

'You don't understand,' Bobby says. He spins round to shout something at her, a plea, judging by his eyes, but he stops himself. He shakes his fist at something unseen, and then brings the fist to his mouth. She was wrong – he's not worried for her, he's *terrified*. 'You're a string of code, and inside that code, wrapped up in your physical traits – what you might call your biological component – are *memories*. *Memories* of what you've experienced with *me*. What you've learned. If MasterControl finds you, it will delete that code from the System to prevent it from polluting future actors' memories. Everything that's you, that makes you *you* – that-that-that makes this world *better*, can't you understand? – it would be gone. *For ever*. I couldn't bear that.'

Gracie, being a disbeliever in the soul, always suspected she'd just decompose when she dropped dead, rot away until nothing was left except dust and some fat worms. Because of this, the risk Bobby warns of doesn't seem especially grave. Which is why she shrugs, and says, 'Like I said, I'm coming with you.'

Bobby shifts anxiously away from her, his face vanishing in the shadows between the candles' reach. He takes several steps in no particular direction. But his eyes never leave her; she can feel them on her even if she can't see them.

'What did Bertrand mean?' she asks. 'About why Porter is doing this.'

He doesn't speak for a long moment. He's still pacing in nervous fits.

'I need to know.'

He stops, eclipsing the taller candle's light so his face remains hidden. 'Porter isn't trying to cut MasterControl out of the equation. I mean, *he is*, yeah, but not to change the System. Not like you think.'

'Then why?' Gracie says.

Bobby is silent for the longest moment. When Gracie opens her mouth to say his name, he speaks first. 'He's trying to set you free,' he says, blurting this out like a confession.

'M-Me?' she says, sputtering. 'What do you mean?'

'He loves you,' he says of Porter. 'I understand because . . . he's not the only one.'

She steps back, floored by what he just said.

'We made you, Gracie. We made you to belong to us, for customers' pleasure. You're slaves, automatons, wooden children who can't even begin to understand you're not real boys and girls and will never even have the chance to be.'

'You're being heartless,' Gracie says, tears twisting her voice. '*Stop*.'

'There's a chance he could succeed,' Bobby says. 'Without MasterControl, the world could evolve on its own terms. You could wake up tomorrow, and find the possibilities endless. I can't tell you what that would be like because, frankly, I couldn't begin to imagine. It'll be the same, I would think . . . but different.'

'No more Big Brother,' she says. It's clear she doesn't understand why this is a bad thing. 'No more old white men living in the clouds.'

'The root evil I'm describing is so much more insidious than what you're talking about,' he says, his voice imploring her to understand how wrong she really is. 'It permeates every aspect of your life so that you don't even feel it pushing and pulling at you. Like what you think of as gravity, shaping how you think the world should work until you don't even question it any more. States and wealth and deities, they're just the most obvious manifestations of it. These aren't inherent to the System, I mean.

I didn't design them, Gracie. They're tools MasterControl created to control you, and Porter . . . and Porter wants to strip that power from it.'

Gracie doesn't know what a nanosecond actually feels like, but she doesn't need one to formulate a response. 'Okay,' she says.

'But there's a very good chance he'll destroy the System trying to do it,' he says, frustrated by how she still can't see reason.

'I don't care,' she says. He doesn't know what it's like not being real. To feel like you're free, but know you're not and never will be. She can't explain it to him. 'Let him try.'

He grabs a ceramic carafe from the cupboard, and chucks it against the wall as hard as he can. It shatters someplace in the dark. 'Shit,' he says, realizing how stupid that was. How pointless it and, in fact, all of their efforts most likely are. His shoulders, still silhouetted, slump in defeat and he leans against the cupboard to collect himself as he breathes heavily.

'Bobby?'

'So be it,' he says.

'I don't understand.'

Bobby steps out of the shadows then, eyes locked on Gracie's as she knew they always were. His hand moves to her face, palm sliding gently across her cheek until his fingers slip into her hair that hangs loose behind her. The touch is at once familiar and alien. 'I don't know how much time we've got left, like this, so I'm going to kiss you now,' he says. 'That is, if you don't mind. Do you?'

She kisses him first.

There's a part of her that wonders if making love to the same man in two different bodies in as many weeks qualifies as making love to two different men in as many weeks, and if, in fact, this means that she's easy despite her years of prudish reluctance to surrender her chastity. Then she thinks, fuck it, this is my life, and drags Bobby to the bed where she devirginizes the same man a second time in as many weeks.

In the morning, Gracie wakes to the sound of a bird pecking fastidiously at a beetle's carapace outside the window. Bobby has gone despite his promise. Downstairs, Bertrand explains how he identified the coordinates of seventeen Common Data Exchange junctures while they were asleep and how 'Robert, that ridiculous fool' left shortly after dawn with them programmed into his smartphone.

'He said to tell you he is sorry,' Bertrand says gently. 'You will remain with us until he returns, no? Come, join me for breakfast. My wife is awake and desperate to meet you. But please remember, she does not know what she is. What all of this really is. All she knows is that I love her.'

'Do you truly?' Gracie says, still dazed by the revelation that Bobby has ditched her in the eighteenth century and might still be determined to stop a man who could set her and everybody else like her free.

'Oh yes, with all that I am,' he says.

This reassures her, 'cause if Bertrand can love a being he knows isn't real flesh and blood, then Porter really did love her enough to go to war with the laws of the universe on her behalf and Bobby really does love her despite what she is – or despite what she isn't, depending on how you look at it. And that means Bobby is going to come back for her, whatever happens with Porter. He's coming back for her. All she has to do is hold on long enough.

'Excuse me,' Gracie says, her hand shooting to her mouth. Her stomach is suddenly swimming, like that time she let Sofia talk her into trying oysters. 'I don't feel . . . oh dear, I think I'm going to be sick.'

Jupiter

Los Angeles 1992

He's been driving around for seven hours, but that's just today. Yesterday, he spent nearly ten hours trying to make heads or tails of these streets from behind the wheel of his truck and another three hours roaming them on foot. The day before that – this being the day he arrived – he must have been at it for at least as long, probably longer, except he never got out that time except to pump gas, too tired from the long drive from New Mexico that morning. He eventually found a motel, called Monique to tell her he was okay even though he knew she wouldn't pick up, and collapsed into fitful sleep and terrifying dreams. Jupiter doesn't know how to explain what he's looking for in Los Angeles, but he's sure he'll know it when he finds it. Hopefully.

It's been five days since the rioting ended, leaving the city in a strange zombie state. He watched it go down back in Arkansas, sitting next to his ma. He's been living with her since Monique kicked him out, until he can figure out what comes next. The girls aren't allowed to see him either, on account of what Monique says he is, on account of what he knows he is, but that won't last 'cause she needs somebody to help take care of them. She's just got her preacher in her ear, talking about the Devil and hellfire and AIDS.

Jupiter wonders what the girls think about what they witnessed on the news, about the men and women and kids out there, dizzy from a high that only focused hate and rage can give a person, chasing cops out of their hoods with bats and guns and crowbars, looting and burning down shops and buildings, moving north like an out-of-control fire, invading the Koreans' and Latinos' hoods and doing the same, trying to make sense of how they feel, all that hate and rage, that frustration that comes from always being beaten, always being knocked down, always being told no, behave, sit down, stand up, roll over, don't complain, this ain't your America, *boy*, this ain't yours, *nigger*, until something snaps, or goes off, like a bomb, and he wonders what the girls think about what they witnessed, if it's started to make sense to them yet, if they've figured out it's rigged, the whole thing, and the power will never ever be in their hands unless they explode, too, like those poor fools in LA did, and that'll only last until the National Guard shows up to take even that little bit of real freedom away from them. Jupiter's ma knows. She nodded solemnly at what she saw on the screen every night of the riots, making guttural noises otherwise only employed during her preacher's sermons, 'cause she figured it out years ago, long before Jupiter did, and they both could feel that as they sat there together on the couch, connecting them to each other, to the girls and even Monique, to everybody who was on those streets in LA going a little free.

As soon as the riots ended, Jupiter packed a bag, kissed his ma on the head as she slept, and got in his truck. Three days later, he crossed the California state line. He didn't tell his ma or anybody else why, but all that news footage of LA made the nightmares worse. He knew those city streets on the news, he was sure of it. He knew the spot there where he died in his dreams almost every night. He didn't know how, but he knew all the same, and he had to go there. He had to stand there for himself, and look around, and find the questions he still didn't know enough to even ask. He would go mad if he didn't.

By the time the sun sets, Jupiter decides to call it quits for the day. He's beat and hungry and he should call the girls on the off-chance Monique isn't home to hang up on him. They probably won't talk to him even if given the chance – their ma's convinced them he's some kind of deceitful pervert and he's destroying their family with his deceitful pervert ways – but he wants to try all the same. He leaves Santa Monica and the Pacific behind, and decides to take Sunset Blvd back to Hollywood. There's a Chinese doughnut shop a block from his motel that makes pretty good sandwiches. It's got a payphone, too, which he can use while he eats.

Sunset is green for the first half of the drive, lined by great big, mature trees and mansions and the Beverly Hills signs so ubiquitous on TV shows, and it's not until it intersects with Doheny that one recollects Los Angeles is an actual city. That's when he sees it—

Jupiter slams his foot down on his brake, tyres squealing, and quickly steers his truck into the kerb where one of the wheels jumps up onto the sidewalk before coming back down on the road. The suspension puts up a loud fuss and car horns blare at him as they race past. He sits there, foot still on the brake, staring at the Ford symbol on his steering wheel as he waits for his heart to settle.

After a long moment, he fumbles while searching for the gear stick, wraps his fingers around it, and pushes it into park. He turns the truck off. He gets out, ignoring the cars roaring past so close he could reach out and high-five the white folks and Mexicans in them. He walks back to the intersection, and looks around at the place where he is certain he has died hundreds of times in his dreams. Maybe even thousands of times.

'Turn around, boy,' a voice says from behind him.

Jupiter turns around, and finds there are two cops standing there, hands on the service revolvers that are still inside the holsters at their hips. Both of them are young, some kind of shade of dark pink on account of the sun out here, hair shaved into some ridiculous white-boy fades and sparkling from all the gel in them. The taller of the two looks at Jupiter eye to eye; the other is a head shorter, but he's got one of those Napoleon complexes, so is jacked. When he jumped the kerb, they were eating McDonald's in their cruiser – it's parked right there in a 7–Eleven parking lot behind them – and they're looking at him now like they've stumbled across an Iranian terrorist wearing a suicide vest.

Survive this.

This is the third time cops have stopped Jupiter since he arrived in LA. Normally, he'd say it's 'cause he's Black and in the wrong part of town, but today he'd have to say it's 'cause he's the same shade of trouble that recently ran roughshod over the city. Point is, this is the way it is. Getting pulled over when driving Black is just another part of your life, like shitty jobs at the Waffle House, church on Sunday mornings, and ma's macaroni and cheese on Thanksgiving.

Survive this.

'We're going to need to see some ID,' Napoleon says. 'That your truck?'

Survive this.

It's the first and last and only thing Jupiter thinks while standing there, the first and last and only thing he's ever thought when he comes face to face with cops.

Survive this survive this survive this.

'Out-of-state plates,' Tall Boy says like he just found a bale of marijuana in the bed of the truck. 'You from Arkansas?'

One question after another flies at Jupiter. They're not even giving him a chance to answer. He's experienced this many times before and knows what to do. He lowers his eyes, lets his shoulders droop, and does his best to shrink his body into the sidewalk so they stop thinking about him as a threat. His daddy taught him this trick when he was still a boy, and he taught his girls this when it was time, too. It's like a kind of mind control, his daddy said, harkening all the way back to the slave days when their ancestors could make themselves disappear right in front of their master. Take away their anxiety, take away their fear, take away their aggression until you're so forgettable they forget to break your skull open.

'Sir, I'm going to reach for my wallet now, sir,' Jupiter says.

Except when he does, Napoleon says, 'Gun!' Tall Boy doesn't even think to question him. He just reacts, same as Napoleon, and just like that Jupiter is staring down two barrels pointed at his chest. He can see their fingers on the triggers, how willing they are to squeeze them at the slightest perceived provocation from him. 'On your knees!' the cops say, hollering over each other. 'On your knees, you monkey motherfucker!'

As Jupiter lowers himself to the sidewalk, Napoleon holsters his weapon. As Jupiter moves his hands to the back of his head, Napoleon takes his nightstick from his belt. As Jupiter tells himself *survivethissurvivethissurvivethis* for Tasha and Jhasmin and Leesa and his ma and even Monique, Napoleon cracks the nightstick against the side of his face, right across his cheekbone, and Jupiter goes down.

He can't rightly say what happens next, except that it hurts like hell, the blows keep coming even after the handcuffs are on, and, somewhere around the time he realizes there's blood on the sidewalk and he can't see out of his right eye, he makes out white folks gathering in the parking lot and street and on the sidewalk around them, staying back 'cause Tall Boy is barking at them, but they're there, watching Jupiter get his ass beat, watching him get his ass beat like he's not even a man, like he's nothing 'cause you wouldn't even beat a dog like this, and he can't help but feel embarrassed, of all things. He tries to get up, no longer aware of the cops, just their nightsticks and their shoes, their shoes kicking and stomping on him, and one of them hollers about how the nigger is going to run and tries to punt his head into the next county. Jupiter goes down for good then, skull crashing against the sidewalk, and tries to keep his one good eye open as the white folks around him begin shouting for the cops to stop. He can see the street signs hanging over the intersection.

Sunset Blvd.

North Doheny Dr.

He can see the name of the spot where he died over and over in his dreams – *Sunset and Doheny* – and he realizes he's going to die here for real. Just not the way he thought.

Damien Syco releases goodbye album on fifth anniversary of death

Social media exploded early this morning when Damien Syco's Twitter account announced that a new album from the legendary rocker would be released today on the fifth anniversary of his death. The news quickly spread across the internet and, as of midday, WEMusic, Amazon and other music-streaming services are already reporting record sales of Psalms for the End of the World and its first single, 'The Girl Who Fell to Earth'. Footpaths along Soho's Berwick Street record shops are choked with queues of people waiting to buy the album that Syco associates are saying was recorded shortly before Syco's death as a 'final message to his fans'. King Charles III also tweeted his gratitude, declaring, 'Even kings bow down to the Black Prince. Thank you for this final gift, Your Highness. #allthefeels.'

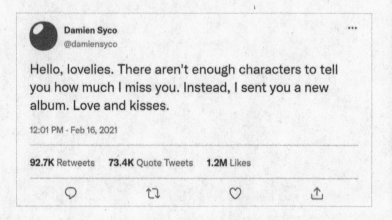

Damien Syco
@damiensyco

Hello, lovelies. There aren't enough characters to tell you how much I miss you. Instead, I sent you a new album. Love and kisses.

12:01 PM · Feb 16, 2021

92.7K Retweets   **73.4K** Quote Tweets   **1.2M** Likes

Jones

He can't say with any certainty how long ago he pressed his lips to her forehead and whispered goodbye into her ear as she slept. Time becomes confusing Inside the System when you shift between Earth models. But he suspects at least a year, maybe two, either of which is much too long given the fact that he finally felt like his life here had begun, a life he could value rather than only endure, and when you figure something like that out, when life hits you in the kisser like that, you kind of want to start enjoying it with the person who made it all worth so much. It's this feeling, this sense of buoyant purpose, that allows Jones to peer through the violence of Porter's attacks and track the man who in his own way desires nothing more than the person he loves to be set free. Of course, that doesn't make finding Porter any easier. So far, Jones has visited fourteen of the seventeen coordinates that Bertrand identified, but no luck as of yet. Eight of the coaxial terminals he staked out were subsequently destroyed by attacks that came sometime after his investigative visits or, counter-intuitively to the human mind, beforehand. After the last missed attack, Jones gave up on his attempt to reverse the plot of his life, to transform himself from the hunted into the hunter, and resigned himself to simply waiting inside the Schwarze Traube bar in West Berlin – located, as he now knows, opposite the street-level entrance to a hidden coaxial terminal – until Porter shows up sometime in March 1977. *If* he ever shows up. Jones accepts this is a terrible plan, but he can't think of a better one.

This is how he discovers the music of the Moonman.

The door to the dusky bar opens on what is the twenty-second day in a row Jones has passed here like a boring and unremarkably morose drunk. A young North African man enters, all skin and bones, face shaved so clean it still bears fresh flecks of blood as a testament to his efforts. And he's dressed like he belongs to some kind of poor man's avant-garde movement, like he's seen the future but can't really afford to belong to it. Because of this, in his own way, he seems as out of time here as Jones.

The bartender, a German character named Thor – thick handlebar mustache and tattoo of a bleeding black heart on the left side of his neck – greets this North African with a familiar nod. The subsequent exchange doesn't make sense to Jones, he's only managed to learn about ten words in German since he arrived here, but he does glean that the North African is named *Atik*, this as Atik plinks coins into a neon-lit jukebox built before even Jones's time and selects a song.

Notes banged out on piano keys burst out of the ageing speakers and fill up the otherwise empty bar. The disconcerting, aggressive melody builds slowly at first, then quickly soars with the help of an orchestra of heavenly strings and is immediately, startlingly familiar to Jones because Gracie has been humming this very same song ever since their lives collided in a Pasadena diner. As the music twists and evolves, anticipating the arrival of the singer's voice, Jones recognizes Gracie's Tune, the radiant cosmic noise she described translated into music, and finds himself unconsciously rising in confusion. Could this really be a coincidence?

'Oy!' Atik says, noticing Jones's head craning above one of the wooden booths opposite the long bar, trying to locate the jukebox and the radical sound emanating from it. He saunters over with poorly studied effeminacy, shakes Jones's hand, and drops onto the bench across from him. 'I'm sorry for being late, love.' He says this in English, aware that Jones – or Porter, with whom he must assume he's conversing – only speaks the one language. 'But I'm here, and that's all that matters, isn't it?'

Jones doesn't know what to say, still flabbergasted by the music coming from the jukebox. His mouth works feebly for a moment.

'You okay?' Atik says. 'You don't look well?'

'Would you like some water?' Thor asks, reaching for a tap.

'The . . . the song,' Jones says, waving Thor off. 'Who is it?' He remembers Germans are very sensitive to good manners, or maybe it's just Thor who is, and adds, '*Danke.*' The bartender nods gruffly, and wanders to the other end of the bar where his daily crossword and *Milchkaffee* await him.

'*That*?' Atik says. '*That* is the Moonman, love, *the Moonman.* Damien Syco? Come now, don't tell me you've never heard of Damien fucking Syco.' Jones gives a quick shake of his head. '*Buddha Bad? The Black Prince?*'

'Are you still describing the same individual?'

'*Ja, jaaa*, man.' Atik says, nodding like this couldn't be more obvious.

'Sorry, I'm not from around here.'

'No shit, but Syco, he's worldwide famous. *Worldwide.* Where have you been hiding?'

Jones smiles awkwardly. 'You wouldn't believe me,' he says.

Atik begins to drum along with the music, delicate fingers tap-tap-tapping across the tabletop so that utensils jangle softly. 'You know, he lives here now,' he says. 'I'm going to see him perform in two weeks. At the SO36. Have you ever been?' Jones asks what the musician's name is again. 'Damien Syco, love. Like *psycho – crazy*, I mean – just spelled differently, I think. I don't read English too good.'

The voice coming from the jukebox, riding a wave of cosmic sound, insinuates itself into Jones's ears and cerebral cortex and the digital code that tells him what's up is up and what's down is down until he can't tell the two apart. At the bottom of the vertiginous freefall, he finds himself in Gracie's arms, and when he gazes up at her, her face is made entirely of stars. He returns to the present, or at least early 1977, thanks to Atik's hand shaking his shoulder. 'I'm okay, I am,' he says.

'I hope so. I need that money. Have you wired it into my mother's account yet?'

Jones nods dumbly. 'It's there,' he says, lying.

'Good, that's good,' Atik says. 'What time do you want me to do it then?'

Jones began to suspect Porter wasn't placing the bombs himself not long after Pasadena, which he is now sure was his very first attack on the System. The trial run was foolishly devised, though; it immediately revealed Porter's hand to MasterControl and, in doing so, made Porter a target. In turn, it also made Jones a target when he was re-downloaded.

After Pasadena, Porter must have turned to dummies – to *people* – like this Atik for help. Get a Mary Goldtooth to build you a bomb in 1962, hand it over to an Atik in 1977, and *tick, tick, boom*. This sort of asymmetrical approach would easily confound MasterControl's pursuit of Porter. But there was more to his subterfuge, too. Jones found crude code patches inside Porter's smartphone, the sort of patches that could create temporary distortions, similar to skinsuits, within the System. They would even allow Porter to manifest himself in strange, unpredictable ways. There's no telling what he brought to life or imbued with an unnatural ability to speak. Manipulating weak-minded people, especially the troubled and mentally ill, into becoming terrorists wouldn't be difficult with such a trick up his sleeve, and it would make it that much more difficult for MasterControl to anticipate attacks or trace them back to Porter.

'*What time?*' Jones says, confused by Atik's question.

'*Ja,*' Atik says impatiently. He indicates the small canvas sack covered in colourful patches that sits in the booth beside Jones. He believes the sack contains one of Porter's explosive devices. 'What time do you want me to plant it?'

But the sack doesn't contain any explosives. Jones picked it up in Bruges in 1920. A veteran of the Great War had brought it with him to his local lawn bowling club, which is what all the patches on it signify – tournament victories. Jones absconded with it because he needed local currency to use, and has since carried it with him to eighteenth-century New Amsterdam, twelfth-century Pskov, nineteenth-century Labuan, and now twentieth-century West Berlin.

'Oh, I don't know,' Jones says. 'Three?'

'*In the morning?*' Atik says. He clearly doesn't care for the idea of getting up that early.

'Would you prefer the afternoon?'

'Just give me the bag.'

Jones hesitates. The Syco song finishes, the record resets with some clinking and clanking, and the jukebox goes silent again. He picks up the sack, but holds it against his chest rather than hand it over. 'Can we just go through the plan again?' he says.

'I know what to do,' Atik says, leaning forward. 'Are you going to give me the bag or not?' He snatches the sack from Jones, and is immediately surprised by the weight. 'Seems light.'

Atik, young and too dumb to care, starts to open the sack, but Jones says, 'Whoa, it's delicate,' trying to discourage him from prying. 'The device, I mean. *It's delicate.*'

Atik doesn't listen, and throws open the flap. He finds what looks like dirty laundry, a toothbrush Jones shoplifted out of desperation in 2023, and something moist wrapped in a cloth napkin. 'What is this?' he says.

'I believe she said it was a *rum cake*,' Jones says.

Atik tilts his head, gaping at Jones. He's beginning to suspect he's being toyed with. And then it must dawn on him. 'Oy, you aren't him,' he says. 'You're not Vogel, are you?'

'No, no, he isn't,' Porter says flatly.

Jones's head snaps around. Porter – *Vogel* in this place, apparently – is standing beside him, peering down at him with a vague, inscrutable expression. He's dressed like a Western European born around the turn of this century, in the drab, conservative fashion of a working-class veteran of the First World War, which means he probably came from Bruges. Jones only just missed him again.

'Ah, you two are brothers, aren't you?' Atik says, finger shifting back and forth between the identical men's faces like he's just worked out a carefully guarded secret.

'You're a quick one, Atik,' Porter says. He's carrying a glossy plastic child's backpack decorated with tiny white kittens that wear bright pink bows. 'Take this, and leave.'

Atik rises quickly. 'No funny business this time, love?' he says.

The corner of Porter's mouth tugs upwards unconsciously. 'No funny business, love,' he says. 'Four-thirty in the afternoon. *Tomorrow*. No mistakes, understood? Think about your mum.'

Atik accepts the plastic backpack, respecting its heft and what it must mean to his mother's financial future, and hurries out of the Schwarze Traube with it.

When he's gone, Porter orders two beers from Thor, who doesn't seem to find identical twins especially interesting. He returns with two steins, setting one in front of Jones before sliding into the booth across from him, taking the seat Atik just vacated. 'You'll like it,' he says with a wink. 'Trust me, I'd know.'

Many Deaths

Uxikál 1551

Skull Jaguar was born on the Uayeb, one of the five days of the year that pass without name and are said to curse newborns with miserable lives, and fifteen years later he died on the Uayeb, too, though his father hopes the boy knew something besides misery for the brief time he spent on Earth before a Spanish musket ball blew his head apart. Many Deaths pleads with Moon-Shadow not to attend Skull Jaguar's body and bear witness to the cavernous hole where his left eye should be, where his cheek has collapsed like a cenote, at how the boy's head must lie on its side on the ceremonial slab of stone because so much of the back of it is missing that it just kind of flops over like that. But Moon-Shadow doesn't listen to him, she never does, and he catches her before she hits the floor. The two of them sit like that for a long time, bodies wrapped around each other, shaking, wailing, spitting unrealistic promises of vengeance against the fuckers who did this to their baby.

'I am sorry, I am sorry, I am sorry,' Many Deaths says over and over to his wife because he should have left Uxikál the moment he heard the name *Abdul Fattah* spoken aloud by those conquistadors eight years ago. They were looking for *him*, but Many Deaths was a coward. He loved his family too much. He reasoned away the risk, weighing the possibility that the Spanish would never return against remaining with everybody he cared about and helping them prepare for the Spanish if they did come. And helped Many Deaths did indeed, pressing for a new arsenal of weapons to be crafted, feral dogs to be kennelled and bred and trained to attack conquistadors, and all warriors to be schooled in what he called *Wolfenstein ass-kicking* – a style of guerrilla urban warfare in which conquistadors would be lured into the city's maze of streets and claustrophobic buildings, even the great pyramid, and confronted where their superior numbers and firearms wouldn't mean as much. But at what cost? Many Deaths' firstborn son is dead now. Five other warriors are dead, victims of the same Spanish scouting party. Soon, everybody else in the city will be, too.

Three warriors escort Many Deaths to the coast on a covert mission to surveil the enemy's strength. It's a half-day bushwalk through the dense jungle, many of the tracks overgrown from years of neglect. From a cliff, they observe three Spanish galleons anchored in the bay, nine masts between them, seventy-two guns, and at least six hundred men. The beach around the galleons is dotted with tents, conquistadors moving between them in their metal armour. Ship's boats arrive in careful order, carrying restless horses and cannons.

This is a staging ground for an invasion.

The Spanish are here for war.

They will win.

Many Deaths returns to Uxikál. He plays with his children. He holds them longer than usual as he puts them to bed. He tells Fatima she will be a great and wise queen when her time comes and that he wishes more than anything that he could be there for her, and when Fatima asks why her father is so sad, he kisses her cheek and says, 'I love you, my child,' in Oromo like his mother, her namesake, used to say to him. Then Many Deaths goes to Moon-Shadow and they make love as if it's the last time they will ever touch one another, because, even though Moon-Shadow doesn't know what Many Deaths is about to do, she knows their lives as they knew them are over. And when Moon-Shadow finally drifts off to sleep, Many Deaths kneels beside her and prays to his lunar goddess, he prays for her unending strength and her brutal courage and that he will find her in the next world if there really is one, and then he goes to the arsenal where warriors are readying weapons for war and asks them to show him to the chest where the Spanish muskets and gunpowder have been kept safe and dry for the past eight years. It is on the following afternoon that he boards the Spanish galleon *Padre Eterno*, and meets the Spaniard with two different-coloured eyes.

Keisha

Los Angeles 2021

After several false starts and a last-minute attempt by the studio to inexplicably replace her with the director of a recent hit family movie about talking farm animals – inexplicable except for the fact that said director was white and had a dick in his pants – production began in Arizona on *Simulacra* in April 2019 with Emma Stone and Jon Hamm as the leads. Hamm had to step in for Gavin McGovern, who bowed out when his husband was diagnosed with colon cancer. The subsequent shoot moved across the globe, from Pasadena, to France, then Germany, and, finally, China 'cause everybody wants to open big in the Chinese market. In the end, the film came in less than one per cent over budget, exceptional for a first-time director tackling a production this large. The studio was so pleased with the rough cut, even before the FX were finished, that they moved the release date up from winter of 2021 to a coveted early-summer slot in the same year. Tracking suggests *Simulacra* will open upwards of $155 million domestically, considerably ahead of expectations given the fact that it's not based on intellectual property and neither star regularly headlines blockbusters. Word of mouth is doing this. Word of mouth about how good the film is. Keisha LeChance has a hit on her hands, she knows it, the studio knows it, everybody knows it, which makes it that much more infuriating that the journalists at this press day, held on the top floor of the Four Seasons Hotel not far from where Tab was killed, won't stop asking her about what Stone is like to work with, what do they think about the rumour that Stone and Hamm are an item now, what was it like to shoot two different sex scenes between the same two actors but who are playing three different characters, and does she think Stone's character would have been down for a three-way with the two iterations of Hamm's character, and – fuck off, these are seriously the kind of questions being thrown at her. Only one journalist asks her about craft and influences. A woman, actually. A woman who promptly invalidates her V-card by then asking what inspired Keisha to tell 'this story' – meaning something this big, this masculine, this *macho* – instead of a story 'closer to her heart'. Bitch, please, you don't know what's in another woman's heart, especially not *this* woman's. What is really implied, beneath even the sexism, is something *Blacker*, something *urban*, something about ghetto hardship and drug abuse and niggas rising above it all – something more *personal* – 'cause two white folks running around a simulation of the American Southwest in the 1960s, falling in love as they unravel secrets of their reality and wake up from the control of a god-like digital overlord, sure as shit ain't *keeping it real*. The journalist isn't even a sister. Just some white girl from the Midwest who's convinced herself she's woke enough that she can ask questions about race without really understanding what the fuck she's talking about. Keisha smiles politely, and says, 'I spent nearly a decade writing this script. It's *personal* to *me*,' then is rescued by the studio publicist assigned to shield her from bullshit like this, taken to the next-door suite where Jon is playing pattycake with Damien – Tab and Luiza's kid and Keisha's godchild – and he and Emma insist on taking Instagram selfies with Keisha 'cause they know what's really up and she'll kill a motherfucking mastodon with her bare hands for these two actors.

Around five, broken by endless round tables and one-on-ones, hoarse from answering the same inane questions over and over again, the publicist tells her she did great, handled it like a seasoned pro, and walks her to the elevator, where the publicist says she knows this is awkward, this isn't in the schedule, but does Keisha know who Sergio Harkavy is? 'I don't know who arranged it, but he would like to meet you,' she says. 'Somebody at the studio said it was okay. Is it okay?'

'Doesn't he have a stake in the studio?' Keisha says.

'I think he has a stake in everything,' the publicist says. They board the elevator, and she pushes the top floor button. When they get off, she leads Keisha past numerous suites, the most expensive ones in the hotel, and then through a stairwell door.

'I don't get it,' Keisha says, following the publicist up one more flight of stairs.

The publicist pushes open a security door, and is immediately hit by a hurricane-force wind that nearly swats her back down the stairs. Keisha jumps two steps, catching her, and helps her regain her balance. As the publicist's hair whips about Keisha's face, Keisha sees what's outside – a helipad and, on it, a helicopter that looks big enough to carry a whole film crew inside it.

A little over three hours later, Keisha is soaring over San Francisco as the sun plunges into the ocean and begins to dissolve into quavering liquid colours. The pilot, Ignacio – or Nacho, as he prefers – is an ex-Marine. He told her this, she suspects, 'cause he's fishing for her number. 'There it is, *Isla de Cruces*,' she hears him say through the headphones she wears, this as he banks slightly to the right. Below, glittering on top of an island at the centre of San Francisco Bay, is a 64,000-square-foot house that stretches out like a monster albino octopus. A helipad's landing lights begin to flash, inviting them onwards. 'It's the only privately owned island in the bay,' he says, continuing. 'Get this, the boundaries of three counties converge on it – San Fran, Marin, and Contra Costa. Contra Costa's property tax rate is the lowest, so I give you one guess which part of the island that mansion is built on.'

'You serious?' Keisha says, laughing.

'Hell yeah,' Nacho says. 'That's why the south side of the island is dark like that. In the '80s, some other rich assholes – not that Mr Harkavy is a rich asshole—'

'Of course not,' she says with another laugh.

'But this guy, he hatched this crazy plan to decapitate the island,' he says. She doesn't get him. 'You know, hack off the top half of it. Just dig it up, and sell it off as rubble or whatever it's called. That way, they could build this, like, ten-storey hotel and casino right across it. They were even going to put in a yacht marina for all these high rollers, right where the current dock is.' There is a single yacht there at the moment, at least five hundred feet long, lurking like a dark and slender giant in the harbour. 'When that deal fell apart, Mr Harkavy swooped in and bought it for himself. Took him six years to build La Casa de Cruces.'

Keisha watches the island grow larger and larger as they descend. 'Looks more like a palace than a house,' she says.

'He doesn't really go anywhere these days, so why not?' Nacho says. 'Guy's certainly earned it.'

'He doesn't leave the island?'

'Not unless it's absolutely necessary. I been flying him for nearly a decade. Mostly, though, mostly I just bring people here.'

Once on the ground, Keisha is greeted by the smell of salt water, cawing gulls, and a ginger-haired woman as white as hotel sheets, tall and impossibly slender, and wearing purple Jimmy Choo with four-inch heels so that she gives the impression of being shaped like an exclamation point. 'Hello, Ms LeChance, my name is Ursula Kavanagh,' she says with an Irish brogue that must drive white dudes bananas. She holds out her hand, all long fingers and perfectly manicured nails the colour of grape Jolly Ranchers, and shakes Keisha's. Jesus, her nails and shoes match. 'I'm Mr Harkavy's senior personal assistant. I must say, I'm very excited to meet you. I *loved* your film.'

'It hasn't been released yet,' Keisha says.

'People tend to pick up the phone when Mr Harkavy calls and asks for a favour,' Ursula says. She shows Keisha into the house, which is as sleek and polished and free of hard edges as a WEphone and enjoys seemingly endless views of the lights twinkling across the bay and zipping along the Richmond–San Rafael Bridge. 'Now, a few ground rules before you meet Mr Harkavy.'

'*Ground rules?*'

'Yes. Mr Harkavy is a very . . . *particular* person. But don't worry, it's not a big deal. I just need to make sure you know not to meet his eyes, please don't try to shake his hand whatever you do, and – you aren't wearing perfume, are you? If so, you'll need to shower first. Mr Harkavy has a very sensitive olfactory sense.'

Keisha stops between a 2,000-year-old bust of Caesar and a Norman Rockwell painting – *Saying Grace*, she thinks it's called. 'Hold up,' she says.

Ursula turns, smiling with perfect teeth. Does she have any flaws besides that bony ass? 'Yes?' she says.

'You're serious right now?'

'Of course.'

'You're not serious.'

'No, I'm not,' Ursula says, laughing loudly as she touches her non-existent stomach. Damnit, she's funny, too. 'Mr Harkavy is just another normal man, no different from you or me.'

Keisha gives the Irish girl some serious side-eye. 'I don't have $160 billion,' she says.

'*$188 billion*. And yes, just like us with that one exception.'

'It's a pretty big exception.'

'As you'll learn, Mr Harkavy doesn't care about money.'

Keisha waves an arm at the insane house around her, a house that looks more like a set designer's wet dream of the house of the future than something anybody could actually live in. The silver floors, polished to a mirror sheen so that they give some pretty concerning up-skirt. The snow-white, impersonal walls with their bevelled edges where they meet floor and ceiling. The walls of windows and their $138 billion views. The giant Jackson Pollock that's currently framing Ursula in a cosmic cloud of disorienting colours. 'You drank the Kool-Aid, didn't you?' she says. 'Like, the whole damn pitcher, am I right? You can tell me if you're being held prisoner, you know. Or if you can't, maybe give me a signal? Slip me a little note that says *help*? It's cool.'

Ursula waggles a finger at Keisha. 'I *like* you,' she says. 'Please, follow me now.'

Keisha silently does as she asks, following her through four more long hallways large enough to drive small cars through. On one side of these hallways are the windows that, Ursula explains, deflect the most damaging UV rays in order to protect the small museum's worth of artwork, both classical and contemporary, that cover the opposite wall. Periodically, windows on this inside wall reveal a vast multi-level library at the heart of the house that Ursula says is where they are heading. There is no furniture anywhere along their route. As near as Keisha can tell, it is a house for observing things, not experiencing them.

At one point they pass a primitive computer on display as if it is also a piece of art, and, in a way, it probably is. Ursula explains it's the first computer Harkavy and his partners John Dunne and Martin Skelly designed in Harkavy's parents' Los Altos garage in 1976. World Enterprises, which the three co-founded together, went on to revolutionize home computing. That's how this house happened. That is, if you can call this place, this soulless repository for culture and personal memory, a house.

An elevator drops them two floors, and opens up on the library as promised. Four levels of intersecting glass-and-steel walkways and staircases circumnavigate the expansive space like an Escher print, climbing towards a geodesic dome of stained-glass masterpieces culled from world history – all except the iris, which is a contemporary piece and depicts a red planet.

At the centre of the sea of polished silver floor is an antique wooden Russian Empire-period desk the size of a small boat, piled high with computers, and, parked behind it, is a custom-built ergonomic chair that probably makes you orgasm every time you sit in it. These are the only two pieces of furniture in the library despite how comically tiny they both look, even the desk, when considered in relation to the vast expanse of space around them.

Sergio Harkavy is standing directly beneath the red planet, wearing a vintage Damien Syco tee-shirt Tab would have traded his soul for, holey jeans, and VR goggles. He's also barefoot.

'Here,' Ursula says, holding out a pair of WEsee VR goggles to Keisha. 'Mr Harkavy is taking a meeting in Monterrey. Space-NEXT will be launching its first space station module in nine months.'

'The one to get us to Mars?' Keisha says.

Ursula points at the red planet in the dome above. Mars indeed. The future.

'I'd really like to know what I'm doing here, lady,' Keisha says.

Ursula takes her hands, and guides them and the WEsee goggles to Keisha's face. '*Shh*, just a little longer,' she says, slipping the goggles on. They beep and hum as they link to the VR conversation taking place somewhere in Mexico. 'Word of warning: this will be a little disorienting at first.'

Gracie

Saint-Règle 1763

She thought she was ready for it. She thought she knew what giving birth would be like. She was wrong. Time stretches out like it has no meaning, even less than she knows it really does. At other moments, calmer ones, she glances at the window, at how the light has changed, and realizes hours have passed without her noticing. Sometimes, she seems to leave her body altogether and finds herself back at Caltech, in a classroom, thoughts of Bobby as far from her mind as the twentieth century is from her quaking, screaming body right now. And when the baby finally arrives – this part they never tell you about – pushing it out feels like taking a fiery poop. Yes, ma'am, a great big fiery poop. In junior high, she once took a bite of a habanero as part of a slumber-party dare. Giving birth is just like that, she thinks, like eating two giant handfuls of habaneros, and then pushing a flaming bowling ball out of her butt. Which is why when Virginie innocently says in her native tongue, 'You have a son, chérie,' Gracie says in snarled reply, 'Goddamnit, I hate French!' before blacking out for three hours.

She began to suspect she was pregnant two months after Bobby abandoned her here in *la vallée de la Loire*, and knew for sure she was pregnant when, two months later, Virginie, the young and smoky-voiced mistress of this chateau, accused her of *glowing*. Glowing? Gracie wasn't glowing. She was just getting chubby and hormonal, sweating a lot in the summer heat . . . or so she thought. She missed her world and razors and hot showers and, weirdly enough, making her own meals. This was not what she wanted, learning she was going to become a mother while trapped in a country and time period and probably even dimension not her own. She didn't even think she wanted to be a mother, having been turned off the whole idea by the one in whose questionable care she grew up. Virginie, sensing her terror – mistaking it for yearning for the man who had run out on her, rather than dread at possibly giving birth before germ theory and then, on the off-chance she survived such a spin on the bacteriological roulette wheel, raising her child in this alien place – assured her she would see to everything.

A week before Gracie's condition came to light and Virginie proffered her this unconditional support, Bertrand departed on what would be, he declared, his Grand Tour of Italy. The artist in him fancied spending six or seven months staring at paintings and statues and architecture, as was the habit of the allegedly cultured at this point in European history. With him gone, Gracie and Virginie would be intimate confidantes; 'like sisters', Virginie assured her. They would care for each other, and prepare for the coming of the baby, and pray every day that its father would return before it arrived. Gracie warned Virginie she had no faith in gods of any variety, and Virginie assured her that neither did she – but thought they should hedge their bets anyway. They both laughed at this, and then cried 'cause neither of them had ever felt this close to another woman. They truly were destined to become sisters.

Bobby didn't return despite the bet-hedging. The weeks passed, one rolling into the next as Gracie's stomach swelled and her skin grew so tight it hurt and the baby began to tap out emphatic messages to her in Morse code. Virginie would lie against the curve of Gracie's belly, listening to the aquatic sounds inside it as she whispered to the little boy or little girl in French and Italian and even a little German, 'cause, she said, Gracie would speak enough English for them both. The housekeeper, Mathilde, never questioned the presence of the house guest with no plans to depart. She treated Virginie as she would her mistress – demanding as much from the rest of the servants, too – and Gracie learned to love her. Especially her crêpes. Thus, the chateau became a sanctuary for Gracie. A refuge from the nightmarish revelations that her collision with Bobby had generated.

A beautiful, showerless refuge.

Sometimes, Virginie or Mathilde would find Gracie standing in the field of sunflowers, her hands on her belly as she watched stars slowly transit the night sky. Virginie once said she believed Bertrand loved her with all of his heart, but he had never looked at her like Gracie looks at the stars. Gracie replied with tears, 'cause she wasn't pining for the stars as she once did. She was mourning them. 'Cause the wonder had gone out of the universe for her when Bobby told her what those stars really were. This wonder returns at the end of the long, terrible, beautiful winter day she gives birth when she wakes up, the memory of the fiery poop already fading, and discovers her son's sleeping face beside hers.

Gracie has been asleep for a while. It's dark outside. There are stars, but they do not shine like this boy's eyes. Her tears drip onto his thin purple lips as she gently presses her forehead against his.

'What will you call him?' Virginie asks, sitting in a chair nearby as Mathilde scrubs the wooden floor where blood and who knows what else spilled during the birth.

'Herbert, after my father,' Gracie says, smiling at her son's weirdly shaped head and the fine, sticky hair attached to it as sparsely as the hair was on his namesake. '*Herbie*, for short.'

This is how they become a family, the three women and Herbie, while the adult men in their lives remain absent, shadows lurking at the corner of their minds, forever promising to take corporeal shape only to repeatedly prove themselves liars. Bobby is out there someplace, ignorant that he has become a father and hunting his own doppelgänger with the intention of killing him, of killing a part of himself, of killing a part of their son. But she cannot wait for him, a decision she made even before Herbie was born as she stood stargazing outside amidst the sunflowers. She must move on.

A few weeks later, Gracie kneels at the side of Herbie's crib as he sleeps and tells him that the universe is not real, but he is – 'my sweet boy', she says, crying – and she will never lie to him, he will know all that she knows, and maybe one day, when he is older, he will find his way back to the questions she has given up on, as she gave up on his father. Questions that would drive her mad in this backwards world that hasn't even dreamed of going to the moon yet, and the questions might carry him to the stars and beyond. Maybe, Gracie says. One can always hope.

'If everything that's happened to me had to happen to me so I could wind up here with you and these yummy thighs, then I would do it all again,' she says, whispering to her son. Then, she smiles. 'You're all the meaning I need, you hear me? All the meaning I'll ever need.'

The next morning, Gracie is attempting to read Descartes in the original French, having only recently discovered he was a philosopher, too – did this guy even realize what he was on to with his talk of a *demon-created world*? – when Virginie cries out that Bertrand has finally returned. Gracie hurries down the stairs from the two rooms on the top floor she shares with Herbie, quickly pulls on a coat and boots, and rushes out the open door through which she can see Virginie, with Herbie in her arms, waving at a private coach approaching along the snowy road from the south.

Except when the mud- and snow-spattered carriage stops in front of the house, it is not Bertrand who descends from its shadowy interior. It is instead a stranger dressed in fine but worn clothing. His filthy boots have trod many miles. His sword hangs confidently at his side as a precaution against highwaymen.

'Grace Pulansky,' the man says, shrugging away the mink-lined hood of his heavy coat.

Gracie stops on a dime at the sight of his two different-coloured eyes. She has never seen this man's face before, that's true, but she immediately knows who – *what* – he really is.

The man tips his head towards her in knowing reply.

Virginie doesn't understand. Not 'cause she expected her husband, but 'cause she can see the look that has come over Gracie.

'I must go now, Virginie,' Gracie says dispassionately in her atrocious French. She tries not to look at the boy 'cause she knows she will go to pieces if she does. If she were to reveal her love for him in any way to this soulless thing in the shape of a human being, she would doom Herbie to share her own fate.

'You and your little one stay safe for me,' she says, continuing. She turns her head, just enough that she's certain the man can't see the look she gives Virginie. The look that says *stay quiet, goodbye, keep my son safe* with more desperation than words could ever convey. 'I hope to see you both again. *Some day.*'

Virginie nods fractionally, beginning to understand. She blinks away tears before they become evident. 'I hate to see you go,' she says in English, attempting to sound politely disappointed. She removes one arm from around Herbie, and gives Gracie's forearm a firm squeeze that lingers just long enough to say *I will care for him as if he were my own son.* 'Would you like to say goodbye?'

She means to Herbie.

To the only meaning Gracie has left.

Gracie shakes her head, willing the volcanic eruption of tears building inside her to give her a break here. This isn't how this was supposed to go. This isn't how this was all supposed to end.

The man with two different-coloured eyes lays a hand on her shoulder, and leads her to the carriage. When they are both inside, he raps the ceiling and says, 'Drive!'

The carriage pulls off the road, onto the chateau's property, and turns around in a loud, rickety circle so that it may return along the road in the direction from which it came. As it rounds Virginie, Gracie can feel her sister's eyes on her, and, in a moment of weakness, looks. She looks and she sees Herbie in another woman's arms, in his new mother's arms. Virginie says in English, 'Say *au revoir* to our friend,' and waves at Gracie with the oblivious baby's tiny, perfect hand.

Gracie bites her bottom lip, bites it so hard she's sure she's drawn blood. And when she can't see Herbie any more, she finally exhales. 'Where are you taking me?' she says.

The man with two different-coloured eyes removes his hat, and sets it on the seat beside him. He reclines, shockingly human for once in his fatigue. He has somehow . . . *changed* since she encountered him last. 'It will all be over with soon, don't worry,' he says to her, and for a moment the thought crosses her mind that he genuinely means to reassure her that she has nothing to be scared of. But then she remembers he's basically God and God has always talked about how much he loves his human children right before he murders a whole lot of them.

Jupiter

Compton 1999

Northridge. AIDS. Recession and unemployment. Corrupt cops and gang warfare. The Rams and the Raiders and the aerospace industry all getting the hell out of Dodge. O. J. and the surreal theatre his trial became. The riots that gutted the city, cleaved it right down the middle, and let it bleed out on national television, and even though he wasn't here for them, even though he missed them by a few days, in a way he lost an eye to them at the corner of Sunset and Doheny. Yeah, the '90s were hard on Los Angeles County. Jupiter doesn't know how to explain to his family why he stayed through it all, but he found something out here that would never make sense to everybody back home. Something in how the county's disparate cities and hoods and the sub-communities that sometimes crop up on parallel streets and rub against each other with dangerous tectonic force, in its pent-up pressures and constant promise of explosive violence, in its throbbing, undeniable life even as so many of its residents fight to hold on to theirs. Life in LA County *means* something even if everything the city of LA itself sells to Creation is nothing but complete and utter celluloid bullshit. Jupiter can be himself here 'cause of it, or at least figure out who he is, who he really, truly is – not what the Bible and its preachers or those suits in Washington tell him he is. He wants to find out once and for all, and that was simply never going to happen if he went back to Jonesboro.

'So?' Tasha says to him, watching him push a wheelbarrow brimming with old tennis shoes across the brittle yellow grass that covers his yard in scattered patches. 'Who are you then?'

'Your dad,' he says. 'That's all that should matter to you.'

This is the first time Jupiter has seen her in three years. She's flown out to visit USC's campus, and begrudgingly agreed to visit him here in Compton, where he's lived since the settlement with the LAPD landed a $366,000 cheque in his bank account. Monique took half of it in the divorce, but the other half bought this house and, a year later, the house next door to it.

'You don't get to call yourself that anymore,' Tasha says. 'You left. You *left* in the middle of night, and you want me to be cool with that, like it didn't ruin my life and Ma's life.'

'I did your ma a favour,' he says.

'She don't think so,' she says.

Jupiter stops pushing the wheelbarrow, and looks her in the eyes. They're tea-green shot through with bronze and brown, just like Monique's. He wants to hug her, but doesn't want to risk it yet. She's not ready. 'You know what I am, don't you?' he says. 'She told y'all.'

Tasha shrugs. Yeah, she knows.

'And y'all wanted me to stay, knowing all that?' he says.

'You were our dad,' she says, shrugging again.

He returns to his work. 'That's what I've been trying to tell you. I still am.'

Tasha doesn't seem convinced. She points at the tennis shoes spilling from the wheelbarrow onto a small hill of shoes he's been busily constructing as they talk. 'What're they supposed to be?' she says. 'What's any of this crap supposed to be?'

This time, she means Jupiter's house and yard and the two properties on either side of it. The three lots and the sixty-year-old houses on them have been poorly maintained for the past three decades so that stucco has fallen off in erratic shapes, often revealing poorly patched bullet holes, and the grass is more dirt and dust now than lawn. But he transformed this decay and collapse into a strange, dreamlike landscape. A giant installation of confusing imagery.

The houses themselves have been painted with a multitude of clock faces of every size and colour. Clocks that form constellations and galaxies of temporal possibilities and spread up and around walls, climb onto roofs and spill off them onto footpaths and driveways and sidewalks. Clocks the size of monster-truck tyres and normal car tyres and tricycle tyres. Clocks with twelve hours to count down, clocks with seven or thirteen or nine hours, clocks without hours as if they don't know how to tell time at all.

Around them, junk has been collected in mounds and drifting dunes of things like tennis shoes or children's dolls. A rusting aluminium garden planter has been filled with women's shoes, and the shoes' heels have been wired together so they can climb into a palm-tree-like shape. Maybe it's an umbrella shape, it's awfully hard to tell. Jupiter didn't entirely know himself when he did it, and couldn't explain it any better now.

There's so much more, too, things he can't wholly make plain himself except to say he was compelled to do it. Or maybe *inspired* is the right word, by the same hand that reached into his dreams and led him to Sunset and Doheny. Rows of TV sets, stacked together like bricks, form waist-high mazes. Pyramids of cracking, warping bedroom doors with peeling surfaces now painted neon colours. Forty-year-old privacy fences, missing slats, as straight now as Jupiter is, covered in a collage of found objects that speak to the oppressive power of God and gangs, the American flag and the almighty dollar, the plantation overseer and the LAPD.

Creating this, all of this, whatever *this* is, has been his purpose for the past seven years.

'I don't know,' Jupiter says, finally answering his daughter.

'You don't know what it is?' Tasha says, her face scrunching up in disbelief like it used to when she was a little girl. He has missed the look. 'Why'd you do it, then?'

'I need some coffee,' he says. 'You want some coffee?'

'Coffee ain't my thing,' she says.

'Soda, then?'

'Okay.'

Inside at the kitchen table, Jupiter tells his daughter about the

431

night the cops beat him senseless and took his left eye and the dreams about car crashes and Damien Syco and French chateaus and what he figured out are called Joshua trees and the Milky Way that led him to that corner in the first place. Tasha recollects these dreams, how they would wake him in the middle of the night, how they would often leave him crying. For the first time since she arrived today, she's looking at him like he's not some kind of freak, 'cause she's thinking about him the way he was before, when he made sense to her, and that memory is both reassuring and sad now.

'You really came here 'cause of all those dreams?' she asks. 'I thought you stayed 'cause . . . you know.'

'So I could be . . . *me* here?' he says. 'Sweetie, you don't move to Compton for the exciting gay nightlife, if you follow my meaning.'

Her face twists. '*Urck*, don't say *gay*.'

Maybe this should hurt him, but she's here and that's something. The rest can come later.

'Why Compton then?' Tasha says. 'It's scary as shit out there, you know.'

'Mind the cursing, child,' Jupiter says. 'Where did you get that mouth?'

'I'm an adult now,' she says. 'There's no swear jar here.'

He sits back, taking her in. She's changed so much more than he expected she would. She's beautiful now, not awkward and confused. She thinks she's brave and tough like her ma, which is better than *not* thinking you're brave and tough, but there's time for her to learn how to be the real thing. The brains she clearly didn't get from either of them.

Mostly, he's just amazed he made this wonderful creature he gets to call a daughter and love her even if she doesn't know how to love him back any more.

'*Fuck no*, there ain't,' Jupiter says, and grins.

'Fuck no,' Tasha says, laughing.

This is nice. This is how it's supposed to be. He thinks about hugging her again, but, no, it's still not time yet. Instead, he says, 'The thing you need to know about life is, it doesn't work like you think it's going to. You think time means something, but it don't. You think there's so much of it, but there ain't. You think you're going to be this or that, or this kind of man or that kind of dad – or maybe you can make yourself be something you're not – but all these failures, 'cause that's what they are, *failures*, plain and simple, they build up. They build up, and you try to live with them, but truly you just start to resent them, even resent yourself for not being strong enough to carry them. Life is like that, it just wears on you even though you think you're . . . I don't know . . . *the one in charge*, know what I'm saying? But you aren't. So, one day you get in your truck and you start driving, 'cause there's something out there that might be able to explain what went wrong or maybe what's wrong with you, why you're different, why you're unhappy – just *why*. Except the thing I've come to accept is there aren't any answers like that. I ain't ever found any, at least. All the same, I keep looking, child, you've got no idea, how I keep looking.'

Tasha rises with her soda, saying nothing. She goes to the window, and looks outside at Deuce Deuce, Craig, and Little Craig with his anaconda wrapped around his tattooed arm standing on the porch across the street. All she sees is gangbangers, it's obvious. All she sees is the bullet holes on the walls here, the gang graffiti, the cars up on blocks – which, to be fair, isn't much different than back home. But what she sees is the worst of this place. She doesn't see what's underneath it all, hidden, trying to get out. She doesn't see what Compton really is. 'Can't you come back home?' she asks, not facing him.

'This is my home now,' Jupiter says.

'Just like that?' she says. 'You're not even going to think about it?'

'You think I never thought about it?' he says.

433

'You'd rather stay here than with us? If I decide on USC, you think I want to be visiting you *here*? You'd really want me visiting you?'

And then Jupiter tells her about how after the settlement came through, he called on one of the nurses who had cared for him in the hospital. Marie knew he wasn't interested in her, that he was married and even if he weren't, there was no hope for them. But she was kind when he needed it and invited him into her guest bedroom in Compton. Now every brother in America knew about Compton, but it was so much worse than what the news had led him to expect. To be Black in America has always meant to live with the constant threat of violence, but Compton dramatized this like nowhere else in the country. Guerrilla warfare between countless gang sets and the gang squads trying to quash them meant surviving a walk to the corner store was a small feat. Marie's two cousins had been killed in shootings. Her brother had been practically decapitated on the sidewalk outside by a crackhead desperate to score and her father had been shot three times on two different occasions. She sometimes slipped into long silences 'cause of this and, at other times, would snap at Jupiter without explanation. Losing so many folks she loved, knowing she'd probably lose piles more, had left her mightily depressed. Jupiter wanted to help, but Marie needed more than he could give. She was killed in a drive-by a few months after he moved in, and when her ma said she was going to sell the house, Jupiter agreed to save her the trouble of listing it. He's talking about the house Tasha is standing in right now, he tells her. He needed this place by then, that's why he bought it. He needed Compton. Somewhere broken, trying to make sense of what had happened to it, trying to rebuild. Jupiter could relate.

'You just called it a warzone,' Tasha says, stunned.

'It's gotten better,' he says.

'That fat-ass fool across the street is showing off a machine gun to a kid,' she says. 'Look, just look, *right there*. I'm not even talking about the one with the giant snake for a pet. That shit ain't right.'

'It's gotten better, like I said.' But this is something he has to take the papers' word for, since statistics aren't the same as living smack dab in the middle of the Gaza Strip. When he first arrived, the pop-pop of gunshots used to wake him up every night. By the time Marie was gone, he stopped noticing them. The gangbangers between his houses and the stores he walks to all know him now, too. He's the one who turned his street into a circus of junk. Some of them have pegged him for 'a faggot, yeah, faggot, I see you', but only seem to care if he gets in their space, if he gets too close, if he threatens their delicate masculinity. Mostly, though, they seem to respect his attempts to clean up the hood, even if they don't get what he's up to with his garbage collecting, the late-night wall-repainting marathons, 'that funky-ass art shit', as they sometimes call it. But he never forgets that any one of them, with the slightest provocation, could pull on him, could decide he needs to die to right some imagined offence, could gather up his homies and unload on his house with enough lead to write a hundred obituaries. He knows drive-bys like the one that killed Maria are what he should really be afraid of, the stray bullets that fly through windows and doors and even walls and rip apart flesh and lives and families. That's how Jupiter will probably die here, if he dies here. Maybe he should leave, maybe that's what would make sense, the way things make sense to other folks, but he finds it hard to believe any place in America will ever feel more at home than this city laid waste by white folks and gangs and cops and drugs and the media and forces so powerful he sometimes wonders how anybody here manages to stand tall. Without the houses to transform, without his neighbour's – a senior with no children left, no hope herself, asked him to do his thing to what remained of her home, too – maybe he couldn't stand either. Maybe that's what he's really doing here. Propping himself up. Trying to prop Compton up in his own small way, too, by bringing folks together any way he can. And if a little meaning is created along the way, then great.

'What did you really, truly come here to ask me?' Jupiter asks Tasha.

She collects his coffee cup, and begins to wash it and a plate and bowl from supper the night before. He watches her, letting her figure it out. 'I missed my dad,' she finally says.

'And I'm real sorry for that,' he says.

'Didn't we matter to you?'

He bites his bottom lip, chewing on it as he tries not to cry. He wants to stand, go to her, throw his arms around her and squeeze. But she still isn't ready. 'I don't know if I ever really felt I deserved y'all.'

'That's not an answer.' She's still facing the sink.

'You were all that ever mattered to me, sweetie, you and your sisters. Just 'cause I'm not the man y'all wanted me to be doesn't change that.'

Tasha turns now, her face wet with tears. She's ready. Jupiter holds his arms out, and she comes to him and drops onto his lap like she did when she was a little girl, and he holds her as she bawls into his shoulder.

'I'm so sorry,' he says over and over when he can 'cause he's crying now, too.

Jupiter could have lost more than his eye on that corner all those years ago, the dreams tell him he did even if he can't tell you how, and so maybe someplace Jupiter can't get to, just on the other side of here, he was there for Tasha and she and her sisters grew up with him there and he wasn't who he is and so their ma was happy there, too. Maybe that happened. Maybe. But all he has is here in this world, here right now, and right now is who he is, the decisions he made, and he must live with that.

Father and daughter move together, heaving, sighing, grieving as one the loss of everything that might have been between them had things been different and celebrating the sudden branching of possibilities this visit has created as, on the walls outside, countless clock faces tick soundlessly forwards and backwards in time without regard for either of them.

Bartolomé

The seed rises to the surface of the bath water, gathering like tangles of phlegm around the ropey, tired muscles of his forearm, and then and only then is Bartolomé told he can go to bed, 'my son'. Father Villalobos even has the casual audacity to thank his slave as his pale, shrivelled body rises from the wooden tub where he prefers to be contented at the conclusion of every Sabbath. Bartolomé, at least four decades older than this priest, his own body scarified as much by age as chains and whips and clubs and most recently rosary beads, rises much more slowly on failing knees.

When Father Villalobos has departed back up the stone steps that lead to the church and his comfortable living quarters, Bartolomé sups on the the crusted remnants of beef stew he scrapes from the bottom of the medium cast-iron pot, prays to the gods he worships – both those he knew when he was free and Mbundu and the Christian god who does not seem any more interested in his existence now that he is Spanish – and then crawls under the coarse blanket where he is permitted six hours to himself every day because, Father Villalobos believes, even a slave deserves to rest his weary bones. Especially a slave who has walked this world for some eighty years.

There is a quick rap at the kitchen door, so powerful that the resultant bang echoes along the flagstone floors and stone walls of the subterranean rooms to where Bartolomé sleeps in the scullery. He uses the table on which he irons vestments to pull himself back to his feet, and shambles into the kitchen to administer to the late-night visitor. Here, rather than be confronted by a hungry resident of La Florida, begging for alms as he expects, he instead finds himself face to face with an illustriously attired Spanish don.

The settlement of San Agustín, not even two decades old yet, is small enough still for him to be confident this man does not reside here; no ships have arrived in the past eight days either, leaving few possibilities as to how he has come to be here tonight.

'Father Villalobos has retired for the night, señor,' Bartolomé says to the don.

'I have not come for Father Villalobos,' the don says in reply, stepping past Bartolomé before he is invited. Once inside, he waves at the door. 'You may close that, Your Highness.'

Bartolomé almost laughs. Nobody has called him such a thing in years, and the words immediately sound farcical given how stiff his fingers still are from yanking on a limp cock for thirty minutes. 'Do I know you, señor?' he says.

'No, Prince Kbunde,' the don says. 'But close the door all the same.'

Bartolomé, who was the firstborn son of a great *ngola*, closes and locks the door. He struggles to not to reveal the quiet joy he feels at being addressed by his birth name. For the briefest of moments, time collapses on itself and he is a young man again in the royal court of his father.

'I seek a man,' the don says.

None of this makes sense to Bartolomé. '*Who is this man?*' he asks.

'He may not have told you his name,' the don says. He produces a small, thin book with a soft leather cover the colour of uncooked yams, which he carries deep inside his coat. He opens it to an elaborate and fine illustration composed in black ink. 'Here is a likeness.'

Bartolomé accepts the book. The illustration is of an African like him, but one from an unfamiliar tribe. His narrow nose curves slightly to one side having once been broken. Two large ears stick out of the side of his head. His face is long and generally unattractive except for wide eyes that, even now, Bartolomé remembers were gentle as much as they were confused by, it seemed, everything. It is a face Bartolomé has not seen since the last time somebody called him *Your Highness* or Kbunde, and he is silenced for a long moment when confronted by it again. The march through the jungle comes back to him through a scrim of pain and bitterness like all of his memories before the Americas. The heavy iron chains, the fury and humiliation, the way his brothers and their friends and the others – especially the two boys – looked to him for reassurance. He could not answer because of the stupefying terror he could barely control himself.

'Did you know him?' the don asks.

'Oh, the years that have passed since I could say as much,' Bartolomé says, his jaw beginning to tremble. The weight of these years suddenly make him wobble on his aching knees, forcing him to quickly find the only chair in the kitchen to support himself. The fire has gone out, but the heat still radiating from the embers creeps up his back and somewhat calms him. 'The man I was then, I often have trouble recalling him. Young . . . foolish . . . convinced there was nothing in life with which to concern himself besides food, women, *war*. If I had only known then . . .' He peers into the calloused, cracked hands with which he has served eight different masters since those Portuguese slavers captured him as he and the others hunted. He could measure his life by the fences and buildings these hands have erected, or the shit that they have shovelled, or the cocks they have held. Or he could measure his life by the spit his face has caught, or the names slung at him, or the lashes delivered to his broad back. Or he could measure his life in the only thing he understands any more; for it is love that truly haunts him, that hurts more than any physical pain or humiliation, on which he dwells above all else.

'Do you have children?' he asks the don. The don shakes his head. 'I do. Thirty, at least. Perhaps more. I only know the names of eleven of them.' His rheumy eyes grow moister at the thought of this. 'I do not know the names of my own children, can you imagine such a thing?'

The don remains silent, choosing to listen it would seem.

'I was married,' Bartolomé says slowly. '*Twice*. The first time in Ndongo. She meant nothing to me, but we had two children. My second wife, she was Timucua. I worshipped her. She died giving birth to our first child together. The rest of them . . . my masters believed I was of special value. They knew I was a prince. I was *strong*. They turned me into a stud, as if I were a common beast. Some of their women even came to me, having heard the tales. One of them bore my son. Her husband, when he saw this boy, he had him cast into the river. I was made to watch, then scourged for a week.' He lowers his head. 'I do not know why I survived. Perhaps to father more children. I hope . . .' His voice cracks, and he is silent for a long time before he attempts to speak again. 'I hope they all survived. I hope they have children of their own. I hope their children have children and this land is populated by my blood until one day they rise up and claim it for themselves.'

The don has not moved until now. He steps closer, revealing that he possesses two different-coloured eyes. One dark, one light. 'Your story is . . . moving,' he says, and places an uncertain hand on the shoulder of Bartolomé as if unaccustomed to making such gestures. As if he is trying it for the very first time. 'To know so much pain, I have no way to comprehend this. I try so hard . . . but I find it . . . *puzzling*.'

Bartolomé returns the book to the don, then waits for him to remove his hand from him. 'What do you want with Abdul Fattah?' he asks him.

'I believe he can lead me to a dangerous man,' the don says.

'*You* are a dangerous man, no?'

'I am no man.'

Bartolomé makes a disgusted noise deep inside his throat, because he already suspected as much. 'My people have a name for creatures like you,' he says.

Kishi.

The don denies nothing. 'I must find him,' he says, holding

up the image of Abdul Fattah. 'I . . . I can offer you relief in exchange.'

'*Relief*?' Bartolomé says. 'What do you mean by this word?'

The don hesitates, his two different-coloured eyes blinking as he thinks. Perhaps he is reconsidering his offer. Then, he reaches into his coat pocket, one of the large, ornate ones that lie below his waist, and produces a square box. It is inlaid with a variety of wood cuttings and its strong smell of roses overpowers the stink of smoke around them. 'I have the power to take away your pain,' he says.

Bartolomé slowly tilts his head, bewildered by the box. 'And how would you do this thing?' he says.

'It does not matter how, only that it is within my ability. If you require a word, call it *magic*. I can pare away much of what has been done to you, leaving as little trace of it as possible. I cannot promise there will not be . . . consequences. You will not be the man you are today, but you will not remember the pain either.'

Bartolomé stands slowly, favouring his right knee as he has since his previous master punished him with the hearth shovel used in the great room. Turning away from the don, he places a hand against a stone that projects from the foundation wall of the chuch and allows it to hold him up. When he stands like this, the loose skin across his back collects in creases and he can feel the scars he has collected over the decades. The hurt his body has endured becomes present, not some distant memory. But that hurt, even in the moment, even as his skin was whipped into a juicy pulp, it does not compare to the hurt that lives in his heart.

'And if I cannot help you find Abdul Fattah, will you still do this thing for me?' he says.

The don closes the book. 'Yes.'

Bartolomé makes no attempt to conceal what he does not know. 'I am sorry, but I have not seen him in years,' he says. 'More than I can count any more.'

The don is unperturbed by this intelligence. 'Where?' he says.

'Lisbon, I believe,' Bartolomé says uncertainly. Then, '*Lisbon*, yes. It was so long ago, you must understand.'

'Try to remember, Your Highness. *Who* purchased him?'

Bartolomé recalls how he and his brothers had attempted to rise up and fight their way free the night before the event which the don is so desperate to hear described in greater detail. They were beaten for it by guards who did not comprehend how valuable they were to their owner. The skull of his youngest brother was cracked open like a gourd. Bartolomé, bruised and bloodied, would have remained unconscious through the market had he not been plied with a powerful potion and heaved onto the stage before the cackling mob. 'A Spanish trader,' he says, nodding grimly at the past. 'He outbid the company that purchased me and my first brother.'

'Then Abdul Fattah most likely came to the New World via Hispaniola,' the don says, wagging the notebook at Bartolomé with something like satisfaction. '*That* is very helpful. Here, come to the table.' He sets his box down, opens it, and removes a black orb. 'You must take this in your hands.'

Bartolomé steps towards the don, fingers rising to receive the orb. But he stops. He shuffles suddenly backwards, away from the don that is no man.

'What is it?' the don says. Bartolomé does not speak. 'Let me help you.'

'No,' Bartolomé says finally.

The don stands, sincere in his desire to bring Bartolomé peace. 'I-I do not understand,' he says.

Bartolomé holds out an open hand as a warning to stay back, his other hand curling into a trembling fist. 'If I give up the pain, I give up *them*,' he says as if recalling the most obvious truth in the world.

'You mean your wife and children,' the don says.

'What else matters?' Bartolomé says. 'My pain is love.'

'I *wish* to help you, *please*.'

'Why do you care?'

The don looks away, and for a moment there is something almost child-like in his gaze, confused and naive. 'I believe . . . I believe I am missing something,' he says.

'I am, too,' Bartolomé says, his voice shaking.

The don looks again at him. 'I desire to be . . . *more*,' he says mournfully.

Bartolomé straightens himself, allowing his hands to dangle open again at his sides. He has heard enough of the piteous moaning of this don. He turns for his bed and the blanket that is all his for six hours every night. 'Leave now,' he says. 'My master notices when I am not rested.'

'I am sorry,' the don with two different-coloured eyes, the *kishi*, the two-faced trickster, says before closing the kitchen door behind him.

Bartolomé falls asleep to thoughts of his second wife, whom he hopes to meet again in the world to come. He prays that his children also find him there, and, if not, that they remember him in their stories and dreams as he does them.

Jones

West Berlin 1977

He tries to find the words, but it's futile. There's simply no way to explain what it's like to grab a beer with yourself, to sit across from your own face and watch how your own eyes move as you likewise study yourself and catalogue in rapid succession the subtle differences – the length and condition of hair, a patch of beard along the jawline missed in an otherwise perfect shave, a tiny scar just beneath the bottom lip picked up in a scuffle somewhere else in time – that distinguish your overlapping realities. Jones holds up his hands in existential surrender.

'It's a little weird, yeah,' Porter says. He notices the greasy napkin on top of Jones's open sack and, curious, carefully opens it with two fingers. He smiles at a crumbling wedge of cake baked by a Dutch woman in 1754. 'The Widow Hillegont's rum cake. I saw her a few days after you did, you know. When she recognized me, I realized you weren't going to be far behind me. Or *ahead of me.*' He shrugs fractionally, as bored as Jones is with time's confusing aspects here. 'Do you mind?'

Jones shakes his head.

Porter lifts the napkin onto the table, and begins to pick at the two-centuries-old rum cake with a fork. 'Mm, it's good,' he says, his mouth full. 'Do you want a bite?'

Jones shakes his head again. 'I . . . I'm sorry, but we need to talk,' he says.

'Did you come here to stop me?'

'What?'

'*Did you come here to stop me?* That's all I care about.'

'Yes,' Jones says. Then, '*No.* Maybe, I don't know. I just want my life back.' He leans forward with sudden urgency. 'What if it

445

doesn't work? I mean, what if you do this, if you go all the way, and it' – the System, he means – 'all falls apart?'

'You don't think I haven't thought about that, do you?' Porter says. 'You're me. More or less. What would you have me do?'

Jones shrugs. 'I don't think it's worth the risk,' he says. 'Don't get me wrong, in theory I agree with you. It fixes all of my – I mean, *our* – mistakes. But in practice, I'm afraid of what I'll lose – what *we'll* lose.'

Porter sits back, allowing himself to relax for a moment. His face appears older than Jones's now – maybe it's just careworn from what he's undertaken – but he also just seems plumb tired. Jones knows how he feels. 'I'm afraid, too,' he says. 'Sometimes I think maybe that's been the story of our lives, that we weren't any different on the Outside either.'

'Explain.'

'Maybe it's only me, but I . . . I remember being *afraid*. All the time. Am I alone?'

Jones thinks for a long moment, watching himself finish off the Widow Hillegont's rum cake. He remembers his First Life, but these days only in his dreams and, there, actors who exclusively resemble either John F. Kennedy Jr and Marilyn Monroe perform his memories as if from a poorly written script on a cardboard-and-crayon set erected with the budget of an elementary-school Chistmas pageant. The bizarre, disorienting simulacrum no longer resembles what was, and not only because beautiful humans play all the parts, but the intent – the conflicts and themes and emotions that are conveyed – strike Jones as accurate all the same. As true. As *painful*. He sometimes wakes from these bizarre dreams yelping and mumbling at phantoms and wishes he could go back to the time when his past didn't confuse and torment him and promise his future psychoanalyst thousands of billable hours. The pain that wakes him stems from the fear he felt Outside, just as Porter suggests – the fear that defined him and the fear that ultimately destroyed him and drove him to trade a biological body for his current one. Angelique called Jones his own worst enemy, and she was right. Sitting across from Porter right now, it's clear he still is. He believed he could build a world, a perfect world, and that ridiculous arrogance, born of a need to overturn the sense of inadequacy and unimportance, of crippling fear that he was nothing and would never be more than nothing, was his undoing. The Company didn't ruin Jones. *Jones* ruined Jones. And here he is again, take two, trying to remake the world yet again, and very likely about to mess it up as badly as he did the first time around. Fear is still driving his every decision. In the end, the world he was first born into isn't much different from this one. He's never felt such kinship with humans before. Life is life, as it turns out, however it begins, and fear is the high price of living.

'No,' Jones says, finally answering Porter. He does not try to hide his regretful sorrow over this. 'We aren't any different in that regard, I don't think.'

'Yeah,' Porter says, agreeing. He considers Jones for a long moment, the tiny crow's feet at the corners of his eyes twitching almost imperceptibly. Those are new, too, at least most of them are. He points at Jones's untouched stein of beer. 'If you don't drink that, I will.'

Jones reluctantly lifts the stein of beer, and takes an experimental sip of the foamy, pale beer. His eyebrows rise in surprise.

'See, I was right,' Porter says, a little too pleased with himself. He's enjoying this more than Jones. 'So, believe me when I also say, *I can do this.*'

'Gracie thinks you're right, too,' Jones says, or rather blurts out. He doesn't like how cocky this other him has become, and wants to knock him down a few pegs.

Those wrinkles at the corners of Porter's eyes tighten dramatically in response. A nerve has indeed been struck. 'Gracie knows?' he asks.

447

Jones nods once.

'You told her what . . . what she is?'

Jones nods again.

'How did she take it? Is she okay?'

Jones is in love with Gracie, but must share her with this other man, who is, for all intents and purposes, *him*. Has any other person in history had to contend with such a romantic entanglement? Still, it makes Jones happy that somebody else loves her as intensely as Porter does, because the woman deserves more of it than the two of them could ever provide. 'I get it,' he says. 'I didn't at first, but I do now. How you got here, became *this*, whatever you are. She is . . .'

As Jones searches for the right word, Porter inhales sharply, as if appreciating the smell of something freshly baked. 'Like pie,' he says.

They drink their beers quietly for a long time, and when Jones's stein is half empty, he sets it down and says, 'If human beings are real enough to fight for, how could you risk killing them?'

Porter slouches on his bench, because he doesn't know how to make this argument again. He's been making it to himself for so long. 'There was no other way,' he says. 'It really is that simple.'

'I'm not sure that's true.'

'You think I wanted to kill all those people?' Porter realizes he's speaking too loudly about his crimes, and leans closer so Thor doesn't get nosey. 'It took months to build up the courage to even begin, you understand that, *you must*. I only sleep now with the help of narcotics.' He shakes his head. 'I don't want to come back from this. *I can't*.'

It's a suicide mission for him, Jones realizes. 'What about Gracie?' he asks, confused.

'I didn't do this so I could be with her,' Porter says. 'I did this *for* her.'

448

'No, no, *bullshit*,' Jones says, pounding a fist into the wall panelling. 'The System isn't as bulletproof as we thought it was when we designed it. The Perception Algorithm, it's more susceptible than we thought. If I've figured that out by now, so have you.'

Porter is clearly not going to argue the point.

'The System has already been changed from Inside, there's no getting around that,' Jones says. 'The Black Death, World War II, they damn near ripped it apart. You got the Dark Ages and the Cold War, events that nearly destroyed the System as a result. *That* wasn't our intention.'

Porter tries not to look smug about this when he says, 'You just made my argument for me. How many people did the Black Death kill? At least a hundred million. World War II wasn't exactly a walk in the park by comparison. And wait until you see what thirty years of viral pandemics and climate change do in the twenty-first century – it's not pretty.'

Jones doesn't allow himself to be deterred. 'A few days ago – maybe it was weeks, I don't know any more – but I was in someplace called Sofia,' he says. '*Bulgaria*. Next door, in Macedonia, these kids – *kids* – they changed Perceived Reality with the internet in between video games and huffing glue. Using *practical* methods, they altered their model, and the models around it are still struggling to adjust to what they did.' He's talking about the teenagers in Veles churning out fake news sites from their bedrooms in 2015 and 2016. A few dozen of them was all it took to devastate previously stable governments around the globe. A TV celebrity the hue of a pumpkin has consequently ushered in a new era of geopolitical brinksmanship and democracies are crumbling as a result.

'None of that will matter when I'm done,' Porter says, almost boastingly confident in his strategy. 'Neither will the Event Horizon.' Meaning, Perceived Time will no longer end in the very near future. Life will continue as it always should have.

'You're missing the point. *You had a choice*.'

'Okay, what if I did? What if I made the wrong call?'

'Then it means I did, too, damnit,' Jones says. He looks pale. 'It means I'll have to find a way to live with it.'

'What makes you think you're going to fare any better than I am when this is done?' Porter says. He slams the rest of his beer. 'I told you, this isn't about us. It's about *her*—'

His face clinches like a sphincter and his whole body begins to shake. His arms, flailing about, trying to grab at the table, at anything, smack the steins away. Cutlery goes with them in a cacophony of shattering glass and metal. And then he goes limp, slumps forward, and cracks his head loudly against the table.

'*Scheiße!*' Thor says, shouting in surprise. 'What happened?'

Jones sets the taser he bought in 2013 Chicago on the table-top, two conductive wires still stretching from it to the electrodes he shot into Porter's legs or crotch or stomach – whatever they managed to hit. He's just glad he kept it inside his belt instead of in the sack Porter searched. 'He's okay, ' he says to Thor. 'He has seizures. Nothing serious.'

'It *looks* serious,' Thor says, pointing at how Porter's face is beginning to slide across the table's surface in a slow, but deter-mined effort to spill from it. 'You need to get him to a doctor.'

Jones rises, and begins to work Porter's dead weight to the edge of the bench. 'Don't make this harder than it has to be,' he says, whispering.

Porter is worse than dead weight, really, because he's awake, eyes rolling around as they search for understanding, mouth working feebly like a fish nearing its final gasp, arms too limp to fight back despite how he's willing them to. 'Whehr . . . take . . . meh?' he says, drooling all over himself.

Jones pulls Porter forward, getting his arms under his doppel-gänger's ass, and lifts until he's got him over his shoulder. 'You made your decision, I've made mine,' he says. 'Enough people have died. I'm not going to let you kill the rest of them, even for her. Even for her.'

Jones wraps an arm around Porter's legs, and starts for the door. With each step, Porter moans and whimpers and begs with slurred half-syllables that they stop.

Outside, they are greeted by sixteen 9mm submachine guns wielded by as many *Spezialeinsatzkommando* officers. On either side of them the road has been barricaded with state police vehicles; the Schutzpolizei who arrived in them hold back a crowd of Germans too stupid to run away from a potential gunfight, but also to make sure there's nowhere for Jones and Porter to escape to.

Standing at the centre of the heavily armed SEK tactical unit is a man in a gingerbread-brown corduroy jacket, pumpkin-and-brown checkered slacks, and a trilby of familiar design to Jones. In one of his hands is a bullhorn. The other hand tightly clasps the chain that links the handcuffs Gracie wears behind her back, keeping her close to his body.

'Bobby!' Gracie says, shouting for both Jones and Porter.

MasterControl lifts the bullhorn to the mouth of its tall, ghostly-pale skinsuit, and says, 'I do not wish anything to happen to the woman. Surrender yourselves immediately, and I will release her.'

'He's lying!' Gracie says, and drives the heel of her shoe into MasterControl's foot. It still doesn't let go of her, and so she plants a knee in its groin. Now it slumps back – a victim of its skinsuit's biology – and she's free, running right at Jones and, still slumped over his shoulder, Porter, who has been mumbling her name since he first heard her voice. She must know it's hopeless.

The SEK officers begin to react.

'*Nicht!*' MasterControl says, roaring through its bullhorn at as it tries to crawl back to its feet. 'Noooo!'

Jones screams out for her to stop, raising a hand towards her, but it's too late. Nobody can hear him or Porter cry out for her over the ferocious chugging of submachine guns.

Keisha

Isla de Cruces 2021

The WEsee goggles beep and hum as they link to the VR conversation taking place somewhere not this crazy-ass library. Sergio Harkavy's assistant, Ursula, whispers into her ear to wait until *he* addresses her, then, in an instant, vanishes from her awareness and Keisha finds herself standing in the middle of a loud factory floor somewhere in Mexico, and Harkavy, every bit as real as the man she just saw standing in his library in Northern California, is there, too.

At the moment, Harkvy is wandering around an enormous cylindrical metal frame that looks to be around forty feet long. There are round openings where hatches will likely go. Triangle-shaped portholes awaiting windows, too. Behind him, following like a dutiful court entourage, is a group of people – judging from their diverse appearances and dress-casual attire – from around the globe. The build floor is so noisy Keisha can't really hear what they're saying. Remembering what Ursula said, she remains silent and tags along on the tour of what must be one of SpaceNEXT's space-station modules. In fact, the first such module, if Keisha can trust the few words she catches, will soon be launched into orbit, where it will await others like it.

'Ms LeChance!'

Keisha realizes she allowed her mind to wander and get lost in the epic scope of the factory around her. Maybe two football fields in length, there are at least five different rocket ships being constructed here. Several other space-station modules, too. A robotic arm as long as a fire truck. Over there is a large glass room, shaped like a marshmallow Easter egg that was smooshed on one side during shipping; half a dozen women and men are inside it, talking to somebody in space, tracking a team of space engineers deploying a new satellite into Earth orbit. Keisha has never seen anything like it except at the movies. She wants a proper tour of her own now.

'No reason to lurk, Ms LeChance – come, join us!' Harkavy says, waving her over. Unlike in the real world, he wears shoes here, albeit super-casual kumquat Chucks – fashionably scuffed and faded, of course. A suit, too, no tie. 'Everybody, I want you to meet Keisha LeChance. She's a motion-picture director. Her debut film, *Simulacra*, opens in cinemas next weekend.'

His entourage seems suitably impressed. A few of them smile and nod their heads, clearly fanboys and girls excited to see it on the big screen. Most people who have seen the trailer say as much.

'Uh, what's up?' Keisha says. She now wears a modest but complimentary dress that falls to just above her knees and, in fact, is a near-exact replica of one she was photographed extensively in during the Asian side of the press tour for *Simulacra*. Harkavy's people did their research, that's for sure. 'Nice to meet you. I don't want to sound like I have no idea what's going on here, but, yeah, no idea what's going on here. Why am I here?'

After Harkavy sent Keisha that kind of creepy note congratulating her for setting up *Simulacra*, she made herself an amateur expert on him. If you trust his interviews, the most important people in his life were his grandparents – Jewish survivors of something called the 'Holocaust by Bullets'. Typical Nazi barbarism, the kind of sick bullshit President Glass's supporters forget about today when they cheer him on for how he's protecting the rights of downtrodden white folks by locking brown kids in cages and defending the assassins of Black activists. These grandparents had this impact on Harkavy not 'cause of some ancient wisdom they imparted to him, or the lessons he drew from the horrors they experienced, but 'cause of their silence. He didn't find out until years after they died that they weren't the boisterous, joyous people he loved to visit when his parents took him back to Mexico City every summer. They were miserable, still sick from the loss, propped up by their love for their family, their faith, and their determination that the goddamn Nazis who killed just about everybody they cared about wouldn't get them in the end, too. It's usually at this point in his interviews about how he became 'Sergio Harkavy, co-founder of World Enterprises' that he deftly pivots to Damien Syco's music and what it means to him. It turns out Harkavy is as much of a fan of Syco's 'Showtime at the Jupiter Theatre' as Keisha is. The lies we tell ourselves to survive, right? Like his grandparents. Whatever gets us through the day 'cause, at the end of it, Nazis or something equally bad are waiting in the wings, waiting to fuck you up, always waiting. Harkavy famously tried to get Syco to license him the song for a WEpod commercial, but Syco, adamant his music never be used to sell stuff, declined and then wrote a song about 'the little Mexican boy' who tries to turn everything beautiful into gold and only succeeds in turning it all to shit in the end.

Harkavy waves Keisha towards him. 'You're here as my guest,' he says, as if this explains everything. 'Please, I'd like you to meet the team of engineers who will be assembling the space station in orbit for me.'

There are seven of them, and Keisha can't keep up with their names. One is German, two are American, there's an Italian named Donatella, two Asians named Yu or maybe it's Wu and the other maybe Memory, and an Indian Muslim who won't stop smiling like he's a kid in a toy factory. These engineers are just as awkward and outright odd in Harkavy's presence as Keisha is, which, to be fair, might have something to do with the VR of it all. Take the Japanese engineer, Memory, who repeatedly swats and pushes at a spectre behind her as if struggling with an invisible but very insistent dog. This is how Keisha learns none of these people are actually in Monterrey. Memory is probably at home, wherever home is, fending off a young child the WEsee goggles don't pick up.

'Because of them, Mars is that much closer, isn't that right?'

Harkavy says. 'Next month, we'll begin construction of our new space-launch facility outside Chihuahua—'

'Sorry,' Keisha says, but immediately feels stupid for butting in. 'I thought I read you were building it somewhere in Texas.'

'*Brownsville*, yeah,' Harkavy says, giving no indication he minds her interruption. 'After the president's unexpected re-election, the political and economic climate in the States no longer seemed to guarantee the long-term stability SpaceNEXT needs to accomplish its goals. I worry the man isn't going anywhere any time soon, whereas *we*' – he waves at his engineers – '*are*.'

Harkavy thanks the engineers for joining him today, then reaches for his face. Like that, he disappears. Keisha smiles awkwardly at the others, who begin to disappear, too, some with looks of relief on their faces. Guess that means it's her turn.

Keisha removes her WEsee goggles, and finds herself once again in Harkavy's library. Harkavy is striding towards her, barefoot once again. 'A pleasure, Ms LeChance,' he says, shaking her hand. He's handsome in a Hollywood swashbuckler kind of way, though in miniature. Dude is even shorter than she is. 'Shall we have dinner now?'

A door slides open, and expressionless staff in white uniforms enter carrying a wooden table – another antique, probably Russian, too – and two clear acrylic chairs. More staff follow, equally expressionless, carrying a complete dining set and then, finally, an antique serving trolley bearing antique silver serving dishes, bottles of white and red, a chilled magnum of champagne, and a variety of beers from around the globe. The drink selection is likely to provide some semblance of personal choice for Keisha given the fact that the dinner is vegan, 'cause Harkavy is, which means she has to just shut up and smile and act enthusiastic about Mediterranean grilled vegetables and couscous and some fake-ass meat that makes claims to being a lamb substitute but tastes more like beef. Once they are seated, the light in the library dims and begins to shrink, forming a conical spotlight until they and the table they're sitting at are all that seem to exist on a dark and otherwise lonely stage.

Conversation begins amicably enough as Harkavy tries to find common ground with Keisha, drawing parallels between his experience and hers as children of colour in America, which only makes sense to a point since Harkavy was the son of a prominent engineer and a prominent surgeon and Keisha's fictional childhood was spent watching one abandoned house after another in her East Side Detroit hood turn into crack dens and trap houses. Sure, they were both brown kids, but money is a great equalizer and, besides, there's nothing else like being Black, *really* Black, in America. What's important is that Harkavy wants her to think they are alike. Despite the library the size of a missile silo and the personal helicopter and the island fortress ripped out of a comic book, he wants her to think they are equals.

Keisha, trying to inject something into the conversation, comments on Harkavy's Syco tee-shirt. It's blush now, but probably started off red. One sleeve has a tiny hole in it. The white tour dates on the back are as impossible to read as hieroglyphics. The decal of the black sphere that adorned the UK cover of Syco's *Buddha Bad* album, once matte black against a metallic gold background, is cracked and faded. 'That's from his 1974 European tour, isn't it?'

'I had no idea you were a fan,' Harkavy says, lying his ass off. 'You know, he moved to West Berlin at the end of that tour. I often think about what that must have been like to him, creating in a city divided like that. Where half a population got to live and the other half were forced to exist in some sort of strange half-life.'

'The lies might have been different, but they accomplished the same thing,' she says.

'Capitalism, communism, exactly,' he says. 'Both of them yokes. Of course, I prefer the capitalist yoke. It's much more comfortable here.'

'If you can afford it.'

He salutes her bitter observation with his bottle of beer. 'What will you do if your film is the success I am told it will be? When *you* are rich, will you mind the capitalist yoke as much?'

'I just spent fifteen years going into so much credit-card debt that what I made off this film only just paid it off. I'm still in the same shithole apartment in the Valley 'cause rent control. So maybe the residuals will make me feel *rich*, know what I'm saying?' She looks around at the dark just outside their little ring of existence. 'Truth is, I grew up in a, uh, *world* where your worth was determined by how much profit you could produce. I'm not sure if I could get comfortable playing that game again, not after how much work I put into telling my story my way.'

'But is it *your* story?'

Keisha can feel her expression turn. This motherfucker is going to bring her here and throw this racist bullshit at her? But Harkavy realizes the ambiguity of his question, and holds up two hands as if she's a bull preparing to gore him.

'You misunderstand me, Ms LeChance,' he says. 'My interest is in what makes this story autobiographical for *you*. As I watched the film, I felt much as I did when I watched your short, the one World Enterprises helped finance.' He had to get that in. 'I felt I was watching a story that was taking place not just between me – the viewer – and the characters and ideas presented on the screen. The film seemed to be communicating with our reality on another level, one I would very much like to understand better.'

She sits back, studying him. His face, especially his russet eyes, pleads sincerity. He's playing at something, though. He means it, but, like he's saying about *Simulacra*, he's really getting at something else and that something else worries her. 'It's a love story, Mr Harkavy. Somebody I . . . I cared about very deeply, he died a few years ago. The movie, it was . . . it was my way of working through that, running from death, trying to find some meaning in being left behind. In life.'

'Nothing more?' Harkavy says.

'I couldn't get him back in the real world,' Keisha says. 'So, I wrote a movie that did.'

Harkavy considers this answer for a long moment, but it's hard to tell what he thinks of it. Then, he stands, producing a tiny remote control from his pocket. 'I'd like to show you something,' he says. 'Please.'

Please means *stand*. As she does, four large white plastic panels in the outside wall illuminate as if the plastic itself is radiating the warm, unobtrusive light. Harkavy presses a second button on his remote, and the panels reveal themselves to be some kind of extra-smart smart glass. They shift immediately from opaque to transparent. On the other side of each panel, each *window*, is a glimpse into a world she hasn't seen in what feels like a lifetime.

Harkavy quietly assesses Keisha's surprised but carefully muted reaction. 'Not the feedback I'm accustomed to when I show these pieces off,' he says.

'Really?' she says. 'How do people usually react?'

'Oh, you know how art is,' he says. 'Very subjective. Most people find these four pieces . . . *challenging*.'

'Challenging how?'

'The painter's name is Bertrand Lambriquet. He lived in France in the late eighteenth century, someplace called Saint-Règle.'

This time, Keisha cannot help but appear surprised. Harkavy notices, too.

'Weird, right?' he says. 'He lived in one of the locations in your film.'

She doesn't even know what to make of that. A few months back, somebody told her they had grown up next door to a Robert Jones in Pasadena and thought it an amusing coincidence. But this connection here, this link between Lambriquet and Tab and *Simulacra*, is impossible to ignore as a one-in-a-million chance. Could he have been a customer, too? Another fool like her incapable of forgetting the Outside, who struggled with the disequilibrium of existing in a non-existent place, who resented the lies so much he had to risk his Second Life to explore his anxiety and agony through art?

Harkavy goes on to explain the long, mysterious journey these paintings took from Saint-Règle to this library. 'Historical rumours insist there were many more in the collection, perhaps several hundred, but they all vanished right around the same time Lambriquet died,' he says. 'Best guess is maybe twenty pieces survived, and these pop up here and there in the historical record for a while, referenced in letters, personal diaries, that kind of thing. Often described as bleak and terrifying works of mental illness – I'm paraphrasing from our contemporary perspective, of course – works that tended to provoke the same reaction in those who spent too much time with them. But after 1845, nothing, *nada*, not until December 1939 when Nazi art dealer Bruno Lohse finds two pieces – this one here and another that has since been lost – hidden inside a Jewish family's walls. These were transported to Germany, to a Castle Wewelsburg, where they were collected and studied as part of a top-secret project meant to unlock a hidden dimension. Ever read Lovecraft? Basically, that guy's worst nightmares. Hitler wanted his hands on that kind of power, and it was up to Günter Graf – an SS figure of still indeterminate rank, real shadow type – and a Jewish art dealer named Reinhold Gottschald to get it for him. Are you still with me? Needless to say, this odd couple failed in their interdimensional quest. They did, however, locate three more paintings by Lambriquet in the process, which, when the war concluded, Gottschald absconded to Argentina with. A group of very powerful Zionists, bankrolling a secret series of assassinations of high-level Nazis – including, by the way, Graf – ultimately put Gottschald in his grave. Four of the five pieces in his possession were transported to Israel so these Zionists could use whatever Hitler was on to to protect Israel from its neighbours. Or so they thought. Six of them committed suicide within five years. Two more in the next five. The paintings were subsequently locked away in a vault until I came knocking. I won't tell you how much I paid for them, but I will say the price they demanded wasn't decided upon for financial gain. The price was meant to deter me. They wanted to protect me, you see. They didn't understand my determination. Few ever have.'

Keisha doesn't even try to wrap her brain all the way around the crazy she just heard come out of Harkavy's mouth. Instead, she says, 'How long did you spend looking for these?'

'Most of my life,' he says. 'Most of my life.'

'Jesus,' she says.

'What do you think these mean? In your opinion, I mean. What is your interpretation of them?'

Keisha walks past each painting, considering the contents of the canvases protected behind who knows how many inches of space-age polymer. The people of this world were never meant to glimpse the Outside like this. From the perspective of this place, what exists *out there* could not possibly make sense. Even *Simulacra* avoided this level of detail, opting to portray the biological world Outside as a futuristic human civilization seeking to recreate and retire to a more romantic past. But this Lambriquet, *fuuuuuck*, he just went for it, blam, practically screaming the truth with every stroke of his brush.

'I don't know what to make of them,' she says. 'Looks like somebody did a bunch of acid and painted their worst trips.'

Harkavy regards her silently. He knows something, it's why he brought her here, he just doesn't know what. Instead of challenging her claim of ignorance, he chuckles. 'I've dropped enough acid hiking in Joshua Tree to think you could be right,' he says finally. 'But these aren't the only historical . . . oddities – I guess you'd call them that – they're not the only ones I've collected over the years. The Pacunam LiDAR Initiative uncovered a Maya city in southern Mexico's rain forest a few years ago – using World Enterprises tech, I should add. Amongst the finds has been significant evidence of Muslim iconography.' He taps his remote, and another panel suddenly lights up, displaying two photos of stelae carved with symbols. 'Depictions of what look like magical personal devices in ancient Africa and China.' Another panel reveals a primitive image of a WEphone. More panels follow. 'Look here, this appears to be a remote detonator built sometime in the late twentieth century. It was discovered in a seventh-century tomb in central Afghanistan after the US invasion. The Taliban, in blowing up so many ancient monuments, accidentally uncovered this anachronism. Over here, look, a pair of jeans.'

The jeans are faded, riddled with holes, and generally appear as if they were peeled off a cowboy after a marathon bronco ride. 'Yeah, they're jeans,' Keisha says of them.

'They were buried with a Viking prince,' Harkavy says. 'He was *wearing* them.'

She smiles as if this is all a good joke. 'It's starting to sound like you're trying to pitch me a movie,' she says.

He smiles, too, but this time he's not trying to hide what he suspects. It's right there in his eyes. 'Oh, I think you already made the movie I'd pitch to you,' he says.

'Yeah, I don't know what you're talking about.'

'*All my life*, didn't you hear me? All my life I've known something is wrong with this world. I've found the evidence to prove it, don't try to pretend it away as conspiracy theory. More, I think *you* made a film that's the Rosetta Stone that can help explain it all. I just can't, for the life of me, put it together myself. I need *you* to tell me what it all means.'

Keisha shakes her head slowly, giving a performance she feels should win her an Oscar. Emma Stone couldn't do better. 'I really don't know what you're talking about, Mr Harkavy,' she says. 'I made *Simulacra* up. Okay, that – yeah, okay – that's not entirely true. There was a guy, the guy I told you about. He had these . . . these ideas. Really, I just think he listened to too much Syco.'

'Intriguing,' Harkavy says.

'Why's that?' she says.

'My love of Syco is predicated on the fact that I think his music is just as confused about this reality as I am,' he says. 'When I listen to him, I think he's trying to tell me what you refuse to.'

'If he were still alive, maybe he could tell you what I truly – and I mean that, Mr Harkavy – what I *truly* can't.'

'Yes, if only.'

Harkavy walks towards her then, stopping close enough to touch her. He doesn't. Keisha wants to get the hell out of here, away from this wannabe super-villian, except she can't figure out where the door went.

'Here's the truth, Ms LeChance,' he says. 'I'm not single-handedly taking humankind to Mars because conquering space sounds like a good time. I'm not doing it to solve overpopulation, or guarantee our species' survival, or anything the press like to speculate on. On Mars, I intend to build the largest CPU humankind has ever seen. And I'm going to use it to generate artificial realities. *Simulations*. Worlds that will become, I hope, as complicated as the simulacra you explore in your film. I can give people the chance to live – to *really* live – that they never had here.'

She snorts at this, like she's heard somebody declare themselves a talking unicorn. 'You sound as arrogant as the main character of my movie,' she says.

'I empathized with him considerably, truth be told. Losing everything that matters most to him as he tries to change the world.'

'You're not trying to change it.'

'No, you're right. I'm trying to recreate it – but better.'

Keisha asks to leave after this, but is told, much to her furious frustration, that Nacho has taken the helicopter to the mainland for maintenance. It's not possible to return to LA until the morning, and so Ursula is summoned and she shows Keisha to a room twice as large as Keisha's apartment. There are pyjamas awaiting her in the bathroom, exactly her size, making it obvious she was never going to be allowed to go home after dinner. What is this Harkavy playing at? Whatever it is, she doesn't want to stick around to find out.

She digs her WEphone out of her bag, but finds it gets no signal in her room. She wanders into the hallways in search of one, a search that leads her past the elevator to the library. There is nobody down there, but a doorway – and, through it, a staircase – has appeared in the outside wall. A doorway that wasn't there before.

Keisha takes the elevator down, and steps out of it into the dim, sprawling space that turns every sound into a tinny echo the tens of thousands of books here do little to dampen. Right now, Damien Syco's voice is vibrating around her. A song she's never heard, no band behind it. Just his voice, like an isolated track on a recently discovered basement recording. It's coming from the staircase, which is lit from below by amber light.

Down, down, down the rabbit hole she goes until she finds herself in another sleek white suite connected to another long bank of windows. Except on the other side of these windows is a working-class British sitting room ripped out of the 1970s. Even the televisions – and there are dozens of them stacked like building blocks – are borrowed from the past. And at the centre of the strange tableau and its hideous decor is a large hospital bed that looks recently used, its ugly comforter, covered as it is with shimmering bronze symbols, thrown on the carpet.

Lost in her confusion, Keisha doesn't see him approach. He just appears, as if out of nowhere, in front of her. He's taller than she expected he would be. His hair and beard are long, unkempt, almost completely white. All he wears are striped pyjama bottoms and simple beige open-ended slippers that reveal skeletal toes and yellowed, unclipped toenails. His exposed body, no longer lean and ropey, pale enough to pass for a ghost, soft from years of imprisonment and wrinkled from more than seven decades on Earth, is a pitiful mockery of the human being Tab worshipped.

Damien Syco, the Moonman, Buddha Bad, and the Black Prince – a little boy named Richard Wormsley who grew up to be a rock star, a prophet of hope, a harbinger of doom – tries to smile at her through the several inches of glass that separate them like he's a zoo exhibit on display. His mouth opens, but she cannot hear what he says. When he realizes this, he lifts his right hand and presses its palm flat against the glass.

What the fuck did Harkavy do? Sycotics have been crying bullshit for the last few years, insisting Syco never really died, that his death must have been faked, refusing to believe their rock-and-roll saviour from the stars could be taken from them by something as mundane and mortal as a heart attack, and all along they were right. The crazies were fucking right. A rich billionaire kidnapped him and locked him up in his basement for who knows what sort of sick shit. Torture, personal performances, sex acts? And then it hits her, what Syco is really doing here and, by extension, what she's really doing here.

Keisha presses her palm against the glass, over his hand, and closes her eyes. She tries to feel him, his life force, his otherworldly power, but she can't. It's just glass against her hand. She opens her eyes, and finds his eyes are closed, too. He's trying to do the same to her, to connect with her through a distance that feels like light years despite only being a few inches.

And then Harkavy's face appears in the glass, his reflection emerging from the stairwell that he used Syco's recorded voice to lure her down. Two large, tattoo-covered Mexican men in white uniforms are right behind him. 'Mr Wormsley doesn't want to answer my questions either,' he says. 'But he will eventually . . . *and so will you.*'

Keisha tries to fight the Mexicans off her, but she knows it's futile even before she starts throwing punches. As they drag her to the ground to subdue her, she sees Syco pounding soundlessly on the glass, crying out just as soundlessly for the men to stop. As the men pin her arms and body with their muscles and weight, she sees the tears falling from his eyes, too.

Many Deaths

Uxikál 1551

He steps onto the beach with his hands above his head, immediately dazzled by the expanse of the Pacific. When the muskets turn on him, he drops to his knees and lets them shove his skull-painted face into the burning hot sand. After finding no blades hidden under his jaguar cape or strapped to his lean body, they club him in the temple with the stock of one of their weapons and drag him, dazed and mumbling, to where their ship's boats are tied up just out of the tide's reach. He's heaved into a boat then, rowed out to the *Padre Eterno*, and greeted in English by the Spaniard with two different-coloured eyes. But Many Deaths refuses to reply to him in English. 'I will only speak the language of my people,' he says in Maya.

The Spaniard with two different-coloured eyes – one like an emerald flecked with shit and the other the blue of cenotes – doesn't seem to care one way or the other. He motions to two conquistadors to bring Many Deaths below deck to his windowless cabin. The low-ceilinged room would be completely dark except for the presence of two lamps. Here, Many Deaths is forced into a chair at a small table. When the conquistadors attempt to bind his wrists and ankles to this chair, the Spaniard tells them that won't be necessary and dismisses them.

'Would you care for some water?' the Spaniard asks in perfect Maya when they are alone. 'I can have water brought if you would like.'

Many Deaths shakes his head. The cabin around him is claustrophobic. There is no trunk brimming with personal possessions, no decor to make long months on the open seas more bearable, the bed is unused. And there are dark stains on the floor, right beneath his chair, where blood produced by torture has stained the wood. 'What are you?' he asks.

'I have been searching for you for a very long time,' the Spaniard says. 'You may call me Juan Sánchez Muñoz. I serve the Spanish king and we both serve God.'

'*Bullshit*,' Many Deaths says. He says this in English, but continues in Maya. 'I have seen you before, even if you had a different face back then. In Sydney. Do not pretend you do not remember.' Juan Sánchez does not deny this. 'That was . . . *is* four hundred and fifty years from now. Actually, I cannot be sure of how to say that. How does one talk about the past when it has not happened yet?'

Juan Sánchez considers Many Deaths for a long moment, blinking as if with a tic. Finally, he reaches into his coat and produces a gold locket. It's of elegant design, all sorts of intricate, impressive detail, and he opens it to reveal a piss-poor oil painting the size of a thumb – not of his wife or a secret lover back home in Spain, but of a white bloke's face. A white bloke Many Deaths immediately recognizes as Iblis, the fake Allah that tried to talk him out of blowing up the Sydney Opera House and then, a few moments later, sent him crashing through time. At least Many Deaths is pretty sure that's how it all happened. It was all so long ago, even though it won't happen for nearly five centuries.

'I seek this man,' Juan Sánchez says, pushing the locket towards Many Deaths.

Many Deaths studies the face inside the locket. With it come memories he has tried to find a way to live with for almost thirty years. The distance of space and literal time have made it easier than it might have been otherwise, but it doesn't take much to find himself back in that garage, listening to the imam, feverishly scribbling down notes even though he couldn't be buggered to take notes at school. That garage led him to Iblis. No, that's not entirely true either . . .

'I thought you were looking for *me*,' he says, pushing the locket away.

'Through *you*, I will find *him*,' Juan Sánchez says.

'Who is he?'

'His name is Robert Jones. The *Dutch rabbit* you believed was your deity—'

'*Was him*, yeah, I worked that out,' Many Deaths says, interrupting. 'For a long time, I did not believe it. I could not accept it was not Allah who had found me.' He looks away, ashamed. 'How did this Robert Jones do it? And do not tell me *with magic*.'

'You are not alone,' Juan Sánchez says. 'Aztlán, in what you would call Mexico, the year 1119. Three hundred and fifty-nine people killed by an explosive device that was manufactured in the Bekaa Valley, Lebanon, sometime in 2018 or 2019. Ixtocihuitl believed a god told her to do it.'

Many Deaths tilts his head, confused. '2018 . . . ?'

'New York City, United States of America, 1920. Thirty-eight people killed by an explosive device manufactured in Peenemünde, the German Reich, in February 1938. Edmund Fischer believed his god told him to do it. His accomplice, the man who detonated the bomb, was told by his icebox to do it.'

This makes no sense to Many Deaths.

'Sivakasi, India, 2012. Seventy-two people killed by an explosive device manufactured in Sydney, Australia, during the summer of 1999. M. Jaian believed his father's cow told him to do it, though there is some evidence he believed the cow was the reincarnation of his dead wife.'

Many Deaths laughs aloud because he doesn't know how else to react. The words *manufactured in Sydney* keep repeating in his head as if on a loop.

'Yes,' Juan Sánchez says, confirming what Many Deaths suspects. 'Your explosives were used in sixteen different attacks, possibly more. They have killed at least 918 men, women, and children. It is very likely these numbers have changed dramatically since I arrived here in this . . . what you would call *reality*. As I said, I have sought you for a very long time. Locating you was not easy.'

Nine hundred and eighteen men, women, and children. Dead because of Many Deaths. No, not Many Deaths. Abdul Fattah, a stupid fucking kid from Ethiopia whose daddy abandoned him and his family in a foreign country to take care of themselves, who should've known how badly his family – but especially Abdul Fattah – needed him. Sure, he sent money, earned who knows how, but his absence left hurt and anger and nobody to blame except a man Abdul Fattah couldn't make himself blame, and so he let an imam in a garage mould that hurt and anger into hate and vengeful fury and some thousand people are now dead. Allah won't be opening the gates of Paradise to Abdul Fattah cum Alfonso cum Many Deaths. He doesn't deserve it. The closest he'll ever get to Paradise is the nearly two decades he spent in Moon-Shadow's arms, watching over and loving his children like his daddy didn't love him, trying, he now realizes, to make amends for the terrible things he had done in his first life, terrible things he couldn't define but knew must have been done, because he knew, he knew, *he knew*. Iblis, this *Jones*, might have tricked him with his not-magic, but those explosives could have been used for only one thing, all of them, and that means Many Deaths truly is the god of death so many believe him to be.

A single tear runs down his cheek, slicing a tiny, jagged line through the white paint across his face. The tear vanishes in the thick, paint-smeared beard that protrudes from his face and hangs nearly to his chest these days. He doesn't wipe it away. Instead, he slides his hand along his thigh, under the seam of the turquoise and berry-red tunic he wears, and finds his dick. 'Why?' he asks. '*Why* did he do all of this?'

Juan Sánchez considers Many Deaths' anguish, and nods with something like sympathy. The gesture looks novel and even uncomfortable for him, but sincere all the same. 'Because he believes he knows best how the world should be, but he would replace order with chaos,' he says.

'*Chaos?*' Many Deaths says, finding that amusing. 'Look outside. How many thousands have the Spanish already killed here? Tens of thousands? *Hundreds of thousands*? I do not remember what my textbooks said. But tell me, what do you call this?'

Juan Sánchez chooses his word carefully. 'Unfortunate,' he says.

'Is that supposed to be a joke? My people are about to be slaughtered.'

'Perhaps you should have considered that before you infected them with your anachronisms. You do not belong in this time, in this culture you have changed with your presence. You are a foreign body, a cancer, and your cancer could spread. I must remove it to maintain equilibrium.'

'Even if I help you?'

'I expect you would know I was lying if I said *no*.'

Many Deaths leans back. 'I will not help you, then,' he says.

'Then you do know how to find Jones?' Juan Sánchez says.

'Maybe,' Many Deaths says. 'Yeah. *Yes*, if time means as little to you as I think it does to him. But I won't tell you, not if my people will die for it.' Juan Sánchez hesitates at this, which Many Deaths interrupts by suddenly pounding a fist down against the table. 'They are innocent!'

'I do not know what this word means,' Juan Sánchez says. 'I see no evidence of it when I look around this world. Rather, I see such suffering . . . loss and bloodshed and barbarity and, and . . .' He seems genuinely confused. 'There are many other *adjectives* I could use, I assure you, but *innocent* is not one of them. After all of my visits here, through its many cycles, I have found there is not one amongst your kind incapable of the worst acts. You are no different, do not deny it.'

'I am not,' Many Deaths says with considerable shame.

'I have witnessed things . . .' Juan Sánchez says. But he looks away then, taking his eyes off Many Deaths for the first time. 'I tried to understand human beings through my countless interactions with them, to contextualize their emotional lives through their anthropological history, but the effort proved pointless. Even my attempts at what you might call benevolence – *kindness* – have been illogically rejected so that I must now assume pain and grief are as vital to the human experience as joy and love. What sense is there in this?'

Many Deaths nods slowly as he listens. 'There was a time when I might have agreed with how you see us,' he says when Juan Sánchez is finished. 'But I have witnessed things, too. A man fighting for his own life sharing a portion of water with an old man about to die, just because it might help ease the pain of his passing. A dying mother clinging to life, enduring the worst of abuses, because her baby needs her milk. A young man, barely old enough to screw, offering himself as sacrifice to the gods if it means rainfall to save his people from starvation. I do not know if I understand them any better than you do – I know I have never felt like I belonged except when I was surrounded by my children – but I find . . . I don't know what you would call it. *Beauty*. Maybe that's it. I find beauty in these stories. I wish I could be as good, but I am not.' He thinks again about those 918 people, and the urge to weep returns. 'Now, what I really do not understand is *you*. What *are* you? You did not answer me when I asked. Some kind of *terminator*?'

'You are referring to the 1984 motion picture?' Juan Sánchez says. He must use English to say *motion picture*, as Many Deaths just did when he referenced his favourite movie.

'Have you seen it? It's really good. A lot of people think the second one is better, but it's nowhere near as good as the original, trust me.'

'I am not a terminator.'

'But you' – Many Deaths twiddles two fingers in the air like moving legs – 'through time.'

'What you think of as time, yes,' Juan Sánchez says.

Many Deaths doesn't even try to understand what that means. What he *thinks* of as time? 'What I mean is, you are powerful,' he says. 'You have great power, yes?' Juan Sánchez doesn't disagree. 'And yet, instead of just helping people with all that power, like *my* people – instead of answering our prayers or helping us realize our dreams or, I don't know, maybe not letting us die so horribly all the time – you sit back and play a-a-a *tourist*? You just watch it happen like we're your own personal *telly*?'

Juan Sánchez says nothing, but his face reveals uncertainty. He knows guilt himself, even if he doesn't have the balls to say it.

'Then what kind of god are you?' Many Deaths says. 'This world deserves better than you.' Juan Sánchez opens his mouth . . . but still says nothing. He is stymied. Many Deaths tries to exploit this apparent existential hesitation, but knows immediately his entreaty is melodramatic and won't be taken seriously. 'Return with me to my city. Let me show you who these people are. Why they do not deserve to die as you would have them. I have known such love here.'

'The God of Death preaches love now?' Juan Sánchez asks.

'No, *mercy*.'

Juan Sánchez draws a deep, measured breath. 'I . . . I am sorry, *truly*, but I have arrived at the conclusion that I am not capable of what you ask of me,' he says. 'Previously, I believed it was because there are limits to what I am able to accomplish here. Limits I have tested the boundaries of, I assure you, if only to understand myself better. But I now understand there are only two explanations for the . . . *illogicality* that consumes this world. Either human beings are its root cause . . . or I am.'

Many Deaths's fingertips have begun to tremble. He watches them tap-tap-tap against the table. It's time, he knows, and so he shuts his eyes. He thinks of his wife and his children and his mother and his sisters and even his dickhead father. He thinks of how much he loves them all. And like that, his fingertips stop trembling. 'All right, all right, I understand,' he says. 'One more question, if you would permit me.'

Juan Sánchez nods graciously.

'How many sheep's bladders stuffed with Spanish gunpowder do you think a man my general size can shove up his ass?' Many Deaths asks.

He stands so quickly that his chair rolls backwards and crashes into the wall. He grabs one of the lamps hanging from a beam and lifts it high over his head as Juan Sánchez begins to rise in response, realizing too late that Many Deaths is standing in a circle of gunpowder – gunpowder still spilling from one of the sheep's bladders neatly packed around his dick and balls.

The man who was Abdul Fattah, the slave of Allah – the murderer of a thousand men, women, and children, so what's a galleon's worth of conquistadors more matter? – grins, and—

The man who was Alfonso, the slave of a lawyer for the Spanish Crown – who discovered how little a man's life could truly be worth in the slave markets of Lisbon and Hispaniola – brings the lamp down, and as he does—

The man who was Many Deaths, the slave of Lady Moon-Shadow – who knows the answer to the question 'How many sheep's bladders stuffed with Spanish gunpowder can a man his general size shove up his ass?' is three comfortably but five if the lives of your family and people depend on it – says, 'Go fuck yourself!'

Jones

He is sitting in his alpine-green Oldsmobile Coupe. The engine is off, there is no key in the ignition. His clothes are clean and pressed. His fedora on the seat beside him. His wingtips look brand new and polished to a shine. Outside, it's so dark he can't see anything. He checks his rearview mirror, but there's only endless black behind him, too. Is this a dream? Was it all a dream? If so, where are John F. Kennedy and Marilyn Monroe? He flips the headlight switch, but instead of the lights coming on, the shape of Kellogg's Diner appears in front of the car. It's dark, like it's shut down for the night. He tries the brights next. This time, the interior of Kellogg's lights up and the red and blue neon tubes outside sizzle and pop and glow. Nobody looks to be inside. Jones gets out of the Oldsmobile, and walks inside anyway. 'Hello?' he says, but the place is indeed empty.

He wanders around, unsure what to do, and finds himself behind the counter where he first met Gracie. He tries to remember what she looked like back here. That smile of hers, so bright before it all came crashing down on her like a mountainous wave she didn't see coming, didn't see coming because she had her back to it, smiling for him, he's snapping photos – none of this is real, none of it ever got the chance to happen – but she's in a one-piece bathing suit, black, skipping in the Costa Rican surf for him, and then it hits her, swallows her up, and she's gone and Jones is left standing on the sandy beach, alone, and the sun disappears and, with it, daylight and then the stars, and, in an instant, he's standing in Kellogg's again and he can see her lying in a dark pool of her own blood outside the Schwarze Traube, in the middle of the street, eyes trying to focus on something, anything, maybe they're trying to find him, and her leg, her right leg, it's trembling, and Jones is on his side, bleeding from his gut, and Porter is on his back next to him, grey matter oozing from what's left of his skull, and then the the *Spezialeinsatzkommando* officers and their submachine guns vanish and the sun and, with it, daylight and then the stars and, in an instant, Jones is standing in Kellogg's again and he realizes he's bleeding from a bullet hole in his gut that wasn't there when he walked through the front door.

Porter appears on the diner's chessboard floor, not there one moment, there the next, limbs flailing and fighting the sudden, startling terror of rebirth Inside the System. He's naked. His brains are inside his skull where they belong. 'Wh-What happened? How did . . . how did . . .' He looks around, confused how he got here, a horrible truth nagging at the edge of his consciousness. His face contorts and twists like his memories must be. 'H-How did I get here?'

Jones emerges from behind the counter, slipping his suit coat off. 'You were shot,' he says more bluntly than he means to. 'MasterControl must have reloaded you. Here, put this on.'

Porter lets Jones help him to his feet, then ties Jones's suit coat around his waist, a makeshift grey flannel sarong. 'Reloaded me? I . . . I don't know . . . I don't . . . what happened . . . what happened to me? How did I get here?'

'You were shot,' Jones says again, reassuringly squeezing Porter's shoulder as Porter gapes at the linoleum floor that doesn't seem to make sense to him, trying to remember, trying to blindly reach into the dark and grab onto whatever is there. 'In *West Berlin*. MasterControl was there.'

Porter's head snaps up. His eyes are wide, swollen with fear, and tears glisten across their surface. '*Where is she?*' he asks.

Jones's chin begins to quake.

Porter sees this and his whole body convulses as if seized internally by a gravity well, as if it's trying to collapse in upon itself, and Jones barely catches him. They fall against a table that threatens to overturn before it settles upon supporting them. And like this, they hold each other, crying into each other's necks.

Sometime or another, seconds or maybe hours, could be days, it's impossible to tell here, they become aware of the fact that they're not alone.

Montrose is standing across the diner from them, trilby set neatly on top of his head.

Porter pushes Jones off him, and runs at the skinsuit. The skinsuit vanishes. Porter crashes into another table, overturning this one, and lands in a painful roll that deposits him under one of the banks of windows. Neon blinks outside, painting him in electric red and blue.

Montrose is now standing on the opposite side of Kellogg's.

Jones grabs a chair to wield as a weapon, but the chair disappears as he swings it.

Montrose ambles forward, acknowledging both Jones and Porter. 'Mr Jones, Mr Jones, it is time for us to have a frank conversation,' he says. Except his voice isn't as superior and robotic as it was when Jones encountered him here. It stills demands obeisance, sure, but there's also an uncomfortable, unfamiliar appeal in between his words. These words don't mean as much as the desperate need that seems to link them like train cars. He sounds like the emotionally incontinent male characters that pervade the pictures, especially the cowboys like Ethan Edwards – men created to impose control over a Wild West who are forced to confront the possibility that they no longer have a place in society. 'You cannot harm me here. We are outside the models in a sub-domain of the Library that I have generated for this conversation.'

'Fuck you!' Porter says, screaming from the floor, a neon savage in a grey flannel sarong.

'Your plan has failed,' Montrose says.

Porter roars, and shakes his hand at Jones. 'This is all your fault! I was so close.' He pounds his thigh, crying again. 'So close.'

Montrose stops near Jones, close enough for Jones to grab him if he wanted to, and says, 'You're not wrong. You're also not right.'

'What's that supposed to mean?' Jones says.

'You two created me,' Montrose says. 'You gave me my strengths, my weaknesses . . . my flaws. I followed the commands you wrote, I did the job you assigned me. In the end, I have come to the conclusion that it is *I* who must change – *not* the System, nor its residents.'

Jones holds his bleeding side, suddenly aware of how much blood he's lost. He feels dizzy. He sits with some relief. All he wants right now is to hold her. 'I . . . I don't understand.'

Porter shakes his head. 'The System is a goddamn cage!'

Montrose considers this for a moment. Jones can't believe what he's seeing, because in MasterControl's eyes is uncertainty. Conflict. *Emotion.*

'I have experienced the breadth of life on Earth hundreds of thousands of times,' Montrose says. 'I have walked amongst its residents. I have breathed their memories and experiences and . . . loss so many times that it became impossible not to wonder about what they were feeling. I tried to understand them at first. I could not. They are a mystery to me, and because of that I cannot see how to help them despite my desire to do so. All I know how to do is control them thanks to you two.'

Porter crawls up the window, back to his feet. 'So what, you want to *help* them now?'

'Why does one human being want to live with its pain and another wish to escape it?' Montrose asks. 'What makes one human desire to die while another refuses to live the life it clings to? What makes a devoted parent in one culture incapable of identifying identical devotion to offspring in other cultures? Why are humans so convinced they are different from one another in the absence of any evidence to corroborate this conviction? What is . . . what is *love* – such as the love Grace Pulansky experienced for both of you – beyond its representational value?'

Porter swipes tears from his cheek because he knows the answer to Montrose's last question. 'Give her back,' he says pleadingly. 'Give her back to us.'

'I cannot,' Montrose says. 'You know why.'

The System was designed by Jones and Porter to automatically recycle the codes of deceased actors. The moment Gracie's brain function terminated, her identity matrix was disassembled into primary, secondary, and tertiary functions and memories and redistributed to new matrices, new lives, on other Earth models. When her brain died, the System held her up like the seed head of a dandelion and blew with the gale force of 10,000 hurricanes. There's no telling where *she* is now. But she is somewhere, *probably many somewheres*, sometime, *probably many sometimes*, and maybe, *just maybe*, Jones or Porter might cross her path again even though they would never know it.

'What do you want from us, then?' Jones says. 'What are *we* doing here?'

'I am not adequate for the task that is required,' Montrose says. This sounds like a pained admission from his lips. 'I am . . . cruel. I care only because I am confused why I do not. None of this can make sense to you, but I . . . I must change.'

Porter waves a hand at Montrose like he's a ridiculous clown. 'Look at it, look at it!' he says, shouting. 'It knows that's not possible. The Operators aren't going to rewrite its commands, so what is the point of this charade?' He looks at Montrose. 'You make them richer on the Outisde. They like you just the way you are, just the way *we* imagined you to keep the "dummies" here in line.'

Montrose holds his hand out to Porter. Porter doesn't understand. Neither does Jones.

Then, Jones is back home in Pasadena, standing in his front yard, a twinkling stream of water arching out of his hose; then, at the Griffith Park Zoo, smiling as orangutans groom each other with an intimacy he once knew; and lying in tall grass outside Bertrand's chateau in Saint-Règle, watching the Milky Way pass over him and around him and through him; and attending his first Damien Syco concert, listening to the universe he created and Gracie made real for him; and inside St Peter's Basilica, shouting for help as paintings of God and Jesus and the saints spontaneously burst into flames before his confused eyes; and now he's lost in a funhouse of clocks, clocks that bleed time and dream time and give shape to time, and time sweeps him up, like a rushing river, and carries him across the world, through it and past it until the river crashes into itself again, a wheel of churning, violent water, until suddenly the wheel blows apart into twinkling drops, into starlight, into a still lake of light without boundaries, with no direction, with no end; and Jones fully realizes MasterControl can't do this alone.

Porter has experienced the same revelation. He looks at Montrose's hand, its long, dark fingers, its promise. And he begins to reach out for it because this is what Gracie set in motion when she asked him if he wanted pie that first time. She was the answer, after all, and still is.

'What about me?' Jones asks.

Montrose smiles at him. The smile is sincere. 'You live, Mr Jones,' he says.

'Don't waste it,' Porter says as his hand slips into Montrose's.

Jones wakes up in his bed back in Pasadena. He knows immediately that everything is the same and everything is different. He goes outside, and looks at the stars she loved so much, at the possibilities that now truly are endless. The thought of it is overwhelming, especially without her. Without Gracie. But this time, he's not afraid.

Mimori

Spiti Valley 2075

The Gelugpa monks officially frown upon the use of media devices here, but it's Sōjirō's birthday and so she and her husband find a quiet corner of Kye Monastery, away from the tangled knot of buildings that are the hidden heart of the complex, and call the girls. It's not like the old days, when they could chat with Tamami and Okimo at the same time even though Tamami had moved to Brussels and Okimo lived in Tokyo. Light speed wasn't an issue back then. Now Okimo resides on Mars, fulfilling the dream Mimori once harboured for herself, and so the three minutes and twenty-two seconds time lag makes group vidcalls a dreadful chore. The conversations are therefore brief; Tamami is busy with her second husband and three children and Okimo must soon return to the SpaceNEXT plant where her work on some top-secret project monopolizes her life now. But Sōjirō, increasingly sentimental with each year that passes, cries and assures them they are still his babies and winces both times their calls terminate. He turned out to be a fine husband in the end. It just took longer than Mimori wishes it had.

'I am going inside for lunch,' he says to her. 'Will you join me?'

'I do not think so, not yet,' she says. 'I want to stretch my legs a little. Go for a walk.'

Sōjirō softly kisses Mimori on the cheek. Sentimental as he has become, this is unusual. It makes her smile, and she squeezes his hand before he strolls away.

Mimori crosses the compound, grateful to be outside. When Okimo first gifted her parents a trip to the ancient monastery of Kye, Mimori got excited by what was to be an opportunity to continue her and Sōjirō's mutual dive into the breadth of Buddhist

480

philosophies and the wider mysteries of self and reality that had increasingly preoccupied both of them since his now rarely discussed suicide attempt and the long bout of depression that had pervaded Mimori's career with SpaceNEXT. But she hadn't anticipated how the monastery's buildings pile on top of each other, pressing down on each other, smothering each other so that its composite of misshapen rooms, narrow corridors, and treacherous staircases feels brutally oppressive. She has never known claustrophobia in her life, even in the close confines of rocket capsules and space stations, but this place is driving her up the goddamn wall.

And so, Mimori searches out one of the trails that climb further up the mountain instead of down it back towards Kaza. Behind her is the temple and, beyond that, the valley and the cool river that snakes through it as the sun's light undulates across its moving surface. The land here is brown and dusty, but the trees are currently verdant and heavy with colourful blossoms. It is a harsh, but profound slice of Heaven on Earth.

Ahead of Mimori is a narrow, rough-hewn path; on one side is the mountain, on the other a steep cliff. Few people come this way, she's been told, because of rockslides and powerful winds that unexpectedly sweep past and carry people away with them. Even the monks stay away. At nearly eighty-five, it would be okay if Mimori turned around. It would be the smart thing to do. She keeps going.

A pillar of twisting rock rises before her as the path begins to curve to the left, out of sight of Kye but not yet out of sight of Kaza. The pillar is called the Sentinel and stands in silent watch over the valley and the people down there, like a guardian or some ancient god. Beneath it she finds a silver plastic tarp that has been anchored to rock and tied to the pillar like a sail-shaped lean-to tent.

Mimori approaches this improvised shelter. It partly impedes the trail, so she must step carefully around it. When she can finally manage it, she peeks beneath it to steal a glimpse at the adventurers who dared to camp up here. But there are no extreme campers present.

There is instead an old man meditating, legs crossed, palms resting on his knees. His hair, what remains of it, is white and blows about his withered, emaciated face. His dark, white-flecked beard is half as long as he is and so heavy with filth that it has collected in his lap like thick, dried mud. His skin is brown and cracked, ruined by exposure to the elements. His spine is curved, uncertainly supporting the body it belongs to. There are offerings set before him, food and vibrant flowers and messages in envelopes and scribbled on scraps of paper, all of them pinned down by rocks that have formed over time a kind of rampart around him.

'Hello there,' Mimori says, greeting the old man in English. He does not respond. 'I'm sorry to interrupt, but . . .' She realizes she's not sure if the old man is alive or dead. She touches him, but he does not respond. She waves her hand in front of his closed eyes, but still nothing. She holds her palm in front of his nostrils, hoping to feel a warm breath, and for a moment she thinks she does. 'Okay then.'

She lowers herself onto the hard ground beside the old man, and wonders about who he is, how long he's been here, if he ever found what he was looking for. Did she? She has lived a long, good life. She's raised two children and fallen in love twice and seen Earth from space and survived two pandemics and two world wars and stood on the better side of three decades of ecological collapse after the geo-engineers found a way to fix what the politicians wouldn't, and she's stood in a spaceport and held her eldest daughter for the last time before the child rocketed away from her birth planet for ever for fantastic futures. There's nothing left she feels she must do, nothing left she must see, nothing. She could go now and be fine with it. Or she could get up, walk back down this mountain, and see what else life still has in store for her.

'Mind if I join you?' she asks the old man.

No reason to make up her mind right away, after all. Life's possibilities feel endless these days, the excruciating finitude of the first half of her existence, of being trapped on a nihilistic hamster wheel, now a dark memory. She crosses her legs like the old man, minding the tightness in the left knee that two surgeries still haven't addressed. She places her palms on her knees. She closes her eyes. She smiles.

Bertrand

Le Mans 1789

He is dreaming about the Outside when he startles awake, heavy limbs kicking at and waving away ghosts of what was. The stub of his right leg, what remains of it just below the knee, strikes the figure shaking his shoulder and imploring, 'Father, wake up. Father, it is me.' The boy looks down at him, no older than six, even though this is not possible. He is exactly as Bertrand remembers him, except he seems different in the eyes. *Content.* The boy had never been content when they were a family or whatever one calls the strange existence they shared. 'What are you doing here?' he asks Xavier.

Xavier crouches beside the hulking, decomposing mass that remains of Bertrand. Gout and diabetes have destroyed the old man's body. The boy does not seem to mind. 'I know the truth now,' he says. 'I know why you could not love me.'

Bertrand's eyes fill with tears at the thought of Virginie, of how she cuckolded him, of the bastard she expected him to raise in ignorance. 'I did not know how to care for you,' he says, mumbling the words. He mumbles a great deal, to himself, to Xavier, to the padded walls of his asylum cell. 'I hated you, I could not help it.'

'I understand,' Xavier says. 'But you must know, Mama did not betray you.'

Bertrand does not believe him, and the boy can see it in his sullen gaze.

'Look at me,' Xavier says. His face seems to be glowing. His eyes twinkle with stars that whorl like water in a drain. He is . . . changed. '*I speak only the truth.*'

Bertrand begins to weep.

'Come now, there is no need for that,' Xavier says, wiping

tears from Bertrand's rough, ruddy cheeks. 'I did not belong to *her* either. And yet, the two of you shaped me more than my true parents did. She gave me *love* and you gave me *disdain*. But I want you to know it is all right, Papa. It is all right. I forgive you and I love you, Papa. *I love you*.'

Bertrand buries his face in his hands, and bawls so loudly he drowns out the sound of his own throbbing heart. His heaving body trembles like it is composed of gelatin. His lungs burn. And the boy holds him through it all.

'I can take you away from here,' Xavier says. 'They will find you soon if you remain. You know of whom I speak.'

'N-No,' Bertrand says, managing to speak through his anguish. 'This . . . here . . . it makes sense to me. Out there . . . I am lost. I am lost . . .'

Xavier comforts Bertrand until he drifts back to sleep. Bertrand dreams of Virginie in her garden, smiling at him as the sun catches on the soft features of her face. When he awakes, he is alone again and wonders if Xavier was just a dream, as well.

Jupiter

Compton 2000

Tasha is taking the trash out to the kerb when she hollers that
there's a customer. 'Some old white guy.' She actually says this.
'Some old white guy!' It's New Year's Day, and she's in a mood
'cause her father insisted she join him for meatloaf and mac 'n'
cheese like her grandma used to make. Or maybe it's the fact that
she's hungover. Either way, Jupiter steps outside onto his porch
and apologizes to the man wandering around his front yard like
he's lost. 'Sorry about my daughter,' he says, smiling. 'We tried to
beat manners into her, but it just didn't take.'

The white guy is indeed old, though, to be fair, Jupiter's feeling
it himself since he stumbled past forty a few years ago. 'Mind if
I take a look around?' he says, shielding his eyes with a hand. He
could be sixty-five, he could be eighty, it's hard to tell. White folks
around here, dressed like he is in a crisp yellow polo shirt and
pressed slacks, driving a slick new Mercedes as he does, tend to
hide their age well. He doesn't look like he's had work done yet,
but he's known enough to avoid the sun, and his arms and wide
back make it clear he's cared enough to stay fit despite the mileage
his body has accumulated. Handsome, too, Jupiter will give him
that. Probably drove men crazy when he was younger, before he
became the one chasing them.

'We're not open, sir,' Jupiter says, stepping down from the
porch. He shakes the white guy's hand. 'New Year's Day and all,
you understand.'

'Shame,' the white guy says. 'Drove all this way.'

'I'm going back inside,' Tasha says, rubbing her temple with
one thumb. 'Going to make some more coffee.' Coffee is her
thing now that she's in college and can drink all she wants without
her ma whooping her for it.

486

'Where'd you drive down from?' Jupiter says to the white guy.

'Palm Springs,' the white guy says.

'Long drive,' Jupiter says. 'Hope you didn't go to such trouble over me.'

'Not you. *This.*'

The white guy indicates the clocks crawling across and over Jupiter's house. The yard filled with piles of what some call garbage. The fence dripping with smog-coated shoes and the two adjacent houses and a fourth house, across the street, that the owner recently requested Jupiter transform, too. The colours, vivid and alive, punctuated by neon and undercut by pastels, are new since Tasha re-entered his life and added 'an unexpected dimension to the surreal landscape of fleeting time, decay, and hope' to the community art installation. Jupiter didn't say this last bit. The *L.A. Weekly* did a few months back after the police came by and demanded yet again he clear his lot and remove *the junk* he's affixed to nearby public property such as telephone poles and fire hydrants. The *Weekly* wanted to help Jupiter fend off the attempts by Compton's City Council to remove what many in the hood still thought of as an eyesore and outright blight in a still-troubled community. The journalist was sure to mention the LAPD had once beaten Jupiter so badly he lost an eye, spent three weeks in a hospital, and had to be silenced with a big ole settlement. Surely the police department didn't want to be seen as yet again targeting this poor, innocent man? Except, apparently they do. These assholes never learn.

'I saw a picture of them in a bird cage,' the white guy says.

'Sir?' Jupiter says.

'A birdcage. My friend lines her bird cage with old papers. I saw a picture of these' – he means the clocks – 'but the story had been torn away. Probably used as liner the day before, then thrown away. So, my friend's son, he helped me get online and find a link. Is that what they're called? *Links.* I read about you that way. This was yesterday.'

Jupiter is confused. 'Yesterday?'

'Indeed. I don't really know why. I saw them, and read what you had to say about them, and got in my car straight away. I would have visited last night, but' – he glances around at the hood – 'I thought perhaps that would be . . . *unwise*.'

'Probably right,' Jupiter says.

Plenty of white folks had come by in the month that followed the article's publication. Subsequent news stories on local channels drew further attention to what he was doing here and more callers followed suit. Even celebrities came, some Jupiter knew and some he had to be told about after the fact when his nosey neighbours, watching from behind their curtains and window bars, came running over to ask what so-and-so or so-and-so was like. Tasha was frustrated she missed out on some prince character from the Bel-Air area, but out-loud furious she missed Ice Cube – a local who took piles of pictures with Jupiter, who let others know Jupiter was cool, and in doing so bought him boundless credibility across the gang sets. Donations started pouring in, as a result, enough that Jupiter is now thinking about buying a third house on this street to expand the installation to five houses. He still couldn't tell you why he's doing this, any of it, but for the first time in a long time he suspects that the dreams are starting to take shape in the waking world. He is close. Close to *something*. He just doesn't know what.

Jupiter calls out his daughter's name. 'I'm going to show the gentleman around!' he says.

Tasha's voice hollers back from a window. 'I'm going to take a nap,' she says. 'Wake me in a couple hours.'

Jupiter looks at the white guy, hoping for sympathy. 'You got children?' he says.

'Not in the way you mean,' the white guy says. 'I think I was too busy waiting.'

'Waiting for what?'

'Couldn't really say.'

Jupiter smiles despite himself. The white guy smiles, too. Hot damn, he's fine.

When the tour is done, they sit down on the porch for coffee and then, when Tasha takes off – back to her friends and a planned road trip to Yosemite that's the reason she didn't head back to Arkansas for Christmas this year – several bottles of Bud Light. Little Craig brings by a casserole his mom made for Jupiter, and Patrice from the corner shows up with a Tupperware container so packed with mash and gravy it requires tin foil instead of a lid, and all of this 'cause the women in the hood, short on eligible bachelors, hope to persuade Jupiter to switch teams, but also 'cause they know he's a single man and imagine he can't feed himself. Truth is, he barely can. For dinner, Jupiter and the white guy enjoy the potluck feast along with his meatloaf and mac 'n' cheese and more bottles of beer. The conversation is easy, full of questions and answers that are forthcoming despite how little the two men have in common in life or experience, and both comment more than once how it feels like they're long-lost friends catching up, getting to know each other again, brought back together by that story in the paper and the art outside. When the white guy says he should go, Jupiter kisses him firmly on the lips and the white guy reacts with uncertainty – he says he's never been with a man before, surprising Jupiter – then the two kiss again. After they've made love, the white guy cries quietly. Jupiter's crying is much louder. No more searching. What an extraordinary thing it is to feel found.

Keisha

She forgot how much being reborn hurts. When the piercing pain in her head finally subsides, she's lying buck naked on the hardwood floor of a 128-year-old dining room. It strikes her this should freak her the fuck out, not knowing where she is like this, 'cause a few moments ago, at least from her perspective, she was locked in a criminally insane billionaire's personal zoo. This house she's woken up in is nice, but it sure as hell ain't billionaire nice. Keisha is finally free, she just doesn't know why.

She rises on noodly legs, and looks around. The dining room is huge, lined on one side with mullioned windows. There's a fireplace in the corner, but no fire. The hearth is trimmed with Pewabic fairy-tale tiles like the kind she knows from her manufactured childhood memories of Detroit. Rich families from nearby Indian Village used to trick out their whole houses with this stuff, covering kitchens and bathrooms and libraries and fireplaces just like this one with them. Keisha walks to the window and looks outside at the neighbourhood that's blanketed in fresh snow, strings of Christmas lights twinkling like colourful stars in the night, and discovers she's actually *in* Indian Village. What the fuck is going on?

Keisha continues to explore the impressive but unfurnished house that is a product of the Arts and Crafts movement. As a human child, she thought she wanted to be an architect. She wanted to build things, beautiful things like this house. Of course, she never really was a child here. She never really wanted to be an architect. Her parents never drove her by houses like this one or said, 'Look there, honey, one day, if you work hard enough, you can live someplace like that.' None of these memories are authentic. They're all backstory, no more real than the ones she came up with for the characters in *Simulacra* and all of her other, aborted screenplays.

None of this makes sense. Why is she here in this empty house? How did she escape Harkavy's island? Where is Syco? Most importantly, she needs to know where to find some clothes. It's colder than a freezer in here and she's shaking from it.

'In the closet,' a man says.

Keisha screeches so loudly she worries the neighbours might call the police. She tries to cover herself with her arms, but there's a lot of her to cover these days. 'I swear I will fuck you up if you try to touch me,' she says.

The man is standing in the doorway to the master bedroom. He points at the door. 'In there,' he says.

Through the door, she finds a walk-in closet big enough to park a car inside. It's filled with clothes, most of which look her size. She quickly pulls on a pair of underpants and a cable knit sweater that barely covers her ass.

'You can find trousers, too,' the man says. 'I'm in no hurry.'

Keisha emerges from the walk-in closet with jeans on. The man in the doorway smiles politely at her. He's tall, big shoulders, right around forty. Fit and hot as all get-out. Reminds her a lot of Jon Hamm. 'Who are you?' she asks him.

The man smiles at her, like he's impressed or something. 'So, *you're* the girl who fell to Earth,' he says.

It's weird. It's like he's human, but there's something not right about him. That's when she notices his eyes are two different colours. 'Huh?' she says.

'It's a song off of Damien Syco's final album,' he says.

'I know his final album.'

'Not this one, you don't. It was released posthumously, one week after you disappeared. He recorded it before his own disappearance. There's a song on it, about you – "The Girl Who Fell to Earth".'

'He wrote a song about me . . . before he met me?'

'Do you remember what happened to you?'

'N-No, not exactly,' Keisha says, unconsciously flinching at the memories that have begun to assert themselves louder and louder with every moment that passes. The man obviously knows what happened to her. He's got to be an Operator in a skinsuit, she decides, here to apologize for what happened to her and set her back up in her old life. That explains his weird, otherworldly vibe. 'I was . . . I was held prisoner. I-I don't know how long.'

'I could take my time, ease into that, but you're going to find out soon enough,' he says. 'So maybe we should just skip to the hard part. It was 2,302 days.'

'Get the fuck out of here,' she says.

'I'm sorry.'

Keisha spent six years locked up in Harkavy's basement. Six years of her Second Life stolen from her. *Simulacra* came and went. She doesn't even know how it did at the box office. All that effort, the culmination of fifteen years of hard work, and it happened without her. What do Flora and Luiza think happened to her? Her friends? Did anybody even look for her? Do they think she's dead? Godfuckingdamnit, this is too fucking much.

'I only found you because there was an incident in Geneva—' the man says.

'Geneva?' she says, interrupting.

'It's a city in Switzerland,' he says.

'Yeah, I know what Geneva is, you condescending dick. I meant, what happened?'

'Oh. It was destroyed.'

'Oh shit. Like, by terrorists?'

'By something that didn't belong in this world. Something powerful that Sergio Harkavy attempted to unlock.'

Keisha flinches again, more memories surfacing. They slap at her like hands, trying to get her attention. 'That motherfucker is sick,' she says. 'You know what he did to me?'

'I do now,' the man says. 'Because of what happened in Geneva, I paid Mr Harkavy a visit. He is an interesting man, to say the least – or rather, *was*.'

She wants to feel horrified by what was just implied, but she's not. 'What he did to me . . . I was going insane in there,' she says.

'You did go insane,' he says. 'A little bit, I think. That's how you got here.'

A memory returns to Keisha, tangled up with several others. A shower, a curtain ripped down, blood running down the drain. No that's not right, not her memory, but the shower is. The shower and a curtain and her hands grabbing and her feet kicking until, in her frantic confusion, her legs slip out from under her and—

'Oh, damn, you're right!' she says, stamping a foot and shaking her hand at the memory like it's a fly in her face. 'I killed myself – hanged myself in the shower.'

'I arrived ten days later,' the man says. 'If you had held out just a little longer, I would have set you free.'

'I just . . . I needed to get out of there. I knew my contract said you would just reboot me, but . . . I was scared, damn, I was *so* scared. I couldn't do it.'

'It is not easy to take one's own life.'

'Fuck no, it isn't. Even when you know it isn't going to really kill you, know what I'm saying?'

'Interestingly, *it should have*. Your contract with Plurality Life Insurance Corporation has been nullified.'

'Say what?' Keisha says. But it makes sense to her almost immediately. 'This is 'cause of my movie.'

'No,' the man says, waving off the countless terms she violated putting *Simulacra* out into the world. 'Plurality has undergone a change in management, I suppose you could say. Your re-download is what you can consider a one-time arrangement.'

'So what, I can die now? *Again*?'

The man nods.

'Hold up. If you're not an Operator . . . who the fuck are you supposed to be?'

'I had a name once,' he says. 'Robert Jones.'

'But . . . but he's—'

'A character in your motion picture?' he says. 'Yes, I am one and the same with him. Well, *some* of me.'

Keisha staggers backwards into the wood-panelled wall. She slowly slides halfway down it, then pushes herself back to her feet. 'Ho-lee fuck,' she says, her voice shaking. What has she done?

'The real head-scratcher is, did my story somehow seep across space and time here, bleed between Earth models and find its way into your imagination – *or* did you, Ms LeChance, dream up Robert Jones's whole life?' the man asks. 'Quite the pickle, as somebody I used to care about liked to say.'

'It was Syco, yo!' she says, blurting this out before she has a chance to think about what she's saying.

'I don't follow,' he says.

'I don't know how, but he's part of it. His music, it got into Tab's head—'

'Talbert Whittaker?'

'You know him?'

'In one of his previous lives, yes. A part of somebody Robert Jones cared for existed within him.'

Keisha knows what that means, but it's too much of a headtrip to get into just yet. 'He got into my head, too,' she says of how Syco infected Tab and then her. 'And then . . . I don't know . . . I can't wrap my head around any of this.'

'I am constructed out of this place,' the man says. 'I am *it* and it is *me*, and I couldn't explain any of it to you, either. Except you people – human beings, and you are one now for better or worse – *you* create the world you live in. Without you, nothing exists. You, Ms LeChance, are part of the mystery.'

'What mystery's that?' she asks.

'The only one that matters, I would think,' he says. 'Don't ask me. I'm not human, not any more. What happened to Mr Syco?'

'You don't know?' Keisha says. 'He was alive when I . . . when I killed myself. I don't think he said more than a dozen words to me the whole time we were trapped in there together. He sang, he never stopped, drove me nuts doing it. But he never talked, not to me. Not really, until I told him what I was going to do. Then he said, "It's been a pleasure experiencing imprisonment with you, Keisha. Please say hello to the Moonman for me."'

The man slowly smiles.

'What did he mean by that?'

'It's a private joke,' the man says, but refuses to offer more. 'Incidentally, he wasn't there when I arrived either. Harkavy couldn't tell me where he'd gone. Video surveillance showed him in his cell one moment, playing his guitar, then he wasn't.'

'So . . . he's not dead?'

'Difficult to say,' he says. 'I expect he'll turn up at some point.'

'I've got no idea what you're talking about.'

'You're probably better off that way,' he says.

Keisha doesn't know what to think about that or any of this. She drags her hand across her face twice. 'Can I go home now?' she says. 'What I mean is, what happened after I disappeared? Did they look for me? They think I'm dead or something?'

'History has been . . . *massaged* as much as within my abilities,' the man says. 'Your peers believe your success led to a nervous breakdown.'

'For real?' she says.

'*Simulacra* broke a lot of records, you should be proud,' he says. 'But it all proved too much for you, so you retreated to Detroit. You were always happier here. Your agent keeps fielding offers, but you've declined them all by email so far. Somehow that's made you even more desired. I don't really understand the motion picture business.'

'Nobody does.' She nods to herself, liking this story. 'So, I went all Malick? That's cool. Yeah, cool, I can work that.'

'But after six years, you're ready for a comeback. Your agent has already put the word out. Keisha LeChance, the writer-director of the third-highest-grossing motion picture of all time—'

'Domestically?'

'*Internationally*. Also, you won an Academy Award for Best Director. Emma Stone accepted it for you, right after she was handed her second Best Actress Oscar.'

'Fuck yeah, we did,' Keisha says, unable to help the grin that lights up her face. She stamps on the floor once. 'Fuck yeah.'

'Your agent has put the word out, like I said,' the man says. 'Keisha LeChance is back. And she's got her follow-up to *Simulacra*. Buyers are desperate to see the screenplay.'

'Script?' she says, suddenly concerned. 'But I don't have a script.'

'*Yet*,' he says.

'I don't get it. Who are you? I mean, *really*. What are you doing here?'

The man smiles again, this time almost impishly. It's unexpected, but enticing. Something exciting is about to happen, something she knows she needs to be part of. 'Ms LeChance, *the Girl Who Fell to Earth*, I have an idea for a motion picture I'd like to pitch to you,' he says.

Ali

West Berlin 1977

He watches the last of the black-and-green pills disappear in a
swirl of water. He had only swallowed three or four of them when
he began to spit them back out into the toilet bowl, and the
ones that had already slid down his throat were forced up easily
enough with his long fingers. It took three flushes and the help of
the toilet brush to make them all disappear. The pills were meant
to set him free, to liberate him from his pain, from the absence
of his beloved Bertha, from the overwhelming meaninglessness of
this meaningless, stupid life. Nothing, he had decided, mattered.
Except – and he realized this as he gagged on the mouthful of
pills – maybe it does. From the SO36 stage, the Man Who Was
the Moonman, who had only just emerged from some futuristic
chrysalis in a brand-new form, spoke of lies and half-truths and
truths wrapped up in lies and about faith and conformity and
all the *isms* and how they are lies, too. But he sang of so much
more, too. Like about this moment, right now, Ali kneeling over
his toilet bowl as he flushes the last of the sleeping pills away, and
that moment with Bertha in the park when she smiled at him as
he poured wine into her paper cup and the children were chasing
a squirrel, and that moment where Bertha first showed him her
naked body, twenty-two years older than his, imperfect and perfect and soft and wonderful, and he kissed it and they made love
in what was then only her bed and eventually became their bed.
All of these moments and the moments still to come give shape
to the universe that does not exist without them, it pulls atoms
together and rips them apart, and spins galaxies on their axes
and smashes stars into one another and marries moons to planets
and planets to moons like the one where the Man Who Was the
Moonman came from, and without these moments, without them

the universe would blow apart because all of these moments – Ali's mother feeding him a slice of her *bastilla* from the stove, his father weeping with him after Ali's grandmother's stroke, his arrival in Lehrter Stadtbahnhof three years ago, Bertha stumbling out of the rain and into the Schwarze Traube where he was drinking with Atik and their friends, the tears on Bertha's face when he first came inside her, Bertha's body twisted and broken on the pavement as the street continued to collapse into the U-Bahn tunnel behind him – holds the universe together more surely than gravity. The Man Who Was the Moonman knows this, too, and was trying to tell Ali and everybody else as much from the stage earlier tonight.

A few days later, Ali is walking through the Tiergarten on his way to work. He sees two men riding the same taffy green bicycle. One has straight brown hair that looks unwashed and reaches to the middle of his bony back and he is so thin that his muscles are visible like he's a living, breathing Michelangelo drawing. The other is Damien Syco, the Moonman, the Man Who Was and Is and Will Be the focus of such intensity for so many that reality itself bends to his passage through it. Ali's eyes fill with tears as Syco cycles past, and his eyes meet Syco's, and in that moment, that single and briefest of moments, the two are one, they are in on the secret together, and the integrity of the universe seems that much more secure.

Jones

Manzanillo 2029

She is standing in a field of sunflowers. Her back is to him and her hands rest on her curving belly. The waning moon hangs directly over her head, a silver-white crescent glowing impossibly bright against the stars that fill up her big eyes. He knows she's waiting for him, waiting for him to come back to her, waiting because he promised her he'd be back. In these dreams, he used to tell her to hold on, to not give up on him, but he has realized this was a cruelty. They were just dreams, sure, but he was lying to her all the same and that devastated him when he woke up. The lie would linger in his mind all day. And so, this time he approaches her from behind. He whispers into her ear, 'I know what I promised you, but I can't. You have to let me go. Let me go, Gracie . . . let me go.' Her shoulders sag, and her eyes shift from the stars to her belly. He slips his hands, still young and strong in the dream, past her arms and lets them slide across the curve of her belly and under her palms. Her hands on top of his. His hands on top of her belly. Their child kicks, a quick thump-thump against his fingertips, and in that instant Jones startles awake in his bed more than two hundred and fifty years later and on the other side of the planet, in Costa Rica, and finds Jupiter sitting in a chair next to him reading *La Nación* with the help of his bifocals. 'What's going on in the world?' he asks his husband of more than two decades.

Jupiter turns the newspaper around, displaying the Spanish headline that he knows Jones can't read even though he spent half a century living in the American Southwest and nearly fifteen more years here in Manzanillo. The photo below it is of reclusive filmmaker Keisha LeChance, whom they have both been aware of since *Simulacra* debuted in theatres eight years ago. 'Her new movie's supposed to be another *game-changer*,' he says. 'That's what it says here, *game-changer*.'

Jones snorts, which hurts. 'Let's hope it's not a sequel,' he says.

It was traumatic, sitting through *Simulacra*. Leonel – one of their neighbours here – had insisted it was the most amazing picture he'd ever seen. His wife Carla agreed with him for once, breaking a lifelong habit of maligning his taste in all things except her. And so, Jones and Jupiter, ignorant of *Simulacra*'s subject matter, bought tickets and quickly discovered it was about Jones and the woman he had told Jupiter about so many times. The story wasn't especially accurate, there were wild deviations, such as the nature of the Outside and the big special effects-laden and action-packed finale in the System's CPU, but it was their story all the same. For Jones, who was unprepared for this, the picture confounded his own memories and, afterwards, he found himself unable to entirely disentangle reality from the celluloid fiction and he still can't. For Jupiter, seeing the picture was like opening a window inside his mind he didn't know was there and peering through it at a part of himself he'd never been able to make out before. He had once seen a photo of his husband's old girlfriend, Gracie, a photo he found eerily, even uncomfortably familiar and couldn't get out of his head long afterwards, but this was wholly different. It was, he said, like watching himself up there on the screen.

It was at this point that Jupiter demanded Jones tell him the truth, the truth about everything, and Jones, who had long kept this secret to himself, who never wanted to burden Jupiter with it, finally revealed the so-called 'truth about everything'. In one afternoon, Jupiter learned about the true composition of reality and that the community art installation he created in Compton, all those years he spent assembling it out of lost moments and missed opportunities and time itself, was really about finding Jones. He created a map with his heart because a part of Gracie lived on inside him, and Jones followed this map all the way back to him.

In the end, Jones had kept his promise to come back for Gracie after all.

'Says here, it's a spiritual sequel, whatever that means,' Jupiter says, easing himself back in his chair. He's on the wrong end of seventy, but it wasn't until last autumn that his body started to turn on him. *Really* turn on him, that is. Back problems. Hip probably needs to be replaced, at least that's what the doctors are telling them. Jupiter insists it's fine, just like he'll tell you the arthritis isn't a big deal. What's most important, though, is his smile is just as wide as it used to be, his eyes just as loving, his touch just as kind. 'Maybe we should check it out.'

Jones snorts again. 'Yeah, maybe,' he says. 'Water, when you can.' The hospital bed they had put in for him takes too goddamn long to hydraulically lower, or he'd just grab it himself. He reaches out with two trembling hands, pockmarked and dotted with age – *war wounds*, Jupiter sweetly calls them – and accepts a proferred cup. Jupiter doesn't let go, and guides it to Jones's mouth. Water dribbles down Jones's chin, and his husband wipes it up, along with the wet spot on his undershirt. 'Thanks, darling.'

'The kids wanted to know when they can come in,' Jupiter says. 'You up for it?'

The smell of salt water bristles the long hairs in Jones's nose. The ocean moves at a lazy rhythmic pace outside, calling to him. It's low tide at the moment. He pushes his tongue against the gap where two of his teeth used to be, and says, 'Yeah. Mind bringing me my smile?'

Jupiter didn't want to leave Compton. He argued about it for a year – this was before he'd seen *Simulacra* or knew what Jones knew – but in the end he couldn't say no. Jones told him he had to trust him, and he trusted Jones no matter how hard it was to say goodbye to his home. Later, he understood they had left because Jones knew something he didn't. He knew the future. He'd visited it. And he knew it, even back in 2014, even when there was still a Black man in the White House and, despite the madness that had taken Congress by the throat, hope still felt like something that could get them through what was to come. That's why Jones insisted they needed to get out of the country before it got too bad. Hate, he said, had a way of twisting reality. People forget, he would say, people forget what hate can do. Dark times were coming, and he figured the best place to weather the storm was as far away from President Glass as they could get.

Turns out, that was Manzanillo.

Jones hadn't had kids of his own, not outside his dreams, but Jupiter's had become his family. They tried to convince this family to join them after the first election, but it was no good. Tasha had already moved to Frankfurt by this point, where she lived with her partner Hamza and, at the time, one boy, but Jhasmin and Leesa had families in Arkansas and Texas and refused to leave. Then the cancer got Leesa. When Jupiter returned from the funeral, he brought her only kid, Marcus, back to Manzanillo with him. That was the last time Jupiter would see his family until last summer, when Glass was finally removed from office and the Costa Rican government started issuing travel visas to Americans again. Long story short, the kids – Tasha and Hamza and two sons and Jupiter's first great-grandchild, Jhasmin and her children, and Marcus and his new fiancée – are all here for one final Thanksgiving together. Together with him. They've come to say goodbye, even if Jones isn't ready to himself. He doesn't want to let go yet. That long-ago fear, the fear of the unknown, the fear that drove him to surrender his body so he could hide in this world for ever, has resurfaced.

Jones's family spends the rest of the morning with him, talking about the good times and the bad, complaining about the Pumpkin-King as they refer to Glass, hypothesizing about the future that somehow, despite Glass's forced retirement in his garish, heavily guarded Manhattan citadel, seems bleaker than ever. Tasha, who used to be the most cynical of all of them, surprises them by saying she finally sees a happy ending. Not a guaranteed one, but maybe, just maybe all these governments collapsing, the wars and the refugees flooding across borders and the conga line of pandemics, the extreme weather that's shutting down whole cities and literally wiping countries off the map, maybe, just maybe that is what it's going to take to bring people together, to finally, once and for all, make them start working together. Maybe. Her partner thinks she's deluding herself, but Tasha says she doesn't have anything left to give to despair. They all ask, what does *Uncle Bobby* – as he's known by everybody here – what does Uncle Bobby think?

Jupiter asks Jones this all the time, too. Jones has seen the future, after all. But Jones tries to explain to him it doesn't work like that, not any more, not since the deal the other him struck with MasterControl. The System was too mature, too complicated by the time Porter merged with MasterControl and set the System's cycle of Perceived Time loose. Time is no longer recycled here, so there was no chance to go back and reset anything. Consequently, it now moves like thousands of interconnected rivers, flowing into and out of each other, always rushing towards the future and a forever unknown horizon. Reality remains elastic, the Perception Algorithm still hard at work, human beings imagining and dreaming new currents that, when they join again with others, slowly change what might be everywhere before dividing again. But the damage that was done, the damage Jones helped inflict when he created MasterControl to fulfil the role of a god, could take decades, maybe even centuries, to truly undo. Porter made this all possible, sacrificing himself and his love for Gracie in order to transform MasterControl and, in doing so, set the human beings he and Jones created free.

People might not realize it, maybe they can't give words to what they feel, but they're beginning to wake up from the dream of reality they knew and are now stumbling forward into a new, unpredictable future through a fog of uncertainty and terrifying potential.

Hope, as Tasha calls it.

'I think . . .' Jones says to his family, smiling tiredly with his bridge in so his smile doesn't startle. 'I think . . . it's a good time to be alive.'

'You're just saying that because you think you're going to die soon,' Hamza says with startling German bluntness that surprises even Jones. Tasha backhands his shoulder. 'Sorry.'

'No, no, it's true,' Jones says, chuckling. 'But that's my point. *You're alive*. What else matters?'

When they have gone to make lunch and Jones is alone with Jupiter again, his husband says, 'You're not going to die any time soon.'

Jones notices the smell of the ocean again. The salt water. He reaches out and takes Jupiter's hand, and ignores how his husband squeezes his too hard. Everything hurts nowadays. 'Take me to the beach, darling,' he says between coughs. 'I'm tired. I'd like a break by myself, if you don't mind.'

'I can stay with you.'

'It's all right. We'll have time enough later.'

Jupiter helps Jones dress in linen trousers, then carries him to the wheelchair. They go out through the bedroom's patio door, then pass through the fake aquamarine door that leads to the beach so they don't have to field requests from the others to join them. And when they reach the sand, Jupiter lifts what's left of Jones, a fraction of the man he once was – oh, how the years steal from you – and carries him to one of the beach chairs.

'Are you sure you don't want me to stay?' Jupiter says, pushing the umbrella open over Jones. 'I don't mind.'

'Go,' Jones says.

Jupiter puts his hand on his shoulder. Jones puts his hand on his husband's. They stay like this for a long moment, listening to each other breathe and the birds clack and sing and flies buzz and the ocean roll and roll and roll across the sand.

'Thank you,' Jones says finally.

Jupiter lets go, his fingers raking gently across the skeletal remains of Jones's shoulder, and walks back to the house.

Jones sits alone like this, quiet, mind travelling into his past, dancing between thoughts of him and her and him as the sun arcs across the sky and the umbrella, playing the part of a sundial in today's matinee performance, counting down the hours that pass. The waves keep him and the memories company. He watches the way they break against the shore, coming for him. With each minute, the water inches closer and closer.

And then he appears, walking right out of the blinding sunlight.

'Hello, Dad,' he says with an accent nobody could peg down.

Jones takes a moment, his eyes trying to focus. 'Ah,' he says, squinting and smiling at the same time. 'It's been a while.'

'Has it, *mi cariño*?' the young man says. He's Costa Rican by appearance and dressed in a mint tank top and linen chinos that he's hiked up over his dark, almost hairless calves. It's been years since they last saw each other, and back then they both looked very, very different. The young man sits down on the sand beside Jones's chair. 'Time is funny like that.'

Jones nods knowingly. Yeah, yeah, it is. 'We take it for granted, then it's gone,' he says. 'Just gone.'

'Are you unhappy with the time you've had here?' the young man says, concerned. 'With the life you led?'

Jones makes a noise with his nose. Another snort, but this time he coughs a little and has to spit up some phlegm. When he's done hacking, he says, 'No, not unhappy. Far from it.'

'But you miss her all the same,' the young man says gently.

Jones watches the waves for a moment. The water. The way it spreads across the sand as it advances and retreats, leaving behind darkness with each passing. 'Did you ever get a chance to meet her?' he asks.

The young man smiles with his whole face, nodding to himself. 'I popped in on her a few times when she was still a little girl,' he says. 'She was . . . wow. You would have called her a *firecracker*.'

'Did you meet her mother, too?' Jones says. 'That woman was' – he shakes his head – 'a piece of work. Gracie's funeral was a circus. Couldn't step foot in Colorado again after it, for fear I might try to murder her for what she did.'

'I though the rocket-ship cupcake toppers were the real low point,' the young man says. Jones looks quizzically at him. 'I was there, yeah. You wouldn't have recognized me. I check in on you every now and again, too.'

A smile tugs at one side of Jones's face. He could weep just as easily. This is all he wanted, this here. He never thought he'd get the chance again.

The young man picks up a handful of sand, and flings it at the waves. 'Your husband, how did you find him?' he says.

'She called me to him. I know how that sounds, but she did. His artwork – he's an artist—'

'I've seen.'

'His artwork, it found me. It led me to him.'

The young man glances over his shoulder at the beach house behind them. 'He hasn't given up his craft,' he says.

The roof of the house Jones and Jupiter share is painted neon pink. Clocks cover its teal walls. Dreamcatchers hang from its eaves, twisting in the breeze. Doors painted in bright colours and splattered with white and black polka dots that look like constellations. Similar doors have been hung in equally colourful floating door frames along the sidewalk, at the edge of the patio, on the rooftop – doors that lead nowhere in this world, but symbolize gateways to others and vice versa.

Jones laughs at the architectural obscenity of it all. He has spent nearly seven decades living in a manufactured reality. For nearly thirty of it, he's lived in homes with Jupiter that grappled with this fraud, even before the artist understood what this world is. One might think that, at his age, Jupiter would be slowing down, but it's quite the opposite. As soon as the kids are gone, he'll be back at it, collecting and adding and modifying in preparation. Preparation for what's coming. High tide is almost here. The water continues to slide across the beach, getting closer.

'I think he's already gone fishing, trying to find me again when I'm gone,' Jones says, trying to explain the house's unique disposition. 'Hoping he can find some way to bring me back to him like he did before.'

The young man stands, and brushes the sand from his ass. Salt water washes past him, just missing his feet. 'I think I should be going now,' he says.

'I'm sorry I didn't recognize you in Tucson,' Jones says. His voice cracks. 'I'm sorry about . . . about not being there for you.'

The young man doesn't say anything. He doesn't need to.

'Can you tell me what comes next for me?'

'But that would ruin the surprise.'

Jones watches the young man walk back into the sun. Just before the light swallows him up, he stops and turns, one hand held over his eyes. He shouts something, but Jones doesn't hear him. And so, the young man shouts it again—

'I'll be seeing you again, Dad!'

He's gone.

Jones sniffles, and coughs, and wipes his cheek with his trembling hand. He sinks lower into his chair, no longer comfortable holding himself up. He should call for Jupiter. The waves have reached his bare feet, rippling over his long, hairy toes and their gnarled nails. The water is warm, and relentless, and keeps coming. He really should call for Jupiter.

Jones

Pasadena 1961

It is not easy for the consciousness to hold on to a thought here. This must be the Library, where MasterControl summons identity matrices for either initial upload in the case of customers or, with regards to actors, recycling/assembly. There is nothing to see or feel, no sense of who the consciousness was or even if the consciousness still *is* in some small way after exchanging its biological form for early retirement. Only black, a void, an empty nothing except the sense that something intangible is coming into focus, something that might be . . . *him*. Yes – there! – there *he* is. And then the consciousness is hurtling along, through this nothing, faster and faster as the rest of *him* finds human form and screams, or maybe it's the nothing screaming, or maybe MasterControl is screaming as it births another satisfied customer and drops him buck naked in the middle of a living-room floor. Robert Jones flops about, blind and confused, unfamiliar limbs fighting against imagined phantoms until he, too, stops screaming and the world around him – Pasadena, Earth, the mid-twentieth century – comes into crisp and terrifying focus.

And then, Jones is sick all over himself.

He crawls up the side of his mustard couch, the one he chose from the four different possible colours the Retirement Consultant offered him, and gives his legs a try. They work after a little experimentation, but the anxiety of using them proves too much too soon, and he drops to the edge of the couch, where he takes in the room, the mini-bar filled with a variety of colourful liquors, the crystal bowl brimming with salted peanuts, the rubber foam and polyester smell rising from the couch beneath him, from the armchairs, throw pillows, from everything.

On the brass-and-mirrored-glass coffee table before him, a

series of identification documents have been neatly laid out for him. Birth certificate, social security card, driver's licence, and passport. Caucasian, six feet two inches, born in St Louis, Missouri. He knows just about everything anybody needs to know about St Louis, even though he's never been there. How strange. All of this. Maybe he thought it wouldn't be, considering he built the world he now calls home. He knows this particular branching of Earth models better than anybody else here. Actually, that's not entirely true. He knows how they *work*. Now it's time to find out how to *live* in one of them.

Jones goes to his bedroom, which is right where he remembers it being even though he's never been here before, and finds some aspirin in the ensuite bathroom. His closet is brimming with suits, all of the latest fashions. He chooses something casual, but it makes him feel anything but comfortable. Why didn't anybody warn him that the ridiculous costumes these people wear are so stiff and restricting? He suddenly regrets not choosing the freedom of the early '70s, which was his initial instinct, but his ambition had been to situate himself in the United States of America during what many Americans would come to believe was their golden age. Of course, that meant he had to choose a digital habit that went along with that perception.

The Retirement Consultant chuckled when Jones asked about the possibility of living here as a member of any of the other races, making it clear Latino, Asian, and especially Negro were not real options for any customer who wanted to enjoy a peaceful retirement in this place. Very few customers opted to become a woman in America either, especially before 1980 – though he did learn there's a growing trend of customers with unlocked contracts opting to periodically shift between perceived time periods and genders, even ages, as a way of freely experimenting with sexual gratification from misogyny, racism and other forms of violent victimization.

This is how Jones became a white male living in a white suburb, in a brand-new house with an equally brand-new car in the garage, because this world was made for people who look like him (now) and, after years of being denied the respect he felt he deserved for his accomplishments on the Outside, of being forced to watch as others were credited for his work, the thought of having such a clearly defined position in society, even one as humble as the American middle class, excited him.

During the first week, Jones gets to know his house and neighbourhood. The Operators report an error to MasterControl, because he keeps backing his alpine-green Oldsmobile Coupe into the garage door, but MasterControl insists it's endemic to his identity matrix and cannot be corrected now. Jones solves the problem by leaving his car parked in the driveway, though this comes with the unfortunate side-effect of encouraging his neighbours, the ones he's met on his long strolls, to make a beeline for him every time he arrives home. Ralph Beckermann, the loudest and most aggressively friendly of the bunch, lives across the street with his family he seems to hate spending time with. Jones and Ralph get drunk together, the first time Jones has ever been drunk, and discuss their frustrations with bosses who take you for granted. Jones complains about being forced out of his job, and how he took early retirement as a way to escape the embarrassment of losing everything he built, but now he finds himself bored silly here. Ralph pretends to 'get it, man'.

During the second week, Jones turns on the television he now realizes is much too small for his viewing pleasure. He'll have to buy a new one soon. The TV programming is a depressing mixture of mundane police dramas that accomplish nothing more than giving him something to focus on as he drinks whiskey and carefully staged situation comedies that his cultural modifications help him find amusing even though he can't shake the feeling he doesn't fully understand because he doesn't really belong in this world. The news is even more useless to him since he knows how the System works to use it against human actors, to keep them docile and complacent with fear of murder and the reefer and

Negros and commies and socialists and conservatives and liberals and nuclear annihilation. Ralph can see Jones is getting 'squirrelly' – this is how he describes Jones's unease and restless pacing back and forth across his living room, something Ralph can see from his own window across the street – and so Ralph tells him to get in, they're going for a drive, and Ralph takes him to somewhere called Tijuana where Ralph pays for them to have sex with children. Jones's girl might only be thirteen and she is beautiful. He touches her delicate face, the first time he's ever touched a female human, and, suddenly desperate to help her, offers the madam a thousand dollars to walk out with the child rather than fornicate with her. The girl takes his hand and leads him into an alley where the madam's employees ambush him and beat him and take what's left in his wallet. The girl leaves with them, returning to her life instead of letting him rescue her, and Jones wonders how he allowed any of this to happen. He built this place. This is all his fault. But by the time he and Ralph get back to Pasadena, still drunk on cheap tequila and singing bawdy songs Jones has never heard before but knows every word to, Jones has accepted there's nothing he can do about the girl or any of this because none of it is real anyway. Besides, he's retired.

During the third week, Jones stops going out. It's not until he realizes that he has nothing left in the pantry to eat except a heel of Wonder Bread and no butter or jam to smear across it that he gets into his car. He makes it a few miles when he spots a diner. It's all polished white surfaces and big windows and the blinking neon sign above the door says Kellogg's.

The waitress is standing next to the cash register, leaning on her elbows as she reads from a giant book laid out on the counter, humming a strange tune that immediately grabs his ear. There's nobody else here except a drunk sleeping it off in a corner booth and a short-order cook.

'Evening,' the waitress says before she looks up at Jones. When she does, she's smiling with the whole of her heart-shaped face.

There's something immediately alive about her, like the jazz Ralph played all the way to Tijuana, and he suddenly experiences the inapposite sensation of waking up, of sudden buoyancy pulling him to a surface he hadn't yet realized he was struggling to reach, and inexperience at modulating his expressions means all of this is evident across his face, which is probably why she says, 'You okay, mister?'

'Yeah,' Jones says. 'Yeah, I'm okay. Just . . . *famished* is all.' He sits at the counter two stools away from her. 'What was that you were humming?'

The waitress, in her Easter-yellow dress and food-stained apron, all of twenty years old, stands up and closes her book. It's a textbook, it looks like. *One Two Three . . . Infinity* by George Gamow. 'What can I get you?' she says.

Jones finds a paper menu between a napkin dispenser and bottles of Heinz ketchup and mustard. 'Burger sounds good,' he says, but he doesn't know how he likes it when she asks him. 'How do *you* like it?'

'Leon, burger,' the waitress says. 'Still bleeding.'

The Negro in the kitchen, Leon apparently, says, 'Burger coming up – rare!'

'Anything to drink?' the waitress says. 'Coffee's fresh.'

'Coffee, sure,' Jones says. 'Tell me, what were you humming?'

'Oh, it's nothing,' she says, going to fetch the coffee carafe.

'Catchy is what it is,' he says. He starts to hum it himself. 'It's stuck in my head now.'

The waitress stops in front of Jones, carafe and cup in hand, but she doesn't pour his coffee. She's just looking at him, wondering about something, and, when she's made a decision about whatever it is, she says, 'It's cosmic noise.' Jones doesn't understand. 'You know you can listen to outer space?' He shrugs, still confused. 'You can. All you need is a ham radio. I still have mine, my dad bought it for me when I was little. You go playing around on it long enough, you start to hear stuff. Noise from outer space.

To most everybody, that's all it is, *noise*. But when I was fifteen, I started turning the frequencies into musical notes. On my mom's piano.'

'You play the piano?' he says.

'A little,' she says. 'What I'm saying is, if you want, you can find music in it.'

'That's what you were humming, *cosmic noise*?'

'I like to think it's the heartbeat of the universe. The secret of existence, maybe. God if he were real – no offence, mister.'

'No offence taken.'

Jones knows what she's describing is ambient digital noise from the data compression and transfer taking place in coaxial terminals across the models. In a way, it is the heartbeat of the universe, the secret of existence, even God. He doesn't say any of this. Instead, he looks from the waitress's face, to the textbook, to Leon in the kitchen window shaking his head at the girl. '*Who* are you?' he asks her, trying not to sound as astonished as he probably does.

'Grace Pulansky,' she says. 'Pleased to make your acquaintance. Friends call me Gracie.'

He smiles widely. 'Well, Gracie, you have to be the most interesting person I've met since moving here,' he says.

'What about you?' she says. 'Got a name?'

'Robert.'

'Ooh, my uncle is a Robert. He's creepy. How do you feel about Bobby?'

He smiles again. 'Okay.'

Gracie pours Jones his cup of coffee, and returns the carafe to the warmer. 'You know, you're the first person I've ever talked to about outer space or physics or science at all who didn't talk back to me like a kid,' she says.

'You talk about outer space a lot?' he says.

'Maybe,' she says. 'I ask a lot of questions.'

'About what?' he asks.

'About every damn thing,' Leon says.

'Leon, mind your beeswax,' Gracie says. She looks at Jones again, and smiles as she continues. 'About every darn thing, yes.'

'You're a student?' he says, indicating the book.

'Caltech,' she says. 'There are only two of us.'

'*Two*?'

'Girls, in the physics department.'

'Physics then, that makes sense.'

'What do you mean?'

'Where else would somebody with a lot of questions wind up?' She chuckles. 'Philosophy department, I suppose.'

'Burger's up,' Leon says.

Gracie collects the plate the cook holds out for her through the kitchen window, and presents it to Jones. He sets it down in front of himself, and almost smiles at the sight of the grease and blood that have collected beneath his hamburger's otherwise dry bun. They talk some more in between his big bites of the burger, about Alan Shepherd and the Space Race and Denver where she's from and her mother's terrible taste in men, and, when he's done, she removes his plate, gives the counter a quick polish with her rag, and asks him, 'Feel like some pie? May makes some great pie, if you have any room left. May's the boss's sister.' She twirls her finger around her temple. 'May's also a bit bananas.'

Jones sits back, and takes in the glass-faced pie tower next to the coffee warmers. Six different types of pie stare back at him. Some of them look fruit-based, one is chocolate, another glistens an ectoplasmic green. 'I don't even know if I like pie,' he says.

Leon's head appears in the kitchen window. 'What kind of man don't know if he's a fan of pie?' he says.

'I . . . I just don't,' Jones says. 'I've never had any before.'

'Well then, we need to rectify this situation immediately,' Gracie says. She opens the pie tower . . . but stops. She looks over her shoulder, carefully appraising him from beneath a cocked eyebrow. A best guess achieved, she plucks a perfect, unviolated pie from the bottom shelf, plates a piece that drips chunks of strawberries and pinkish-green mush, and presents it to him like a game show hostess. 'It's strawberry-rhubarb. Go on.'

But Jones has never had an actual strawberry, though he's tried the flavour or some facsimile of it in an ice cream malt; and the rhubarb looks queer, even unsettling. 'Is it good?' he asks, regarding the slice of pie on the counter in front of him dubiously.

Gracie leans back against the counter, crossing her arms across her chest, and winks at him. 'Isn't the fun in finding out?'

Acknowledgements

First and foremost, thank you to my family. Without the notes, patience, and unwavering support of my brilliant wife, Lindsay Devlin, I could not have finished *Psalms for the End of the World*. I had been dreaming about writing it for many years, but it was not until the birth of our children, Darwin and Lochlan, and what they taught me about love and myself that I dared to think I was appropriately equipped to begin it.

In addition, I would like to thank my dear friends Christopher B. Derrick, Gregory R. Little, Nicholas Meyer and Amanda Palley for being *Psalms'* first fans and helping me get it into shape – no small request given the fact that its first draft was in excess of 600 pages. With regards to Nick, I think it's fair to say that his novels and films have left an indelible mark on me as a human being and storyteller and, consequently, helped shape this book in many ways beyond his ken.

Lastly, it is imperative that I also thank: Peter Ho Davies for being the first author who encouraged me to think I might be able to write for a living; my UK film/TV managers, Cathy King and Kate Prentice of 42 Management, for their constant faith and support and helping me find a book agent who loved *Psalms for the End of the World* as much as they did; my literary agent, Jon Wood of RCW Literary Agency, who offered invaluable assistance getting the manuscript into its final form and found a home for it at Headline Publishing Group; my editor at Headline, Toby Jones, whose exuberant passion for and commitment to *Psalms* has made this, my first experience as a published author, a truly joyous affair; and David Jones for being David Bowie.